# THE OFFICER

## BY ETHAN RABIDOUX

**LOVE...LOYALTY...REVENGE**

Copyright © 2014 Ethan Rabidoux
First Edition – February 2104

Editors: Sharon Crawford
and Kat Exner

**ISBN**
978-1-4602-3330-6 (Hardcover)
978-1-4602-3331-3 (Paperback)
978-1-4602-3332-0 (eBook)

This book is a work of fiction. While some of the novel is based loosely on real life events names, characters, places, and incidents either are the product of the author's imagination or are used fictitiously.

All rights reserved.

No part of this publication may be reproduced in any form, or by any means, electronic or mechanical, including photocopying, recording, or any information browsing, storage, or retrieval system, without permission in writing from the publisher.

Produced by:

FriesenPress
Suite 300 – 852 Fort Street
Victoria, BC, Canada V8W 1H8

www.friesenpress.com

Distributed to the trade by The Ingram Book Company

Madame Bancroft,

"When you gaze long into the abyss, the abyss gazes back into you."

Enjoy "The Officer".

Merci!
EGR.

This book is dedicated to the gallant workers of
Electro-Motive Diesel in London, Ontario.

History will vindicate your struggle.

# CHAPTER 1

**HE** moved quickly through the hallways of his prison, walking so fast he was practically running. It was an ordinary day. The halls were crowded with awkward teenagers—the boys slurring their usual chest-thumping machismo, the girls, gravitating towards the finest faker in the crowd.

For just one time, he didn't want to be noticed. Just once.

That smell peculiar to high schools—a mix of raging pheromones and the foul tang of pubescent body odor—wafted through the confined space. They all had ten minutes before second period began. The bell rang three minutes ago. Seven minutes left. The schmoozing started instantly. Instantly, that is, for the alphas and the omegas of the school corridors: the overlords of all creation at Wellington Secondary School.

He was not one of them. He was an untouchable in the high school caste system. A good day meant invisibility and those days were few and far between. So far, it had been a good day but it wasn't even lunch hour yet. That was usually when things happened. For now, he just wanted to make it from math class to biology with his head down.

He made a hurried stop at his locker, his fingers frantically fumbling for the combination. After three tries, the lock mercifully opened. He exchanged books, stuffed them into his backpack and rushed to his next class.

All around him, conversations raged. He sometimes wondered if he was the only member of his generation who could hear. Everyone else his age seemed to yell everything they said, even to people standing right next to them.

*Just don't let them see me.*

The two-minute warning bell finally rang out through the school. The students slowly began shuffling off to their next class. So far, so good. Nobody had noticed him. Despite that, he was still tortured. His proactive tormentors were nowhere to be seen but the passive antagonism of his scantily clad female school chums was relentless.

Their low-cut, skin-tight tops and extremely short skirts showed off the firm curves of young feminine beauty. Beneath his beta male stoicism, hormones raged just as fervently as those of the most masculine jocks in the school. They had a shot at getting in those short skirts. Not him. The girls were usually nice enough to him but their genuine adoration went to the very people he hoped were blind to his presence.

At last, he arrived at biology unscathed and unnoticed. He took his seat at the front of Mr. Bergman's science class. She sat next to him.

"Hi, Dylan," she said, with her usual bubbly smile, her long brown hair falling sleekly past her shoulders.

He smiled meekly to acknowledge the acknowledgement.

She was one of those girls that reminded him every day of his second class status on that thousand-person planet. Ashley Hood was a goddess.

Worse still, she was kind. She was always pleasant towards him and never treated him as her inferior. But he was, and he knew it. Every time she smiled and said hello it was a reminder of what he would never get.

The final bell blared through the school. Anyone who arrived to class now would be late.

"Good morning, class," said Mr. Bergman. "Pick a partner, someone sitting close to you. Today we're dissecting pigs."

His brown eyes met with her blue eyes by accident. Ashley's tanned skin further accentuated her piercing irises. He froze. She smiled, moving her desk towards his.

"You want to be my partner, Dylan?" she asked.

*Oh, do I ever—in every sense of the word.*

As Dylan stood to get the fetal pig, Ashley bent over her desk to flip through her notebook. Her shirt hung low and he gazed upon what seemed like heaven and the Promised Land rolled into one. She was wearing a black bra with pink hearts on it. Probably a matching thong too, but he would never know.

He snapped out of the trance and plucked one of the baby pigs from the pail of formaldehyde. When he came back she was still leaning over the desks flipping through her notebook—her tits still on display.

It was a long class.

# CHAPTER 2

**ACROSS** town, Staff Sergeant Lionel Stockwell closed in on his prey. The target was a local methamphetamine dealer named Willie Hogan. He'd been dealing to high school students for years. The cops had never been able to pin him down ... until Lionel took over the file. In three months, he'd nailed the bastard.

"First squad, follow me," Lionel commanded into his headset as his teams took their positions. "Second squad, prepare to come in the back entrance on my mark. Let's bust this son-of-a-bitch."

Two squads may have been overkill to arrest a local junkie but Lionel left nothing to chance. Rumor had it, the guy was heavily armed and a frequent abuser of his own product. Two SWAT teams was the bare minimum Lionel would accept for the operation.

"Is everyone in place around back?" Lionel asked over the radio.

"Rock and roll, Sergeant" replied his gung-ho second-in-command, Sergeant Elijah Hunter.

Lionel took a deep breath. If Hogan was armed, there was a chance a few of the officers wouldn't live to see the end of the raid. Nothing cut to the soul of a police unit like the loss of a comrade in the line of duty.

Lionel shook off the concerns. It was part of the job.

"All right gentlemen, on the count of three we move in," he said as adrenaline levels spiked. "One ... two ... three, bust it!"

The two squads burst through the front doors and the back doors simultaneously. Pandemonium ensued. Lionel could hear a woman scream, a baby cry and dozens of voices yelling as the two teams converged in the house.

Lionel arrived first on the landing. The top cop noticed a short staircase heading upstairs and a long staircase heading down to the basement directly in front of him. He heard the crying and the yelling but couldn't see anyone. Lionel could already smell the marijuana. Sadly, it masked the foul stench of the house. The place was an absolute dump. Dirty dishes were piled everywhere, garbage strewn all over, cigarette burns dotted the floors and the walls looked like they hadn't been painted since the Seventies. The bathrooms emanated an absolutely putrid smell. Bottles of drain cleaner, brake fluid, lye, along with the rest of the ingredients and utensils needed to prepare meth for the market were scattered throughout the house as were several needles and bongs. Hogan lived in pure filth.

Lionel's SWAT teams arrived behind him on the landing.

"Squad two, move downstairs and comb the area," Lionel ordered. "Squad one, follow me."

Just as he said that, a hail storm of Uzi 9mm bullets rained down on their position. Lionel spun around. He saw Hogan in the kitchen firing at them from behind a table he'd flipped over for cover.

"Get the fuck down now!" Lionel yelled at his men.

Willie Hogan knew how to use an Uzi. He could empty then reload a magazine with clockwork timing and precision.

The baby's cries in the background grew louder and more desperate as the Uzi's roar ripped through the house. The unknown woman's screams became hysterical. Bullets landed all around the officers. They shredded the walls, floors and doors surrounding their position.

All at once, Constable Eric Dejong flew back against the wall like he had been cow-kicked in the chest. Dejong was the youngest member of the team, joining the force only one month earlier.

"Jesus Christ, Dejong," Lionel said, as he crawled over to the twenty-two-year-old cop. Dejong's eyes were closed. Lionel placed his hand on the rookie's neck. His pulse was still strong but he had blood all down his chest.

"Get him the hell out of here," Lionel ordered.

Two other police officers removed their young comrade from the scene. The Uzi continued to pound their position with hellfire. Lionel had had about enough of this. Hogan was coming with him dead or alive.

*If Dejong dies, I'll have him pleading for a lethal injection.*

"Everyone get behind me," Lionel shouted over the gunfire.

He readied his assault rifle, flicked off the safety then turned right into Hogan's flurry of bullets. Time slowed down to a crawl. Twenty-two feet separated Lionel from Hogan. He could hear the bullets whiz past his head. The officers behind him stood mesmerized. Sergeant Hunter yelled at his leader to get down but his screams were muffled in Lionel's ears.

Hogan's clip emptied. He locked eyes with the officer approaching his position behind the flipped table. It caused the notorious drug-dealer to hesitate for the briefest of moments. This officer surprised him. The man was either crazy or fuckin' ballsy . . . or both.

Lionel raised his gun. He was now within ten feet of Hogan. The red laser on his rifle aimed squarely at his target's center of visible mass. Lionel exhaled half his breath then gently squeezed the trigger. He unloaded four rounds into the dealer before he could reload.

Hogan staggered backwards then collapsed. The whole exchange felt like an eternity to Lionel but it had lasted less than three seconds.

"Fuckin' A, sir! That was awesome!" yelled one of the men from the landing.

# THE OFFICER

"Call an ambulance," replied Lionel, focused on the task. The woman's screaming had stopped when he shot Hogan, but had started back up, reaching an ear-splitting shriek.

Lionel noticed some movement out of the corner of his right eye. She charged out from around the corner with a butcher's knife, running straight at the staff sergeant. The woman was high as a kite and strung out. She looked pale, gaunt and anorexic. Her eyes were lifeless and surrounded by dark bruises. Her hair disheveled. The hag screamed like a banshee. She was physically alive, but mentally absent. Needle marks and cutting scars alternately adorned her arms.

Lionel squeezed off one round at point blank. She was luckier than her man; it only hit her shoulder. She fell to the ground with a shattered collarbone. Two cops jumped on her and arrested her before she could get back up. They didn't know what she was on. If it was PCP, she could get back up without feeling any pain from the entry wound.

The second squad stormed the basement. They found a massive marijuana grow op, along with a meth and ecstasy lab. Hogan laced his weed with ecstasy without telling his customers. He also targeted youth. He would charge them normal street value for the first deal, then jack up the prices when they came back for more. If they tried to buy it from some other dealer, the customer would never get nearly the same high with natural weed. They would always come back to Hogan.

Four of Lionel's men administered first aid to Hogan until the EMS crew arrived. The woman was arrested and taken out by two other officers. The house was now quiet except for the crying baby.

"Where the hell's that coming from?" Lionel called, partially to himself and partially to the officers around him. He followed the baby's cries up the stairs.

"Hunter, Miller, follow me."

"Yes, sir," they replied in unison.

Lionel walked up the stairs, kicking dirty laundry out of the way as he side-stepped ashtrays and syringes, among other things. He wasn't exactly sure what was smeared all over the walls but it looked like human feces. At the top of the stairs, Lionel scanned the hallway. The baby's cry grew louder and clearer. He continued towards the baby's cries. When he arrived at the open door where the sound was coming from, he signaled to Hunter and Miller to take up position and be ready for anything. Lionel took a deep breath. After all he'd seen that day, nothing would surprise him.

But it did.

Lionel jumped into the open doorway, his rifle at the ready but all he saw was an adorable blond haired girl standing in a crib. She was no more than eighteen months old and utterly terrified. She had good reason to be. All around her crib was Hogan's arsenal: Two dozen sawed off shotguns, four submachine guns, ten handguns, a 12-inch hunting knife, a few hand grenades and an RPG-7 for good measure. He'd had no intention of going without a fight.

"Jesus Christ," Lionel gasped. "What's wrong with people?"

He shouldered his firearm, entered the child's room and carefully lifted the little girl out of her crib. She stopped crying immediately. The child looked tiny in the arms of the burly, six-foot-four police sergeant.

"Elijah," Lionel said to his second-in-command. "I want you and Miller to take the girl back to the precinct and make sure she's taken care of."

"Yes, sir."

As soon as he handed her off, the tears started to flow again. The officer gave her a big smile.

"There, there, little one. It's going to be okay," Lionel called softly after the baby as she disappeared down the hallway in the care of the two policemen.

The sirens on the police cars and ambulances lit up as Hogan and his sweetheart were wheeled off. Lionel led a sweep through the rest of the house.

Meanwhile, a crowd had gathered outside. The media was all over the area looking for an interview and as soon as Lionel walked out the front door, the hyenas in the press went crazy. Journalists shouted incoherently, cameras clicked and flashed incessantly. Leading the pack was Jonathan Pickett — an ambitious reporter with the Philipsville Herald.

"Hey Sarge, I hear that itchy trigger finger of yours was even twitchier than usual," the cocky, banty rooster redhead yelled at him. Lionel ignored him as he walked along the police tape towards his cruiser. "I need an interview for this article. Gimme five minutes!"

"Not a chance," replied the staff sergeant with disinterest.

"Oh, c'mon," Pickett whined. "I've got a 4:30 deadline. At least give me a quote."

"Get a job."

Pickett snickered then scribbled it down on his note pad.

"Thanks, Sarge! I'll call you later today at your office. I'm sure you'll have more time to chat then." Pickett then disappeared into the crowd. Lionel shook his head. He knew the little turd was already scouring the earth for another source, any source to talk to and that he would take flak from the armchair generals in the media for shooting Hogan but he really didn't care. Bad press got to many officers but not to him.

Lionel removed his Kevlar vest. He set it in the police cruiser then pulled out a bottle of water. He took a deep breath and tried to block out the commotion.

Chief John Paul O'Reilly arrived on the scene just as the house was secured. He walked up to his most trusted soldier. Lionel, engrossed in watching his men do their work, didn't even notice him.

O'Reilly put his hand on the broad shoulder of the most decorated member of the Philipsville Police Department. "You've proven yourself again Lionel," said the Chief with admiration in his voice.

"Thank you, sir."

O'Reilly smiled as they stood shoulder to shoulder, taking in the scene. It was still chaotic. The crowd lingered, the press jackals circled the wagons but at least the threat had been neutralized. This was relative calm by police standards.

# THE OFFICER

"Listen, when you get back to the station stop by my office," O'Reilly said. "We need to talk."

Lionel turned to Chief O'Reilly, a little concerned. "I'm listening. What's on your mind?"

O'Reilly shook his head. "No, we'll talk later. You need to get that wound looked after first." O'Reilly motioned to Lionel's forearm. It was oozing blood. He had caught a bullet from Hogan's Uzi and hadn't even noticed.

"Oh my God," Lionel sighed in amazement. He searched the police cruiser for a towel but couldn't find one.

The Chief patted him on the back. "Here, take this." O'Reilly removed his tie from around his neck. "Stick out your arm."

"You're kidding right?"

"It's just temporary to stop the bleeding," the chief replied. Lionel reluctantly stuck out his arm and O'Reilly wrapped the wound. "Now, get yourself to the hospital when you're done here, then swing by the office before you head home tonight."

Lionel was still leery about O'Reilly's cryptic request for a meeting.

"What's wrong, John Paul?"

"There's nothing wrong Lionel," he replied. "Nothing at all. Just come by my office before you leave for the day but get yourself to the hospital first." The chief jumped back into his car and was about to drive off when he poked his head out of the window. "By the way, Constable Dejong is fine. He has a cracked rib from the bullet hitting his vest but otherwise he's good."

Lionel was relieved to hear that piece of news but something didn't make sense.

"Hey, John Paul," Lionel shouted as O'Reilly was about to drive off. "He couldn't only have a cracked rib. He was bleeding."

Chief O'Reilly laughed and shook his head. "Trust me Stock, he wasn't cut." He pointed towards Lionel's arm. "That wasn't his blood you saw in there."

# CHAPTER 3

**THE** school bell blared throughout Wellington High, signaling the end of third period and the start of lunch. Mr. Bergman's students had spent the whole class dissecting fetal pigs and documenting everything they saw. After the bell rang, Mr. Bergman assigned homework.

"All right class, your five-page analysis of today's dissection is due Monday at the beginning of class."

The class groaned.

"Oh, come on," he said, half-mocking the grade eleven students. "It will take you guys thirty minutes to complete. I only need one analysis per pair."

The class started emptying out for lunch. Ashley, who had been chipper all class, now seemed miffed. She had plans for the night. "How am I going to get this done," she complained. "I don't have time tonight."

Dylan knew where this was going; he had been down this road before. Not just with Ashley but with other girls in school. "Don't worry, I'll take care of it," he surrendered. He knew it would do absolutely nothing to ever improve his chances with her but he had to do it anyway.

Ashley smiled. "Thanks Dylan!" she said, with renewed exuberance. "I don't want to burden you. Did you have plans tonight?"

The honest answer was no. He knew it. She probably knew it too but he would try to save some face. "Yeah, I've got a few things going on but it'll be fine," he said, forcing smile.

"Well, thanks for doing this. I owe you one." She then walked out of the classroom and off to lunch. He watched her leave. She didn't look back but it was still a beautiful sight.

Dylan Stockwell stood in the classroom all by himself, psyching himself up. He had remained invisible so far but nobody could hide in the cafeteria. He just hoped his tormenters would be quick about it, whatever it may be today. It changed daily. They possessed a seemingly endless supply of humiliation methods.

Dylan would have loved to sit with Ashley but he knew that was a pipe dream. Hell, he would have settled for any friendly company to join him over lunch hour but they had to approach him. He didn't have the stomach to handle a rejection. Someone else had to take the chance.

The school cafeteria was a zone of different groups, separated by invisible walls. The stoners had their tables, as did the jocks. The young skater punks sat closest to the windows. They usually split after twenty minutes, running outside in good weather, their boards under their arms, to practice new moves. The artsy students sat together. Dylan always found them agreeable but eccentric. The science geeks also banded together as did every other sub-culture and nobody interacted. A subtle form of apartheid was alive and well at Wellington High.

Dylan inhaled deep, composing himself before exiting the science class.

*Here we go.*

Head down, Dylan navigated the crowded corridors as best he could. He opened his locker to grab his lunch bag. Other students had pictures, bumper stickers and articles in their lockers but not him. His was bare out of fear of expressing himself; it would be an invitation for abuse. Someone higher up on the high school food chain could decorate their locker with the exact opinions, interests and beliefs of Dylan Stockwell and their reward would be flattery. Girls would swoon and their friends would think it was totally awesome. If he did it, there would be a different reaction. It would reaffirm his current status on the bottom rung. Dylan would rather not be reminded.

The cafeteria doors loomed large as he approached them. Like a soldier storming a village in an unholy war, Dylan thought to himself;

*What am I doing here?*

But he moved in anyway.

# CHAPTER 4

**ANDREW** Walter Reed came from money. Lots of it. The sixteen-year-old had received every break in life imaginable, yet always felt entitled to more. His father, Walter, owned multiple country clubs across the nation and made shrewd investments in the stock market. His mother, Betty, was a homemaker. Andrew was the oldest of four siblings.

Deeply religious, his parents made the kids attend church every Sunday. Walter, at Betty's insistence, tithed weekly. He was also a deacon of the Third Day Baptist Church in the community. Their eldest son learned to play the game early. He never whined or complained about going to church. He dressed up nicely every Sunday and smiled at every member of the flock. His parents fell for the guise as did everyone else.

Many mothers at the church quietly, while others not so quietly, hoped Andrew would notice their daughters. Truthfully, he had already "noticed" many of them. A few repeatedly, but their parents would never know. In the eyes of his family, he could do no wrong.

Andrew Reed stood six-foot-two and weighed 210 pounds. He started hitting the weights when he was fourteen years old and the steroids began six months later. Reed's fearsome temper was legendary. It wasn't the steroids either; he had a short fuse as a toddler and his folks did nothing to change it.

Betty and Walter never said no to him. Girls never said no to him. A few tried but that didn't stop him. Andrew learned early on that people jump out of a bulldozer's way.

His size and brutal aggression made him a star Wellington Warlock football player. He was the starting Offensive Tackle for the Warlocks and had won several awards for his prowess on the field. Rumors abounded that certain American universities had noticed the young pit bull and were preparing offers. Reed's coaches partially feared the boy but he was good at what he did, and the pressure from the school administration to win was too powerful.

It was school policy that nobody could play on a sports team if their academic score fell below a B average. Reed was lucky to get a C on any assignment. Often he got Ds or Fs. That was if he handed in the assignment at all but

# THE OFFICER

Wellington High obligingly looked the other way. Walter Reed was a wealthy alumnus and his son had duplicated his old man's success within the smaller universe of high school. Andrew Reed ruled the roost. No student, teacher, coach or school administrator could stop him.

# CHAPTER 5

**THE** school cafeteria was a zoo, the tables divided into their usual groups. People sat, more or less, in the same spot day after day. The cafeteria was jammed to the rafters. The smell of grease emanated from the kitchen. French fries with gravy, pizza, cupcakes and cola were served up in endless supply by the cafeteria broads. And yet, school officials always wondered why the students were borderline comatose in class immediately after lunch.

For many students, lunch time in high school was one hour of ruckus before classes resumed. It was a chance to catch up with friends in other classes—the highlight of the school day. Not for Dylan. He closed his eyes, hoping beyond hope that he could just be left alone, for once, to finish his lunch in peace. He entered the cafeteria and made a beeline for his usual spot at a table in the corner. It was as isolated as he could possibly get.

On his way there he saw them: the Philipsville Vipers; the resident bad asses of Wellington High. They were a group of people you didn't want to cross anywhere in the school.

They were five friends, all from wealthy families, who fancied themselves the epitome of all that was cool. Three of them played on the football team, the other two played lacrosse. Their sense of invincibility oozed out of every pore in their skin and the Vipers never fought a fair fight. Once, after a long night of drinking and multiple hits of acid, they jumped a man on the street and beat the shit out of him purely for entertainment.

They were Dylan's tormentors. They haunted his mind. They kept him awake at night. When he would fall asleep, they ruled his dreams. Their leader, Andrew Reed, was the worst of the bunch. A mean muscular son-of-a-bitch, he would cross the street to be nasty to someone. His icy blue eyes could burn holes through people.

Reed was a well known supplier of marijuana, meth, shrooms and even cocaine in the school. His four minions skulked around him, worshipping the ground he walked on and helping him with his dirty work.

Many untouchables relished the thought of pounding on Andrew Reed for all the misery he put them through but those fantasies were always crushed by the reality that Reed never fought alone. His buddies would jump in if needed, and frequently, even if it wasn't needed. Your best option was to endure the abuse.

Dylan got to his seat without incident. He had never gone a full lunch hour without something happening, let alone a full day and as he unwrapped his tuna fish sandwich, it started. He could feel it gathering like a storm in the distance. They were roughly thirty feet away.

A red Skittle flew through the air and bounced off the side of his head. He'd been noticed.

"Hey, faggot," Reed yelled at him. "If you got a problem we can take it outside."

A handful of Skittles crashed all around him. A few made contact.

The message was crystal clear: sit there and take it or get the living daylights knocked out of you. Dylan looked down and tried to ignore them. He had been told his whole life that bullies would leave him alone if he just ignored them. He knew this was bullshit but it was a Catch-22. He couldn't force them to stop, and ignoring them only encouraged their behavior. In moments like this Dylan lived life minute to minute, second to second.

The Vipers laughed maniacally, sounding like wild animals encircling their wounded prey. Another six or seven Skittles bounced around him, hitting the wall behind his head. "Oh man, so close," moaned Bobby Johnson. "Pass me another bag."

Dylan pulled out his book, *Oliver Twist*, and flipped it open. He was reading it for a book report in English class but right now it was a façade. There was no way he would be able to focus on it in the cafeteria. He just wanted to give the impression that nothing was bothering him, that he was oblivious to the bombardment.

More Skittles came his way. One landed in his pudding. Another hit him in the eye, causing him to wince. The Vipers hissed with delight.

"Nice one Bobby," commented Reed.

They would never throw all the Skittles at once. The Vipers preferred to throw a few at a time. It prolonged the humiliation. Reed would pull antennae off insects as a child. It was more fun than squashing the bug quickly. Some things never change.

They lobbed another handful, each taking turns.

"Ok boys, everyone take a handful of what's left," Reed instructed, realizing they were running out of ammo. They passed out the rounds evenly.

"On the count of three, we all throw at once. One . . ."

Dylan called forth all his strength to suppress all emotion.

". . . two . . ."

He swallowed hard, trying to remain casual and calm, as though nothing was happening.

"Three!!!"

With that, dozens of Skittles landed all around him. Many bounced off his head and face, whipped hard enough to sting. A few left welts on his body.

The hissing glee of the brood reached a fever pitch bordering on sexual. These guys got off on spreading pain.

Dylan went numb trying to ignore it. He could feel the anguish and the tears knot in his throat but he cut it off with a violent choke. With all his remaining strength he repressed the whole encounter. The Skittles were unique but the degradation was old hat. The Vipers always found new ways to humiliate Dylan.

All around the cafeteria, conversations continued uninterrupted. Everyone pretended not to notice, nobody said anything. It was like the whole thing never happened. But the welt on his neck and the Skittle in his pudding left no doubt that it was real.

# CHAPTER 6

**ROBERT** Taylor Johnson III was the eldest of three brothers. He inherited his full name from his father who, in turn, inherited it from his father. It was one of many heirlooms Bobby stood to benefit from over the course of his life.

Bobby's family was old money. His grandfather struck it big back in the forties and fifties buying up land in Texas and Alberta. He bought it for pennies, only to learn later that the land teemed with oil and the family had been comfortable even before this discovery. They soon went from well-off to fuck-you rich. When Bobby's grandpa died, he left a fortune for Bobby in his will; the kid was already a millionaire and not even eighteen years old.

The family owned a huge ten thousand square foot mansion in Philipsville and a three-storey cottage in the Hamptons, as well as a chalet in Provence. They had a maid and a butler on staff, as well as gardeners for his mother's roses all around the house. Bobby had never even had to make his own bed or work a part-time job in his whole life.

His family placed a high emphasis on sports. Bobby played football and baseball growing up but found his true calling was on the lacrosse field. He was a middie—Midfielder—for the Warlocks. Despite his passion for the sport, Bobby was as an average player. He wasn't nearly good enough for a full scholarship in the NCAA, a fact his father refused to accept.

Robert Taylor Johnson II, Bobby's father, ruled his home with an iron scepter. He was into wealth management and had done very well for himself independent of the inherited wealth. He had been a rabble-rouser when he was Bobby's age, so his father, Robert Taylor Johnson I, sent him off to military school, which straightened him out in quite a hurry.

Robert Johnson II was a natural athlete; he had played football for the Crimson Tide at the University of Alabama. He wanted his sons to follow in his footsteps more than anything. They definitely loved sports as much as their old man but lacked his killer instinct, natural talent and the will to win at any cost. These shortcomings followed Bobby throughout other parts of his existence. He was fine in school but no scholar. He was fine on the sports field but no star. Aside from the silver spoon in his mouth, Bobby was nothing special and he knew it.

Bobby always felt like he was in his father's shadow. His sense of inferiority came from everything his dad had accomplished in his own right. His father's one Achilles' heel was his need to be accepted by others. His dad operated the household with an authoritarian streak but Bobby soon realized that so long as he never did anything publicly that would embarrass the family, his dad didn't really care what he did. It was all about image.

Bobby and his brothers all picked up on this. They could do pretty much what they wanted at home and could do whatever they wanted when they were out with friends, so long as it never got back to Big Bob. Ignorance was bliss. Robert and Dawn Johnson never even suspected that he was anything other than an angel because they never heard a bad thing said about him. Truthfully, other parents, coaches and teachers had expressed concerns to them about the group of people Bobby hung out with but Robert and Dawn would hear none of it.

# CHAPTER 7

**DYLAN** returned to the comfort of his own invisibility following lunch hour. His next class was English which went by without incident. His last period of the day that semester was phys ed. Nowhere was the divide between the Morlocks and the Eloi of high school more pronounced than in the damp locker rooms of Wellington High. To make matters worse, two of the Vipers, Bobby Johnson and Lucius (Boomer) Simons were also in that class.

Time always seemed to fly when he had something to dread. In that sense, gym class was a partial blessing for Dylan. Classes ranged from bearable to awful but at least it made the rest of the day feel shorter.

The school bell ended English class. He had ten minutes to walk the Baton Death March to the locker room. Dylan always tried to get there early and change into his gym clothes before anyone else arrived. It reduced the chances of something happening before class. Usually Bobby and Boomer were just loud and obnoxious, but on some occasions they would up the ante.

Dylan would never forget the time Bobby chased the fat kid, Will Harburn, around the change room with a damp towel trying to snap him on the ass. The kid had showered and was in his tighty-whities when Bobby decided it would be a fun thing to do. Even Dylan had laughed. Will seemed to be a good sport about the whole thing and laughed it off. Something always happened in the change rooms after class. Dylan just hoped he wouldn't be the target today.

In gym class they were learning basketball. Most kids in the class didn't know how to play and Dylan was able to blend in. Mr. Coleman was the teacher. He seemed like a decent guy. He could be rough on the students but he was fair. He even mocked the Vipers a few times.

At the end of class, Mr. Coleman informed the students they would learn wrestling the following week. Dylan was horrified. Having his face in someone else's crotch and armpits wasn't his idea of a great way to end the day. He knew nothing about the sport but he was pretty sure it would be one more excuse for the bigger kids to whip his ass. When they learned lacrosse, Dylan could barely walk by the end of class from all the body checks, slashes and tackles he took during the game. Both Bobby and Boomer were on the lacrosse team and they had thoroughly enjoyed that class. That's a sport where physically destroying your opponent is only a peripheral goal. In wrestling, it's the whole objective.

Mr. Coleman dismissed the class so they could all get showered and changed. The moment they got back to the change room, it began.

Bobby walked up nonchalantly to a kid in the class named Tim. "Hey Timbo, flex your abs. Let's see 'em."

Boomer came over. "Dude, what are you doing?" he asked Bobby.

Bobby put his arm around Tim. "This kid is ripped," he explained to Boomer, with Tim not sure what to make of it all. "You got to see it. He's wiry as fuck."

Boomer shrugged and turned to Tim. "All right, let's see it."

Tim lifted up his shirt and did his best to flex his stomach muscles. Dylan watched out of the corner of his eye. He wasn't sure what the Vipers were up to because Tim definitely didn't have anything to brag about.

"C'mon man, flex harder," said Bobby. "Concentrate!"

Tim, determined to impress the Vipers, mustered every ounce of strength in his body to flex his abdominal muscles. His entire body was locked up, his lungs full of air, his hands clenched in fists. Without any warning, Bobby sacked Tim in the groin with the back of his hand. The kid hit the ground in pain and everyone lost it. Even Dylan had to smother his laughter. Boomer and Bobby were on cloud nine. They couldn't believe Tim fell for it.

Tim was sucking wind. He crawled to the bench and pulled himself to his feet, more than a little humiliated. The pain from his groin spread like fire through his body. Even his gums throbbed. The Vipers were euphoric.

Dylan decided to shower before heading home. He tried not to look at Tim. The kid had already suffered enough but Dylan hoped Tim had borne the brunt of the Vipers' abuse for everyone and that they would be satisfied for the rest of the day.

He was wrong.

Dylan walked into the shower with the towel around his waist. Boomer watched him. "Hey, nobody drop the soap," he yelled out at the top of his lungs. "Stockwell's in the shower."

Everyone laughed again and Dylan would have joined in if someone else was the butt of the joke. Boomer was about to make an already awkward situation worse. If there was ever a time Dylan did not want to attract attention, it was in the showers at Wellington High, but he stepped in anyway and started the water. The steam filled the shower area and eventually the whole locker room. At first, Dylan was alone in the shower. After three or four minutes, Boomer and Bobby made their way in. They had found two plungers next to the toilets and were having a lightsaber duel with them. Dylan pretended not see them. He wanted to get in and out as quickly as possible.

"Hey, Stockwell," Bobby shouted with urgency. "Check this out!"

Dylan did a one-eighty and stuck his face into the wrong end of a plunger. Bobby had it pointed right at the back of Dylan's head. He did a face plant into the suction cup the moment he turned around.

"Oh, shit!" Dylan exclaimed, recoiling from the plunger.

# THE OFFICER

Bobby laughed hysterically at the gag. Before Dylan could turn around, Boomer knocked his soap to the ground.

"Are you going to pick that up would you like me to?" he asked.

Dylan froze; there was no right answer. Boomer stood there with a grin on his face. The Vipers never grew tired of hurling insults like faggot, queer, or dyke at anyone. Finding new and revolting ways to depict someone as a homosexual was an Olympic sport for them yet they enjoyed horsing around in the showers a lot with themselves and others. Dylan was tempted to point out this contradiction but thought twice. He didn't want to die there and then.

Before he could answer he noticed a strange feeling on his right leg, a sensation slightly warmer than the water flowing from the shower head. In shock, Dylan looked down and then slowly looked back up at Bobby. It took him a moment to process the image: Bobby was urinating on his leg. Dylan's eyes bulged. It was one of those, "is this actually happening?" moments. Finally, his brain sent the necessary response to the rest of his body.

"What the fuck, man!" was all Dylan could muster as he grabbed his towel and darted out of the shower, feeling no cleaner than before.

Bobby and Boomer were in hysterics again.

"I was wondering how long it was going to take him to notice," said Boomer, gasping for air between laughs.

"Hey, dude, you forgot your soap," yelled Bobby. "You should come back and get it."

Dylan was moving as fast he could to get out of there. He put his clothes on without drying himself. He'd had enough for one day. Bobby walked out from around the corner naked, wet and holding Dylan's bar of soap.

"You dropped your soap, man. I picked it up for you," he said to him. "You missed the show."

Dylan didn't look up at him. He finished dressing and moved to the door.

"If you don't want it, can I have it?" Bobby asked with a smirk.

Ignoring him, Dylan walked out of the change room.

"I'll take that as a yes," Bobby said to himself, returning to the shower with Dylan's soap.

It was Friday. Dylan had earned two days of freedom from the hell that was Wellington High. He now had the weekend to help restore his sanity.

# CHAPTER 8

**BETWEEN** his imposing physique and a decorated service record, Lionel Stockwell cast a long and respected shadow on the Philipsville police force. Although raised a Catholic, Lionel adhered more to the Calvinist principles of frugality, discipline and duty above all. He turned a tough, unemotional face to the world of crime.

Taking down murderers, rapists and drug dealers (like Willie Hogan) was the most satisfying part of being a cop for Lionel. It wore him down some days but the adrenaline rush was perversely addictive. He also knew he could never live without the camaraderie of the police force; The Brotherhood-of-Arms—one of the world's largest fraternities. They got paid to bust bad people. For him and the vast majority of his peers, it was a vocation. Driven by an iron clad sense of duty, Lionel Stockwell was unrelenting in his pursuit of criminals on the streets of Philipsville.

He was completely different around his family. He and his wife, Dana, moved to the suburbs to raise their son, Dylan, the pride of Lionel's life. He was their only child. After years of trying, they had given up on having kids. Then one day, Dana woke up feeling nauseous and weak. A visit to the doctor confirmed what they'd previously thought impossible: she was pregnant.

They had heard that Philipsville was a peaceful, quiet and affluent city. That's why they had moved there shortly after Dylan was born. Although housing prices were a little beyond their financial reach, it was worth every penny if it meant that Dylan could grow up in peace. Failures like Willie Hogan seemed few and far between. Every town, no matter how big or how small, has problems. It was tough for Lionel not to become cynical and jaded when all he dealt with were the bad parts of society but he always knew they had it good there.

Wellington Secondary School was a no-brainer for their son. It had a tremendous reputation for success. Great facilities, outstanding athletics and ninety percent of all its graduates went on to university. The vast majority of the kids at the school came from wealthy families who contributed a lot to the school. There was a strong sense of pride and school spirit at Wellington High.

When it came time for Dylan to go to high school, Lionel and Dana sent him there confident it would be the perfect spot for their son.

# CHAPTER 9

**LUCIUS** Willard Simons was the youngest of two children. His older sister had graduated from Wellington High the previous year. She now attended Penn State on a full volleyball scholarship. Not that she needed it. Their family had piles of money.

Lucius's father Abner was a powerful corporate attorney in one of the country's biggest law firms. He had worked there for over twenty years, becoming a full partner after just five years with the company. Abner Simons was the mergers and acquisitions guru, handling some of the biggest takeovers in the business world. He was frequently featured on the cover of various legal magazines.

There was a price he paid for success. An ordinary day meant sixteen hours at the office. He was known to go three or four days straight without stopping. After his wife died of breast cancer ten years earlier, Abner further buried himself in his work to escape the pain. His kids never saw him.

Lucius harbored a quiet, simmering resentment of his father. He hated him for being absent all the time. As a baby, Abner had given Lucius the nickname Boomer because of his lung power. When Lucius cried in his crib, Abner said the walls shook. Boomer was now seventeen-years-old and the moniker was more fitting than ever. With puberty having finally settled in, Lucius's once squeaky tone was replaced with a powerful, commanding voice. Another gift from his dad.

To compensate for his absenteeism, Abner gave his children everything they wanted. Both kids had their own cars. They also both had Visa's in their own names with dad paying the bill at the end of every month, no questions asked.

Each Christmas, spring and summer break, the kids would go on multiple trips, fully paid for by Abner. Boomer spent six weeks touring Europe and then two weeks at the end in Cancun the previous summer. The rest of the Vipers had joined him in Mexico, wreaking havoc at their five-star resort with complete impunity.

The family owned a cottage in the Muskokas in Ontario. Boomer and his sister used the cottage for parties whenever they wanted. If the place was a mess afterwards, the kids hired cleaners to come in and put it all back together, charging it to their credit cards as usual.

Boomer was a striker on the Wellington High lacrosse team. He was definitely a skilled player but his sister inherited most of the athleticism in the gene pool. Their father never attended a single one of their matches. The Warlocks had made it to the regional finals the previous year in lacrosse but Abner hadn't even bothered to show up. Boomer had scored twice but the Warlocks still lost four to three.

After the game, there had been a party at the home of one of his teammates. Boomer got smashed and started ripping into his dad for never being around. His friends chalked it up to the weed and excessive amounts of malt liquor. It couldn't have been a genuine rant. They saw how much Boomer got from his father in the way of designer clothing and a Chevrolet pick-up truck, among many other things. They assumed he was just a little too hammered for one night.

It was a cry for help. Boomer knew how good he had it but it was still not good enough. He also knew he would never find a sympathetic ear because he had everything in life because of his father, yet he still wanted more from his dad. He wanted his attention and a little affection. He wanted to hear his father mention how proud he was of his son and how much he loved him but it never happened. Even when Boomer got in trouble at school or tried to cause problems at home his Dad never took the bait.

The anger and the resentment built daily. Boomer took it out on others. He was mad at the world.

# CHAPTER 10

**LIONEL** Stockwell drove from the hospital back to the police station. The doctor wanted him to stay after bandaging his arm but Lionel felt fine, so he left.

As he was driving across town, he received a text message on his BlackBerry. Willie Hogan had survived. His big-shot New York City lawyer was already complaining about police brutality and threatening legal action. Hogan's junkie sweetheart also survived except she was too strung out to either confess or deny any accusations.

Complaints about police tactics never bothered Lionel. He was satisfied with the truth; as long as it was on his side, everything was fine. He was rare in this regard on the police force. The shameless opportunism of certain lawyers and the deliberate, ideological stupidity of various politicians and journalists infuriated many police officers but not Lionel Stockwell.

One exception was the perennially ignorant question, "Why didn't you shoot them in the leg?" It was asked every time an officer fired his or her gun. It annoyed Lionel but anyone who has used a firearm understands the absurdity of the question, which is why he was able to let it roll off.

However, he was by no means passive or docile in the face of vicious and unsubstantiated allegations levied against him or any of his comrades. A few years earlier, he was in a media scrum, surrounded by journalists. They fired question after question at him. Earlier that afternoon, he had Tasered a man who was high on PCP. The loser was a known wife abuser and had charged at one of the cops with something in his hand. It turned out to be a butter knife. The man went into cardiac arrest after the Tasering and was rushed to hospital. He was still alive but it had become a public-relations nightmare for the police force.

Jonathan Pickett had hounded Lionel during that scrum, asking Lionel why he used a Taser on a man armed with only a butter knife.

Lionel didn't even hesitate. "He charged at a member of my team and wouldn't obey our commands to get on the ground," he told the group of reporters. "I'd do it again in a heartbeat."

"Even with the hindsight that he only had a butter knife?" asked another reporter.

"Especially with the hindsight that he only had a butter knife," responded Lionel.

"But why a Taser," Pickett persisted. He was always trying to get under Lionel's skin hoping he would get angry and say something stupid. It would make for a better quote. "Don't you have other options at your disposal?"

"Yeah," Lionel said, without a hint of sarcasm in his voice. "I could have shot him." Lionel had allowed that comment to sink in as the reporters waited for a punch line that never came. "And if we didn't have Tasers, that's exactly what I would have done."

The answer was honest but failed to win over the headline whores. He was roasted the next day in the media but Lionel had no regrets. He'd used his Taser since that incident whenever it was required without hesitation. Lionel's overriding philosophy on the matter was simple and he drilled it into every new recruit:

*At the end of the day, the good guys go home.*

The staff sergeant finally arrived back at the police station. He had some paperwork to take care of. Otherwise, he was done for the day. He just needed to speak to the chief. He hadn't the foggiest notion what John Paul wanted to chat about.

He was on a first-name basis with Chief O'Reilly despite their different places on the chain of command. They went back a long time and each had a strong respect for the other. John Paul was Lionel's staff sergeant when he first joined the force as a green, idealistic constable ready to take on the world. O'Reilly had never seen a more talented and versatile police officer. He knew the young man would make a great cop.

Lionel loved working for John Paul because his whole life was devoted to the police force. As their chief, John Paul defended his officers without fail. His ambitions were not for some higher office. He hated politics and was motivated by a very simple, basic impulse of duty just like Lionel Stockwell. For this reason, Lionel knew he could always count on the chief's support when the self-righteous and the willfully ignorant in the cheap seats lectured him on how to do his job.

Lionel approached the chief's office and knocked on the door. O'Reilly was expecting him.

"Come on in, Lionel," came the chief's booming baritone from the other side of the door.

Lionel entered the room and stood at attention. Even though they were close friends he still gave his chief the formal respect owed to the rank. The Chief's office was decorated with family pictures and medals he had received during his thirty-year career.

"Grab a seat Lionel, take it easy."

"Thanks John Paul," he said, pulling up a chair. "What's all this about?"

O'Reilly reclined in his chair with a half-smile on his face. He pointed at Lionel's arm.

"Have you told Dana about your arm yet?"

# THE OFFICER

Lionel had been dreading going home all day for that reason. He knew Dana was going to freak out. For the most part, Dana navigated her marriage to a police officer with a "don't ask, don't tell" policy. She was always supportive and understanding, but constantly worried about his safety. She could suppress the concerns except on the rare occasion when Lionel would come home with a black eye or a bloody nose after breaking up a fight or arresting a noncompliant. That always hit a little too close to home for Dana's liking. His being shot would drive her over the edge.

"No, I haven't," he said after a long pause.

O'Reilly smiled and nodded. He had been in Lionel's position, down in the trenches. That was truly where he belonged but he started working behind a desk when the broken bones and bruises became too much for his wife, Mindy, to bear. She begged him to leave the force. For John Paul, that wasn't an option. But for the sake of his marriage, O'Reilly opted for a leadership role in the department and had a knack for it. He had now been chief of the Philipsville Police Service for five years.

"Lionel," the police Chief said, seriousness in his voice. "You turn fifty soon. You've been on the front lines for nearly thirty of them. Have you ever thought about changing gears?"

"No," snapped Lionel, even though the opposite was true. He had given a lot of thought to taking a position in the unit where he could keep a lower profile. Not out of desire but because Dana's patience for the profession, much like Mindy's, had worn thin. O'Reilly called his bluff.

"Yes, you have," he said. "Every warhorse thinks about it at some point."

Lionel still wasn't sure why he was in his boss's office; he didn't like where this conversation was heading.

"What do you want from me, John Paul?" he asked, leaning forward across the chief's desk. "Are you offering me an early retirement package, or what? If you're firing me, could you not have picked any day other than the day I'm shot to hand me my pink slip?"

Chief O'Reilly shook his head. "You're not being fired, Lionel, and you know it," he said. "On the contrary, I need you here by my side."

Lionel was now completely confused, but before he could ask anything more, O'Reilly spoke again.

"James Regan gave me his letter of resignation today," he said, referring to his deputy. "He's decided to retire to the golf course, and spend more time with his wife and grandkids."

"Good for him," said Lionel. "What does this have to do with me?"

"I'm offering you his job. You interested?"

The proposal caught Lionel off guard. He and Dana had talked about retirement, thinking they might be able to manage it within the next five years. Dana was a nurse at the local hospital. They had managed their money well. Their home was completely paid off and Dylan's college fund was where they wanted it to be. They could afford to pay for his entire post-secondary education but they wanted him to carry half the burden so he would appreciate it more and learn the value of money. They were well positioned to retire.

"I'm speechless," was all Lionel could muster. It was a huge promotion and a big pay jump but there was a downside; his days as a street soldier were over. He would work behind a desk for the rest of his time with the force. O'Reilly then leaned forward on his elbows, a somber look on his face.

"There's something else, Lionel," he said, then hesitated. "I won't be here much longer either. By this time next year, I'll have also retired." O'Reilly stood up and looked out the window. Lionel could see the emotion in his eyes. "If you accept this promotion, you'll be a shoo-in to replace me." O'Reilly paused to see if he was making any headway. He turned from the window and sat back down, looking his top officer square in the eye.

"Lionel, there's nobody else I trust more with this police department than you. If I could leave this position in the care of an honorable man, I'll be able to retire in peace. I can't see myself leaving until I'm sure my police officers are in good hands."

Lionel didn't say anything. He stood up slowly, took a deep breath and walked over to the sink in O'Reilly's office. He poured himself a glass of water and pondered the whole thing. It was a lot to take in.

He thought about Dana and Dylan. He thought about all that happened that morning. It was a decision that would permanently change his life. He would never be able to go back to the action once he left it. That thought alone forced a knot in his throat. O'Reilly knew exactly what was going through Lionel's mind. He had been there himself five years earlier. He stood up, walked over to Lionel and put a hand on his shoulder.

"What do you say, old friend," he asked. "This city needs you, the police out there need you. Your family needs you . . . and so do I." O'Reilly appealed to Lionel's sense of duty. "In all the years I've known you, you've never faltered in the line of duty. Now I need you to seriously consider this offer for both of our sakes."

The staff sergeant took it all in but his decision was already made.

# CHAPTER 11

**DYLAN** arrived home from school. The walk home was tranquil. He was actually able to think and reflect on the day. Nobody roughed him up; he didn't have to run from pine cones hurled at his head like he did the previous week. All in all, not a bad day. Definitely not the worst.

The house was empty when he arrived, both parents still at work. After six hours of repressed teenage hormones clashing with the visual stimulus of teenage eye candy, he was about to burst. He went into his room and turned on his computer. He signed on to Facebook, the opium of his generation. Username: dylanisking@hotmail.com; Password: AshleyHood69.

With that, he now had access to the greatest supply of soft-core pornography on the planet. He had over six hundred Facebook friends. Dylan wondered where those friends were at lunch time in the school cafeteria.

He scanned his profile. There was nothing new. No messages, no wall posts, no photo or status comments. Just as before. He then got down to the real reason he'd logged on.

"Ashley Hood," he said to himself as he typed her name into the search option. Ashley was one of his Facebook friends. She'd even posted on his wall—twice. Both were always thank-yous for birthday wishes. Her comments were kind but brief. Regardless, he never let that ruin this moment. It was the only quality time he ever got to spend with her.

Ashley had recently posted three photo albums from her recent trip to the Dominican Republic. She was tagged in several others.

Dylan opened the first album. Halfway through, the pictures went from her and her friends in airports to Ashley and her friends on the beach in bikinis. He clicked from picture to picture, to picture. Her athletic, tanned body in a white two-piece captivated every inch of him.

He got to the end of the first album then opened the second. In this one, she was wearing a red, strapless bikini. In one picture she was lying on the beach smiling, the next was a close-up of her face. The next five or six showed her fooling around on the beach with friends, swimming in the blue ocean then walking out dripping wet. There were other pictures of them out for dinner or at the bars. Dylan skipped over them, focusing on the beach pictures.

He clicked open the third album; his heart rate already pounding from the first two. A black bikini was now the wrapping on the gift. He clicked through picture after picture until he came across his favorite one on the entire Facebook network—Ashley and her friend Sarah Jane, hugging each other on the beach, their breasts pushed firmly together, as they posed for the picture. Dylan went rock hard.

He gazed at the picture for another five seconds then went over to his bed, unzipping his jeans.

In his mind, he's on that beach with her. Just the two of them. Otherwise, the beach is empty. She's wearing the black bikini, his favorite, as she swims out of the ocean. Every part of her is soaked. He stands up and walks towards her. She walks towards him. They meet halfway. She starts making him happy.

She gets on her knees in front of him granting him visions of paradise. She keeps going while she unties her bikini to expose her firm breasts and large erect nipples. Dylan tells her what to do. Feel them. Pinch them. Push them together. She does as she's told. He is, after all, king.

After he's had enough, they both strip completely naked. He takes her from behind. She's beyond aroused. She can't get enough of him. She loves him and loves every minute of it. She needs it.

Dylan pulls out just before climaxing, turns her around and does her one more favor. He explodes on Ashley's sweaty bosom, marking its territory. Not like he has to. She doesn't want it from anyone other than him. Not after getting fucked by The King. Everyone else would be lesser mortals by comparison to Dylan.

Ten seconds later, his head cleared. Reality returned. It was the most redundant lesson; he knew it would never happen.

The house was still empty. Dylan opened his door ever so slightly to ensure nobody was there, then wobbling off to the bathroom to clean up. He had homework to do in a few subjects but he would tackle biology first.

# CHAPTER 12

**JONATHAN** Pickett typed feverishly at his computer. His fingers flew across the keyboard in rapid-fire sequence. He had thirty minutes to go before deadline; this was going to be tight. Pickett worked for the Philipsville Herald. There were thirty-five reporters on staff and he was by far the most accomplished in his short career.

Empty coffee cups, chocolate bar wrappers and cans of Red Bull littered his cubicle. A Marlboro burned away slowly in the already overflowing ashtray on his desk despite many "No Smoking" signs around the office. Pickett lived and breathed his job. He worked endless hours, skipping meals and sleep. He had a bottle of Jack Daniels in his desk to calm his nerves. It was three quarters empty and resting next to two other bottles of J.D. One empty, the other full.

Pickett hailed from the Eastern Seaboard of the United States. He grew up in the Bronx. Being a small, red-headed kid, he learned to throw fists early in life. His parents had frequently expressed their exasperation at the kid's energy levels. He never slowed down, settled down or quieted down. He discovered journalism at the age of fourteen and channeled his frenetic activity into that one vocation. While other kids were trying out for track, learning to play guitar or auditioning for the drama club, Jonathan Pickett was editor of the high school newspaper. He earned the respect of his classmates by covering everything that happened at the school. He would always be found at any sporting event, drama production, bake sale or science fair with a camera around his neck and a notepad in his hand.

Pickett eventually distinguished himself while away at post-secondary, earning his MA in journalism from New York University. His writing was decent but it was his risk-taking ventures that got him noticed. While at university, he dyed his red hair black, put in dark contact lenses, glued on a long fake beard and flew himself to Iraq to embed himself in the civilian population. He wanted to study the actual effects of the international sanctions on the country without the bias and spin of the mainstream media. Despite a few close calls he emerged unscathed and wrote a feature article that appeared in *The New Republic* about the devastation the Iraqi people suffered due to the embargo. That put him on the map. Over the next ten years, Pickett racked up the awards and honors for his incisive, investigative writing. And there was no target he loved more than the police.

Pickett made it his mission to expose police abuse, corruption and wrongdoing, real or otherwise. It became his shtick while in New York. He wrote venomous critiques of the New York Police Department while interning with the *New York Times*.

Despite his success, Pickett's combative personality clashed often with editors and coworkers alike. They found him rude, vulgar and arrogant—three traits Pickett fully acknowledged with pride. There was also a large amount of jealousy from his fellow reporters at the newspaper. Pickett was very good at what he did, his work ethic was unmatched and people resented him. As complaints about his style and his poisonous interactions with work colleagues piled up on the Editor-in-Chief's desk, Pickett's days at the *New York Times* were numbered. The editor didn't fire him since that would have led to a lawsuit from the hard-nosed reporter so he reassigned Pickett to the Arts section instead.

He quit the paper the next day which is exactly what his editor had expected. Pickett was a crime beat reporter to the core. After an intense, expletive-laced tirade in his boss's office, Pickett stormed out of the building but he wasn't unemployed for long.

The *Philipsville Herald* was hiring and approached the young scrapper about joining the paper. Philipsville was much smaller than New York City but it was still a decent size. Pickett accepted the offer not thinking he would stay there for longer than a year but when he arrived, he found the Philipsville Police Department to be a perfect foil for his own interests and ambitions. He had developed a particular hatred for one of the rising stars on the force, Lionel Stockwell. Pickett hated the guy's approach to criminal justice. It reminded him of former New York City mayor Rudy Giuliani's attitudes towards law enforcement that, Pickett believed, trampled on civil liberties, encouraged police brutality and targeted visible minorities.

However, he could never get any insider to dish the dirt on this one cop. Pickett could often get police to divulge information to him anonymously but Lionel Stockwell was the one that always got away. Whenever he asked his contacts about the staff sergeant, they would clam up. It drove him crazy.

The clock in the newsroom read 4:17 p.m. He had thirteen minutes before he had to file. This story was going to be big. Lionel had repeatedly shot a man and woman in their own home while leading a SWAT team. This was the story he had been waiting for. He hoped it would force one of his inside sources to speak to him on the record about Lionel Stockwell when the story hit the front pages.

He knew that was unlikely but Jonathan Pickett was undaunted.

# CHAPTER 13

**ANDREW** Reed and his buddies went back to Boomer's place after school. There was a big party planned for that night at Sarah Jane Harnick's house. Her parents were apparently out of town for the weekend.

The Vipers never received an official invite to the kegger but they didn't need one. They showed up to whatever party they felt like crashing. They once barged in on a party where they knew nobody at all. One guy asked them to leave. Reed cracked him in the face. The guy didn't dare ask them to leave a second time.

Boomer had broken into his father's liquor cabinet. They had been drinking since 4:30 p.m. that afternoon and smoking cigars from Abner's humidor. They already had a good buzz going when Andrew Reed pulled out his gift to the group.

"All right, boys," he said, holding out his hand. "Enjoy yourselves."

He had ten pellets of acid, two for each of them. Reed was a well-known dealer within certain circles in the city. He dealt to his buddies but never charged them. They often helped him deal it out and enforce contracts around school and in the community. The least he could do was share the wealth.

"Wicked," said Rocco Palermo. "You're the man, Reed!"

"You got that right, Rock!" said Reed, grinning. "All right, c'mon you pussies, take the hits and let's get this night started."

"Bitchin'! Who gave you this stuff?" asked Carl Hicks, the token brown-noser of the Vipers. His parents were wealthy and apathetic. From the time he was eleven years old, Carl had no rules or responsibilities. His father had been a star with the Wellington Warlock football team thirty years earlier. Out of loyalty and because his father was a wealthy alumnus, the coach secured a spot on the football team for him. Carl never played, which suited him just fine. He didn't even like football but it kept his dad happy.

"The usual," responded Reed. "Old Man Hogan dealt me quite the supply a month ago but you guys had better enjoy it. It's the last of my stockpile for a while." The four other Vipers looked surprised. Reed had a seemingly endless supply of narcotics. "Hoagie was greased today by the goddamned police," he snarled. "Those fucking pigs broke into his place then shot him and Veronica."

Bobby chuckled.

"Well, I guess we owe them a favor for shooting that bitch."

Reed punched him in the shoulder.

"Hey, man, shut the fuck up. This isn't funny." Reed had been racking his brain ever since he heard the news about Hogan. He didn't know what he was going to do.

Drug money made him a king. Despite being underage, he could bribe his way into any bar, nightclub or casino. He would purchase liquor and tobacco with impunity and gamble compulsively. His parents gave him lots of toys like his car, laptop, PlayStation and countless other gadgets. He got whatever he wanted but they were oblivious to his darker habits. Reed feared they would become suspicious if he spent their money on these pursuits so he raised his own money instead. Until that day, his drug money covered his extracurricular activities but it was about to dry up.

All five of them popped the LSD tablets at the same time. Twenty minutes later, things were all fucked up. Someone kept tilting the world on them. Bobby accidentally knocked a Bible off the coffee table. Carl got down on his hands and knees, gathering up all the words that had fallen out of the book, and spent the next ten minutes trying to put them all back together.

They sat around drinking and playing Xbox. It was hard playing Grand Theft Auto when the graphics looked like nothing but black oscillating blobs on the screen.

"Hey, where we going again tonight?" asked Bobby, about two hours after taking the acid.

"Sarah Jane Harnick's house," replied Boomer.

"Oh, man, she's so hot! I'd fuck her," slurred Bobby. "I think she's looking for cock. I'll feed it to her tonight."

Rocco chimed in. "You can have Harnick. I've heard she's received a lot of dick in her time. She's all yours."

They all laughed at Rocco's observation. He had his eye on someone else.

"Is Ashley Wood going to be there tonight?" he sputtered.

"Yeah," the other four shouted in unison.

"She's mine," said Rocco. As he went to stand up, the room moved on him and he fell over. The others laughed. "Yup, if she's there I'm going to tear that pussy apart. Shit, I don't know if she can handle me. I may bust her in half."

Boomer, Bobby and Carl started laughing but were cut off by Reed who flew across the room and tackled Rocco, pounding him relentlessly in the face until blood was gushing from his nose and mouth.

"If you fucking touch her, I'll cut your balls off and stuff 'em down your throat," he screamed. "You got that?"

Reed had wanted Ashley for years but she was one girl who had resisted him. She had gone to two semi-formals with him at school and he piled on the charm—flowers, dinner; he had even sprung for Veuve Clicquot one night. She was always sweet and said thank you but never demonstrated gratitude the way Andrew Reed believed a woman should when graced by his presence.

"And that goes for the rest of you too," he hissed.

Rumor had it that Ashley was still a virgin and Andrew Reed was determined to deflower her. He loved the tightness of a pure girl and the peace of mind that they didn't have STDs. He hated condoms; they cut the pleasure. This way was better.

Reed punched Rocco one last time for good measure. He stood up and left the room, pushing Bobby out of the way in the progress. The other three didn't say a word. They could hear Reed snorting with anger. Rocco pulled himself up to his knees, spitting out blood onto the floor. He couldn't see out of his left eye.

Carl looked over at the clock. "Hey, boys, let's roll," he yelled to break the awkward silence. "We've got bitches to fuck and hoes to pimp."

"Shotgun!" shouted Reed, returning to the room. He either drove or sat in the passenger seat. Bobby once sat in the front seat and Reed dragged him out by the hair. None of the Vipers said or did anything without Reed's say-so.

Rocco staggered to his feet. His nose gushed blood, a tooth was knocked out and he had a black eye.

"Hey, guys, wait for me," he pleaded. "I just want to splash some water on my face."

"C'mon, you twat," yelled Reed. "We don't have all night."

In his stupor, Rocco grabbed a curtain and yanked it off the rod, thinking it was a towel. He stumbled into the kitchen and splashed water on his face. He swore he had only been at the sink for ten seconds. Apparently, it was more like five minutes. With a violent jerk, he was dragged by the collar of his shirt through the house and out the front door by Reed, then tossed in the back of the pickup truck.

"When I say move, I fucking mean it," he yelled like a father scolding his child. "You're pissing me off tonight, Rock."

Rocco sat in the back of the pickup, humiliated and broken. He could feel the tears welling up behind his eyes. None of the other Vipers did anything to intervene. They didn't want to get an ass-kicking either. It seemed like one of them always got beat up every night they were about to head out and party. Rocco absorbed more punishment than the others.

Rocco didn't want to go to the party anymore but he knew he would get another beating if he backed out now. He did the only thing he could do in this situation, which happened frequently for each of the Vipers.

"I'm sorry, man," he muttered pathetically to his superior. "I didn't mean to ruin your night."

Andrew Reed walked to the side of the pickup truck. He looked at Rocco curled up in a ball with tears starting to form in his eyes. Reed ruffled Rocco's hair with his hand.

"It's cool, dude. You know I love you," Reed said with absolute sincerity. "You're my bro, I'd never do anything to hurt you. You know that, right?"

Rocco suddenly felt better. Andrew Reed did have a peculiar charm where he could make someone feel like the lowest form of life on the planet then lift them up and make them feel special.

"I know that, Andrew," Rocco said, taken in by him, tears rolling down his face. He felt so unworthy of Reed's friendship. Reed offered him his hand.

"Come on, get off of there and get in the truck," Reed said, helping Rocco climb down and giving him a brusque hug. "C'mon, let's tear up this party and have a great fucking time!"

Rocco giggled as he wiped away the tears. He then climbed into the pickup truck where the other three Vipers waited quietly and patiently. Reed climbed in. Boomer plugged in his iPod and blasted the music. They drove off laughing, singing and cheering as though nothing had happened.

# CHAPTER 14

**DYLAN** was finishing up his biology assignment when his mother came through the door.

"Anybody home?" Dana called through the house.

"Yeah, I'm in my room, Mom," Dylan shouted.

She ran up the stairs and knocked on his door. When Dylan opened his door, she engulfed him in a big hug.

"Hi sweetie, how was your day?"

Dylan cringed when his Mother called him sweetie, but as long as she didn't say it in public he could bear it.

"It was fine." He was hoping his disingenuous answer wouldn't be noticed. His mom kissed him on the cheek.

"Good to hear. What are you working on?"

"Biology. I'm almost done."

"Good for you," she said, smiling. "I'm making hamburger casserole tonight for dinner. Is that all right?" It was a ridiculous question. Dylan was the least picky eater ever. He ate anything, which was remarkable considering his tall, lanky physique. Dana was determined to put some meat on his bones.

"Yeah, that sounds great," responded Dylan. "When's Dad getting home?"

"He should be home soon. You know your father."

"Yeah, I know him all right," he chuckled, rolling his eyes.

Dylan could never believe the rough-and-tumble stories people told him about his dad. Around the house his father was a gentle soul. He treated Dana with the utmost respect. They seemed to fall more in love each day even though they had been married for so many years.

Dylan was a mama's boy but he idolized his father. His dad was who he wanted to be: the gentle warrior, completely at ease with his masculinity. It never seemed like his father was trying to prove anything. The man had been a hockey star in high school. His whole adult life had been devoted to the protection of those in society who couldn't stand up for themselves.

Could Dylan ever live up to his father's legacy? He worried about it constantly and wrestled with feelings of inadequacy even though his parents never put any pressure on him. Dylan changed the subject.

"I'm almost done my homework," he said. "I'll be down when I'm finished."

Dana sensed there was a problem but didn't want to pry. She suspected he was keeping something from her. Dylan always seemed out of sorts after school. She feared he was being picked on but he would never tell her if he was. Much like his father, Dylan would suffer in silence when going through tough times.

"Okay honey, I'll call you for dinner."

She closed the door and walked down the stairs to the kitchen.

Dana Stockwell was a strong woman with a mountain of enthusiasm. She stood five foot seven and weighed 115 pounds soaking wet. Dylan got his height from his father and his build from his mother. Dana's personality and optimism amazed everyone in the palliative care ward at Philipsville General Hospital.

All day, every day Dana worked with people who were on their way out of this world and the families they left behind. Somehow, it never seemed to get to her. When she was studying to become a nurse, she had hoped to work in the maternity wards but every other nursing student wanted that posting as well. No one wanted palliative care.

Dana was often how she could be so positive about life when she was surrounded constantly by illness and death. She never knew how to answer. It just came naturally to her. She never had to make an effort to stay positive. In her mind, you could either live life happy or unhappy.

She got this attitude from her mother Betty. Dana was the second oldest of four sisters who all shared the family matriarch's cheerful determination. Betty insisted that all of her daughters go to university. She had always wanted to attend post-secondary and become a teacher but she came from a different generation. Her parents never saw the need for women to pursue higher education. Betty vowed, if she ever had daughters, they would all enter the workforce, armed with a university degree.

Betty's husband, Donald, was a quiet, hardworking factory man. Dana and her sisters adored him for his gentleness and integrity but he was aloof and he worked long hours. Betty became the role model for their daughters, constantly encouraging them to work hard and aim high. When Dana flunked a math test in grade five, Betty sat with her for hours, helping her master the multiplication table. Her daughter aced her next math test, and Betty proudly taped it to the refrigerator for everyone to see.

Betty would always read to her girls when they were young and had them read to each other as they grew-up. Dana absorbed her mother's thirst for knowledge and belief in education. She was a top-student going into high school and made the honor roll every academic year.

Dana met Lionel in high school during their junior year at a post-hockey game party. Dana was with the yearbook committee. She took pictures of the hockey team then interviewed Lionel, the team captain, at the after-party. She was so nervous around him that she stuttered through her first two questions. He smiled and put here at ease with his smile and gentle demeanor. In many ways, he reminded Dana of her father except Lionel was far more talkative.

# THE OFFICER

They spoke for hours. Dana knew he was a handsome, talented player but she was mesmerized by how different he was from the jock stereotype. He was thoughtful, sincere and actually quite well-rounded. He enjoyed more than just sports and they had a lot in common. Lionel asked her about the yearbook and how it was going. He always looked her in the eyes which impressed Dana. Most males in high school would look at her chest when speaking to her. Lionel got her phone number that night, promising to call her later that week. She was already in love with him but didn't think he would follow through.

The feelings were definitely mutual. Lionel was drawn in by her shameless optimism and endless energy. He was more of a cynic. She possessed an eternal supply of patience and enthusiasm. Lionel was infatuated after that night at the party and determined to woo her. He called her that week and they went out for coffee. A couple weeks later, they were officially boyfriend and girlfriend.

When Dana went off to university to become a nurse and Lionel went to the police academy, they continued dating despite the distance. They made it work and were married right after Dana's graduation. They had never looked back since and that had been twenty-seven years earlier.

Dana made her way down to the kitchen. She had mixed the casserole together in the morning before work. It just had to be cooked. She tossed it into the oven. Less than twenty minutes later, the house filled with a wonderfully appetizing scent. Dylan smelled it all the way upstairs and grew hungrier by the minute.

# CHAPTER 15

**ROCCO** Antonio Palermo sat in the backseat of Boomer's truck right behind Andrew Reed. He was holding a towel to his nose to stop the bleeding. His right eye throbbed and his rib cage was killing him. He heard a snap when Reed tackled him. Rocco had been wheezing ever since. It would turn out to be a cracked rib.

Carl was sitting next to him. He was concerned for Rocco but didn't say anything. He didn't want to set off Reed again. Besides, all five of them were laughing, singing along to the music blaring from Boomer's speakers. They hooted and hollered at every female pedestrian they passed. Even Rocco seemed to be having fun. Carl decided to say nothing.

Indeed, Rocco was a survivor. The seventeen year old's parents were first-generation immigrants. His father came to Philipsville from Italy while his wife was pregnant with Rocco. They already had a son and a daughter. Rocco would be their last. The family was piss-poor at the time. Giuseppe Palermo had been a laborer in Italy. He wanted to escape all that and become rich in the New World.

Settling in Philipsville with his family, Giuseppe went to work right away at any job he could find. He worked three menial jobs, saving every penny he could to open his own restaurant. Rocco and his siblings never saw their dad. He worked endless hours and times were tough.

Bernadetta's, named after Rocco's paternal grandmother, opened when he was five years old but his dad didn't slow down. The whole family was conscripted into making the operation successful. Rocco was peeling potatoes in the kitchen at the age seven, as his siblings washed dishes and kept the place clean

The restaurant developed a reputation around town as having the best Italian food in the area. It became so successful his father opened up four more restaurants across the region and into the bigger cities. He then turned it into a franchise. Within fifteen years, Giuseppe Palermo was a multimillionaire.

The family now had plenty of money but Giuseppe was always working in order to keep his empire afloat. He was a powerful man with jet black hair, dark eyes, a deep voice, and thick accent, all of which made him very intimidating. Rocco inherited all his father's physical traits but none of the mental toughness.

# THE OFFICER

The elder Palermo was a ballbuster. He demanded the best from his family and his workers. He was a strict disciplinarian and he wasn't afraid to get physical; abusive by modern North American standards. Rocco and his siblings alternately respected and feared their father.

One night, Rocco's brother, Anthony, was brought home by the cops. Anthony was drunk and had been caught urinating on a light post. After the police left, Giuseppe slugged his oldest son in the face and tossed him down the stairs. Rocco had been in bed but he remembered the sound of his father screaming at his brother. Rocco pulled the blankets over his face to hide. His dad was livid. Rocco had been on the receiving end of his father's wrath but nothing like what happened that night.

"Siete un disonore," his father yelled over and over again at Anthony. His brother was sixteen years old at the time and sobbing like a little girl. Anthony never pulled a stunt like that again. That had been five years earlier.

Rocco's mother, Adriana, was a devout Roman Catholic. She made her children go to Mass every Sunday. They were old-school Catholics, attending service in Latin. She knelt with all three of her children every evening before bedtime as they said the rosary together

Rocco adored his mother. She was a beautiful woman with long dark hair, olive skin and perhaps the gentlest demeanor he had ever seen. Rocco was shy by nature and, as a boy, would hide behind his mother's leg in crowds. A stay-at-home mom from the moment her first child was born, her children were her whole life. For Adriana, the sun rose and set on them.

Giuseppe's love was harder to earn. He placed a high premium on family honor and work ethic. To him, kids in North America were lazy and spoiled. Yet, as the family prospered, his kids got all the breaks in life he had never received.

They lived in a huge home in Philipsville with an indoor pool and owned three cars. They had another home in Pigna, Italy for when they visited family. His kids had the best clothing, each had their own room and the latest electronic gadgets. It was light-years away from the poverty and hardship Giuseppe endured as a boy, but he seemed to resent his own offspring for getting every break in life, even though he was the reason for all of it.

He was harshly critical of his children whenever he felt they hadn't lived up to his standards.

"Monelli guastati," was repeated constantly, accusing his children of ingratitude.

Although she endured her share of wrath, Rocco's sister Ella got off the easiest. She was a daddy's girl, the apple of her father's eye. Rocco and his brother could never be good enough and their father went to great lengths to remind them of this. Their school grades were always too low, their rooms were never clean enough. He felt his sons never worked hard enough at life and would get them out of bed early on Saturday mornings for no particular reason. He just didn't like the idea that they were sleeping when they could be doing something, *anything*, with their time.

Anthony was never able to redeem himself where his father was concerned but Rocco started playing football when he was ten years old. His parents were die-hard soccer fans but American football was fine too. Rocco wasn't the biggest guy on the team but he enjoyed playing. His dad was in the stands when Rocco scored his first touchdown. His team won that game by three points. Afterwards, Giuseppe took Rocco out for ice cream and told everyone there that his son had won the game. Rocco had never seen his father happier.

From that moment on, Rocco poured everything he had into being the best football player he could be. He trained his heart out during practices and hit the gym religiously to get bigger, stronger and faster. He watched his diet closely. It wasn't until he got in with the Vipers that he started taking alcohol and drugs. His father never knew his son was into that stuff and Rocco couldn't let him find out.

His dad never missed a home game. Rocco was a wide receiver and could run faster than anyone on the team. He dominated the little leagues and was a no-brainer for the Wellington Warlocks once he got to grade nine. Easily the hardest working member of the team, he was very skilled but the coach doubted he was good enough for the NCAA level on full scholarship.

That broke Rocco's heart but he kept trying. He never told his father what the coach had told him. The gridiron was the one place he could gain his father's approval. If he couldn't get a scholarship to play in college, how would he bond with his father after high school?

Adriana and Giuseppe shared a genuinely loving and romantic marriage but Giuseppe demanded absolute subordination. Growing up, Rocco had twice seen his father strike his mother in an argument. Rocco cried both times it happened. He tried to fight his dad the first time, and Giuseppe tanned his ass because of it. Rocco didn't even bother the second time.

Rocco didn't consider the marriage abusive despite what he had seen. It only happened twice and his mother never seemed unhappy in the relationship. As he got older though, he realized it wasn't right and vowed to take on his dad if he ever tried it again, but it never happened. He always felt shame for being unable to defend his mother, and wondered if he had the guts to take on his Dad. He hoped his father would give him a chance to prove his manhood but it never came.

The shame nagged away at Rocco. The older he got the more he resented his old man. He wanted to believe he was tough. He so wanted to stand up to his Dad and prove it. Yet, whenever his Dad ragged on him for something Rocco folded every time but he was sure he wouldn't fold if his Dad hit his mother again. That's what he kept telling himself. He wouldn't let *that* slide. The opportunity never came though, because it never happened again. Rocco didn't get his chance to take the crown from his father.

This simultaneous desire to impress his father and fight him left Rocco confused and angry. It burned him up inside. He knew he was a tough guy so why couldn't he defend himself?

# CHAPTER 16

**DANA** was reading the *Philipsville Herald* waiting for dinner to cook when she heard Lionel pull into the driveway in his Ford Taurus. Dana knew something was up. He entered the house with a lavish and fragrant bouquet of flowers in one hand and a bottle of Nicolas Feuillatte champagne in the other.

"Hey, gorgeous, I'm home," he said, with a smile.

Dana saw the flowers and ran down the hallway. She jumped into Lionel's arms and they embraced. Lionel winced as she bumped his bandaged arm but he shook it off. He was wearing a jacket that covered the injury. He didn't want to take it off yet or Dana would notice.

Lionel passed the blooms to his wife. Dana was puzzled. There was nothing special about the day . . . There were no anniversaries or birthdays.

"They're beautiful, thank you," she said. Dana took the bouquet then pulled Lionel towards her for another kiss. They stood there in the hallway of their modest home embracing. Dana smelled her flowers then smiled at her husband. "So," she asked. "What's the occasion?"

"Well, actually, I was hoping to take advantage of you later," Lionel responded sarcastically. "I figured this would be a good start." Dana hit him playfully then went to find a vase in the kitchen. She filled it with water and set the flowers on the living room table.

Lionel took a deep breath and removed his coat. It was time to tell her everything. "Grab a seat honey," he said as his tone turned serious. "I have something to tell you."

They sat down on the couch in the living room. Dana took her husband's hand. "Is everything all right, Lionel?" she asked. At that moment, Dana noticed his forearm wrapped in a field dressing. "Oh my God, what happened?"

Lionel didn't hesitate. "I was shot today." Dana jumped off the couch.

"What!" she shouted. "What do you mean? What happened?"

"I was in a shootout today. My SWAT team had to storm a house in town. I'm honestly fine, sweetie. I promise."

Tears welled in Dana's eyes. Lionel knew this would happen. He couldn't blame her. He reached up to bring her back down on the couch but she resisted.

"Lionel, you can't keep doing this to me," she said, her voice cracking. "We need you. Dylan needs you. You almost orphaned him today."

Lionel stood up. "Come here sweetie," he put his arms around her. The tears were now flowing freely.

"Why didn't you call me when this happened," she asked, looking at Lionel's bandage.

"I didn't want to alarm you. I'm okay, I promise." Lionel decided it would be best not to tell her that he had actually stopped by the hospital to get his arm checked and asked the staff not to tell her he had been there. They had obviously kept their promise.

"Lionel, you could have been killed today," she said. "What if you had been shot in the head?"

"I know, Dana," Lionel said in a soothing tone. "There's something else. Please, sit down with me." The two sat back down on the couch, Dana still crying. She had long resented the police force but not because she didn't respect their work. She was well aware of Lionel's protective instincts long before they married.

In their senior year, Lionel broke up a fight at a high school dance. Five kids were gang beating a fellow student because he was gay. Lionel ran into the melee and pulled them off. He then made sure the kid on the receiving end of the abuse was all right. The five aggressors were shocked that the Captain of the hockey team had stopped them. When Dana asked him later why he'd intervened, his logic was simple. "It was wrong what they were doing. Nobody has the right to hurt someone else just because they're different." She knew he was a natural protector but that didn't make the strains of his profession any easier.

Her resentment came from the intensity of his devotion. The police force felt more like a mistress than a career. The hours could be long and unpredictable. She was afraid to ask for too many details about his day for fear of hearing something she didn't want to know.

The worst was that feeling she got every time he was at work and her phone would ring. A part of her always wondered if this was that one dreaded call where she would be told that something had happened to him. She was proud of her husband but it had taken its toll on her.

Lionel knew this. He owed it to her and Dylan to get out of the line of fire. It was time to tell her. "Sweetheart, I've got some good news," he said. She looked up at him through the tears. "My days on the frontline are done."

"What do you mean?" Dana asked, confused.

"John Paul offered to promote me to deputy today and I accepted. I'll serve the rest of my days at a desk away from the fighting." Dana stared at him, not sure if he was being honest.

"Are you telling me the truth, Lionel?" she asked wiping away the last of the tears.

"Absolutely," he said. "That's why I brought the champagne home. We're going to celebrate tonight."

# THE OFFICER

Dana saw he was being serious. She was relieved but knew he would be conflicted by the move. She was so thankful he would be off the frontlines but she also knew how much it meant to him. "Are you going to be able to live with that?"

"I'll be fine," he said with a smile. Inside, Lionel was hurting but he knew it was time. "This was my decision."

Dana smiled and hugged him. He put his strong arms around her. There was nothing she loved more than when he wrapped his arms around her and held her tight.

"I love you, Lionel," she said. "I'm so proud of you."

Lionel smiled at his wife, the love of his life. The woman who gave him his son, supported him in his career every step of the way. He looked forward to growing old with her and being grandparents together. Many of his friends from high school were now divorced. Some more than once. He'd lucked out and he knew it. More importantly, he could never have lasted as long as he had as a police officer without her constant support. He knew his job tore her up at times. Despite that, she had never wavered.

"I love you, too, Dana." Lionel closed his eyes and kissed the top of Dana's head. "More than you'll ever know."

\* \* \*

The clock timer on the back of the stove buzzed. Dinner was a simple meal of hamburger casserole and corn. Dana called Dylan to the table. A few minutes later Dylan made his way downstairs and into the kitchen. The family ate together, as they did on most nights, unless Lionel was working the afternoon or evening shift. The conversation was lively between Dana and Lionel, but Dylan remained quiet for the most part. Lionel sensed something was wrong but decided he would wait until after dinner to talk to his son about it. They finished off dinner then moved on to dessert – the lemon meringue pie.

"Did you hear about what happened to your father today?" Dana asked Dylan, as Lionel cut the pie and served it. Dylan shook his head.

"No, what happened?" he replied. "Does it have anything to do with the wrapping on his arm?"

Lionel burst into laughter. He didn't mean to laugh since there wasn't really anything funny about it. He just knew that's not what Dana meant. She gave him a playful, yet dirty, look, an indication to Lionel that her initial shock about her husband being shot had subsided.

"No," she said, trying to bring the conversation back to the good news. "He can tell you about his arm later if you're interested. Your father was promoted today to Deputy Chief of Police."

"Wow," Dylan replied. "That's huge Dad! Congrats!"

"Thanks," Lionel answered, then handed his son a slice of pie.

He had taught his son all the officer ranks when Dylan was younger. For some reason it stuck. Dylan could recite them from memory. He immediately understood the enormity of the promotion.

"You must be happy as well, Mom," Dylan said. "You don't have to worry about this loser getting killed anymore."

"Ha!" Lionel laughed, again, not meaning to do so. "Those were your mother's words exactly."

"They were not!" Dana shot back. "Granted, I probably did call you a loser but you deserved it."

"Oh, is that a fact?" Lionel responded, as he set down the knife and the rest of the pie.

"Yes, that's a fact."

"You're going to be sorry you said that."

"Why? What are you going to do?" she asked.

Lionel knew his wife was extremely ticklish under her arms. She hated being tickled; it would actually cause her to scream. He would only use the tactic in retribution, usually for an insult she'd hurled his way. Lionel made his way around the table. Dana was sitting and couldn't move fast enough.

"Don't you dare…" she started to say.

He pounced. Dylan shook his head as he watched his mother squirm out of her chair, screaming and laughing. They always kept each other young. Tonight was unique. They seemed younger than ever.

"You bastard!" she squealed, tears rolling down her face. "Stop it! I'm going to pee my pants." They were now on the floor. He had her pinned on the ground.

"Say you're sorry," Lionel demanded. He paused briefly so she could apologize. When it didn't come fast enough, he continued the torture.

"Okay, okay, I'm sorry."

"That's right. And don't you forget who the boss is around here!" Lionel stood up and went back to the table. He sat back down at the dining room table across from Dylan, who was rolling his eyes at him. "How's the pie, son?" Lionel acted as if nothing had happened.

"Gee, I don't know, Dad," he replied sarcastically. "I was too distracted by you two idiots and your foreplay."

Lionel chuckled and shrugged. Dana finally composed herself and went back to her seat. She looked at the piece of lemon meringue pie he had cut for himself, sitting on the plate right in front of him. He was about to cut into it when Dana pulled the oldest prank in the book.

"So, you're the boss, huh?" she asked.

"Damn right," Lionel replied, sticking out his chest for extra effect. "Was it ever in doubt?"

"Oh my God," Dylan moaned, as he placed his head on the table. "You two are unreal."

"Well, would the boss leave that over in the corner?" Dana pointed towards the corner behind Lionel. He turned around and Dylan raised his head to see what his mom meant

# THE OFFICER

"What are you talking about?" Lionel asked as he turned back around. "There's nothing over there . . ."

He was cut off mid-sentence as Dana slammed the pie in his face then ran away from the table. She was laughing every step of the way. Dylan's eyes enlarged as he took in the scene. His dad slowly removed the pie. Dylan finally cracked up but his dad simply nodded his head.

"If you'll excuse me, Dylan, I have to go kill your mother." Lionel then jumped up, ran out of the kitchen and up the stairs, in hot pursuit. He used his wife's hair and shirt to wipe his face.

Dylan watched him leave. Sitting alone in the dining room, he cut himself another slice of pie and devoured it.

# CHAPTER 17

**SARAH** Jane Harnick and her family were a rare exception in Philipsville. They were Jewish, which was quite the anomaly in a nest of WASP occupants. The Harnicks had to drive a distance to find a synagogue and the city had no private Jewish schools. Sarah Jane and her siblings all went to public school, much to the chagrin of their grandparents.

Her mother and father were both successful lawyers. They had settled in Philipsville for the same reason as the Stockwells: it was quiet, safe and clean. Despite the cultural isolation, they were happy there.

The Harnicks' house was huge with a massive backyard. Mr. Harnick had spent a million dollars over the past fifteen years on the backyard alone. It contained a cabana big enough for several people to sleep in. Modeled on Japanese architecture, it resembled a structure you would find near a Buddhist temple. The backyard also had a pool and a hot tub surrounded by lush gardens, along with an expansive patio area for parties and barbecues.

Sarah Jane and her sisters always held parties when their parents were out of town. Their home had developed the reputation of party central. Tonight was going to exceed them all. With her parents and two younger sisters gone for the weekend, Sarah Jane had the place to herself. By the time the Vipers pulled up in Boomer's truck, one hundred people had already arrived. They ranged in age from fifteen to thirty years of age.

"This is going to be fucking sick," said Carl from the backseat.

"You're fucking right it will," replied Reed. "Come on boys, let's rock and roll."

They emptied out of the truck and walked across the street towards the Harnick's. As they approached the house, they could smell the marijuana. Hip hop music blared through the warm May evening. Bobby opened the gate to the backyard and they all walked in. Everyone was talking, drinking and laughing. Many stopped and looked over as the five of them entered. The Vipers liked to get trouble rolling.

"Good evening, cocksuckers!" yelled Reed to anyone within earshot.

The bravado was working overtime; the testosterone was flowing and all five of them had a good buzz from the acid.

# THE OFFICER

"Where's the booze?" asked Carl.

"It's over there," replied Boomer, pointing at the tables on the patio. He stared at the close to three thousand dollars worth of alcohol sitting there as well as a keg full of Coors Light.

As they moved through the crowd, people shifted out of the way. Reed casually grabbed a joint from someone's hand as he walked by. The guy raised an eyebrow but kept his mouth shut. Reed slapped a girl on the ass as he passed her. She spun around, shocked, and seemed ready to chew out whoever had done that until she laid eyes on the culprit. Reed winked at her.

*That's right. Resist me, bitch. It's better that way.*

The Vipers descended upon the reservoir of alcohol, and were mixing drinks as the hostess approached them.

"Hi, guys," said Sarah Jane. "I'm glad you could make it out."

The Vipers knew her from school and she was looking good tonight in a black dress that showed off her curves.

"Thanks for having us," Bobby replied. He leaned forward and kissed her on the cheek. She smelled amazing.

"You're sweet, Robert," she said. "Now, you guys are going to behave yourselves, right? I'll make you stand in the corner if you cause trouble."

Reed laughed. "Sarah, when have we ever started anything," he asked, with a grin. "We're good boys."

Sarah Jane was about to reply when her best friend, Ashley Hood, joined her.

"Hello, Andrew," she said, with a big smile. "I thought I'd see you here."

Reed was speechless. She was hot on the best of days but she was absolutely stunning tonight in a tight red dress, her hair gleaming just past her shoulders. All the other Vipers were entranced but they knew she was off limits.

"How's it going, Ashley?" asked Rocco from the other side of the table. He was the first to break the awkward silence that had set in with her arrival.

"Hi Rocco," she said, with her usual charm. Reed had to resist the urge to lay another beating on him. "Oh, my God," she gasped upon getting a closer look at Rocco's face. "What happened to you? Are you all right?"

Before Rocco could respond, Reed stepped in.

"He's fine," said Reed, giving Rocco a playful punch on the arm. "The klutz fell down a flight of stairs at Boomer's place. It was actually quite funny."

Reed filled two plastic cups with coke and two shots of rum each. He then reached into his pocket, as discreetly as possible, and pulled out a little white tablet. Reed looked over at Ashley. Her back was turned to him as she chatted with Bobby and Sarah Jane. Reed dropped the tablet into the drink in his right hand and looked around to make sure nobody saw him do it. Old Man Hogan had given him the Rohypnol as a thank you for his good work. Reed had done his best to woo Ashley but she only wanted to be friends. It was a massive blow to Reed's ego and he was determined to have her.

"Here you go, Ashley," he said, handing her the drink with his right hand.

"Oh, thanks, Andrew," she replied, smiling.

Reed's reputation was well-known, but he had always been kind to her. He was well aware of her Catholic devotion to chastity. This just made her all the more enticing to Reed. He had many fantasies of her in a school girl uniform doing all kinds of nasty things to him. She was about to take a sip of her drink when he stopped her.

"Hey, Ashley," said Reed, taking her free hand. "Will you walk with me? I want to talk to you."

Ashley smiled at him. "Sure," she replied. They left the crowd and walked through the huge backyard holding hands as Reed made conversation. He led her around the pool and back towards the cabana on the other side of the yard.

"Hey, what's in there?" he asked.

"It's really cool," Ashley replied. "Have you never been inside?"

"No, never."

Ashley flashed him a big smile. "C'mon, I'll give you the tour."

"Okay, Ashley, but first, may I propose a toast," he said, holding up his plastic cup. Ashley went along with it, raising her cup too. "To a beautiful girl and a wonderful friendship."

She flashed her infectious smile at him. "You are so sweet. You know, people told me you were an asshole. I always told them they were wrong. Thank you for proving me right."

Reed returned the smile. "No, thank you."

"For what?" Ashley asked, still smiling.

"For being beautiful. And for not prejudging me. A toast to us"

They touched the cups together and drank. Ashley took a sip. Reed ribbed her.

"Oh, come on, you wuss," he teased. "Is that all you can drink? I thought you were tough."

Ashley flicked her right eyebrow at him, then chugged the drink down in three seconds.

"Atta girl," Reed said, with a big grin.

Ashley motioned towards the drink in his hand. "How about you, tough guy?"

Reed shrugged. He pounded back the drink and crushed the cup. Ashley took him by the hand as they walked around the cabana and entered through the back. Reed slid the door shut then locked it behind him. Ashley didn't notice.

Inside the cabana, the fragrance of incense added to the Eastern feel. There was a bed, a bathroom and the whole structure was made of cedar. Reed looked at her and sized her up.

"You truly are absolutely beautiful, you know that," he said.

She blushed. "Thank you."

Ashley set down her empty cup. She told Andrew about the cabana, its history and how much Sarah Jane's father paid to have it built. Reed nodded, asked follow-up questions and pretended to be captivated by the information. He was biding his time. When she finished telling him everything she knew about the cabana, Reed changed the subject.

"Ashley, how come nothing ever happened between us?"

"What do you mean?"

"You know I've liked you for a long time," Reed said, taking her hand and sitting down on the edge of the bed. "I love that we're friends . . . I just always hoped we'd become something more."

Ashley looked away.

"I'm sorry, Andrew," she said, not making eye contact with him. "You're a great guy but I just don't feel the same way." Ashley paused then continued. "I thought you were happy with being friends."

"Of course, I want to be friends," Reed said, putting his hands on her shoulders. "I would rather have you in my life as a friend than to lose you completely."

Ashley smiled again. "Thank you."

"I just wanted to be honest with you; that's all. I'm sorry I brought it up." Ashley leaned forward and hugged him. "I'm totally cool with us being friends," Reed continued. "Just know; you'll always be special to me." Ashley squeezed him tight.

Reed had managed to drag the whole conversation in the cabana out for twenty minutes. He didn't know what he was going to do next. Ashley stood up.

"How about we rejoin the party?" Just as the words left her mouth, she reached out for the wall to brace herself. "Whoa," she said, as a wave of nausea hit.

"Are you okay?" asked Reed, feigning concern. He stood beside her. Ashley tried to respond but couldn't. The room tilted to one side then went fuzzy. Her legs turned rubbery and her knees started to give. She reached for something to hold onto but lost her balance and crashed hard to the floor.

Andrew Reed stood over Ashley. She was out cold and motionless. Reed lifted her onto the bed and started removing her dress. In his mind, he wasn't taking anything he hadn't rightfully earned.

# CHAPTER 18

**ONE** hour after the ruckus from dinner had settled down, and Dana had left for the supermarket, Lionel decided to talk to Dylan. He had noticed he had been unusually quiet and gloomy that evening.

"Hey, Dylan," Lionel said, while filling a glass with water in the kitchen. "I'm going to fix the back door tonight. You wanna help?" Dylan declined but Lionel persisted. "Oh, come on," he said. "Is your homework done?" Dylan nodded. "Then give your old man a hand. It will only take half an hour tops."

Dylan shrugged. "Okay, Dad."

They got started right away on the door.

"Hey, Big D," Lionel called to Dylan from outside. "Can you bring my toolbox out here?"

"Where is it?" Dylan responded.

"It's in the closet by the stairs."

Dylan walked over to the closet that held all his father's blue collar trinkets. He found the toolbox and brought it out to him.

"Here you go, Dad."

"Thanks," replied Lionel, opening the box and pulling out the tools they would need to repair the broken hinges. He could sense Dylan's heaviness. The boy carried his pain in his eyes and his shoulders. Lionel had a hunch he knew what the problem was but wanted Dylan to talk about it voluntarily. A moment of silence passed as Lionel organized the tools. He finally broke the ice.

"What's wrong, my boy?"

"Nothing," Dylan replied quickly. "Nothing at all. Why?"

"Well, you haven't been yourself lately."

"What are you talking about?"

Lionel had a gold-plated bullshit detector and Dylan was a bad actor. Lionel had interrogated some tough bastards and polished liars in his time; they always cracked under pressure. Dylan was neither a bastard nor a liar, so Lionel barely had to try.

"Usually you're happy, outgoing, chatty. Lately, you just lock yourself in your room after school." Lionel paused "Is there a problem at school?"

That did the trick. Dylan's body language changed ever so slightly. He took a deep breath and looked away, as if trying to muster the energy to deny the question, but instead he just stood in silence.

"Listen," said Lionel, placing his hand on his son's shoulders. "I'm here for you. You can talk to me about anything. I won't even tell your mom if you don't want me to. What's up?"

Lionel waited.

"There are some guys at school," Dylan said, after a long pause. "They're always doing stuff to people."

"Like what?" Lionel asked.

Dylan told his father about a few things he had seen the Vipers do to other students and about some of the stuff that had happened to him.

"Who are these guys?" asked Lionel.

"They call themselves the Philipsville Vipers."

Lionel had to stop himself from laughing. The moniker was absurd given the city they lived in. It would have fit perfectly in the ghettos of the nation's bigger cities but in Philipsville, it sounded ludicrous.

"Don't tell me," he said. "Rich kids?" Dylan nodded his head in agreement. "What are their names?"

As Dylan listed them off, he recognized a few of the last names as belonging to prominent members of the community, even though he'd never had to deal with them through his job.

Some families in the city were so notorious the cops had them on speed dial. Family problems always existed and the kids were screwed up. The kids would then reach adult age and raise their own generation of failures that a new generation of Philipsville cops would have to deal with.

None of the Vipers fell into that category. They came from stalwart, moneyed families, yet Lionel knew the type. His comrades in the university towns hated dealing with students. They were loud, obnoxious and walked around with a sense of entitlement—spoiled, rich white kids who had never worked a day in their puny lives at an actual job or faced reality on their own.

Philipsville didn't have a college campus but it was extremely affluent. Right away Lionel knew the type of kids Dylan was talking about. The so-called Vipers would go on to university and fit in perfectly with the elite snobs.

"I'm going to speak to the principal on Monday," Lionel said.

Dylan recoiled with horror.

"Dad, whatever you do, don't do that," he said. "They would kill me if they found out I ratted on them."

"What should we do then?" asked Lionel. "Things can't keep going on like this."

Dylan shrugged his shoulders then sat down on the patio with a resigned slump.

"I don't know, Dad. I honestly just want them to stop. Everything would be better if they would just leave me alone. I never did anything to them. I don't know why they come after me."

Lionel sat next to his son.

"Stand up for yourself, Dylan," he said. Dylan rolled his eyes. "I'm dead serious. They target you because they think you're an easy mark. Next time one of them gets in your face I want you to slug him so hard his ancestors will bleed."

"Are you serious?" Dylan asked. "Did you actually just say that?"

"Dylan, if you stand up to them once they'll leave you alone. Your mother and I will always back you up if you get into a fight defending yourself or someone else. If you initiate the conflict you're on your own, but I know you won't do that. Stand up to them or they'll keep coming at you."

Dylan shook his head slowly. "I can't do that, Dad. It will get me killed."

"Listen, Dylan," Lionel continued. "Your mother and I are here for you no matter what. You don't have to face this alone. We'll face it with you. I promise."

Dylan nodded. Lionel stood up and returned to his tool box.

"I won't go to your principal so long as you keep me in the loop," he said. "We'll brainstorm ideas and get you through this." Lionel stood up. "If you want, we'll enroll you in jiu-jitsu classes or something like that."

Dylan exhaled.

"Let me know what you need. Come on, let's fix this door," said Lionel.

Dylan walked with his father over to the table where the tools were spread out.

"We can discuss this more tomorrow, if you want," Lionel said.

"We'll see, Dad," Dylan replied. "Thanks for the talk. Now, what do you need me to do here?"

"All right, take this drill and unscrew the old hinges. We need to replace them."

Dylan took the drill and started removing the screws. Lionel quietly pulled the plug, and the drill died. The plug was around the corner. His son couldn't see what his father had done.

"What the hell?" Dylan muttered. He shook the drill and flipped the switch on and off a few times. Lionel quickly plugged it back in. When Dylan pulled the trigger, it worked again.

"There we go," he said, starting on the second screw. Lionel quickly pulled the plug again, stifling his laughter.

"Oh, come on," Dylan said, slightly louder than before. Lionel could hear him flicking the switch on and off again and violently shaking the drill to make it work. Lionel quickly plugged it back in. Dylan walked over to where his father was standing and saw that it was plugged in.

"Is there a problem?" asked Lionel, with a straight face. He could almost see the steam rising from Dylan's head.

"No, I'm fine," he said as he went back to the hinges. Lionel heard the drill spin perfectly. Just when he figured his son was removing the screw and starting on another one, he pulled the plug again.

"Fuck!" Dylan yelled. "This piece of shit doesn't work!"

Lionel plugged it back in and walked around the corner.

"Here, let me see it, ya amateur."

"I'm telling you, it's screwed up," Dylan said. "It keeps stopping and starting. It's broken."

"It's not broken," replied Lionel, mustering every ounce of strength he could not to crack up. "It's brand new. You just have to know how to use it."

"Bullshit," said Dylan, still fuming.

"All right," said Lionel. "If I can unscrew both hinges without this thing dying, you have to buy me breakfast tomorrow."

"Fine," said Dylan. "I'm telling you it's busted."

Lionel tested the drill. It seemed to work fine. He promptly removed all the screws from the hinges then handed the drill back to his son.

"See?" Lionel said. "You just need the touch. It comes with time, young grasshopper."

A mixture of disbelief and a sense that something was up came over Dylan. Lionel took one look at him then burst into laughter.

"Real funny, old man," he yelled, tackling his Dad.

Lionel was still bigger than Dylan but Dylan had hit a growth spurt in the past year. He probably would never get to be quite the same size but he would at least come close. Regardless, Lionel had trouble fighting back; he was laughing too hard.

"Oh man, you should have seen your face," Lionel said to Dylan, who was trying to suppress a smile. It didn't take long before he was laughing too. After a few minutes of pandemonium, they got a grip on themselves.

"All right," said Lionel. "For real this time, let's fix the door."

"Sounds good to me," replied Dylan.

Lionel picked up the drill and they went back to the toolbox to get the new hinges.

"Oh, by the way," Lionel said, turning to Dylan, "you still owe me breakfast tomorrow, in case you were wondering." He started laughing again.

Dylan shook his head in disbelief.

# CHAPTER 19

**THE** party raged long after midnight. The only people who saw Reed walk away with Ashley were the other four Vipers. Everyone else was oblivious. Even Sarah Jane was distracted by Bobby, who had begun flirting with her the moment they arrived. By 12:30 a.m., Bobby got what he wanted—He was in Sarah Jane's room with her.

At this point, the party had started to move indoors. Bottles of alcohol were strewn all over the place. People made out everywhere. Several bongs fired simultaneously and lines of cocaine were snorted off the kitchen table. The bathrooms were disgusting. Mr. Harnick's beloved gardens would also require a good cleaning once everyone had gone. Sarah Jane's parents didn't get home until Sunday but she would have everything cleaned up long before that time.

Some random guy accidentally spilled a drink on Boomer. He apologized for it but that wasn't good enough. Boomer got right in his face. The Vipers dragged him out front and stomped his ass. The poor guy didn't have a chance. He limped away from the party bloodied and bruised.

Andrew Reed emerged from the cabana at around one o'clock. He had been in there for close to three hours. Reed had taken by force before but never with roofies. He didn't think it would be as good but he liked it. With Ashley unconscious, he was able to have his way with her repeatedly, and she would never know what had happened.

He walked through the backyard and into the house. He found Carl and Boomer snorting cocaine at a table while Rocco was making out with some chick on the couch. Boomer looked up at Reed with the powder still on his nose.

"Where the hell have you been?" Boomer asked.

Reed ignored the question.

"We're leaving," he said. "Give me the keys to the truck. I'm driving."

"Why?" asked Boomer, as he fished the keys out of his pocket.

"Because I'm the least fucked up right now."

"No, why are we leaving?" Boomer responded. "The night is still young."

Reed ignored Boomer. He tapped Rocco on the head and told him to get in the truck. Rocco appeared annoyed but Reed was insistent. He wanted to leave immediately.

"Where's Bobby?" asked Reed.

"Upstairs in Harnick's room," yelled Carl from the kitchen.

"All right, you three get your butts out to the truck. I'll go get Bobby."

Reed walked up the stairs, sidestepping intoxicated bodies and copulating couples along the way. He approached Sarah Jane's room and barged in. She was bent over her desk with Bobby standing behind her. Reed turned on the light.

"Dude, what are you doing!" asked Bobby.

"Finish her off and get out to the truck. You've got two minutes."

Reed tossed Bobby's clothes at him and then left. He didn't even close the door. Sarah was too drunk to mind. He turned around and saw Bobby pulling on his trousers. Reed continued on to the truck.

"Get in; move it," Reed said when Bobby arrived at the truck.

He floored the gas pedal. The tires screeched, then caught traction. They were off like a bullet. Bobby seemed to be still ticked about the interruption.

"Why did we have to leave so soon?" he asked. "I was having fun."

"The cops were on their way," replied Reed. "Considering all the drugs at the party and that none of us are even old enough to drink, I thought it would be smart to get the fuck out of there."

Bobby looked at Reed confused. "That hasn't stopped you before."

"What do you mean?"

"Well, you're usually the last one to leave a party," Bobby said. "When have you ever been afraid of the cops?"

Reed kept his eyes focused on the road ahead.

"Trust me Bobby, tonight's different. Besides, what do you care anyway? You got what you wanted."

Bobby smiled at his leader. "You mean Sarah Jane? Ha! Was it ever in doubt?"

Reed used every back road possible to avoid the police. When they had travelled a safe distance from the party, the Vipers decided to crash at Boomer's for the night.

"Did you guys have fun tonight?" Reed asked the other three in the backseat.

Rocco, Carl and Boomer had already passed out on each other.

# CHAPTER 20

**THE** sun shone bright the next morning. It was a beautiful spring day in Philipsville. The warm weather had returned and the birds were singing in the trees. It couldn't have been more perfect.

Lionel Stockwell took full advantage of the weather. He jogged to the gym at 5 a.m. then blasted his pecs and triceps for ninety minutes. He couldn't understand people who didn't exercise. If Lionel didn't work out for more than two days straight, he started feeling restless, sloppy and moody. Dana never complained about his alarm going off so early in the morning. She also enjoyed the fruits of his labor. At forty-nine, he was in better shape than people half his age.

Lionel hit the gym six days a week. His neck was a thick 21 inches around and he weighed in at 245 pounds. He could bench press 320 pounds, squat 525 pounds and rattle off one hundred push-ups cold, much to the embarrassment of his young, cocky recruits fresh out of the academy.

Lionel never wasted time at the gym. After stretching, he proceeded with his usual intensity. He always had goals for exercising. If he curled ninety pounds on a barbell then he would aim to increase that by five pounds. Once that was mastered, he aimed for one hundred pounds. To him, stagnation wasn't an option at any age.

Afterwards, he jogged home from the gym feeling supercharged, his arms and chest tightening as blood filled his muscles. He arrived home twenty minutes later. He ate a banana and downed a protein shake before jumping into the shower.

After shaving and getting dressed, Lionel grabbed the *Philipsville Herald* from the front porch. The front page screamed the headline, "Police Shoot Man Four Times During Raid." The byline explained everything; the article was written by Jonathan Pickett.

"Oh, Jon-Jon," Lionel sighed. "What am I going to do with you?"

Lionel gave the story a once-over then flipped right past it. The media often knew nothing about the realities of policing and this was reflected in the reporting. For this reason Lionel had stopped reading crime articles years earlier.

# THE OFFICER

Dylan was an early riser like his old man. It was 7:30 when he walked into the kitchen.

"Good morning, sunshine," Lionel said to his son who was still half asleep. "I thought you were going to sleep away the whole day."

"Yeah, well some of us prefer to go to bed *after* the sun goes down, you old fogey," Dylan said.

Lionel didn't care that Dylan made jokes about his age. He could still beat his son in an arm wrestling match.

"All right," Dana yelled from the bedroom. "Which one of you is taking me to breakfast this morning?"

Lionel beat Dylan to the punch. "Actually, Dylan lost a bet to me yesterday and owes me breakfast anyway."

"Nice try, old man," said Dylan.

"You welcher," replied Lionel. "Everyone get dressed; we're going to the Thundering Scot."

"I'll be ready in two," shouted Dana from her bed.

"Thanks Dad but I actually have to pass. I need to be at work for nine o'clock."

"I have to work, too. Don't worry," replied Lionel. "We'll get you there in lots of time."

With that, the three of them piled into the family Taurus and went for breakfast.

\*\*\*

The sun came up on the Harnick residence, but nobody was awake to enjoy it. Sarah Jane was sleeping off the alcohol and cocaine from the night before. The last of the party goers finally left by 8 a.m. and she had no idea they had remained until that time.

Sarah Jane finally woke up around ten o'clock with a splitting headache. As she rolled out of bed and set her feet on the floor, she stepped on a used condom. Bobby left so quickly the night before he just tossed the damn thing on the ground before getting dressed. After an initial flurry of revulsion, Sarah Jane put on her housecoat and surveyed the damage.

"Holy shit," she said quietly to herself, in shock at the disaster that was her home.

She walked around the house taking in everything. The property was a complete mess. Empty bottles of alcohol and plastic cups littered the inside and outside of the house. The living room and kitchen areas reeked of marijuana. Cigarette butts were all over the backyard and her father's garden. Sarah Jane would have to remove every last one or her dad would have a conniption.

People had vomited and urinated all throughout the bushes and gardens. She would have to take a hose to the mess. The puke in the bathrooms would be harder to clean. The toilets had been annihilated, as had the tub. Someone missed both but hit everything in between. The mess had dried and was caked on the bathroom surfaces. The stench was absolutely repugnant.

Her memory of the party was a little spotty after a certain point. She knew it had been huge but had underestimated how bad the chaos would be. Luckily, no vandalism had occurred and nothing appeared to be stolen.

Sarah Jane had her work cut out for her. It would take the whole day to clean everything spotlessly. The pool in the backyard seemed relatively undefiled as did the hot tub. The gardens were a mess and the cabana appeared unchanged from the outside. Sarah Jane didn't think anyone had been in there last night and didn't bother checking the interior.

\*\*\*

The Thundering Scot was a local greasy spoon the Stockwells frequented. It was owned by Duncan Macdonald and his wife, Lily. The couple had immigrated to Philipsville from Glasgow, Scotland, forty years earlier and opened the restaurant shortly after arriving in town. The place had an old fashioned diner feel, and had become a fixture in the community.

Dunc, as he was known to everyone in town, greeted the Stockwells like he did every customer – with a big smile, a booming jolly voice, and a thick Scottish accent. He knew the Stockwells on a first name basis.

When their waitress came around, the orders were predictable. Dana had the French toast, Lionel ordered an egg-white omelet and Dylan ordered the William Wallace breakfast. Dylan's meal consisted of three pieces of toast, four eggs, four sausages and two pancakes. It was a cholesterol-laden platter befitting the burliest lumberjack. Dylan ordered it every time they came to the Thundering Scot.

The sight and smell of all that grease made Lionel gag but he shrugged it off. Dylan was young and skinny. The kid could have ingested Tupperware and his digestive system would have burned right through it.

After breakfast, they drove Dylan to work. Bill and Leona Fitzpatrick, friends of Dana's from university, owned a dairy farm on the edge of town. Dylan did chores for them to earn some spending cash. It wasn't glamorous work but he loved the farm life. He helped milk and feed the cows. They had to be milked twice a day. He also cleaned the pens and changed their bedding.

Once, Dylan had even helped deliver a baby calf. It had been the highlight of his time on the farm. The procedure had involved tying chains around the calf's hooves and pulling until it popped out of its mother. Upon its arrival the young bull had been completely motionless. Bill had moved the calf in front of its mother and she'd licked her baby until his eyes opened and he was roused. Within hours the calf had been up and walking around, a bit wobbly at first but sturdy by morning. The whole thing made Dylan want to be a farmer. University wasn't too far off. He gave serious thought to studying veterinary medicine.

After they dropped off Dylan and said a quick hello to the Fitzpatricks, Dana drove Lionel to the police station. He had some work left over from the previous day that he wanted to finish. It was a twenty-minute drive from the farm. They arrived at the station shortly after 9:30 a.m.

# THE OFFICER

"Thanks, babe," Lionel said to Dana. "I'll call you when I need a ride home."

"I may or may not answer the phone," she replied, smiling. "It'll depend if I'm up."

"You're such a candyass," Lionel said, kissing her on the cheek. He turned to leave the car but she pulled him back and kissed him on the lips. He smiled at her, gave her one last peck on the forehead then jumped out. He turned around just before walking through the front doors and blew her a kiss. She returned it then drove away.

\* \* \*

Sarah Jane spent the morning scrubbing the bathrooms in her house. She wanted to get the worst task out of the way first. It was an ugly job. She then moved on to the backyard. It would take the longest to clean. Sarah Jane dragged a big garbage bag around as she loaded it up with bottles, paper plates, plastic cups, napkins and a whole assortment of other rubbish. She had to be meticulous. Her father was a neat freak.

As she roamed the backyard, memories from the previous night started coming back to her. Sarah Jane remembered snorting lines of coke with Bobby, then sitting on his lap as they each took hits from a bong. It wasn't long before Bobby's wandering hands were up her dress. They sat on the couch making out for half an hour before she led him up to her room.

Sarah Jane giggled to herself as she thought about the encounter. Her head was still sore from the alcohol and drugs but she was feeling good: the throbbing head was drowned out by a euphoric sexual high. Unlike other girls who felt guilty after a one-night stand, Sarah Jane always reveled in the glory. She was well aware that some people attached labels to her but she didn't care. Life was meant to be enjoyed.

Suddenly, Sarah Jane remembered—she had lost track of Ashley early in the evening. Sarah Jane assumed she had gone home early but it was highly unusual for her to leave without saying goodbye.

Ashley and Sarah Jane were thick as thieves. They had been best friends since kindergarten. Their friendship worked because they were the perfect combination of similarities and differences. Ashley was quiet, traditional, conservative and had a bigger heart than anyone Sarah Jane had ever met. Ashley was everyone's sister, always the responsible one who would take care of others. On numerous occasions, Ashley had helped a drunken Sarah Jane home and put her to bed.

Sarah Jane was the polar opposite in many respects. She was loud, flamboyant and opinionated. She had been in a number of short relationships. Her reputation for chewing up and spitting out young males was widespread. She did have a soft, caring side but only her family and closest friends ever saw it. To everyone else, she came off as both a princess and a ball-buster. Sarah Jane's thinly-veiled sense of entitlement enabled her to extract many gifts from adoring, horny high school boys.

Despite these differences, both Ashley and Sarah Jane were star athletes on Wellington High's volleyball team. They were workout buddies at the gym and highly motivated in school. Ashley went to Sarah Jane's bat mitzvah when she was thirteen. Sarah Jane and her family attended Ashley's Confirmation later that same year. They shared with each other all their secrets, hopes, dreams and fears.

"I hope she's all right," Sarah Jane said to herself as she ran inside to find her cell phone. She checked it. She found four missed calls, but none from Ashley's number. Sarah Jane checked her voice mail–only a message from her parents checking in on her. There was also an incoherent text message from Bobby; he wanted to see her again. Sarah Jane rolled her eyes.

"What a wimp," she said with pride. "I swear; men can't fuck without getting emotionally involved."

She had no desire for a relationship with Bobby. Sarah Jane would call her parents back right away so they wouldn't worry but she would let Bobby suffer. It would make him more desperate. She loved it when they got pitiful. The thought of him begging for another night with her gave her guilty pleasure. She knew it was mean but she just couldn't help it.

Sarah Jane wanted to call Ashley before she called her parents back. She wasn't overly worried; however, it was just out of character for Ashley to leave suddenly and not say anything. She scrolled through the extensive list of names in her cell phone, pushing the little green button when it landed on Ashley's name. The phone rang several times then went to Ashley's voice mail. Sarah Jane hung up and tried again. Same thing. She decided to leave a message.

"Hey, lovey, hope you had fun last night. I sure did. Don't know where you went to. Call me whenever you get this. Love your guts!"

Sarah Jane put the phone in her pocket and went back into her yard to clean up. An hour later, she sent her friend a text message. There was still no answer. By 1 p.m., she was starting to actually get concerned. She checked her email and Facebook but still nothing from Ashley. They never went more than a few hours without speaking. They would often text each other from different classes in school.

She sent another text message to Ashley around a quarter to two.

"Hey, gorgeous, hope you're all right. Call me ASAP. Muah!"

Sarah Jane returned to her backyard. She had to refocus on cleaning up because she still had a lot to do. She went to her parents' garage and pulled out the hose to cleanse her dad's gardens. They had to be impeccable.

# CHAPTER 21

**ANDREW** Reed paced nervously in Boomer's living room. Usually cocky, this time he was concerned. The mistakes racked up in his mind. He was positive people had noticed he had gone into the cabana with Ashley. He had watched *CSI Miami*. Thus, he *knew* how police operated.

His mind raced furiously. Reed thought about heading back to the Harnick's house but Sarah Jane probably would have found Ashley already. He logged onto Boomer's laptop and surfed the net. He went to cnn.com for all the sports scores. Reed wanted desperately to think of something else but he couldn't. He didn't feel guilty for what he had done the night before but, for the first time, he was afraid he could get caught.

"Oh, who cares," he said quietly—a little pep talk to himself. "Nobody would believe her if she accused me of it anyway."

That thought gave him cold comfort but he couldn't convince himself of its truth. Ashley came from a well-connected, highly respected family. She had an unblemished reputation. People wouldn't buy the typical "she actually wanted it," rape defense.

Reed decided to look for more information. Old Man Hogan always told his workers to have an alibi or explanation in the bag before any job. It was a gross perversion of the Boy Scouts' "Be Prepared" motto.

Reed went to Google and typed "Rohypnol" into the search engine. Over 700,000 hits came up. He scrolled through the different pages. He was pleasantly surprised by what he learned.

> *Rohypnol has a synergistic effect with alcohol. When taken with alcohol, Rohypnol can cause severe disorientation and a loss of memory. These memory blackouts are typically 8–12 hours long. The victim may or may not appear "awake" during this time.*

Reed chuckled at this little tidbit. "She definitely appeared asleep," he said to himself. He went to another Web site.

> *Many victims raped under the influence of Rohypnol are unsure whether or not they were raped, because they have no memory of*

the event. It can take several days to piece together a story from eyewitness reports.

Reed reclined in his chair and considered the information. If there were no eyewitnesses, it would be nearly impossible for her to remember what had happened. He got an idea.

Reed logged into Facebook. He went to Ashley's account. It showed no activity since she left for the party the day before. He posted a message on her wall.

*Hey loser, hope you had fun at the party. You seemed a little woozy when we chatted. Hope you're feeling better. See you in class on Monday. Andrew*

Reed logged off and closed the laptop. His swagger had returned. He was smiling from ear to ear when Bobby bounded down the stairs in his boxer shorts.

"Good morning, peckerhead," Bobby said to Reed. "And what a fine morning it is too!"

Reed chuckled as Bobby skipped into the kitchen. He tossed two pieces of bread into the toaster.

"Why are you so damn chipper?" Reed asked. Bobby looked at him. Both of them were grinning idiots.

"I nailed Sarah Jane last night," he said, pride oozing out every pore in his skin.

"Yes, I recall. It was good, I take it?"

"Oh, my God!" exclaimed Bobby as he sat down in the recliner. "That girl gives the best head in the world. I swear she has no gag reflex!"

The two shared a good laugh. The toast popped up. Bobby walked back into the kitchen.

"How about you?" Bobby shouted into the living room.

"What about me?" Reed shot back, knowing damn well where Bobby was going with this line of questioning.

"Did anything happen between you and Ashley?"

Reed suppressed a smile. He did his best to keep a poker face while he watched Bobby smear Skippy peanut butter over his toast. He looked up at Reed who still hadn't answered. Reed shrugged his shoulders.

"We had a long chat," he said nonchalantly. "We got to know each other better."

Bobby trotted into the living room, toast in hand and sat back down on the recliner.

"Don't worry man, you'll get her eventually." Bobby took a bite of his first piece of toast.

"Indeed," said Reed, eyeballing the food. "Hey, give me one of those." Bobby looked at him incredulously.

"Kiss my ass!"

Reed stared at Bobby as they shared an awkward silence. Bobby rolled his eyes, leaned forward and handed him the second piece of toast.

# CHAPTER 22

**LIONEL** Stockwell wasn't supposed to work weekends but he always did. There was never enough time during a regular work week to get everything done. He plowed through a mountain of paperwork until noon then turned his attention to the arrest of Willie Hogan. Chief O'Reilly needed the report on his desk by Monday morning. The commissioner would demand answers about why Lionel had shot Hogan during the arrest. The attack dogs in the press were already circling the wagons. O'Reilly needed all the information to placate the media and his superiors.

Lionel's tactics had caused John Paul many headaches over the years. Lionel wasn't a bureaucrat and cared little about image. O'Reilly occasionally had to rein him in for good measure but it was more to satisfy those above him.

Lionel worked away on the report through the early afternoon. He tried to remember as much detail as possible from the day before and their reasons for going into the home. He also checked on the paperwork surrounding the little girl found in Hogan's house. She was now a ward of the state. The process of finding her a new home was underway.

Satisfied, he turned his attention back to the report. Lionel finished it, proofread the whole account and printed it off. He dropped a copy of the final report into the Chief's mailbox and looked up at the clock. It was seven minutes to two. He brewed some coffee and poured himself a cup. As he walked back to his office, he heard the front door of the police station fly open.

"Lucy, I'm home!" a voice boomed out from the end of the hallway.

Lionel let out a hearty belly laugh.

'Hey, dumbass," he yelled out. "I'm in my office."

He heard footsteps running down the hallway. The door opened and Jack Dercho burst into Lionel's office and sat down.

"How's the Stockster doing?" Dercho asked, as he put his feet on the desk.

"I'm fine, meathead. You?" Lionel pushed Dercho's feet to the ground. Dercho did that every time he came in just to piss him off.

"Oh, I feel just capital, thank you."

Dercho followed his nose to the coffeemaker. Unlike Lionel who always drank his coffee black, Dercho loved cream and sugar. He mixed up his cup and came back into to Lionel's office.

Lionel had first met Dercho at the police academy when they were young men. Dercho, in many ways, was Lionel's younger, undisciplined brother. The guy had plenty of talent and passion to spare but he was more hot-blooded than Lionel. Dercho frequently got into fist fights, drank heavily and he had a hard time honoring his nuptial vows. His third marriage failed six months earlier for the same reason as the first two: Dercho was a notorious philanderer. Lionel hated adulterers but overlooked it for some reason with Jack. He suspected Dercho was an undiagnosed manic depressive.

Lionel knew he was a good man despite his flaws. Dercho always had Lionel's back and frequently helped him out even if it meant breaking the rules. Lionel had moved through the ranks with much greater speed than his buddy in large part because of Dercho's inability to control his abrasiveness. The guy would fly off the handle in meetings, argue with supervisors over the stupidest things and he was known to get unnecessarily rough with the people he arrested.

Police officers frequently endured taunts, catcalls and tough-talk. Most of them either considered the source and let it roll off or they absorbed the abuse then burned it off at the gym, in a dojo or through some other method of release. Dercho could never find his equilibrium.

Ten years earlier, he'd assaulted a man wanted for vandalism because the guy called him a pig. A subsequent investigation found Dercho guilty of police brutality. That was also when the police department first became acquainted with Jonathan Pickett. At the time, he was a brand-new addition to the *Philipsville Herald* staff. He was all over the investigation and wrote stinging articles every day about Dercho and the rest of the local police force.

The whole ordeal had been hell for Dercho. He would have lost his job if Lionel hadn't intervened. O'Reilly spared his career but moved him off the beaten path. Dercho was relegated to a desk job over at Intelligence. To everyone's surprise, Intel was a perfect fit. Dercho flourished, channeling his raw aggression towards the infiltration of child pornography and pedophile rings in the area. Dercho developed cutting edge strategies for countering cyber crime of every kind. The man had a sixth sense for anticipating criminal activity and the ability to track suspects for months online without detection.

Dercho's work helped numerous police forces smash multiple crime rings involving everything from narcotics and human trafficking to money laundering and child predators. He had been instrumental five years earlier when Lionel decapitated a powerful biker gang in Canada. Dercho had connected Lionel with an informant who helped him obliterate the entire biker command. The organization crumbled into chaos without its leadership, then closed up.

But Dercho had been moving up at Intel even before the strike against the bikers. The coup five years earlier sent him shooting up the chain of command.

# THE OFFICER

He was now the head of Intel for the region. He gave Lionel full cooperation and that's why Dercho was at the police station on a Saturday.

"By the way, thanks again for your work on the Hogan file," said Lionel.

"Hey, no problem. I hear you greased the son of a bitch!"

"Yeah, the guy had an Uzi. I had no choice."

"Well, you won't get any complaints from me," replied Dercho. "I can't say the same for the liberal pansies who are going to rake you over the coals. Did you see today's newspaper?"

Lionel nodded and shrugged.

"Yeah, I saw it." Lionel knew he was probably going to get an earful from various civil liberties organizations. It wouldn't be the first time. However, he had a more nuanced view of their role in society than Dercho who was still bitter over their intervention on behalf of the guy he roughed up ten years previously.

"Unrestrained power will always corrupt and be corrupted," Lionel said to his friend. "Civil liberties groups have their place too, Jack."

Dercho cringed and moved his hand in a masturbatory motion in front of his groin.

"Whatever," he said. "Those bleeding hearts don't have the first clue how to protect society."

"Agreed," Lionel replied, calmly. "But every group needs a watchdog including us. Now, what do you have for me?"

The police had developed enough evidence to move against Hogan but Intel was having a hard time cracking his network of suppliers and dealers. The department had a list of twenty-five suspected traffickers. The day before the raid Dercho had all their phones tapped so they could be monitored. He had recommended they go in and arrest Hogan then watch the numbers for activity.

It was a risky move. If it didn't work, the police might never be able to penetrate the drug ring. After the SWAT teams moved against Hogan and his sweetheart, Dercho and his team monitored all the numbers closely. The gamble paid off. Eight of the numbers received cryptic phone calls from a ghost caller informing them that "the shepherd had been sheered." The conversations also produced leads for two other suspects not even on the original list.

"I've got gold for you today," said Dercho. He opened his briefcase and removed a dossier. He flipped through it quickly then slid it across Lionel's desk.

Lionel thumbed through the information. It contained the list of the ten drug dealers affiliated with Willie Hogan and every last scrap of information Dercho could drag up on each of them.

"This is impressive stuff," said Lionel, looking over the files. "This information is rock solid?"

"One hundred percent," replied Dercho. "We obviously can't use this in court but we know they worked for Hogan. We'll keep each of them under twenty-four-hour surveillance until we have enough to shatter them in front of even the most lenient judge."

Lionel scanned the list again. None of the names jumped out. They were all a bunch of nobodies. A couple had police records but nothing serious. One name rang a bell; however, he couldn't place it.

"Who's Andrew Walter Reed?" Lionel asked. "I may be completely mistaken but it sounds vaguely familiar."

"He comes from a wealthy family in town," Dercho replied, taking a sip of coffee. "His parents are well-known. The kid's an all-star football player at Wellington High and has no previous criminal record. He seemed like the model teenager until he appeared on this list."

Lionel reclined in his chair. He was about to let it go but he was positive he'd heard this kid's name elsewhere.

"Have you learned anything else about this guy?" asked Lionel.

"Nothing really of consequence as far as we know. Two of our agents tracked him and some of his friends to a party last night over on Rockcliffe Street. Three of them beat the shit out of a kid at the party later in the evening."

"He wasn't part of the assault?" asked Lionel.

"No, he disappeared into a little hut in the backyard with a girl and wasn't seen for several hours. He and his buddies left the party shortly after 1:30 this morning in a hurry. They drove over to Abner Simons's residence on Glebe Crescent where they spent the night."

"Abner Simons?"

"Yeah, he's some corporate big shot. The guy has more money than God. I think his son is friends with Andrew Reed."

The whole thing was driving Lionel crazy. He was positive he knew the name from somewhere but still couldn't quite place it. He racked his brain trying to connect the memory remnant with the file on his desk.

"Anything else?" Lionel asked, scanning the documents on Reed.

Dercho shook his head. "That's about it on him. All our information on each of the suspects is in that folder. I'll obviously keep you posted on any developments."

"Thanks," replied Lionel. He was still deep in thought. He looked out his window then back at the files.

Dercho finished his coffee then slid the mug to the end of Lionel's desk. He stood up and closed his briefcase.

"Oh, one other thing." Dercho smirked. "My two agents covering Andrew Reed told me something. I damn near soiled myself laughing. Do you know what Reed and his four buddies call themselves?"

Lionel looked up slowly at Dercho. He had a feeling he was about to hear the missing link. He hesitantly shook his head.

"No, what?"

"The Philipsville Vipers . . ." Dercho waited for a laugh but it didn't come. "Seriously, have you ever heard anything more ridiculous! Shit, why don't they just get it over with and call themselves 'White Man's Burden?'"

# THE OFFICER

Much to Dercho's surprise, Lionel still didn't laugh. He'd already heard the joke. Lionel could feel the hair on his arms stand up. He quickly pulled himself together.

"Tell your boys to keep a close eye on this bastard," said Lionel. "I want to know everything he does."

"Okay." Dercho shrugged.

Lionel snapped out of his deep thought. He stood up, walked out from behind his desk and shook Dercho's hand.

"Thanks for everything, Jack," he said, pumping his comrade's hand effusively. "I don't know how the hell you do it."

"You don't wanna know," Dercho said. "If there's anything else you need, gimme a shout."

Dercho picked up his briefcase and walked out of Lionel's office. Lionel stood at his desk flipping through the file. He looked at his watch. It was almost three o'clock. He'd had enough for one Saturday. There were a few other things to do but he could take them with him. He called home. Dana answered.

"Ah, you're up! I wasn't sure if you would be," Lionel said. "I'm ready whenever you are."

"I'll be there in thirty. I'm going to pick up Dylan first."

"Thanks, sweetie, see you soon."

Lionel hung up the phone and continued flipping through the file left by Dercho. He tried so hard never to take his job personally but he now had a bead on the culprit responsible for making his son's life miserable. How could he *not* take it personally?

# CHAPTER 23

**BY** five that afternoon, Sarah Jane was starting to worry. She still hadn't heard anything from Ashley. She checked Facebook again and noticed Andrew Reed's posting. She didn't have Reed's number but thought about calling Bobby to see if he or Reed knew where she could find Ashley. Sarah Jane also didn't want to call Ashley's parents, scaring them if there was no real reason to do so. She decided to wait until 7 p.m. If she still hadn't heard anything by then she would start making phone calls.

Sarah Jane's efforts to clean up her parents' property were paying off. The backyard looked great and the local radio station was calling for thunderstorms overnight. That would help clear away anything she may have missed. The bathrooms were spick-and-span. She just had to straighten up the living room, and then she would be done.

Sarah Jane started by picking up all the empty bottles and unclaimed bongs strewn amongst the wreckage. She vacuumed the carpet and wiped down every surface making sure she didn't miss a single inch. She couldn't chance it. Her parents weren't puritans but they wouldn't appreciate drugs in their home. She opened the windows to air out the curtains, hopefully eliminating some of the odor.

Every fifteen or twenty minutes, Sarah Jane checked her cell phone for messages. Nothing from Ashley. By 6:30 p.m. the living room was looking A1, except for the stains in the carpet.

"I guess I can't put this off any longer," she said to herself about the rugs. She grabbed a pail from the laundry room and the carpet cleaner from beneath the kitchen sink. Then, Sarah Jane thought about Ashley again. Her stomach was in knots. She told herself she was overreacting but she wrote her another text message in what she hoped came across in a stern but playful tone.

> *Hey, I'm worried about you. Haven't heard from you since last night. Is everything all right? Call me as soon as you get this.*

She turned on the hot water in the kitchen sink and placed the bucket underneath. She unwrapped a brand new sponge and pulled on a pair of rubber gloves. Sarah Jane no sooner had the gloves on her hands when her cell phone started ringing.

"Shit," she said to herself, turning off the water.

The cell rang again.

She quickly removed her gloves and plunged her hand into her pocket.

The cell phone rang a third time. After four rings it would go straight to her voice mail. She flipped it open and saw Ashley's name. The call was coming from her number. Sarah Jane sighed in relief. She pressed the green talk button halfway through the fourth and final ring.

"Yo, bitch," she said playfully into the phone. "Where the hell have you been all day?"

On the other end there was silence. Someone was there but they weren't speaking.

"Hellooooo," sang Sarah Jane, trying to elicit a response. "Way to leave the party early, you lame-o."

Sarah Jane's smile slowly faded from her face. The breathing on the other end sounded pained and forced. She could hear quivering in the person's voice like they were freezing cold. Sarah Jane's gut told her something was very wrong.

"Ashley, are you there? Is that you? Talk to me."

The response sent a violent chill up Sarah Jane's spine.

"Help me," a tiny voice whimpered. "Help me."

Sarah Jane's eyes opened wide in sheer terror as her concern gave way to absolute fear. She knew that was her best friend's voice; she could never mistake it for anyone else's.

"Ashley, it's Sarah Jane. Where are you, sweetheart?"

"Help me," the voice repeated.

"I am going to help you, Ashley, I promise. Tell me where you're at and I'll come get you."

"I don't . . . I don't know where I am."

"Oh my God, girl. What the hell happened?"

"I don't . . . I can't remember."

Ashley's voice sounded faint and weak. Sarah Jane had never heard her like this before. Ashley was always vigorous and she possessed a seemingly endless supply of energy. Even when ill she put on a brave face. Sarah Jane knew her friend was in serious trouble. She had to hold back the tears, figure out where Ashley was; then bring her to safety.

"Ash, are you inside or outside?"

"I'm . . . I . . . inside I think."

"Okay, go outside and see if you can find something familiar or someone who can help. I'll be there before you know it. Everything's going to be all right."

The phone cut out before she could finish. Sarah Jane could feel the tears roll down her cheeks. She felt guilty for waiting so long when her best friend in the world was in danger.

"Dammit!" she yelled at the phone. "Come on, Ashley. Hang in there."

Sarah Jane ran out the door into her backyard hoping to get a better signal. She flipped the cell open and called Ashley's number again. It rang and rang and rang then went to voice mail.

"Fuck!" Sarah Jane was frantic. She redialed the number, now sobbing uncontrollably. It rang once, twice. "Please pick up Ashley," she said through her tears.

Sarah Jane's cries stopped abruptly when the front door of the cabana opened slowly and a familiar figure slouched out. Sarah Jane stood stunned with disbelief. The cell phone slid from her hand and smashed on the patio.

At the other end of the yard, a zombie-like girl limped out of the cabana and onto the pool deck. She looked like a naked corpse wrapped in a bed sheet, and was unable to walk in a straight line or fully open her eyes. She moved at a snail's pace and every motion seemed to increase her pain. Sarah Jane knew it was Ashley the moment she laid eyes on her, but didn't want to believe it.

"Ashley." She gasped and felt sick to her stomach. Her friend looked as if she'd been hit by a freight train and left for dead. The tears starting flowing again.

"Oh, my God, what happened?"

Before Ashley could respond, she collapsed on the pool deck. Sarah Jane screamed and ran towards her friend's limp, motionless body.

"Somebody help!" she yelled as she ran to her friend. Sarah Jane sat there on the pool deck with Ashley's head cradled in her arms. Fear gave way to panic then utter confusion. Sarah Jane didn't know what to do but scream.

"Somebody help us!"

\*\*\*

The sun descended in the skies over Philipsville that Saturday evening but nobody in the town could enjoy the sunset, in particular Sarah Jane. For years after, she associated unexpected changes to severe weather to the unexpected changes in her best friend, Ashley. It was as if the weather echoed Ashley's situation.

Storm clouds moved in quickly then the rain started. It picked up velocity all night until thunder and lightning marked the storm's crescendo around three in the morning. Ferocious winds pounded the city and relentlessly whipped the countryside. Tree branches snapped and power lines went down. The city slept in complete darkness.

The rain continued through the next morning. Sunday was overcast and gray. It lightly rained, on and off, the entire day. The clouds maintained their dominion over the skies of Philipsville. The garish sun never showed its face.

# CHAPTER 24

**MONDAY** was the first day of June and an unseasonably chilly day. Exams at Wellington High started in two weeks. Dylan would then be free from school for two months to do as he pleased; no invisibility required. He was excited for summer. The next year would be his last year in high school. He was determined to get through it and never look back. Besides, he had much to look forward to.

Dylan's mind had been on the future a lot. His grades were outstanding. If he kept them up, he had a good shot at winning a few academic scholarships from different universities. He didn't know his parents had squirreled away a large chunk of cash for him. He was unaware of this because Lionel and Dana had kept it a secret. It had the desired effect; Dylan was working hard towards scholarships and bursaries, thinking he would have to pay for post-secondary entirely on his own.

Dylan hated going to school in June. It was the hardest month. Sitting in class trying to learn was torture when the summertime weather set in. All that sustained him, and every single one of his classmates, was the knowledge that it would all be over soon. Freedom was just around the corner. That was the mantra he repeated to himself that morning as he prepared for school.

Today wouldn't be too hard to concentrate because of the weather. Dylan ate his breakfast then got dressed. He put on jeans, a hoodie and a Denver Broncos baseball cap.

"I'm out of here," Dylan said to his Mom as he left the house. He figured his Dad left for the gym at his usual time of 6 a.m. and then went straight to work.

"Have a good day sweetie," Dana replied. "I'll see you tonight."

"Thanks Mom, you too." He was about to walk out the door when his mother spoke.

"Hey Dylan, I almost forgot; tomorrow's recycling day. Can you move the boxes out to the curb when you get in tonight?"

Dylan smiled at his mother. "Sure, no problem."

Dylan walked out the front door and began the first of his many daily death marches. He had grown accustomed to this routine. Often nothing would happen which was always pleasant. Other times, he wasn't so lucky. Every morning, he hoped nobody would see him so he could at least start the day off well enough.

Wellington High was a fifteen minute walk each way. Dylan enjoyed the quiet time to think. That was assuming his morning tranquility wouldn't be shattered by a gang of slithering reptiles.

His father's words from Friday night echoed in his mind.

*Stand up to them, Dylan. Stand up for yourself.*

The conversation had played itself over and over again in his mind all weekend. He knew what his dad would do in those situations. His father was not an aggressive man. He simply had what a Sensei would describe as "the fighting spirit." He wouldn't start a fight and he wouldn't necessarily rise to the bait when provoked. Not all fights were worth fighting, but his father would lay another man flat on his back in a heartbeat to protect himself or those around him. Dylan feared he didn't have the same gumption. It was a constant source of shame for the kid.

Dylan was now about five minutes away from the school. It was 8:13 a.m. but he didn't have to be in homeroom until nine o'clock. He found getting to school early often allowed him to avoid any unpleasant confrontations. He would arrive, unpack his stuff at his locker then head up to the library until the bell rang. On most mornings, his walk to school was pleasant and uneventful. Occasionally, it wasn't.

Dylan came within sight of his school's front doors. What he saw confirmed to him that this morning would fall into the "exceptions" category. Carl Hicks and Boomer stood smoking in front of the school.

"Oh shit," Dylan muttered.

Despite the cool temperatures, they were both only wearing "wife-beater" undershirts. Dylan shook his head at the scene. It was the perfect picture of two idiots in action. They were standing outside freezing their asses off, trying their hardest to look tough even though nobody else was around.

Dylan walked towards them as slowly as he could while trying to avoid the appearance of doing so. He hoped they would finish their cancer sticks and leave before he arrived. His father's voice echoed in his memory.

*Stand up to them once and they'll never bother you again.*

As he approached, he did his best to avoid making eye contact and to pretend they weren't there. No such luck.

"Hey, faggot, where you going?" asked Carl.

"And why so early?" added Boomer.

Dylan shook his head as he walked by. That got their attention.

"Did you roll your eyes at me boy?" asked Carl, with contrived incredulity. "I'll fuck you up good if you do that again."

Boomer positioned himself in front of the school's entrance to block Dylan's path. "You know, I still have your bar of soap," he said, with a smirk. "Well, most of it. Don't you want it back?"

Carl joined Boomer standing in front of the doorway. Dylan raised his head and looked them both in the eyes—this was nothing to them. They would laugh about it for thirty seconds afterwards; then go on with their day as though it had never happened. The situation, however, meant a little more to him.

*Your mother and I will always back you up.*

"Excuse me," Dylan said as he tried to walk around them but Boomer moved with him, not allowing him to pass. Dylan felt an upsurge inside of him. He had never felt it before. He put his hand on Boomer's shoulder and pushed him out of the way. "Excuse me," Dylan repeated, in a more forceful tone.

Carl seemed dumbfounded and Boomer appeared equally shocked. Right before Dylan was about to walk through the school's front doors he felt a violent jerk from behind and then heard a loud rip. Boomer had yanked on his backpack, hoping to pull Dylan back outside. Instead, the bag ripped. It wasn't his original goal but he laughed at the results.

"Nice one, Boomer," Carl said as they bumped fists.

Dylan's backpack was ruined. The shoulder strap was completely ripped and a huge gash showed along its side. A couple of pencils, three pens and one eraser had fallen out. Dylan stared at the bag. He'd had it since Grade Nine. It was a gift from his grandparents one week before he started high school.

Dylan looked up at the grins on the two Vipers. They were so smug and self-satisfied. All at once, his brain was flooded with memories of these two and their three buddies antagonizing him. Now, they had destroyed a present from his grandparents. Both had died since he had started high school. Dylan had been close to them his whole life. The final straw had dropped and something snapped.

*Stand up to them, Dylan.*

He dropped the backpack. Dylan walked straight towards Boomer and hammered him with a haymaker to the nose. The kid's cigarette flew in one direction while his body stumbled the other way. He staggered backwards while Dylan pursued. He shoved Boomer, causing him to stumble backwards even faster until he tripped over a bench and fell into some shrubs in the school garden.

Carl's mouth was agape. Blood gushed out of Boomer's nose as he sat on the ground in shock. Nothing was said between the three of them. Dylan stood over the bully, seething with anger. Tears welled up in Boomer's eyes. Carl stood completely frozen. He hadn't moved since Boomer ripped Dylan's backpack.

Dylan spun around, walked up to Carl and got in his face. They stood toe-to-toe, eyeball-to-eyeball. Carl trembled as he looked upon the hate in Dylan's eyes. This had never happened to any of the Vipers before. Carl seemed to still be processing the event as if trying to make sense of it. Dylan still said nothing. Their silent face-off lasted another ten seconds. Dylan then turned around, picked up his backpack and disappeared into the school.

As Dylan walked towards his locker, he held back tears. He wasn't a fighter and his bag remained ripped. It would be impossible to fix. He felt overwhelmed by what had just happened. This was his first fight and he didn't know what to make of it. He'd never imagined he would actually have the balls to throw fists at a Viper. A million thoughts raced through his mind including every worst case scenario but it felt bloody good to tag Boomer. His elation mixed with confusion.

That Friday night when his father had guaranteed him that this approach would end his problems, Dylan had considered it academic. He didn't think it would actually happen but it had. And Dylan had a feeling this fight was far from over.

# CHAPTER 25

**BY** the time Dylan made it to homeroom, his father had already been at work for close to three hours. Lionel wanted to be ready for any possible fallout from the Hogan case and he knew O'Reilly would announce his promotion to the entire staff. Once that information was out, his productivity would plummet. Lionel wanted to get as much done as he could before it all hit the fan.

By 9:30 that morning, the office was fully staffed. Headquarters hummed with activity. Police officers came and went constantly. The phones were ringing off their hooks. There was even a mini-gym in the basement where officers went to blow off steam or just to stay in shape. It was a typical day at the Philipsville Police department.

Lionel had answered all his emails and returned every phone message before people started arriving that morning. Jonathan Pickett was the exception. He had left a few messages asking for a comment from Lionel on the article he'd written in Saturday's *Philipsville Herald*. Lionel deleted them all.

A steady stream of constables made their way to his office to congratulate him for the arrest on Friday. It seemed like everyone already knew. Most likely, the officers on the two SWAT teams had gone out for beers Friday night with other police and shared the story.

Police units are notoriously gossip-filled. It comes with the territory. Police see and hear much they can't disclose to the general public. They have to lean on each other for everything including boasting and venting, which is why news travels so fast. Lionel appreciated the accolades but would have preferred peace and quiet so he could stay focused on work.

O'Reilly wouldn't be in for another half hour. His office was dark and orderly. The guy was obsessive compulsive about neatness. Lionel could see his boss's office from his own. He looked up from his desk and noticed three constables picking the Chief's lock. They opened the door and snuck into his office.

"What the hell..."

He stood up and walked to the doorway to keep an eye on things. The three of them left something on the Chief's desk, then ran out of the office giggling like children. One of them noticed Lionel standing in his office's doorway. He knew what they were doing.

Pranks were commonplace around the police force. It was truly a fraternity in every sense of the word. Everyone was on guard, knowing that someone would try to pull a fast one right when you least expected. He'd been the victim more than once and had even partaken in a few such exercises himself.

A common gag was to flip the badge on a rookie's hat upside down, and wait to see how long it would take for the new recruit to notice. It was the equivalent of having a "kick me" sign on the back.

A few weeks earlier he had almost killed Dercho. He'd been showering in the change rooms at the end of a long shift. Dercho had filled a bucket with freezing cold water then emptied it over the shower curtain. Lionel's voice hit octaves he hadn't reached since puberty. Dercho and all the men in the change room had laughed until they hyperventilated. Lionel had unleashed a string of profanities on Dercho which had only made the whole thing more amusing. Lionel also knew it was funny. Hell, he had done it many times to other people. If you couldn't laugh at yourself, you became an even bigger target for future shenanigans. The best thing in that situation was to laugh it off, acknowledge the defeat, then plot revenge.

As the three constables shuffled past Lionel, one of them placed his index finger over his lips and made the "shhhhhh" gesture to his superior. Lionel responded by zipping his lips, indicating he wouldn't tell anyone what he'd seen. He didn't know exactly what they had done. The boys were always thinking of something new. Regardless, Lionel knew he would hear the fallout in about twenty-seven minutes when the Chief arrived.

# CHAPTER 26

**DYLAN** walked from homeroom to math class. He looked over his shoulder and kept a close eye on his surroundings. The adrenaline from an hour ago still hadn't completely worn off. He usually walked the halls with his head down trying to look inconspicuous. Today, he walked tall with a sharp eye out for the Vipers.

He could have sworn people were looking at him differently all morning in homeroom. He even got a few smiles on the way from homeroom to math class but he ignored them. When people smiled at him at Wellington High, they were laughing at him, not with him.

Dylan arrived at Mrs. Moore's class two minutes early. When he walked in, two girls looked at him and smiled.

"Hi, Dylan," one said in an overly perky manner.

Dylan was suspicious. They had never said hi to him before. He didn't even know them, except by name. He nodded his head, acknowledging them, and took his seat.

*Just what are they up to?*

Jimmy Winslow sat behind Dylan. They had never been particularly close but he had never given Dylan any trouble. Jimmy tapped him on his shoulder.

"Hey, dude," he said. "Is it true you beat the shit out of Boomer Simons this morning?"

Dylan turned around slowly. Jimmy was a well known pothead. He was laid-back about everything in life and didn't seem like the type of guy to listen to rumors.

"How do you know about that?" Dylan asked. He hadn't told anyone.

"Dude, everyone knows about it. You're the fucking man."

"Gee, thanks," Dylan replied, rolling his eyes as he turned back around towards the front of the classroom. He didn't really want to draw attention to the incident. He would prefer the whole situation to just go away now.

"Hey man, that guy's a douche," Jimmy continued in his lethargic tone. "He had it coming. The world owes you a favor."

Dylan agreed but his stomach was still in knots. This conversation wasn't helping. Any attention at Wellington High had always been negative. The knowledge that everyone was talking about him almost made Dylan throw up. What he heard next made him light headed.

"Yeah man, way to take one for the team," Jimmy said in his typical monotone voice. "If I were you I'd grow eyes on the back of my head."

Dylan looked back over his shoulder at Jimmy then quickly turned his eyes towards the chalkboard. He could feel himself breaking out in a cold sweat. He took a few deep breaths and tried to push everything out of his mind. Dylan looked down at his hands—they were shaking. His father had assured him everything would be all right and that he had nothing to worry about.

The bell blared through the school. The first period had officially begun. Mrs. Moore shuffled her round figure to the front of the class and cleared her throat.

"All right class, let's begin."

# CHAPTER 27

**LIONEL** waited for the Chief to arrive. John Paul O'Reilly loved routine and continuity. He led a life of repetition that many privately mocked as boring but it worked for him. He was always at work by 10 a.m. He used to arrive earlier but after he and his wife became grandparents, he insisted on having his mornings free. O'Reilly's grandchildren were the apple of his eye. They would have breakfast with him and his wife each morning.

Sure enough, O'Reilly arrived at 10 a.m., just as planned. In the meantime, Lionel had learned what the boys had done. It seemed every staff member in the whole damn building knew and were waiting for the explosion. The speed at which news traveled at HQ never ceased to amaze Lionel. Telephone, television, tell-a-cop — news travelled equally fast through all three mediums.

As O'Reilly walked towards his office he said hi to everyone along the way. He carried the *Philipsville Herald* folded under his arm and to Lionel he appeared to be in a good mood. O'Reilly fumbled through his keys looking for the one to open his office door. He found it, inserted the key into the deadbolt and turned it counter clockwise. The door swung open and O'Reilly turned on the lights.

Lionel thought it would happen instantly but it took his old friend a surprisingly long time to notice what the constables had done. When he did, the walls shook.

"Judas priest!" The Chief's scream echoed through the building. Lionel, and everyone else within earshot muffled their laughter. "Okay, who just signed their own death warrant?"

Lionel watched as O'Reilly went to each office in the immediate area demanding information. Everyone, including himself played dumb and gave O'Reilly the same response – "What are you talking about, sir?"

The object in the Chief's office was part of the evidence of a recent arrest. The police department had arrested the owner of a local adult store the week before. His store was perfectly legitimate and legal but he was also dealing on the black market. The police searched his home and found crate loads of materials in the basement. He was running everything from birth control and sex toys to underground snuff films. All the contraband had been stuffed into a secure locker until it could be disposed of. There were some items that defied comprehension.

The Chief's voice boomed down the hallway.

"Staff Sergeant Stockwell, get your ass in here now!"

Lionel composed himself then walked across the hallway into the Chief's spacious bureau.

"Sir, you seem distraught," Lionel said, trying to maintain his poker face.

"Who the fuck did this?" growled O'Reilly, pointing towards the big rubbery purple dildo on his desk. Lionel took one look at it and his facade crumbled. He exploded into laughter while the Chief fumed.

"I don't know sir," Lionel said through his laughter. "Did you leave it there before you left on Friday?" They could both hear hooting and hollering from every office all down the hallway. Everyone at HQ was enjoying themselves.

Chief O'Reilly had been a Constable once and had pulled many similar stunts in his time. Lionel leaned on the walls for support as he laughed himself silly. The Chief cracked a smile and shook his head.

"All right," said O'Reilly. "Can you at least get rid of this thing for me?"

Lionel looked at the fake organ on his boss's desk then started laughing again.

"Sorry J.P. You're going to have to write me up for insubordination cause that's one order I'm not following."

O'Reilly wasn't going to argue. He folded the newspaper and grabbed the garbage can from underneath his desk. He used the paper to push the purple pecker into the garbage. He took great pains to avoid making any physical contact with the sex toy. Heaven only knows where it had been. It took twenty minutes to restore order around the building. Once the prank had passed into folklore, they were able to get on with the morning, including Stockwell's promotion.

"You ready for this, Stock?" O'Reilly asked his protégé.

"What do you have in mind?"

"I'm going to check all my messages and emails. Once that's done, I'll send out a memo via email about your promotion to everyone on staff and all our media contacts."

"Sounds good to me," Lionel replied.

He was still adjusting to the reality that he would no longer be out on the street where all the action happened. It still didn't seem real. In less than two hours, everyone would know and there would be no going back. It was the natural progression for a guy like him but he would miss leading his troops into battle.

Lionel turned around and walked back to his office. He had been in the middle of reading Constable Nicole Maloney's report from the weekend. Saturday and Sunday had been, on the whole, uneventful except for one bizarre incident. Constable Maloney was called to a home Saturday night in one of the ritzy parts of town. She paid a visit to 1259 Rockliffe Street. One of the neighbors called in frantic, saying they thought someone had died.

# THE OFFICER

Lionel read the report and remembered that Rockliffe was the same street where the massive party had been that Dercho told him about. The party was on Friday night, not Saturday. He was about to sign the report and move on to the next one but decided to look a little deeper. He flipped through his BlackBerry for Constable Maloney's phone number. She was a rock steady police officer with an excellent service record and the sharpest eye for detail on the force. Lionel found her number, picked up the phone on his desk and called her.

"Hello," Maloney answered after three rings, in her usual no-nonsense manner.

"Hi Nicole, this is Staff Sergeant Stockwell here. How are you today?"

"I'm great, sir. You?"

"Just splendid, thank you." Lionel pulled her report closer to him so he could read it and speak to her at the same time. "I'm sorry to bother you on your day off but I just wanted to speak to you about your report from Saturday. Do you have a few minutes?"

"Yes, sir."

"Terrific. First of all, great job. There's nothing wrong with the report so don't worry. You're not in trouble." He could hear her let out a sigh of relief. Lionel meant it when he told her she had done a great job. The report was the perfect length. No supervisor wants to read a novel. The report captured all the important details in two pages and there wasn't a single spelling or grammar error. Maloney took pride in producing ultra-professional reports for her superiors. It was one reason she was a rising star on the force.

"My reason for calling, Nicole, is that I just want you to walk me through absolutely everything surrounding the incident at 1259 Rockliffe."

"I'll do my best, sir. Let me gather my thoughts."

She had received a 911 distress call shortly after 6:30 Saturday evening from neighbors, saying a young woman was in trouble. Maloney raced over to the house and found two girls in the backyard. One was unconscious while the other was an absolute basket case. The couple from next door, who had called police, was with them.

Maloney had surveyed the scene and instantly determined the problem. She checked the unconscious girl who was in rough shape. She'd had a negative reaction to the Rohypnol and was covered in vomit. The only thing that had saved her from choking to death was her head had been tilted to one side when she heaved. She was also as naked as the day she was born except for the bed sheet around her body but her pulse was strong. Maloney called for an ambulance. When the paramedics took her away, she turned her attention to the sobbing, gibbering sixteen year old.

It was tough questioning her because many of her answers didn't make sense. She told Maloney there had been a party at her place the night before. She thought her friend had left early and gone home only for her to emerge from the backyard cabana a full day later. This caught Lionel's attention.

"Backyard cabana?" he interjected.

"Yes, sir," replied the young constable. "You should have seen this place. The cabana alone was worth more than my whole house."

"I'm aware of the neighborhood," Lionel said, rolling his eyes. The whole community was wealthy but Rockliffe and the surrounding area could get ostentatious. "What is the cabana? Describe it to me."

"It's like a little cottage or cabin in the backyard."

"Like a hut?"

"You could call it that, except that scarcely does it justice. This thing was gorgeous. The cabana looked like something straight out of Japan."

"And that's where the girl was found?"

"Not quite. Her friend watched her exit the cabana around 6:30 p.m., much to her surprise, but that's where she had been for close to twenty-four hours."

Lionel reclined in his chair and looked up towards the ceiling. He had a feeling there could be a big connection with the Hogan file.

Constable Maloney went on to describe the crime scene. She'd called in two inspectors to gather evidence. The one girl had definitely been date raped. Her dress had been ripped off her body and the cabana reeked of vomit. In the room the inspectors found pubic hair not belonging to the girl. The doctors at the hospital ran blood tests which confirmed the presence of Rohypnol in her blood stream. They had also found semen in her long brown hair and she had been sodomized. The rapist clearly had fetishes.

"So, we definitely have a confirmed date rape?" asked Lionel.

"Yes, sir," replied Maloney. "Now, there's some good news and some bad news here. The good news is that because the victim was sent straight to hospital and we were able to inspect the crime scene before anyone else tampered with it, we were able to get DNA evidence. We also have blood tests confirming the girl had been drugged. If we can find the bastard that did this, he's dead meat. The case against him is iron clad."

Lionel understood right away why this was important. Usually, victims of date rape woke up alone with no recollection of what happened. Rohypnol's ability to impair memory was terrifying. The victim, unsure of events, might not report the rape for several days or even weeks, assuming they report it at all. By the time the victim went to police, all the traces of the drug have left the bloodstream. There was no way to prove the victim had ever been roofied and DNA evidence was harder, if not, impossible to collect while eyewitnesses became more difficult to track down.

"Okay, what's the bad news?" asked Lionel.

"The bad news is that nobody has the first damn clue who did this. There were hundreds of people at the party, all drunk and high on several drugs. The hostess was so sure nobody had gone into the cabana that night that she didn't even think to clean it."

Lionel couldn't believe it. "Nobody saw them go back there?" he asked in disbelief. "Somebody had to have seen it."

Someone did.

# THE OFFICER

At that moment, it all snapped together in Lionel's mind. Dercho had mentioned in passing that Andrew Reed was at that party. He had disappeared into some backyard hut. The agents tracking Reed didn't see him again for several hours when he left the party in a hurry with his buddies. Lionel felt a rush of ecstasy run through his body. He didn't want to jump to any conclusions but the coincidence was too big to ignore. With DNA evidence, it would be easy enough to validate or repudiate Reed's innocence.

"How's the girl doing?" asked Lionel.

"She was released from hospital yesterday. She'll live. She doesn't remember a thing. Her family members are beside themselves. I think we should send out a general warning of a date rapist in the area."

"We'll get to that, Nicole but not just yet." Lionel had another idea. "I'm going to speak to Jack Dercho over at Intel. He's going to call you later today. Tell him absolutely everything you just told me along with the names and contact information for everyone involved. Doctors, Inspectors, family members, everyone. I'll fax him over your report."

Constable Maloney seemed a bit confused by her Staff Sergeant's reaction. "If you don't mind me asking sir, what's this all about?"

Lionel paused to consider the possibilities. "I think Jack Dercho knows who the rapist is."

# CHAPTER 28

**DYLAN** sweated his way through math class. He tried to concentrate on the lesson but Jimmy Winslow's words stuck with him. When the bell rang ending period one, Dylan grabbed his stuff and made a beeline for the door. He walked briskly to his locker where he dumped his math books in exchange for the biology texts. He looked over his shoulder constantly making sure none of the Vipers were around.

Dylan slapped the combination lock back into place. He turned around and scanned the entire area—No sign of any threat. His biology class was on the other side of the school. He walked down the hallways of Wellington High and up to the second floor moving as quickly and as calmly as he could.

The hallways were filled with students as they maximized the ten minute break. Dylan worked his way through the unwashed and horny teenaged masses. Today was different; he noticed people looking at him as he passed by them. There were even a few head nods, smiles and one wink. News traveled quickly at Wellington High. This unknown student had risen out of the shadows and delivered a mighty blow to the oppressors on behalf of the oppressed. Many students that day, upon hearing the news that Dylan had made Boomer cry, lived vicariously through the tall, skinny sixteen year old.

Dylan finally made it to Mr. Coleman's classroom. No sign of the Vipers anywhere. He allowed himself to believe for just a moment that maybe they wouldn't come back. Maybe this was truly over. Then he remembered that he would have to face Boomer and Bobby in gym class. They were going to learn wrestling that week. A small part of Dylan was actually looking forward to the sport now. He knew he could handle Boomer on the wrestling mat and Bobby was even smaller. The thought of it made him grin.

The biology class was only half full when Dylan arrived. Mr. Coleman had left to get a cup of coffee from the cafeteria. When Dylan entered, he noticed her immediately but she looked different. Ashley Hood was sitting in the same spot as usual, right next to Dylan's desk but her head was down and a forlorn malaise gripped her entire existence. Dylan barely recognized her. Ashley's demeanor was completely different. He took his seat next to her. She looked up and managed a weak smile.

# THE OFFICER

"Hi Dylan."

"Rough weekend?" Dylan smiled. She looked at him then looked back at the desk in front of her.

*Yikes! I think I touched a nerve.*

Mr. Coleman returned. The class hadn't officially started yet but most of the students had now arrived.

"Okay, class," he said as he opened his coffee. "Take ten minutes to make one final review of your assignments from Friday. Get together with your partners and read them over."

Ashley didn't move. She would usually jump out of her chair and push her desk next to Dylan's before he could even ask her if she wanted to work together. Dylan could see she had zero enthusiasm today. He thought maybe she was mad at him for something. Regardless, they were partners on the assignment so he pushed their desks together.

Dylan flipped open his binder and removed the polished report. Both their names were on it even though he had done all the work. He tossed it in front of her.

"Here, read," he said. This wasn't the first time he had carried the entire load. He knew she was capable of doing excellent work. She was smart, motivated and had made the honour roll every year. Yet, Ashley never had any qualms allowing Dylan to do all the heavy lifting when they teamed up. He figured that was why she always claimed him as a partner. Dylan always went along with it hoping maybe something would click between them. He knew it was ridiculous. It would never happen and he'd now had quite enough of it. This would be the last time he partnered with her.

Ashley flipped through the assignment. "Thank you for doing this Dylan," she said as her blue eyes looked straight into his soul. He was enthralled again. Dylan had looked into those eyes many times only this time, he saw nothing but sorrow. She put her left hand on his right hand. Dylan's heart skipped a beat and his lungs tightened. "I'm sorry for not doing more. It won't happen again, I promise."

*Yeah, bullshit.*

He'd been ready to tell her as much when he first arrived in class but noticed she wasn't herself today. Dylan had an excellent ability to detect when someone was hurting. He got that from both his parents. He could see it all over Ashley. Someone had hurt her badly. He didn't know what to say. She removed her hand from Dylan's then finished flipping through the assignment.

"This looks amazing, Dylan." She slid it back to him. Ashley had never touched Dylan's hand before or ever actually read the work he had done on their behalf. Dylan wanted to say something but couldn't muster the words or the guts. When he finally built up the courage to ask what was wrong, Mr. Coleman piped up.

"Okay, everyone hand in your dissection reports and flip to page 113 in your textbooks."

Dylan took the assignment over to his teacher's desk and tossed it on the pile of other reports. He sat back down wishing he hadn't hesitated. All over the classroom, desks screeched along the floor as all the students moved back into regular seating. Dylan pulled his desk away from Ashley's. He sat down but looked at her out of the corner of his eye.

She seemed aloof and oblivious. She appeared to be in her own little world trying to decipher a mystery. Her transformation from Friday was so stark and so absolute it was disconcerting. Dylan was determined to talk to her after class.

# CHAPTER 29

**CHIEF** O'Reilly sent out the mass email to every staff member on the payroll of the Philipsville Police department. He faxed the memo to every media contact in the region. It was a full page long but the subject line said it all:

'Staff Sergeant Lionel Stockwell Promoted to Deputy Chief Effective Monday, June 1st.'

The rest of the memo praised Lionel for his years of fearless service to the force. It listed his many accolades and accomplishments. It ended with a quote from the Chief:

"There isn't a more honorable man on the entire police force or one more deserving of this promotion."

Lionel was touched by the kind words. In a matter of minutes, phone calls, emails and text messages flooded his office. A steady stream of officers, secretaries and staff members made their way to Lionel's office to congratulate him. Lionel knew he wasn't going to get anymore work done. His inbox was overflowing and even the mayor had called to wish him well. It made the transition to office life a little easier for Lionel. It provided the last tiny bit of reassurance he needed that this was indeed the right move. O'Reilly walked into Lionel's office with a huge smile.

"How's the man of the hour doing?"

"You've unleashed quite a storm," replied Lionel. "I have a mountain of work to do but I'm probably not going to get to any of it."

O'Reilly laughed. "Lionel, relax and enjoy the day," he said as he put his hand on his new deputy's shoulder. "By the way, the *Philipsville Herald* called. The editors want to do an interview with you this afternoon. I said you would drop by around two o'clock."

Lionel wasn't great with media interviews. He felt a little miffed that he wasn't consulted first. O'Reilly picked up on the attitude.

"Lionel, dealing with the media is part of the job," he said. "I know they're not your favorite people. They aren't mine either but we need to get them on board as much as possible."

"All right," said Lionel. "But why two o'clock? I could head over there now if they want."

O'Reilly shook his head.

"No. We've ordered a big cake and balloons. It will arrive at noon. Reporters from all the news outlets are coming by as are a few local politicians. We can't have you miss your own party."

Lionel glared at his superior officer. O'Reilly must have arranged this over the weekend and never told him. Lionel was never comfortable drawing attention to himself and he certainly didn't require a party in his honor. Once again, O'Reilly pre-empted the reaction.

"Trust me; you want to enjoy today, Lionel. There are few days as fun as today when you're at the top." The Chief paused briefly to reflect on his own words. He then continued. "Leadership is lonely and you're often putting out fires wondering if you're making any headway at all. I never said the job would be easy but I know you can do it. So, please, relax and have some fun."

Lionel knew his boss was right. His own wife often told him he needed to relax more at work or he would give himself an ulcer. He was determined to soak it all in for one day. It had been a long time coming. O'Reilly smiled at his new deputy.

"So, I'll see you in the front lobby at noon," he said as he made his way to the door.

"Hey, John Paul . . . Is it worth it?"

Chief O'Reilly stopped in the doorway. He turned around slowly and seemed to ponder the question. O'Reilly looked straight at the new deputy chief. He answered with absolute conviction;

"Every minute."

# CHAPTER 30

IT was a monumentally boring biology class. Dylan and his twenty classmates sat through Mr. Coleman's lecture about the human cell. He handed out a diagram listing the dozen tiny parts that comprise the microscopic organism. The teacher informed his students they had to memorize every part and be able to accurately label a blank diagram. There would be a test at the end of the week. Twenty-one students groaned in unison.

Dylan usually gazed at Ashley during biology just to admire her frame but not today.

Dylan shot several glances her way trying to figure out what was wrong with her. Even Mr. Coleman asked if she was feeling sick. Ashley left class a couple of times to go to the washroom.

The bell rang at exactly ten minutes to noon. Everyone immediately packed up their stuff and made their way to lunch. Dylan usually feared this time of day due to the communal nature of the cafeteria. Today, he had replaced one fear with another. He wanted to talk to Ashley. He was genuinely concerned about her.

They both packed up their books and papers. Dylan finished before Ashley. He did his best to look preoccupied with something else as he killed time waiting for her to head towards the door. At last, she tossed her backpack over her shoulder and walked slowly out of the classroom. Even her walk lacked energy or drive. Dylan watched her leave. She was lost in her own thoughts and he was losing his nerve. The shame of backing away from the challenge was already setting in.

"To hell with it," Dylan said, defiantly.

He ran out of the classroom and scanned the crowded hallway. Ashley was drinking at the water fountain only fifteen feet away. He walked briskly towards her as fear and doubt double teamed him every step of the way. Ashley turned and began walking away from Dylan. He caught up with her and did his best not to tremble or stutter. Dylan had never spoken to her outside of class before. He came up from behind her and tapped her on her left shoulder. She turned around slowly.

"Can I talk to you, Ashley?"

Dylan didn't even know where the words came from. The whole thing felt like an out-of-body experience. His mind was totally blank. He was actually talking to his high school crush outside of class and during lunch hour to boot.

"Sure," Ashley replied.

Dylan sweated profusely and was quite agitated. He was just trying to keep his wits about himself.

"Are you all right?" he asked. "You just don't seem like yourself today."

"Yeah, I'm fine," she said.

He didn't know what to say next but her eyes begged him to enquire further. They stood in silence as Dylan scrambled for something to say.

"Here, come with me," he said.

They walked down the hallway to a fire escape. The staircase was empty and quiet. Dylan looked around to make sure they were by themselves. Convinced they were alone, he went for broke.

"Look Ashley, you and I run in different circles at this school. I barely know you so I probably shouldn't even be prying into your personal life. I know you're hurting right now. I can see it all over you and I don't have a clue what it is. I probably can't help; I don't even know why I brought you here . . ." Dylan didn't know what to say next. He hadn't thought that far ahead. Even if she did open up to him, what assistance could he possibly provide? Embarrassed, he decided to wind down the conversation as painlessly as possible.

"I . . . I just want you to know," Dylan stammered. "I'm truly here to listen if you ever want to talk." He wanted to crawl under a rock and die. His humiliation was now complete. Dylan was mentally kicking his own ass for starting the conversation. He knew he should have just let it slide. This whole adventure would permanently tattoo "loser" on his forehead in Ashley's eyes.

Dylan stood there awkwardly then bowed his head in defeat.

"I'm keeping you from your friends. Get out of here."

Ashley hadn't said a word the entire time. She stared at this guy she had known for three years. They had been in classes together each year since grade nine.

Ashley looked down at the ground. A tear rolled down her cheek. She wiped it away. "There is something Dylan," she said. "I'm just not ready to talk about it yet."

Dylan nodded. Her reaction wasn't nearly as bad as he thought it would be. He wouldn't push it any further.

"I understand," he said. Dylan reached back and opened the fire escape door for Ashley. "Go on, people are waiting for you."

She wiped another tear away and walked through the door. Ashley paused in the hallway and turned around.

"Thank you, Dylan," she said. "Thanks for noticing." She then walked down the hallway, turned the corner and disappeared out of sight.

Dylan shut the door. He leaned against the wall in the fire escape. He had to catch his breath. He was not nearly as smooth as he would have liked but he also didn't completely bomb. His shirt was drenched with sweat. He would clean himself up in the washrooms before heading to the cafeteria.

Dylan walked through the hallways on his school's second floor. He passed by his biology classroom. The lights had turned off and the hallway was barren. Everyone was downstairs eating lunch or they were outside on this chilly June day.

The post-adrenaline calmness was already setting in. Dylan walked into the second floor washroom and went straight for the sinks. Two other guys were standing at the urinals. Dylan leaned over one of the five sinks and splashed water on his face. He couldn't believe all that had happened that day. He also couldn't help but feel some pride in himself. He had crossed two thresholds he hadn't dreamt possible the week before.

Dylan also couldn't wait to tell his Dad. He knew Lionel would bask in his boy's triumphs. Dylan splashed some more water on his face, took a few deep breaths then smiled at the mirror. For the first time in his life, Dylan saw his father in the reflection.

\* \* \*

Outside in the hallway, the Vipers closed in on the bathroom doors. They saw their target go in a few minutes earlier. Reed was the leader but this was Boomer's show.

"This cocksucker's all yours," Reed said to Boomer in a hushed tone. "We won't intervene unless you wimp out again like this morning."

"I still think we should let this one slide," said Rocco, who was still nursing his wounds from the weekend. The other four looked at him like he had two heads.

"What the fuck did you say?" asked Boomer, incredulously. "This faggot almost breaks my nose and we should just let it go?"

Rocco nodded. "That's exactly what we should do. It's not like you didn't have it coming."

Boomer cocked his fist back and was about to send it flying towards Rocco when Reed grabbed his arm.

"Girls, cool it," he said. Reed sometimes felt like he was babysitting a gaggle of four-year-olds. "Boomer, don't be a bitch. Rocco, keep your fucking trap shut. Now, let's go."

# CHAPTER 31

**BALLOONS** filled the front lobby of Philipsville Police headquarters. Local politicians, dignitaries and journalists crammed into the relatively small area along with every local police officer who wasn't on duty. Over the years Lionel Stockwell had made quite a name for himself in the community. The mayor made a short speech praising the police for all their hard work. She congratulated Lionel on the promotion and said she looked forward to working with him.

Chief O'Reilly was next. He praised Lionel in front of the two hundred or so gathered in his honor. He introduced Lionel who was greeted with a hearty round of applause from the crowd. Camera flashes fired; then a hushed silence fell over the crowd. Over one hundred constables were in the audience. They had all been weaned on Lionel Stockwell's legacy. There was no cop on the force more revered than the new deputy chief.

Lionel had prepared a few short remarks. He walked to the platform then spoke straight from his heart.

"Thank you all for coming. This means the world to me.

"You know, police officers have a tough job yet they don't seek praise, recognition or reward. They have no one but each other since they often can't share their experiences or pain with those they love.

"Aldous Huxley once wrote, 'No man can concentrate his attention upon evil, or even upon the idea of evil, and remain unaffected.' With all due respect to Mr. Huxley, I must disagree. The men and women I have had the privilege to serve alongside right here in Philipsville have stared down the darkness of this world without becoming that darkness we all seek to eradicate.

"I'm not saying it's easy to cope with the darker aspects of society. It wears all of us down from time to time but I refuse to allow the worst in this world to drive me away from the best. The only people who will decide when my days as a peace officer are over are all of you— my brothers and sisters who wear the uniform.

"I am honored to be the next deputy chief of the Philipsville Police Department."

# THE OFFICER

Lionel stepped down from the podium. His few words, spoken without any trace of bravado or flamboyance, left the audience spellbound. At first, the room was silent then one officer started to applaud. Every other officer joined in until the whole room was cheering. The ovation lasted several minutes. Lionel noticed tears in the eyes of some of the younger constables.

He worked his way through the crowd, shaking hands and even taking a few hugs along the way. He met the mayor at the giant cake brought in for the occasion. They both took a big knife and started cutting out pieces for all those assembled. Photographers lapped it up. They snapped pictures from every possible angle, as did the camera operators from the regional TV stations.

As they handed out the cake, everyone mingled with those around them. Chief O'Reilly walked up to Lionel and shook his head in awe. He put his arm around the local hero.

"You will make a helluva of a Chief one day, Lionel," he said.

"Thanks J.P.," replied Lionel with a big smile. "I've learned from the best."

"I mean it. I know how to manage but you know how to inspire. That's the final test of any leader. Can they inspire those who follow them?" O'Reilly paused and looked around the room. He was in a nostalgic state. "I'll be forgotten five minutes after I retire but these men and women will always remember you."

The Chief went back to the crowd and continued working the room. Lionel didn't say anything. He was touched by the kind words and by everyone who had shown up. He also just wanted a piece of cake. He was hoping there would be leftovers. He would take it home for Dylan and Dana.

# CHAPTER 32

"**ARE** you feeling sick?" asked one of the students in the washroom. He had been at the urinal when he noticed Dylan splashing his face with water.

"I've never been better," replied Dylan, smiling. "Thank you for asking." Dylan grabbed a few paper towels and dried off. That's when he heard the washroom door open.

In walked Andrew Reed, Boomer Simons, Carl Hicks, Rocco Palermo and Bobby Johnson. One student gasped. Another bystander backed into a corner. They knew this couldn't be good. Dylan looked at them, wiped his face one last time with the paper towel then tossed it in the garbage.

"Hey boys," he said calmly. "What can I do for you?"

"You remember me faggot?" asked Boomer.

"Of course," replied Dylan. "I never forget a mangled face."

Rocco chuckled at the remark. Boomer shot him a death stare. Reed shook his head.

"Come on, Boomer. Cut the foreplay," he said. "Let's get this over with."

Boomer was a terrible fighter. He charged at Dylan straight on. Dylan stuck his leg out allowing Boomer to drive his groin right into his foot. Boomer stopped dead in his tracks. He crouched forward and gasped for air. Dylan banged his two cupped hands over each of Boomer's ears simultaneously, popping his eardrums. He had seen that done in several movies. It obviously worked. Boomer temporarily forgot about his throbbing testicles and focused on the unbearable pain in his ears and throat.

Dylan grabbed Boomer's head. He pushed it downwards as he brought his knee up. His knee collided with Boomer's already delicate nose and broke it for good. Blood spattered everywhere. Dylan kneed him four more times in the face then shoved him back towards his buddies. Boomer tumbled into the other four Vipers a humbled, bloodied mess. The whole fight, if you could call it a fight, lasted less than ten seconds.

Carl caught Boomer and pushed him into the corner. Boomer slowly slid down the wall until he was sitting on the ground with his head resting against one of the urinals. Boomer's mouth was wide open in shock as he tried to breathe with no air flowing through his nostrils. He was completely disoriented from the shattered eardrums, busted nose and his genitals were numb.

Rocco nodded his approval.

*You got what you deserved, you fucking idiot.*

Reed pulled a pair of brass knuckles out of his pocket and slid them on his fingers.

"Get him!" he yelled.

The four remaining Vipers charged at Dylan, ramming him into the counter. The combined force smashed his organs. Internal bleeding started immediately. The pain shot through Dylan's body as he fell to the ground clutching his stomach. Rocco, Carl and Bobby proceeded to stomp on him while he was down. The two other students stood by horrified. They watched as the three Vipers bashed Dylan's face in until it was barely recognizable. Reed stood back and watched the whole thing unfold.

"Get back," Reed said, after close to a minute of relentless, three-on-one abuse. They backed off and stood behind their fearless leader. Dylan's left eye was completely swollen shut. His right eye wasn't much better. Dylan's ribs were cracked and his insides were hemorrhaging. He could hardly breathe from all the pain.

"Have you had enough?" asked Reed. "If so, just apologize to Boomer and we'll be on our way."

Dylan had not come this far in one day to surrender all he had earned. He rolled over on the ground and coughed up some blood. He then reached up, grabbed the counter and with every last ounce of strength left in his body, pulled himself to his feet. He stood eye to eye with Andrew Reed, his nemesis.

Dylan's face was battered. He cradled his shattered ribs and his stomach with his right hand. Three of his teeth were knocked out but something more profound had changed; he was no longer scared of the Vipers. They'd hunted him for three long years. He now stood before them and saw them for what they truly were. Dylan, at last, was free.

Reed stood there in the bathroom, a smug smile adorned his face. He was the embodiment of all Dylan hated in the world. Dylan snorted back snot and phlegm, mixed it with the blood and saliva in his mouth then fired a grotesque wad right into Reed's face. The Vipers recoiled. Rocco stared at him in awe. Reed stood frozen. He lifted his left hand slowly to his face to wipe away the disgusting mess. His hand shook. Reed adjusted his brass knuckles and looked squarely at the wounded.

"Fuck you," said Dylan, through the blood and the pain. "I will get even, I promise you."

"I don't think so," replied Reed.

With that, he unleashed the meanest right hook to the temple of Dylan's head. Everyone in the bathroom heard it crack. Dylan spun around then fell to the ground like a wet noodle. He cracked the back of his skull against the floor. A trickle of blood formed beneath his head. It quickly turned into a reservoir. Dylan looked up at the ceiling, his vision fading.

Dylan's parents flashed before his eyes. He tried talking to them but couldn't muster any words. Dylan had finally stood up for himself and confronted his deepest fears, just like his father told him to. He had no regrets. As the light faded to darkness, Dylan experienced true freedom for the first time in his life. He exhaled his final breath, bloodied but unbowed.

The Vipers stood over Dylan's body. Boomer limped over. The two bystanders whimpered, as if hoping they weren't next.

"My god," gasped Rocco. "What the fuck have we done?"

Reed returned the favor and spit on Dylan's face.

"Motherfucker," he sneered, as he kicked Dylan's head one final time for good measure.

The other four Vipers stood at Dylan's feet confused and afraid. This hadn't gone at all the way they had planned.

"Let's get out of here," Reed said to his brood.

Carl, Bobby and Boomer slowly made their way towards the exit. Rocco stood at Dylan's feet crippled by guilt. He waited for Dylan to come around so he could say sorry. It never happened.

Rocco then felt a familiar pain. Reed grabbed him by his hair and dragged him out of the washroom.

"Are you stupid?" Reed screamed. "Let's get the fuck out of here, now!"

The Philipsville Vipers scurried out of Wellington High as fast as their legs could carry them.

# CHAPTER 33

**ACROSS** town at the Philipsville General Hospital, Dana Stockwell felt ill. She had been working since nine that morning and felt perfectly fine the whole time. All at once, she was overwhelmed by a feeling of dread. She knew something bad had happened.

Two of her nurse friends saw her turn pale. They ran over and helped her into a chair.

She sat down with a glass of water by an open window so she could catch her breath. Dana knew she was overly cautious by nature. Some called it paranoia, she called it maternal instinct. Her nausea passed after five minutes but her uneasiness lingered. She thought about calling Lionel at work but she didn't want to disturb him. She wiped her face with a washcloth then went back to her patients. Dana did her best to suppress the awful feeling in her stomach but it wouldn't go away.

\* \* \*

Ashley walked down the high school's staircase slowly. She was usually excited for lunch hour. It was her chance to hang out with Sarah Jane and their friends but things had changed. Ashley was still coming to terms with what had happened to her. It was tearing her apart inside.

Ashley was shocked that Dylan had noticed. The only person who knew about the incident Friday night, other than her family, was Sarah Jane. Ashley swore her to secrecy about it. All her other female friends were oblivious while every boy in school continued their quest to get her on her back. Dylan was the only one to see something was wrong.

Embarrassment, shame, guilt and denial were only a few sentiments Ashley had experienced ever since Constable Maloney spoke to her Saturday night in the hospital. She refused to believe it had happened to her.

Ashley had thought rape happened to someone else in a different part of the world. It didn't happen in Philipsville.

Maloney dispelled that myth when speaking to Ashley and her family. She told them that, despite forty years of progress, sexual assault remains an insidious, silent widespread crime.

Ashley tried so hard to remember what had happened. Constable Maloney had attempted to extract as much information as possible but Ashley's mind was blank and she was completely exhausted. Her parents were equally delirious. They didn't know how to handle the situation either. They were loving parents who always gave Ashley and her siblings plenty of support. Her parents doted on her when she came home from the hospital. They didn't know what else they could do. Her mother had suggested she stay home from school but Ashley refused. She thought it would do her good to maintain her normal routine and be around people. Instead, it had left her exhausted.

Ashley descended the staircase towards Wellington High's first floor. She didn't want to see anyone. She just wanted to be alone. The wall beside her on the staircase was lined with windows overlooking the cafeteria. She stopped and looked out over the jungle. She could see her friends sitting where they always sat. Their table was right smack in the middle of the cafeteria. Many of the jocks claimed a table parallel to their own. Ashley knew they would start flirting with her the moment she arrived. Normally, she took it as light-hearted fun. She wasn't sure she could do that today.

Her cell phone beeped twice. She dug it out of her pocket. There was a text message from Sarah Jane.

"Hey hun, where are you? Come to lunch. Everyone misses you. Muah."

She shut her cell phone and sat down on the staircase. Half of her wanted to run back up and spill her heart to Dylan. She needed to speak to someone and he was the only one to notice her pain without knowing about the incident. She didn't really know him that well and wasn't sure she could trust him either. She was growing increasingly paranoid of everyone. She felt there was nobody she could trust.

Ashley sat on the steps for another ten minutes. She desperately wanted to know who her attacker was. Then she wondered if she really did want to know. As people walked past her on the staircase, part of her wanted them to ask if she was okay. Another part wanted them to leave her alone.

The confusion was overwhelming. Ashley felt lost in her own world. The school and the city were places she had loved her whole life. She had always felt safe and secure. Now, she was a refugee. Would it ever be the same? Would it one day feel like home again?

Ashley fought back the tears. She wasn't ready to go back up and talk to Dylan or anyone else for that matter but she really wanted him to walk down the stairs and find her. He would stop and ask if she was all right. She would answer in the positive. He would pretend to accept that answer then continue on with life. At least he would try. That's all she wanted.

Ashley looked over her shoulder, up the staircase. It was barren. Dylan never came.

# THE OFFICER

She stood up, took a few deep breaths and wiped away a couple of tears. Her cell phone beeped again but she didn't even bother to check. Ashley knew it was Sarah Jane. As she readied herself to head into the cafeteria, she heard a loud commotion behind her. Ashley spun around and saw the Vipers, all five of them, charging down the stairs.

"Let's go, let's go," yelled Reed. "Move it!" He looked up and saw Ashley. Reed winked at her as they passed by. Ashley stood there confused. They usually stopped to say hi in the hallways.

"Hey, where are you guys . . ." Before she could finish, they ran out the school's back doors and were gone. "What the heck was that all about?" she asked herself quietly.

She decided to join her friends in the cafeteria. That might cheer her up a bit. After school, she decided she would speak to Dylan. Something told her he could be trusted.

\* \* \*

The two agents tailing Reed were surprised to see him and his four buddies leave Wellington High at noon. This didn't keep with Reed's usual routine. They had followed Reed to school then parked their car within sight of the school's parking lot. They expected it to be a long boring day of waiting.

Reed and the rest of the Vipers didn't just leave; they sprinted out of the school, piled into Boomer's pick-up truck and screeched out of there. The agents had already rigged a homing beacon to the bottom of Boomer's truck Friday night while the Vipers were at Sarah Jane Harnick's party. They could track it now on the GPS.

The agents jumped into their car. As they followed the speeding truck from a safe distance, the agent riding shotgun called Dercho to inform him of the development.

"Jack Dercho," said the voice on the other end.

"Hey boss, it's me. The target is moving. He appears to be in quite a rush to get away from the high school. We think something's up. I'll let you know if we learn anything."

"Great, keep on him."

"Yes, sir."

The agent flipped his cell phone shut then switched on the Global Positioning System.

\* \* \*

The two bystanders stood dumbfounded in the washroom. One was fourteen years old while the other would turn sixteen in less than a month. Everything had happened so fast. Neither of them had crossed paths with the Vipers before but they knew the group's reputation. They stood at Dylan's body.

"What do we do now?" the younger one asked.

"We need to tell the office what happened," replied the older student. "Follow me."

The younger student didn't move. "Those were the Vipers," he said, in a hushed and angst-filled tone. "They'll kill us if we rat."

"They'll probably kill us anyway when they remember we were here."

The younger boy hadn't thought about it that way. He looked at the older student. They had never met before. They now shared an unbreakable bond.

"Fair enough, let's go."

They ran out of the washroom and charged through the hallways towards the principal's office. As they burst through the doors, Principal Dan Hayle was laughing with a group of teachers.

"Principal Hayle," screamed the older boy, desperation in his voice. "Call the police! There's been trouble."

The younger boy started crying in the office as his guilt for doing nothing set in.

# CHAPTER 34

**ASHLEY** worked her way through the cafeteria crowd towards her friends. As usual, she was the center of attention. Everyone smiled at her as she walked past.

"Hi Ashley," one girl said as Ashley strode by her table.

"Hi hun," responded Ashley, with a wave and a big smile. She had no clue who that girl was. Ashley put on her best game face. She tried to bury the turmoil so she could enjoy lunch with her friends. They were all laughing and giggling as usual. The jocks sat beside them, thumping their chests the entire time.

Her friends exploded when they saw her. None of them had seen her since the party Friday night except Sarah Jane. They were all rich girls. They wore the latest designer clothing and carried Louis Vuitton's most expensive purses. They had an extended circle of friends but there were five girls at the core. They called themselves the "Fab Five." They could get quite gossipy and catty which Ashley was never a fan of but they were her girls. They had been together since they were kids. She adored them and they reciprocated.

Ashley prayed they wouldn't bring up the party. She couldn't handle that right now.

"Come on, sit down, girl," said Julia McCann. She was also on the volleyball team. "You were effin' hot at Harnick's party! Where did you get to? I looked around for an hour and couldn't find you?"

The comment seared Ashley to the bone. Mercifully, Kendal unintentionally intervened.

"Yeah, we've been talking about Friday night," she said. Kendal St. Julie was a star on the school's field hockey team. "You need to host another one, Sarah"

"Yeah, we'll wait and see," she replied with a poker face. "It was a great party."

Sarah Jane looked at Ashley right after saying that. She smiled at her hurting friend while her eyes begged forgiveness. Ashley was already losing her composure. She was drowning in a sea of thoughts right there amongst all the noise and pandemonium.

One of the jocks at the other table leaned over and poked Ashley in the side of her stomach. Ashley was very ticklish. The guys learned if they poked her there she would jump out of her skin. As soon as he touched her, Ashley cracked. She let out a quick scream then buried her face in her hands.

"Are you all right, sweetie?" asked a surprised Hannah Edinger. She was the fifth member of the Fab Five and a phenomenal female wrestler.

Ashley didn't answer. Everyone appeared concerned. Before anyone could say anything else, Ashley jumped up and ran out of the cafeteria. She wasn't comfortable being touched by people anymore. Normally, that didn't bother her but things had changed.

She walked briskly out of the cafeteria, her friends in hot pursuit. She burst into the corridor and was stupefied by what she saw. There were two police cruisers parked out front and an ambulance. Two police officers exited the one cruiser, entered the school and ran up the stairs to the second floor as fast as they could.

Ashley's friends caught up with her.

"Ash, what on earth is going on?" Hannah asked.

Before anyone else could talk, they saw what Ashley was looking at. The paramedics wheeled in a stretcher from the ambulance and carried it up the stairs behind the officers. Something was very wrong.

"What the hell is going on up there?" asked Julia.

Sarah Jane turned to the group. "Come on, girls. Let's go see what's happening."

They ran up the staircase and turned the corner. The boys' washroom door was open but they couldn't see in. The whole area was cordoned off with police tape. Two large police officer's stood guard, their faces locked in a steel-eyed stoic glare. More were on the way. Ashley picked up an ominous vibe as she approached the one officer.

"Excuse me, sir. What happened?"

The officer didn't answer. He simply shook his head as if to say "sorry, I can't tell you." Ashley noticed both officers were incredibly tense. They looked rattled. Beads of sweat ran down their foreheads. At that moment, Principal Hayle's heavy voice came over the intercom.

"May I have everyone's attention please . . ."

Ashley and her friends didn't listen to Hayle too closely at first. It soon became clear he was talking about the crime scene. They stood there in disbelief. A cold chill descended upon each of them. Downstairs, the cafeteria fell silent. Nobody could believe what they were hearing. More police officers filed into the school. Teachers emerged from the staff room. This couldn't be happening. Not at Wellington High.

Hayle ended his announcement instructing students to vacate the school and wait for further instructions. They were to find their homeroom teachers and stay with them until told to return. Students immediately made their way for the doors. In less than five minutes, the school had emptied.

Outside, a cold breeze blew through Philipsville. The sound of wind whistling through tiny nooks was the only noise that could be heard in Wellington High.

# CHAPTER 35

**LIONEL** held a media marathon in his office after the party. His Editorial Board meeting with the *Philipsville Herald* was scheduled for two o'clock but there were many reporters from other media outlets at the event. Lionel did the radio interviews first followed by television. He then herded all the print journalists into his office and held a scrum.

They fired questions at him for forty-five minutes. Lionel sat there and answered them all until there were no questions left. Much to his surprise and relief, Jonathan Pickett wasn't there. His absence made for a jovial press conference. One reporter asked about Pickett's story on the weekend. Lionel responded that the incident was under review; he stood by every single decision he made that day and that was all he would say. That was the end of it. No reporter broached the topic again.

Unlike previous encounters with the press, this one was very pleasant. The questions focused more on Lionel's background, his plans for the job and future ambitions. He didn't know how long the honeymoon would last. Lionel never cared about popularity but that didn't mean he wasn't enjoying the attention.

"Does anyone else have any questions?" asked Lionel as he looked at his watch. It was close to 1:30 p.m. and he needed to make his way over to the *Philipsville Herald*.

The reporters flipped through their note pads.

"I hate to do this guys but I do need to be going."

They seemed to understand. Lionel had already given them ample material to work with for the next day's news cycle. He walked out from behind his desk and shook all their hands. They filed out of his office smiling at him. He wasn't used to that from the media either. Maybe this was the start of something good.

Lionel was finally alone in his office. He put on his uniform dress jacket and grabbed his cap. He wanted to look absolutely professional heading out into public. Lionel gave himself a quick look in the mirror. Everything was impeccable. He was about to walk out when he decided to take a minute to revel in silence. The whole day had been wonderful.

Many of his friends were in the throes of a midlife crisis. Their careers hadn't panned out the way they had hoped; their marriages were on the rocks and nobody's waistline was getting any smaller. A few of them had empty nests while others had insolent, lazy children. Lionel couldn't relate. He loved his career and adored his family. He was in the best shape of his life and the future excited him. All in all, life was good.

*I'm the luckiest man alive.*

Lionel opened his door, hopped into one of the unused police cruisers and drove to the local newspaper's offices. He smiled all the way there.

\* \* \*

At the hospital across town, Dana Stockwell skipped lunch. She had no appetite. She took half an hour to lie down and rest. Her heart still felt heavy. She had tried to call Lionel on his cell phone but it was turned off. Her calls went straight to his voice mail.

Dana sat up on the couch in the nurses' lounge. She picked up the telephone and decided to try Lionel one more time. She was probably overreacting again but she just couldn't shake her anxiety.

Dana dialled Lionel's cell again. It went straight to voice mail. She decided to leave a message.

"Hey honey, it's me. Give me a call whenever you get this. I'm not feeling well and I want to just see if you're doing all right. It's probably nothing but just call me whenever you're free. I love you."

She hung up the phone and walked over to the counter. She splashed some water on her face and dried off with one of the dish towels.

"Dana, are you sure you're okay?" asked Nancy Logan. Nancy worked with Dana in the Palliative Care unit. They had been friends for over twenty years. "You really look pale."

Dana wasn't feeling well but she knew it wasn't an illness. She decided to walk it off before heading back to work.

"I'm fine, Nancy. I'm just going to take a little walk outside and get some fresh air."

"That's a good idea," Nancy said.

"I'll be back in ten minutes."

The Palliative Care unit was on the fifth floor of the hospital. Dana always took the stairs instead of the elevator. It gave her a little extra exercise. That was probably her husband's influence rubbing off on her. Also, the stairs tended to be empty but the elevators were always busy. Dana just wanted some peace and tranquility to compose herself.

She finally made it to the Emergency Room. It was also the hospital's front door. Dana was just going to stand outside for a few minutes then head back up. As she walked through the lobby, a group of paramedics went charging past her. They all jumped into two ambulances and screeched off in a hurry. Dana didn't think twice about it. That was commonplace where she worked.

She walked past the front desk where Judy Jackson worked reception. She had been at that hospital for almost forty years and was nearing retirement.

# THE OFFICER

"Hi Mrs. Jackson," Dana said, with a big smile at the loving secretary. She was everyone's favorite at the hospital.

"Well, hello there young lady," replied the grandmotherly woman. "How are you today?"

"Oh, okay," replied Dana. "I'm feeling a little under the weather so I'm just going to take a little walk."

"That sounds like a wonderful idea."

"Thanks," said Dana. "By the way, where were all the paramedics off to in such a rush?"

"Oh, we received a call from the local high school," replied Mrs. Jackson. "Principal Hayle was pretty frantic. In all my years, I've never heard him sound liked that. He said one of the students was in trouble."

Dana approached the desk slowly.

"What kind of trouble?" she asked. "Did he say?"

Mrs. Jackson adjusted her reading glasses and shrugged her shoulders.

"He said something about a fight. One of the boys was badly hurt. I didn't push for too many details but it sounded serious."

Dana considered everything. She was positive she had nothing to worry about and did her best to remain rational.

*Everything's fine. Don't do anything embarrassing.*

"Thank you, Mrs. Jackson."

"Anytime, dear."

Dana turned to walk outside. The automatic doors slid open. She stopped in front of them again. She had to know for sure. She walked back to the front desk and borrowed Mrs. Jackson's phone. Dana was going to call Wellington High just to make sure.

She dialled the school number. It rang once, then twice. In the middle of the third ring the receptionist picked up.

"Wellington Secondary School, how may I help you?"

"Hi Shirley, this is Dana Stockwell. May I speak to Dan Hayle please."

Everyone in the office knew Dana because of her involvement in the PTA. Diane Robinson was no exception. She had answered the phone in her usual chipper yet professional manner. Now, her whole demeanor changed. There was a long period of silence.

"Hello . . . Diane?" repeated Dana.

After a little longer, Diane pulled herself together long enough to say, "Hello, Mrs. Stockwell. Can you hold for just one moment?"

"Of course."

The line went to hold. A few minutes later, Dana heard someone pick up.

"Hello, Mrs. Stockwell," Diane said. "Principal Hayle is in his office. I'll transfer you through."

# CHAPTER 36

**THE** Vipers sat silently at Boomer's house. Bobby tried to clean up Boomer as best he could. The kid needed to see a doctor but Reed wouldn't allow it. He didn't want anyone to leave the house until they had figured out what they were going to do. The enormity of what happened was sinking in. Rocco had grasped the situation the moment Dylan died. Bobby, Boomer and Carl slowly clued in. Reed was the last holdout. He had escaped punishment and was certain he could escape it again. The Vipers sat scattered throughout the living room for over an hour before someone finally broke the silence.

"What do you guys want to do?" asked Carl.

"Shut up, Hicks," snapped Rocco.

"What the fuck's your problem?" he hissed in reply.

"Gee, I don't know, Carl. It may have something to with the guy we murdered today."

Rocco's words echoed through the house and hung in the air. Bobby had been shaking ever since they arrived, Boomer was in too much pain to do anything and Carl, as usual, appeared clueless. Reed maintained the stoic facade. Somehow, he was going to get out of this. He just knew it.

"I think we should go to the cops," Rocco piped up.

"Are you fucking crazy?" Reed asked quietly.

"No Andrew, I'm dead serious," Rocco replied. "We're screwed. They may go easy on us if we turn ourselves in and show some remorse."

Reed could tell the words resonated with the rest of the pack. He couldn't allow this to happen.

"We're not turning ourselves in," Reed said in a matter-of-fact manner. "You should all try to control your fear."

Rocco had had enough. "Fuck you," he yelled at Reed. "If you assholes had listened to me, Dylan would still be alive and we wouldn't be in this mess. But I'm not going down for this. I'm going to the cops right now. Who's with me?"

Bobby looked at Boomer and Carl as if waiting for them to make the first move. Neither of them budged.

"You're not going anywhere," Reed stated casually. "Sit your ass down."

# THE OFFICER

Rocco ignored the order. He made his way for the front door. Reed was growing tired of Rocco's cowardice. He had been whining all day. First, he was against going after Dylan, now he wanted to lie down and surrender. Reed grabbed Rocco's arm as he passed by.

"I said sit down, Rocco."

Rocco yanked his arm free. Reed jumped off his chair furious. He ran ahead of Rocco and shoved him back towards the group. Rocco, teary eyed, shoved Reed back.

"That's it, you're fucking dead," Reed growled.

Rocco prepared himself for the ass kicking. Reed was too strong for him to ever beat in a fight. Before Reed could wallop him, Bobby and Carl jumped between them.

"Come on guys, break it up," Bobby said. "We're in this together. Now let's figure out what we're going to do."

"I'm not in anything," Rocco said through tears. He pointed at Reed. "This prick killed Dylan and I'm not taking the fall for it."

Reed laughed. "Maybe you've forgotten but you helped us kill him." Reed's words had a sobering effect on Rocco. "Oh, and by the way, his father happens to be Lionel Stockwell. Does that name ring a bell?"

Rocco went pale. Reed smiled at the look on Rocco's face. He could tell he had gotten through to his panicky friend.

"So, your idea of going to the police isn't going to wash," Reed said. "Now pretty please, with sugar on top, sit the fuck down."

Reed turned around and went to sit back down on the recliner when Rocco challenged him.

"Is that what this was all about?" Rocco blurted out. "Did you use us to carry out a personal vendetta?"

Reed turned around slowly - a scowl on his face and daggers in his eyes but he didn't say a word.

"You son of a bitch," Rocco said in a hushed tone. "You wanted revenge for Willie Hogan, you needed our help and now we're all fucked."

Reed didn't respond. He just glared at Rocco. This was the second time in one day someone had challenged Reed's supremacy. Rocco shoved Reed again.

"You worthless piece of shit," Rocco said, his voice rising. He shoved Reed for a third time causing him to fall back into the recliner. "Admit it. That's what this was all about!"

Boomer, Bobby and Carl gathered around Rocco.

"Come on, man, say something," Bobby said. Reed looked at all of them. The fear in their eyes angered him. He wanted to lash out but knew the other three were with Rocco and not their "rightful" leader.

"I didn't mean to kill him," Reed said quietly.

"Bullshit," Rocco snapped.

Reed slowly stood up and looked his friends in the eyes.

"Fellas," he said as he placed his one hand on Rocco's shoulder, the other on Bobby's. "Old Man Hogan had nothing to do with this, I swear to God." Reed spoke in a calm, reassuring and seemingly genuine voice. "I honestly didn't mean to kill Dylan. I wanted him to apologize to Boomer for what happened this morning. I expected him to do it without a fight."

Reed could tell he was slowly winning the group back . . . except for Rocco.

"Listen, whether you four want to accept this or not, we all killed Dylan and we're all going to fry if we get caught but I'm not going to let that happen. I've never let you guys down before and I don't intend to start now. So, everyone please sit down, take a few deep breaths and let's figure out where we go from here."

Carl, Bobby and Boomer went back to the couches and sat down. Reed could tell Rocco wasn't convinced. He was no longer a believer. They stared at each other, neither one saying a word. Bobby cut the tension.

"Hey, Rock," he called out from the sofa. "Come on, buddy, sit here. It's going to be fine."

Rocco shook his head and chuckled.

"You dumb shit," he said to the naive follower. "Did you all forget there were other people in the bathroom when Dylan died?"

All four of them clammed up. Even Reed hadn't thought about that yet. Rocco got up in Reed's face.

"And while you think about that, think about this . . ." They were nose-to-nose but his words were directed more at the other three than at Reed. "This retard spit on the dead body, which is like leaving your signature at a crime scene except for one big difference; you can't pretend someone else forged your DNA."

Bobby stood up slowly but didn't speak. Boomer and Carl sat frozen. Even Reed's trademark arrogance faltered. It was too late to go back to the school. The police were probably already there. Rocco took a step back as if to gauge the effect his revelation has had on the room. He looked squarely at Reed.

"So, fearless leader, talk your way out of this one."

# CHAPTER 37

**THE** Editorial Board meeting couldn't have gone any better. Lionel laughed and joked his way through the numerous questions fired in his direction. The six editors of the *Philipsville Herald* also enjoyed themselves. Lionel couldn't believe he was getting along so well with the media. On any other day he considered journalists to be arrogant, lazy, egomaniacal, armchair generals. That was starting to change.

Lionel shook all their hands and posed for a few pictures. A photographer had been in the room the whole time snapping impromptu shots during the interview. When all the formalities were done, Lionel excused himself from the boardroom. He walked through the cubicles where reporters filed their stories against the backdrop of a ticking deadline.

Lionel even stumbled upon Jonathan Pickett's cubicle. The new deputy police chief didn't know that Pickett had been quietly cultivating other sources about the Willie Hogan incident. Lionel decided to say hi.

"Hello Jon-Jon," he said jokingly. "Did you miss me?"

Pickett appeared surprised at first. He stood up and shook Lionel's hand.

"Congratulations on the promotion," he replied. "I have a feeling we'll be seeing more of each other in the future."

"I'm sure we will." Lionel was about to leave when Pickett blurted out;

"Did you read my article on Saturday? I would love a reaction from you."

Lionel chuckled. "It was biased, Jon, like everything else you write about the men and woman on my force."

"But was it untrue?"

"Yes."

"Well, please, enlighten me. What did I get wrong?"

Lionel shook his head. "Have a good day, Jonathan. If you need to reach me, my number's still 911."

Pickett didn't laugh or react. He turned his attention back to his computer as Lionel left his cubicle and exited the newsroom.

At last, he was finished. Lionel was so excited to get home and tell Dana and Dylan about the day. He was smiling ear-to-ear. He had even claimed a huge chunk of the cake from his party so he could take it home. Dylan would probably polish it off in one sitting.

As Lionel walked through the newspaper's spacious lobby he thought of his family and then remembered that he had turned off his phone. He dug into his pocket, fished out the cell phone and turned it on. His eyes popped out of his head when the screen indicated forty-six missed calls.

"What the heck?" he said.

He had never seen it higher than five missed calls. Lionel opened his call log and clicked on the "Missed Calls" option. It showed him the phone numbers that had tried to reach him. The list was substantially shorter, closer to six numbers.

"Jesus, someone really wants to talk to me!"

Lionel recognized his work phone number and Dana's work number. Odd. She seldom called him in the middle of a shift. When he checked his voice mail, he received another shock. He had twenty-one unheard messages and two saved messages.

"Oh, man," Lionel said as he clicked the little red telephone button to end the call. "I'll listen to them later."

He flipped the phone shut but left it on. He placed his police hat on his head and prepared to leave the building. As soon as he stepped through the doors, the cold wind stabbed him from every direction. Lionel had forgotten how frigid it was outside.

"Global warming my ass," he muttered under his breath.

Lionel made his way through the half empty parking lot towards the police cruiser he had borrowed. He looked up and noticed a familiar figure standing in front of it.

"Hey!" Lionel shouted, surprised to see his boss. "What the hell are you doing here?"

Chief O'Reilly didn't answer. His body language was completely different from earlier in the day. He stared down at the ground, his shoulders slouched. He removed his police cap as his new deputy approached. Lionel knew there was a problem. Sorrow pulled on the man's face. Lionel's brisk walk slowed to a crawl. He approached his old friend with apprehension.

"John Paul, what's wrong?"

O'Reilly lifted his head slowly, his eyes remaining glued to the ground for some time. "John Paul," Lionel repeated in a stern tone. "Look at me. What's going on?"

O'Reilly looked straight at his long time comrade and best friend. His mouth moved but nothing came out. Lionel could see O'Reilly was holding back tears. Whatever it was, he knew it was serious. Lionel's powerful eyes stared straight at O'Reilly, making the Chief feel tiny. Finally, he spit it out.

"Dylan's dead."

The words rang hollow. Lionel heard them but he didn't connect them to his son.

"Dylan who?" he asked, completely sincere.

# THE OFFICER

O'Reilly looked away, closed his eyes and exhaled. "Your boy, Lionel. I'm so sorry."

It still wasn't clear.

"What? What are you talking about?"

O'Reilly was shaking. "Dylan's dead, Lionel. He was killed at his high school earlier today. I tried to tell you as soon as I heard the news but I couldn't get through on your cell."

Now it registered.

Lionel's eyes remained pointed at his boss but they had changed. His usual intense focus was replaced with the "thousand mile gaze," an early indicator that post-traumatic stress was setting in and he was breaking from reality.

"Lionel, listen to me," O'Reilly continued. "I promise you we're going to catch who did this. We have DNA evidence; we have witnesses and I spoke to Jack Dercho already. He's rounding up suspects as we speak."

Lionel heard none of it. His mind was everywhere and nowhere.

"I want you to go home and just be with your wife. I've been trying to reach her at work but they say she left early in a mad rush. I don't know where she is just yet but where trying to..."

"Where's Dylan?" Lionel asked quietly, his face locked in permanent disbelief.

O'Reilly took a deep breath.

"Lionel, I'm begging you to please, go home and wait for..."

Lionel grabbed his Chief by the jacket collar, lifted him off his feet and slammed him against the car. Lionel's eyes refocused, pulsating with absolute hate.

"Where's my son, John?"

O'Reilly trembled as he looked into the eyes of an unchained beast. "Dylan's body is still at Wellington High. The investigators didn't want to move him until we got every last bit of evidence and..."

Again, Lionel didn't let him finish. He let go of O'Reilly's jacket and let him fall to the pavement. He jumped in the cruiser, fired up the engine and turned on the siren. Lionel smashed his foot against the pedal causing the car's tires to screech. The smell of burned rubber filled the area and Lionel was off like a bullet. His police siren blared at full volume. Cars got out of the way as he sped out of the parking lot.

O'Reilly coughed a few times on his knees in the parking lot. Lionel had knocked the wind out of the Chief when he pushed him against the car. O'Reilly's kidneys would feel the worst of it the next morning. He wasn't angry at his deputy. He would have reacted the same way if it had been one of his children or grandchildren.

O'Reilly got to his feet and dusted himself off. He had known Dylan since he was a baby. The loss tore his heart in half. He couldn't imagine what it was doing to Lionel. O'Reilly knew it would only get worse before it got better. That's assuming it would ever get better. O'Reilly had watched families of victims struggle through the so-called grieving process. The word "process" implied a beginning, middle and end. However, the grieving process was endless.

He climbed back into his car. He needed to get a message out to the police at the Wellington High murder scene.

"To all the officers at the school, please listen up," he said into the radio. "This is Chief John Paul O'Reilly. Lionel Stockwell has been informed of the situation and is on his way over. You would be well advised to stay out of his path when he arrives."

O'Reilly closed his eyes. Every worst case scenario was running through his head. Lionel was fully armed. He knew he would never do anything to hurt a fellow officer but this type of situation changed everything. He might not act rationally. Nothing and no one could stand in Lionel Stockwell's way if he didn't want them to. O'Reilly felt his heart race.

"I'm on my way to the school; I'll be there in ten minutes," he said into the handheld device. "I repeat; do not try to stop Lionel Stockwell. I'm begging each of you to follow my order for your own safety."

# CHAPTER 38

**BOBBY** and Boomer were freaking out. It had been close to an hour since Rocco's revelation about the evidence against them. Carl rolled a joint but it didn't help him calm down. Reed sat in silence. He hadn't said anything since Rocco cut him down. His command over the Vipers had all but dissolved. Reed was a master of bullshit. He had conned his way out of many situations before but he appeared defeated here.

Unbeknownst to the other four, Rocco had slipped into the washroom shortly after confronting Reed. He'd called 911 from his iPhone and told the police everything. He ended the call with the address where they could find him and his four buddies. When he returned to the group, they were oblivious to what he had done. Normally, Reed would have been all over him but he wasn't thinking straight.

The police showed up at 2:34 p.m. Jack Dercho's booming voice called on them to come out of the house with their hands in the air. Bobby wet his pants; Boomer started crying while Carl, stoned on weed, summed up their dilemma perfectly;

"Aw, shit man. We're in trouble."

Reed looked out the window stunned.

The only one whose demeanor didn't change was Rocco. He had been expecting them. Reed looked over at Rocco's calm acceptance of the situation.

"What the hell did you do, Rocco?

Rocco looked at his once fearsome friend with a blank expression and zero emotion. Reed no longer filled him with fear.

"It's over Andrew," he replied. "And it's time to face the music."

Rocco opened the door and raised his hands. The cocking mechanism on a dozen police assault weapons clicked into place. The other four followed behind him. Reed was the last one out. As his friends buckled under the pressure, he had no choice but to follow suit the jig was up.

Dercho ordered them to the ground. The five Vipers got on their bellies with their hands behind their heads. The officers slapped handcuffs on each of them and they were stuffed into the police cruisers. Bobby, Boomer and Hicks sobbed when the handcuffs locked into place. Rocco had prepped himself for this. He knew he would break down soon but didn't want it to be there and then.

Andrew Reed didn't say a word. For the first time in his life, he was speechless. Dercho slapped the cuffs on him. This was personal. Dercho lifted Reed up by his arm, causing enormous pain in his shoulder blade area.

"Now, you have earned the right to remain silent," Dercho said through his teeth. After reading them their rights, Dercho shoved Reed into the back of the cruiser. Reed's head thumped hard on the back door frame. He winced but remained silent. "Let's see how tough you are now," Dercho whispered in Reed's ear. "Where you're going, you're the faggot."

# CHAPTER 39

**THE** halls of Wellington High were empty. So were the classrooms. Abandoned food and half-eaten meals covered the cafeteria tables. The only activity was on the second floor as the police finished their investigation. It would soon be time to move the corpse to the morgue. Four officers stood guard at the scene. The hallways were barren; not a soul in sight.

Two police officers were in the front lobby trying to pacify Dana Stockwell. They wouldn't let her see the body. She was told by the principal what had happened. Dana refused to believe it. It simply wasn't true. It couldn't be true. She had left work early and raced over to Wellington High but she wasn't allowed near the crime scene. Until she saw a body, she would remain convinced the whole thing was just a really bad joke.

Through the front door Dana could see all the students huddled together for warmth and comfort. The news seemed to have a wrecking ball affect on the teenagers. Several female students cried while many of their male friends appeared to struggle to keep their emotions in check. Many of them broke down too. Students held each other as they wept openly trying to make sense of everything. A number of students held hands and prayed.

Off in the distance, came the sound of screeching tires and a siren blaring incessantly. A car approached in a mad rush. The engine grew louder as the car moved closer to the school. The police cruiser finally roared out from around the corner. The siren howled its warning as the cruiser tore passed the shivering crowds. Students backed away from the curb in case the car didn't quite make all the necessary turns. The tires screamed as the driver slammed on the brake at the school's front doors.

The officer jumped out of the vehicle. He walked into the school with a brisk, steadfast determination. He didn't even blink. He was zeroed in on his goal, everything else was racket and white noise. He nearly ripped the door off the hinges as he burst into the school's front lobby.

Dana spun around and saw her husband.

"Lionel!" she screamed as she ran for him. He wrapped his arms around her and kissed her head. "Tell me it's not true," she begged. "They told me Dylan's dead but it's a lie. It's a lie, right?"

Lionel didn't respond. She looked up and saw fear in his deep dark eyes. He had been told the same thing but he didn't want to believe it either. Lionel looked straight at the two officers.

"Where is he?"

The older of the two answered their superior.

"Boys washroom, second floor."

Lionel was off like a flash. He left his wife at the door and ran up the stairs. Lionel reached the top of the staircase and turned the corner. Four officers were guarding the door to the washroom at the end of the hallway. It was sealed off with police tape. Lionel felt a wave of dread wash over his body. He had to see for himself. Nothing on the other side of that police tape could be worse than what he was imagining.

He walked towards the cordoned off area. The four police, to Lionel's surprise, stepped out of his way. Suddenly, Jack Dercho emerged from the washroom. He had rushed over after arresting the Vipers to intercept his friend.

"Lionel, don't go in there," he said as his friend approached. He walked towards Lionel. "Lionel, please don't go in there."

The two met halfway between the washroom and the top of the staircase. Dercho put his hand on Lionel's arm trying to redirect him away from the washroom. Lionel shook off Dercho's grip and continued. Dercho got more physical out of desperation. He grabbed Lionel's shoulders and tried to force him to a stop.

"Lionel, my friend, please listen to me."

Lionel spun around and punched Dercho in the face. Dercho flew back five feet and landed on the ground. The force of Lionel's blow left Dercho completely disoriented and his nose bloody. He crawled slowly over to the lockers along the school walls and sat against them. Lionel didn't skip a beat. Once Dercho was out of the way, he turned around and headed straight for the boys washroom. He tore through the tape, and charged into the crime scene.

There, on the floor, in a pool of blood lay Dylan. His face was mangled but there was no mistaking it. Lionel felt his knees go rubbery.

"No!" he said quietly to himself, absorbing the image. His only son was dead. He couldn't move; he couldn't talk. Finally, panic set in and thrust him forward.

Lionel ran across the washroom. He fell to his knees beside Dylan's body and touched his son's chest. The heartbeat had long since faded away.

"Come on buddy, let's go home," he begged, knowing Dylan wasn't going to wake up.

Lionel positioned himself behind Dylan. He pulled his son's body up and cradled it in his arms. Dylan's head rested on his father's chest. This was how Lionel had sat with Dylan when he was just a little boy. Lionel remembered rocking him to sleep when Dylan had been sick or after a nightmare. He ran his hand across Dylan's face; then kissed the side of his head. He could feel the tears welling up. He sat on the floor of the high school washroom in a pool of Dylan's blood holding him close. Lionel had never cried once during his adult life, not even in front of his wife. Somehow, he held it all in.

# THE OFFICER

Inside Lionel Stockwell, something broke that day. He shouted loud and long at the heavens. The sorrow; descending like an anvil, wrapped around his neck and weighed him down. The tears didn't flow. He wanted them to. Maybe it would provide some relief but they never came. Lionel looked down at Dylan. His son seemed calm, at ease and peaceful.

Lionel looked around the washroom, frantically trying to think of something he could do. Overwhelmed by the situation, he let out another miserable roar. It echoed through the empty school, including outside in the corridor where Dana fainted.

Twenty minutes later he staggered out of the washroom and into the corridor. His face bore a frozen expression and looked paler than that of a ghost. His eyes sunk into his skull. He walked slowly past the group of officers. He didn't seem to see Chief O'Reilly and Dercho who exchanged a brief glance then quickly looked away from each other. Lionel continued his slow walk down the hall; then dragged his feet down the stairs. His heart weighed a metric ton; his stomach felt empty. Every breath was an effort for even his lungs felt constricted.

Two officers helped Dana to her feet. They followed Lionel out. O'Reilly ordered one of his men to drive them home. Lionel stopped at the school's front doors and waited for his wife. Dana, crippled by grief, couldn't even walk. She put her arms around her husband again and wept.

Together they walked out of Wellington High. They had sent Dylan there trusting he would be safe. As they made their way to the waiting police cruiser, a flash popped in front of their faces. Lionel didn't even have the strength or motivation to stop the *Philipsville Herald* photographer from snapping a picture of them in their pain. It would be a long time before he could look at that picture which dominated the front page of the newspaper the next morning.

When the cruiser pulled away from the school, Lionel tried not to picture the paramedics taking his son to the morgue across town for the autopsy. He knew he would never see his son again and he wanted to remember him as he had been when alive.

# CHAPTER 40

IT was ten o'clock that night before John Paul O'Reilly made it home to his wife Mindy. He was much later than usual. One of their grand kids was over. The grandchildren took turns spending the night at Grandma and Grandpa's house. It was well past their granddaughter's bedtime but she wouldn't go to sleep until O'Reilly was home to tuck her in.

O'Reilly was heartbroken. A day that had started out so good had ended so badly. He had managed to keep his emotions in check all day but his thin veneer was starting to crack. It took him an eternity to park his car in the driveway and walk through the front door. He had called earlier saying he would be late because there had been "problems" at the office but he would explain later.

O'Reilly entered his home to a hero's welcome from his granddaughter Trixie. She adored the old man.

"Grandpa!" she screamed as she ran down the hallway and latched onto his leg. She made him smile. All his grandchildren did.

"How are you, munchkin?" he asked as he picked up his three-year-old jewel.

Mindy walked up and kissed her husband on the lips.

"Are you okay?" she asked.

He was far from okay but O'Reilly always did his best not to bring his work problems into the home.

"Before you hop in the shower," Mindy said with a smile. "It's well past someone's bedtime."

Trixie wrapped her arms around her Grandpa's neck and rested her head on his shoulder. O'Reilly knew she was trying to woo him into letting her stay up. Despite thirty-five years spent fighting the worst in society, O'Reilly was a complete softy with his grandchildren. They knew he was an easy mark.

But before he could respond, Trixie started to nod off. They both shared a good laugh at her expense. He carried her up to the guest room and put her to bed. He kissed her good night and left the nightlight on. He looked at the precious little girl lying in front of him.

*What a terrible world we've created.*

He was now finally alone. The Chief was still mentally processing all that had happened. He would have to tell Mindy everything because they were close friends with the Stockwells. He had already delivered enough bad news for one day and didn't want to do it anymore.

O'Reilly walked into the bathroom and shut the door. He started the shower and let it run while he undressed. As the water warmed up steam filled the room. O'Reilly jumped in. The warm water washed over him relaxing every muscle and easing the tension.

In less than thirty seconds, he cracked. O'Reilly put his hands on the wall in front of him. He looked down at the tub drain. The tears started without any advance warning. His chest heaved beneath the steady stream as his sobbing grew more and more intense. The shower was often where he cried. The water camouflaged the noise. At least, that's what he thought.

He'd been raised old school Irish Catholic; his father had never cried and had raised his boys with an iron sceptre. Crying was a sign of weakness. O'Reilly had tried desperately to eradicate the reaction from his existence but he had never fully succeeded. It was a mark of shame for him that had lingered on from his childhood. His dad had constantly belittled him in the hopes it would toughen up his son.

O'Reilly wept for ten minutes. Once it finally passed, he washed up, dried off and put on clean clothes. He then confronted his wife.

"Mindy, I need to tell you something." O'Reilly almost broke down again. He motioned for her to sit down on the couch in the living room. "Something terrible happened today."

"I know," Mindy said. O'Reilly was surprised.

"You already heard?"

"No," she replied, taking his hand. "You're just too easy to read, John Paul. I could tell from the moment you pulled in the driveway there was a problem."

O'Reilly exhaled, searching for the right words. He looked at his wife then looked away. "John, it's all right. Talk to me. What's the problem? What happened today?"

O'Reilly closed his eyes and forced the words out.

"You know Dylan?"

Mindy nodded.

"Lionel's boy? Of course. What about him?"

O'Reilly began to shake.

"He was killed today at school."

Mindy recoiled in horror. She clasped both her hands over her mouth.

"Oh my God! Are you serious?" O'Reilly didn't move or make a sound. "What do you mean? What happened?"

"Bullying incident at Wellington High. Five kids ganged up on Dylan in the washroom."

Mindy gasped. Tears quickly started flowing down her face. O'Reilly finally opened his eyes and looked at his wife. The sight of her crying made him break down again.

"Lionel and Dana must be devastated," Mindy said. "We should head over to their place tonight. They'll probably need our help."

O'Reilly shook his head.

"They'll need our support but I was with both of them earlier today. There isn't anything we can do for them tonight. I'll call them in the morning."

"Are you sure?" she asked.

"Trust me. Lionel wouldn't want us there right now anyway. Besides, he'd probably end up consoling me."

That remark made Mindy smile briefly through her tears. O'Reilly, exhausted from the events of that turbulent day, led his wife to their room.

They went to bed in each other's arms and cried themselves to sleep.

* * *

Lionel had spent years hounding Dercho to come with him to the gym. Dercho was never interested. That night, Dercho went to the small workout facility in the basement of the police headquarters. He wailed on the punching bag for two hours straight. He envisioned Andrew Reed's face as he drove one fist after another into the padded bag.

Dercho then showered and brought twelve of his "closest friends" home with him for company. In other words, he purchased a twelve pack of Budweiser and planned to consume them by himself. He downed one after another, after another, after another. In the darkness of his apartment, Dercho hoped to drown out the memories of a horrendous day and then fall asleep.

He was still tossing and turning at 2 a.m. He wanted to call Lionel to check in on his best friend but didn't dare. There was nothing he could say. Unable to sleep, he called his second ex-wife, Jenna. She actually picked up the phone. He then jumped in the car and drove to her place. He thought getting laid might help him sleep.

Jenna had divorced him six years earlier but was still single. She was never able to fully trust men after Dercho had cheated on her multiple times. He could also be verbally abusive. Yet, she was always up for a one-night-stand every time he called. Her friends all thought he was a prick. They all loathed him as did her family. Dercho couldn't blame any of them for feeling that way. He deserved every bit of their hatred. This was the only marriage Dercho felt guilty about messing up.

She only lived five minutes away in the house they had bought together. As soon as he arrived, the foreplay started. They undressed each other slowly, kissing every square inch of the other's body. She still looked amazing with long brown hair that ran halfway down her back and she was younger than Dercho by nearly fifteen years. Her busty frame could always entrance Dercho but this night was different.

After oral sex, Dercho pulled out a condom and rolled it on. As he got into position, the memories from the day hit him in one swift and sudden motion. He went limp and completely lost his composure.

He sat naked and crying at the end of his ex-wife's bed. Jenna tried to console him.

# THE OFFICER

"Jesus, Jack, what's the matter?"

The image of Dylan's battered and broken body haunted him. The dead, lifeless look in Lionel's eyes as he left the school washroom cut to Dercho's soul. He adored Lionel and owed him everything for saving his ass a decade earlier. Dercho didn't tell his ex-wife any of this.

"Why are you crying?" she asked him. Jenna placed her hand on his groin. "It okay, this happens to everyone from time to time. Give me two minutes. I'll get you restarted."

Dercho shook his head. She didn't understand.

"Why do bad things happen to good people?" Dercho asked Jenna, through the snot and tears.

She rolled her eyes, removed her hand and climbed off the bed. Impotence was hardly the worst thing that could happen to someone and Dercho was far from "a good person."

"Yeah right," she replied. "I guess there's just no justice in this world."

Dercho removed the condom and got dressed. He apologized for his lousy performance and for waking her up. He promised he would call her later in the week and they would go for coffee.

"Sure, Jack," she said, putting her clothes back on. "You say that after every one of these midnight sessions."

She opened the front door and motioned for him to go. He looked at her with begging eyes.

"I'm sorry," he said.

Dercho drove home. He lay in bed staring at the ceiling all night.

# CHAPTER 41

**LIONEL** and Dana Stockwell went to bed as soon as they got home and didn't move. Dana cried. She had started crying at the school and didn't stop. Lionel held her close but didn't say anything. Both were paralysed by an indescribable sense of loss.

Dana's tears grew more intense by the hour. Lionel never knew it was possible for a human being to weep as much as she did. She cried all through the night. He stayed awake holding her. A million thoughts raced through his mind but he didn't speak; neither did Dana. The absolute nature of his loss was becoming clear. He had lost his son forever. Dylan would never come home. Unlike Dana, Lionel was an only child. His family tree would end with him.

These realizations along with many others sent Lionel into the darkest depths of an unspeakable depression. It kick started his insomnia. He had no energy or inclination to go to the gym. He had no desire to do anything but he knew he had to be strong. There was work to be done. He would start it in the morning after sleeping for a few hours.

Sleep never came but the morning arrived as usual. Lionel called all the relatives on both sides and broke the news. They immediately made plans to come down and help out. Dana continued crying in bed non-stop for a solid week, even when her sisters showed up. It was as if they weren't there. The presence of his in-laws enabled Lionel to take care of funeral preparations while they stayed with his wife. He didn't want her left alone and was grateful for their help. They cooked meals for them but she never ate. They couldn't get her to stop crying long enough to ingest some food. Her sisters moved her to the bathtub to clean her up. Even then, she wouldn't stop. Her grief knew no bounds. She literally cried until her tear ducts ran dry.

A steady stream of friends and neighbors stopped by the home to offer their assistance and condolences. Lionel thanked each of them. He was truly touched by their thoughtfulness but it also hurt every time someone dropped in. Nothing was funny anymore and nothing made sense. He felt lost in the wilderness. He had no energy to entertain people. Every movement and every motion made his body ache.

# THE OFFICER

He never imagined misery like this existed in the world. But it did. He saw no way out. As the week dragged on, Lionel's grief ignited a spark of anger inside of him. He wanted justice for his murdered son. This desire would slowly turn into an obsession.

* * *

Principal Dan Hayle's days were numbered. The *Philipsville Herald* covered the murder extensively with Jonathan Pickett leading the charge. He wrote feature after feature on school bullying in Philipsville. Nobody was spared from the wrath of his pen. The students who had been bullied by the Vipers told the media they had reported this to school authorities but nothing was ever done about it.

Hayle tried to fight back against the wave of negative publicity with no success. Pickett kept up the pressure on the school administration as more and more students came forward. It turned out Dylan wasn't alone after all.

None of Hayle's predecessors had had the guts to stand up to the children of wealthy alumni either. The conspiracy of silence started long before he was principal but it didn't matter now. He had been the principal when the powder keg exploded. The school board didn't renew his contract. Two months later, he and his wife moved away from Philipsville to start over. The town people looked for anyone other than themselves to blame. While guilty of his share of sins, Hayle became the scapegoat for the transgressions of an entire community.

Jonathan Pickett was in his glory. His relentless coverage earned him national and international attention. The BBC, CBC and 60 Minutes all produced TV features about bullying at Wellington High over the following year. Pickett became an authority on school violence that all the other media networks turned to. His articles won endless praise and acclaim the world over.

For the time being, the pugnacious journalist backed away from his quest to take down Philipsville's top cop. The truce wasn't out of sympathy but opportunity. Pickett would bide his time until he could return to the target he both loved and hated—Lionel Stockwell.

# CHAPTER 42

**DANA** and Lionel decided on cremation. Dylan's funeral took place one week after his murder. They didn't want to see the body again. It was too painful. Dylan's ashes were spread on Bill and Leona Fitzpatrick's farm. There was no place their son had loved more.

Only family members and close friends were invited to the spreading of the ashes. Dana wept the entire service. She sat in chair while Lionel stood behind her. He noticed how thin and gaunt she had become. None of her clothing fit because she hadn't eaten anything in over a week and had lost fifteen pounds. She wasn't big to begin with.

The police union covered the cost of a beautiful gravestone for Dylan in the local cemetery. The union also hosted a reception after the service. The community was invited. Thousands showed up.

Jack Dercho approached his friend at the reception. Lionel gave him a big hug and apologized for the bloody nose. Dercho put his arm around the wounded giant. He only had one thing to say to him.

"If you ever need anything, and I mean anything . . . call me."

Lionel looked Dercho square in the eye for a moment then nodded his head. He knew exactly what he was talking about but he wasn't at that point yet. Lionel would let the legal system do its thing. O'Reilly reassured him the case was a slam-dunk. He would honor the principles of law and order. They were principles he had spent a lifetime fighting to preserve.

Many local residents stopped by to offer their support. Even Jonathan Pickett dropped in and shook Lionel's hand. He offered his deepest condolences to his old adversary

When all the visitors were gone and there was nothing else to do, Lionel and Dana visited their son's grave one more time. Dana collapsed at the sight of the grey monument. Lionel sat with her as she spilled her pain. She rambled on about her final words to their son on the day he was killed, something about reminding him to take the garbage out when he got home from school. Lionel tried to make sense of it and grew more concerned when she began to apologize profusely for it to the gravestone as if it was Dylan.

"I would give anything for one last chance to talk to him," she said.

## THE OFFICER

Lionel put his arm around her shoulders.

"I know," he said softly. "Me too."

They mourned their son in complete privacy. No relatives, no friends, no strangers and no media personnel were around. Life moved on for everyone else. They were alone. Lionel kissed his boy's gravestone then led his wife to the car. It had been a long day and an endless week. It was time to go home.

# CHAPTER 43

**GEORGE** Schultz strutted down the ornate halls of the District Attorney's offices. His corpulent frame moved with a bounce that morning. He had a smile on his face and a stack of papers under his arm. The Philipsville Police Department had sent the documents over to him that morning. Schultz worked for Rex Hunter, the iron jawed, silver-tongued, ambitious lead prosecutor of the district. These documents were a gift from providence.

It had been thirteen days since Dylan Stockwell's murder. The case had already been sent over to their office and the accused had been arraigned. It was one of the most pitiful exhibitions Schultz had ever seen. Five rich brats sat shaking in front of the judge. They all shed their share of crocodile tears except for Andrew Reed. He maintained his composure.

The only people crying harder than the Vipers were their parents. They sat directly behind them in court and wailed for their darling children. Justice Isaac Devereaux denied them bail which caused a fresh round of self-pity.

After the arraignment, Schultz had witnessed Walter and Betty Reed speaking to the media about the injustice their son was enduring.

"Boys will be boys," Betty Reed had said to the TV cameras. "Andrew has always liked to rough-house. What boy isn't like that? Unfortunately, this went a little too far but these boys aren't murderers and they should be back with their families."

After the arraignment, Schultz listened as Rex Hunter reinforced his explicit instructions to his staff, the same instructions when the case had landed on his desk.

"Take no prisoners," Hunter said. "This is the case I've waited for my whole life."

Schultz knew Hunter's primary motivation on this case was politics, despite Hunter's respect for Lionel. The Vipers file had already attracted international attention. Ambitious lawyers craved publicity the way mere mortals craved oxygen. Hunter wanted a public execution. He wanted everyone to marvel at his legal prowess and tough-on-crime philosophy. However, Schultz reasoned, there was one snag; the defendants were young offenders.

# THE OFFICER

This designation had to be overturned somehow. The media would be severely hobbled in its ability to write about the trial because the identities and privacy of the accused would be protected. So Rex Hunter had made it his number one objective to get the Vipers charged as adults. It was up to Schultz and the rest of Hunter's staff to find a way to make that happen.

George Schultz didn't so much find the solution as the solution found him. In the weeks after Dylan's murder, dozens of people came out of the woodwork to report incidents of harassment, violence and abuse at the hands of the Vipers. The police investigated the claims and filed documents to the prosecution detailing fifteen other acts of criminal aggression by the nasty brood stretching back over five years.

Jack Dercho monitored the investigation closely then recommended police get a search warrant for Andrew Reed's home and the homes of each of the other Vipers. Officers went through their bedrooms and found a gold mine. Detectives found sketched images of a snake on each of their computers. It was the same black-and-white logo with the initials PV, or Philipsville Vipers for short.

Detectives also unearthed images of swastikas, Satanic paintings and Hells Angels' stickers, among many other disturbing decals. They were primarily on Andrew Reed's computer but all the other Vipers possessed them in smaller quantities.

This information, along with the fifteen cases, was sent to George Schultz. He devoured the pages in less than an hour then phoned his boss. He got Rex Hunter's voice mail but his message was brief.

"Hey boss, it's Schultzy. Remember the Vipers case? Well, I've got one word for you – jackpot!"

He knew his boss would grasp the meaning of the message instantly. George Schultz had figured out how to strip Reed and his minions of their juvenile status. About ten minutes later, he received an equally brief voicemail from Hunter.

"Get your fat ass over here now."

As Schultz walked briskly down the hallways towards Hunter's plush, spacious office, visions of legal victory danced in his head. Given the Vipers long history of violence and the common insignia found in their homes, Schultz had an idea; Charge them as a criminal street gang.

# CHAPTER 44

**THE** academic year ended at Wellington High two weeks after the murder. It was a blessed relief for everyone in the school. Ashley Hood became more reclusive. Summer break made it easier for her to avoid contact with people. Sarah Jane tried to talk to her but Ashley wanted distance. She wasn't mad at Sarah Jane. She didn't blame her for what had happened. She just wanted time to think.

The Thursday after Dylan's death, Ashley discovered one of the two parting gifts left behind by her violator from the party. The stress of exams, her sadness about Dylan and the confusion from the rape caused an outbreak of blisters on and around her genitalia. It was grotesque. She felt like a freak. After a few days of denial, Ashley went for testing. The doctor confirmed the obvious; she had contracted Herpes. There was no cure. It would torment Ashley for the rest of her life.

The psychological effect of the Herpes outbreak sent Ashley into a deep depression. She couldn't seem to move, had no desire and slept for eighteen to twenty hours a day. Her parents stood by her every step of the way but she never told them about the STD. The last thing she wanted was more sympathy. Ashley already felt like a burden to her family. She knew that they did not see it that way but she still endured an extra layer of guilt on her already beleaguered mind.

Ashley couldn't keep Sarah Jane away no matter how hard she tried. Her best friend sat by her side all day, even while she slept. They had been through a lot together over the years. Sarah Jane stood by Ashley through this ordeal as well. The rest of the 'Fab Five' stopped by frequently. Sarah Jane did her best to limit the visits. Kendal, Julia and Hannah seemed to understand.

By mid-July, Ashley discovered her attacker's second parting gift. The blisters had long since subsided. She was starting to feel normal again. Sarah Jane brought her breakfast every morning and sat with her all day. Ashley's birthday was July 22nd and her friends wanted to get her out of the house. They all agreed she needed some fresh air and new scenery. Sarah Jane told her that she hoped it would take her mind off her troubles, if only for one night.

# THE OFFICER

In the week leading up to her birthday, Ashley grappled with frequent bouts of nausea. She couldn't keep food down. She didn't have a fever and it definitely wasn't food poisoning. Her fatigue, which had been improving, took a sharp turn for the worse. Ashley's breasts became sore and she constantly needed to use the bathroom.

On one of her daily visits, Sarah Jane walked into Ashley's room and started fishing something out of her purse.

"I had to sneak this into your house," she said as she rummaged through the jungle that was her gaudy handbag. "I'm guessing your parents wouldn't be too impressed with me if I they knew I had bought this for you."

"Bought what?" Ashley asked, sitting up in her bed.

Sarah Jane found what she was looking for and tossed it on the mattress.

"Go into the bathroom and follow the instructions," she said in a no-nonsense tone.

Ashley picked up the pregnancy test kit and studied it. She looked up at her friend and set the box down. She refused to even consider the possibility.

"Nope," she said as she lay back in her bed to rest. "I'm just feeling a little under the weather. I don't need to . . ."

"Go into the bathroom and follow the instructions," Sarah Jane repeated. "It will only take ten minutes. If you're just under the weather, you have nothing to worry about."

Ashley slowly sat back up in her bed. She picked up the box and looked at it for another minute. Every excuse imaginable raced through her mind but she said nothing. Sarah Jane would hear none of it. Ashley couldn't bear the thought of a positive test result. She lifted herself out of her bed. Sarah Jane helped her to the bathroom door. Ashley felt woozy and weak.

"How do I use this?"

"Follow the instructions to the letter," Sarah Jane replied. "It's pretty basic. Trust me. I've had to use them myself."

Ashley acknowledged her friend with a faint nod and headed towards the bathroom door.

"Sarah, I'm scared," she said as she turned and faced her friend. "What do I do if I'm pregnant?"

Sarah Jane closed her eyes. "Ashley, we'll cross that bridge when we get there. For now, take the test and let's wait for the results."

The tears started rolling down Ashley's face. She had been so sheltered and naive her whole life. A month earlier she believed wholeheartedly in the innate goodness of humanity. Her shameless optimism and unbridled energy had been contagious. It touched everyone around her. All of that was gone. She felt hollowed out. Whenever she thought things couldn't get worse, they did. The mere thought of a positive test result made her dizzy.

"I'm sorry," Sarah Jane said. "Take your time. I'll be here when you're finished, however long that takes."

She reached out and pulled her hurting friend in for a hug. Ashley rested her head on Sarah Jane's shoulder. The tears continued to flow. Ashley soaked her friend's shirt but Sarah Jane didn't seem to mind.

"I don't think I can endure too much more of this," Ashley sputtered over Sarah Jane's shoulder. Sarah Jane tightened her arms around Ashley. She pulled her in as close as they could get.

"I know," she replied in a quiet, soothing voice. "That's why we're going to endure it together."

# CHAPTER 45

"**ARE** you insane?"

George Schultz half-expected this reaction from Rex Hunter. He always shot down new ideas until you convinced him of their merit. That's how Hunter ensured bad advice stayed out of his decision-making process.

"No boss," Schultz replied. "I'm dead serious. We can make this stick."

Hunter reclined in his leather chair behind his shiny desk. A whole library of legal books lined the wall behind him. He had removed his suit jacket but his tie was still done up despite the heat. The District Attorney always looked sharp. His tailored suits, cufflinks and neatly coiffed hair were all part of the package Hunter wanted to project—confident, strong and no bullshit.

"This isn't Cosa Nostra we're dealing with here, Schultzy," said Hunter. "It's not the Bloods or the Crips either —"

"It doesn't have to be that extreme for them to qualify as a street gang," Schultz interrupted. "They fit the definition."

"We'll be laughed out of court George. Their attorneys will mock the whole thing and we'll look like fanatics trying to crucify a group of bratty teenagers."

Schultz gave his boss a confused look. "Isn't that exactly what we're doing?"

Hunter let out a hearty laugh. "Indeed it is Schultzy, but we don't want to be so obvious." Hunter stood up from behind his desk and went over to the sink in his office. He splashed some water on his face to freshen up. "Go back to the drawing board, George," he said, reaching for a towel. "This information the police have sent over is great and we'll use it in court but we'll never get the judge to assign the criminal street gang label to this group of pasty white, rich kids."

"And why not?" Schultz asked, anger rising in his voice. "If they were poor black kids in some Detroit ghetto with the exact same history, there wouldn't be any doubt they were a gang. Right?"

Hunter dried his face off and sat back down at his desk. He neither ignored nor responded to his assistant's question.

"Go back to the drawing board, George," Hunter repeated. "This idea isn't going anywhere."

Schultz, undeterred, pressed his case.

"Rex, listen to me! They fit the definition perfectly. They're a group of three or more people; they've got their own colors and insignia as the police found on their computers, and they were territorial. They wanted to intimidate people within a specific geographical region. In this case it was their own community. Maybe they aren't the worst street gang—"

"And that's the problem Schultzy. Judge Devereaux has dealt with the worst of the worst. Our claim will be measured against what he's already seen. He'll never buy it."

Schultz jumped out of his chair and slammed the files down on the District Attorney's ornate desk. They worked well together because Schultz was so passionate while Hunter was stoic.

"Just look at the objective criteria for Christ sakes, Rex! They meet every single component."

"I know they do," Hunter nodded.

"The problem is that people have a stereotype in their mind about what criminal street gangs look like."

"I totally agree, George."

"And communities like Philipsville don't want to acknowledge the reality that they exist in their own towns because they see themselves as above the 'inferior swine' of the inner cities. They just want to maintain their own fucking delusions. That's why people like Dylan Stockwell get killed."

"And you've just argued my point, Schultzy," Hunter replied calmly. "You and I know that's true. The Vipers will be judged by a jury drawn from the very community in which they lived. They may hate their guts but they won't ever accept that a street gang lives in their town for the reasons you just gave." Hunter paused to gather his thoughts. "Unless there is something missing, something that's grievously savage in these pages you've brought me, the jury will basically view them as schoolyard bullies. We need something extravagant to make your idea possible. Until that time George, I need you to lead our staff in thinking up a new strategy for getting these guys charged as adults."

Schultz had nothing else to say. Hunter's brutal realism often conflicted with his own desire to save the world but he had to concede he was right. It didn't stop him from sulking about Hunter's conclusion.

"Come on, George," Hunter continued. "I need you on this. I appreciate what you've brought me today. It all helps but use that brain of yours and mobilize our staff to find another route for making this happen. I need you."

Schultz gathered all the papers he'd brought in for the meeting then made his way to the door.

"Don't worry boss, I'll think of something."

\* \* \*

Jack Dercho was ecstatic. He couldn't believe he hadn't thought about it until that morning. Once he did, he immediately called the laboratory and asked them to compare the samples. The scientists called back four hours later. The

# THE OFFICER

DNA was identical, a perfect match. Dercho pounded his fist against his desk in triumph.

"Fuck yeah!" he shouted. "Thank you, Doctor. Forward this on to the prosecutor's office."

Dercho slammed the phone down and jumped out of his chair. He pumped his fist in the air then clapped his hands together. The case was strong before the connection was made but this was the clincher.

"We got you now, motherfucker," Dercho shouted out loud in his empty office.

Dercho walked out of his office door revelling in the news. He went over to his secretary and sat on her desk playfully.

"Can I help you, Jack?" she asked.

"As a matter of fact, yes you can Shirley."

She pulled out a note pad and a pen. Dercho seldom ever asked for just one thing. Requests usually came in clusters.

"Get me Lionel Stockwell on the phone. I have some big news about the little cocksuckers that killed his son."

Shirley shot him a dirty look. She was constantly referring to profanity as "the linguistic crutch of the illiterate asshole." Usually he tried to rein it in around her but that one slipped out.

"Okay, okay, I'm, sorry," he said, waving his hand around to annoy her. "Before you call Lionel, get a hold of Constable Nicole Maloney. Tell her to call me about docket number 3-4627 from about four weeks ago. She spoke to Lionel about it. She'll know which one I mean."

Shirley scribbled it all down.

"Anything else?"

"Yeah, tell her to call me once she has the docket. We've developed evidence that identifies the attacker in that case. I want her to break the news to the victim."

"That's quite a request," said Shirley.

"It is but the victim's family really warmed to her. Lionel would agree with me."

"Fine, is that everything?"

"No," replied Dercho. "One more thing ... would you rub my feet?" Shirley's face dropped. She was an excellent receptionist but lacked a sense of humor. "I'm just kidding," Dercho said, laughing. "That's everything."

"Only two things? You're going soft in your old age, Jack."

Dercho smiled at her from his office doorway. "I'm in a good mood today."

\*\*\*

As soon as George Schultz had the information, he barged into Hunter's office. It took him less than five minutes to convince his boss to charge the Philipsville Vipers as a criminal street gang.

# CHAPTER 46

IT was a sweltering summer in Philipsville. The heat and humidity packed a one-two punch on the productivity of city residents. It went several weeks without raining. The typically lush public gardens and private golf courses turned brown. Area farmers suffered depression-level crop prices. A general malaise engulfed the entire town as factories, offices and several other workplaces shut down repeatedly, due to the crushing heat.

There were two groups that didn't slow down one bit; the lawyers representing the prosecution and the defence in the Vipers trial. Rex Hunter pushed his legal team of lawyers and interns to the limit. Eighteen hour days were minimal. He wanted to bury his opponents.

The defence was as equally formidable. Brenda Munroe headed a star-studded legal team of four lawyers, hired by Walter Reed and the parents of the other four vipers. The defence team were all battle-hardened veterans but none more so than her. She was Hunter's equal in ambition and zeal. She was his superior in flamboyance and charisma. Munroe loved the cameras and had a knack for snappy one-liners. She had defended murderers, pedophiles, rapists and gang members in the past. She pulled out all the stops for each of them as she genuinely tried to set them free. Her team charged ten thousand dollars a week and they were worth every penny.

Just like Hunter, Munroe issued her prime directive to her legal team at their first meeting;

"Nothing is sacred. No one is to be spared."

The defence was dealt a mammoth blow when Andrew Reed was definitively connected to the rape of Ashley Hood, a little indiscretion the four other Vipers apparently didn't know about.

Munroe scrambled to think of a way to counter the new information. She was going to use the time-honored "she wanted it" rape defense but her client's use of Rohypnol blew that option away. She decided instead to focus her team's considerable legal acumen on building a new narrative of what happened the day Dylan was killed.

The judge presiding over the case was Justice Isaac Devereaux. He was a well-known liberal in the region but no bleeding heart. His appointment was a victory for neither the prosecution nor the defence. He had his work cut out for him: massive egos, tremendous legal expertise and cunning intellects threatened to derail the trial if he didn't exercise a firm handle on proceedings.

\* \* \*

As the lawyers dug their legal trenches to prepare for the September trial, the Stockwells grappled with their grief. Dana made Lionel take her to Dylan's grave every morning. He watched as she knelt by the gravestone. On some days, she would talk out loud to her dead son. On other days, she would just cry. Sometimes she would do both. Lionel sat with her, fearing for his wife. She was breaking with reality. Her conversations with Dylan were disconcerting because she would ask the gravestone a question and then react as if she had received an answer.

They both took a leave of absence from work. Lionel took four weeks while Dana scheduled three months. That was the cause of their first fight. Dana was angry that Lionel would head back to work so soon. He didn't see the need to sit around doing nothing. He missed their son as much as she did but wanted to keep busy.

Their sex life had once been the envy of Dana's friends. After several years of marriage, many couples were caught in the bland, boring daily suburban grind. Her friends, especially the nurses at the hospital, would joke that it was the reason she was always so chipper each morning. It now dried up immediately.

Dana was barely able to function during the day. She would then cry herself to sleep at night. Lionel became more and more preoccupied with his son's murderers. He went online to learn as much about them as he could. He spent hours reliving the murder in his mind, wondering what it must have been like for Dylan. His hatred for the Vipers grew daily.

Lionel would sit down at his computer late in the evening to dig up as much dirt on them as possible. He could never pry himself away. His wife begged him to lie down with her but his mind was elsewhere. With his sleep patterns out of whack, insomnia set in.

Lionel tried to get to the gym but his workouts became sporadic and unfocused. They happened less and less until he gave up entirely. To everyone around him, his remarkable physique didn't change much at first but Lionel felt completely different. His muscles felt loose and sloppy. He became twitchy and restless. His temper shortened as he lost the outlet for his aggression. Testosterone levels declined and his stamina withered.

Friends and relatives helped out as much as possible. Dana's oldest sister recommended counselling but Lionel wasn't interested. John Paul and Mindy O'Reilly suggested the Stockwells join them at church. They hadn't been to church in many years. Lionel went only because Dana told him that it might provide some comfort, but he never paid much attention to what was happening.

He thought constantly about the Vipers. These kids had tortured and tormented his son for years then killed him. His son had told him everything three days before his murder. Lionel would never forgive himself for not doing more. If he had, Dylan would still be alive. The mental anguish was relentless.

One Sunday, the priest at O'Reilly's church opened his homily by thanking the Lord for saving the life of a boy in the congregation who had leukemia.

"The Lord is good," Father Louie Renaud told the flock. "His divine plan rescued young Timothy Fisher because God is faithful. He never abandons the righteous."

He finally had Lionel's full attention. The officer fumed in his pew as the words slapped him across the face.

*That boy is no better than my son.*

Chief O'Reilly and Mindy sat with Lionel and Dana while Father Louie continued his homily. Then the priest dissected *The Lord's Prayer* for the congregation and explained the contract God had made with His people.

"Forgive us our trespasses, as we forgive those who trespass against us. Whenever we say these words that Jesus taught us, we're telling God to forgive us the way we have forgiven others."

Lionel didn't like where this was going.

The priest then read from the Book of Matthew.

"But I say unto you, love your enemies, bless them that curse you, do good to them that hate you, and pray for them which despitefully use you, and persecute you; That ye may be the children of your Father which is in heaven: for he maketh his sun to rise on the evil and on the good, and sendeth rain on the just and on the unjust."

Lionel was livid. He felt his heart rate intensify as the chubby clergyman droned on. His hands trembled and his breathing increased.

"And so, my friends, since God forgives us of our sins, we must also forgive others," Father Louie said in closing. "That is the price of our salvation."

*You arrogant little prick.*

Lionel jumped up and challenged the priest in front of the congregation.

"The Lord didn't save my boy, did he?" he shouted, as Dana sank in the pew. "Why not? That boy's no better than mine."

The priest was frozen behind the pulpit while O'Reilly's jaw hit the floor.

"Forgive my enemies?" Lionel asked, walking up the aisle towards the front. "I'll tell you what Father; when you have a son and you spend every day of your life caring for him when he's sick and watching over him while he sleeps only to have him stolen from you by a gang of thugs who made his life miserable, then and only then, can you have the audacity to say that to me."

People in the congregation shifted nervously. O'Reilly chased after Lionel. When he reached him, O'Reilly placed his hand on the hurting man's shoulder.

"Come on Lionel, let's go," O'Reilly said without anger.

"This guy lives in his ivory tower protected from the real world," Lionel shouted as he pointed at Father Louie. "And he has the nerve to say that I'm no good unless I sell out my son's memory." Lionel looked directly at the stunned cleric. "Fuck you!"

# THE OFFICER

Dana stood up quickly and walked out the back of the church. Mindy chased after her. O'Reilly grabbed Lionel's arm.

"Let's go soldier," he said. "That's an order."

Lionel was angry. His body quivered with indignation. One thousand pairs of eyes observed his antics, unsure of how to react. It was more than a little unorthodox for the conservative, heavily scripted Catholic Mass. A pin drop could be heard. As Lionel cooled off, O'Reilly led Lionel by the arm out of the church. Lionel, remembering where he was, placed his face in his hands.

"I'm sorry John Paul; I'm so sorry."

O'Reilly patted his shoulder.

"Don't give it a second thought, Lionel," he said.

The two found Dana sitting with Mindy on a park bench a block away from the church. Mindy had her left arm around Dana's shoulder and her right hand on her knee trying to soothe the wounded mother's frayed nerves. As they approached their wives, Lionel knew he was in trouble. Dana glared at him but said nothing. Her vow of silence towards her husband lasted more than a week.

The next morning, Dana visited Dylan's grave. Lionel visited in the evening. They both went alone.

\* \* \*

Jonathan Pickett was incensed. An independent civilian oversight committee reviewed Lionel's handling of Willy Hogan's arrest in the months following the incident. The committee was always called in when a civilian was hurt or killed by police. Its mission was to evaluate the situation and determine if police had acted responsibly. If not, they assigned blame.

The panel quietly reviewed the incident. They interviewed all the officers involved then discreetly issued a report vindicating Lionel Stockwell. The committee said the arrest was handled by the book and all the rules were followed. Lionel was cleared of any further response to the incident. The file was closed.

Pickett insinuated that favoritism poisoned the investigation and called for a full judicial inquiry. The reporter tried to fan the flames as much as he could but nothing came of it. His editors eventually told him to cool it and move on to other topics. Pickett officially did as he was told. Behind the scenes, he worked tirelessly to cultivate sources in the Philipsville Police Department who would speak against their former Staff Sergeant.

Pickett hoped that with Lionel out of commission, he could finally convince someone at the police station to dish the dirt about the famed officer. He was closing in on a source. He knew it. It was just a matter of time.

## CHAPTER 47

"ASHLEY, you have to make a choice soon. The window is closing."

Sarah Jane grew increasingly frustrated with her friend. She had been pregnant for two months and still refused to consider all her options.

"Do you really want this?" Sarah Jane asked. "Do you really want to bring that asshole's child into the world?"

Ashley had told her about the new evidence of her rapist's identity after Constable Maloney had informed her.

"It made me vomit," Ashley had said. The Hoods had been informed by Constable Maloney of the new evidence. Ashley had passed the information on to Sarah Jane. They were both shocked.

Sarah Jane vowed to kill Reed if she ever saw him again. If she had it her way, she would cut his balls off and keep them as a trophy to ensure he never did it again.

In the meantime, they had another problem—the fetus in Ashley's womb was growing bigger by the day. Sarah Jane was of the absolute opinion she should terminate the pregnancy. After twenty weeks, it would be harder to find a doctor willing to do the procedure. She urged her friend daily to set up an appointment even though she knew Ashley had opposed abortion her whole life except in instances of rape. Here she was in that very situation yet it didn't seem to make the choice any easier.

Of course it wouldn't, thought Sarah Jane. Ashley's parents were staunch anti-abortionists. They considered it the epitome of all that was wrong with Western culture. They didn't know their daughter was pregnant. She had kept that from them. Sarah Jane knew that Ashley was afraid her parents would either forbid certain options or be exposed as hypocrites. So her friend was coping alone by doing nothing. She could also see the feeling of betrayal in Ashley's eyes. Ashley had cared for Reed very deeply, and had defended him to others including Sarah Jane. Ashley had always believed he was a good guy. Now with her trust shattered, Sarah could see she was growing cynical and more disillusioned.

"It's a simple procedure," Sarah Jane said. "I'll be there with you the entire time and I'll bring you home. Your parents never have to know. How would you support it on your own, Ashley?" Sarah Jane frowned. "You can kiss university goodbye if you keep the baby. You'll never leave Philipsville."

\* \* \*

Ashley tried to pray the rosary at night but she could never finish. She had too much on her mind. Abortion was a sin. She had uttered those words repeatedly before the rape. Now, she faced the prospect of using the very service women had fought so hard to obtain. Ashley used to hate feminists for legalizing abortion. She now realized why they had done it. She wasn't sure if she wanted to terminate the pregnancy but it was reassuring to know the service was available.

Ashley, once again, was overwhelmed. What had the baby inside her done to deserve an early death? This question echoed in her conscience. It was always followed by a reminder of who the father was and how she got pregnant. Her opinion swayed by the hour. She had embraced every word her parents had taught her about Catholicism. Her faith was now completely shaken.

The confusion was unbearable.

*Jesus forgives, right? I've been good all my life. He'd understand, wouldn't he?*

She wrestled with the issue for another two weeks. By mid-August, Ashley knew exactly what she had to do. Her mind was made up and nothing would dissuade her or change her opinion. She was able to square the decision with her faith. And when she told Sarah Jane, her best friend supported her choice.

# CHAPTER 48

**LIONEL** went back to work four weeks after Dylan's murder hoping it would distract him from his misery. It didn't. Lionel couldn't focus on the job. He couldn't muster the energy or enthusiasm to do what his job required. Everyone at the office empathized with his plight but the work had to be done. After two months, there were rumblings within the ranks that changes needed to happen.

Lionel felt as though his brotherhood was turning on him. He was now a rundown, broken down, old warhorse. He felt increasingly out of place at home and now at work, the two places he once relied on for shelter from the storms of life.

At work, Lionel's temper grew increasingly volatile. He would snap for no reason at those around him. It took him days to respond to emails and voice mails. His legendary eye for detail waned and he lacked the intense personality that had once inspired the entire Philipsville Police Service.

Lionel used to leave his door open at all times so everyone knew they could walk in and speak to him. He would do the tour of the office daily to chat with the rank and file. Lionel no longer left his office. His door was closed and locked.

O'Reilly and Dercho couldn't stand the sight. They did their best to defend him internally from criticism but it was a lost cause. O'Reilly moved him out of the deputy chief position and gave him a clerical job. Lionel pleaded with the chief to at least allow him back on the front lines if he couldn't serve as deputy chief but O'Reilly refused.

By the end of August, a new deputy chief was sworn in. There was no party, no fuss and no fanfare. It was a solemn occasion. All the hope and promise in early June were a distant memory. Lionel loathed his new job but he buried himself in his work. It was better than going home. His marriage continued to deteriorate.

As the scorching summer months wore on, Lionel grew shabby. He didn't get fat but his muscle withered up. He seemed scrawny compared to what he was before. This drove him further into the darkness of his mind. He wanted to get back into the gym. He wanted to make love to his wife. He wanted to be the deputy chief of police. He wanted to smile and laugh again. He wanted to make Dana smile and laugh as well but he simply couldn't do any of it.

Lionel would try to hit the gym before work only to sleep through his alarm. He didn't know what to do. He simply couldn't gather the strength to pick himself up off the ground no matter how hard he tried.

Yet he raged away at those who had killed his son. He stood at his boy's grave and promised to exact justice by any means possible. He felt Dana wasn't grieving properly but said nothing to her. He let it fester inside until some petty trigger with Dana unleashed an avalanche of resentment.

He missed his son.

\* \* \*

Dana wept endlessly about Dylan. She was consumed with sorrow. She continued to talk to Dylan's gravestone and apologized daily for her perceived shortcomings as a mother. She also felt her partner was not grieving in the proper manner, but like Lionel, she said nothing. And like Lionel she let the resentment grow inside until something small and immaterial happened. Then she exploded into a bitter fight with Lionel.

It was the only break in the silence she shared, yet didn't share, with Lionel.

She watched with a broken heart as her husband spiralled into oblivion. The two men she loved more than life itself were gone.

She mourned for both of them.

\* \* \*

Lionel spent his summer scouring the Internet for any articles, comments or videos related to the case. While at work, he would surf the net for hours then continue his search when he got home. He also maintained close contact with the prosecution to hear updates on trial preparations. He learned that Rex Hunter had assembled all the people who had ever been beat up, bullied or abused by the Vipers. He secured statements from over two dozen such people who were prepared to testify. They all wanted a pound of flesh and this was their chance.

Hunter also had lined up expert after expert on gang violence. He had assigned two articling law students the task of digging up as much precedent as possible on charging young offenders as adults in murder trials. He had even cut a deal with one of the Vipers just to be safe. Hunter wanted to hammer these four punks from every imaginable angle.

The District Attorney also passed along updates to Lionel about the Defense team. Brenda Munroe had known Hunter for many years and considered him to be completely predictable. She anticipated his every move and went to work preparing a vicious counter attack on behalf of her clients. With the help of her clients' affluent and well connected parents, Munroe organized witnesses who would vouch for the good character and work ethic of the boys.

There were more developments that raised Lionel's ire even more.

Walter Reed conscripted the minister of the Third Day Baptist Church to testify about the righteousness of his son. The elder Reed made it clear in a less-than-subtle way that his substantial donations to the church's various projects would dry up if he didn't get full cooperation. The pastor didn't need to be told twice. He prepared a glowing written statement about Andrew Reed and how he was such a promising, young Christian man.

The head coaches of Wellington High's football and lacrosse teams were also volun-told. They had known for years what the boys were like off the field but said nothing. Their job was to win. The Vipers helped them towards that end. Their parents were generous benefactors of the school and endowment goals had to be reached.

Although these updates hurt Lionel he still insisted that Hunter keep briefing him on the trial. However, the stories Dercho passed along to him from the prison guards about the Vipers summer imprisonment brought Lionel some cold satisfaction.

Lionel learned that the Vipers weren't exactly having a party in prison. They had been denied bail because of the seriousness of the charge. It gave them a taste of prison life and they choked on it. All five of them broke down their first night in the joint. Bobby sank so low as to actually beg the guard to let him see his Mom. Carl's sanity slowly slipped away. Reed wasn't doing much better. He tried befriending the guards but they told him not to bother. He couldn't bluff his way out of this mess.

As the trial date of September 5 loomed less than a week away, Lionel kept a close tab on the online conversations. The blogosphere was dominated by debate about the trial. Discussions in all the local taverns and cafes also revolved around the Vipers, the trial and the victim. Both legal teams rushed to put the final touches on their respective cases. The media vans from all over the world were already rolling into town.

As the lawyers geared up for opening arguments and the town readied for its close-up, Lionel braced himself as best he could for the trial. Although they seldom spoke, he knew Dana was doing the same. They *had* to be at the trial every single day.

# CHAPTER 49

**THE** deadly heat finally broke the night before the trial. The humidity gave way to a massive thunderstorm. Huge drops of rain pounded the city as lightning crashed and illuminated the sky. Lionel didn't sleep at night anymore. He could never ease his mind. Tonight he couldn't even turn on the computer and check any updates on the Vipers, the trial and the media coverage of Dylan's murder.

Lionel stood at the window in his living room and looked out at the storm. The harsh winds caused the trees to sway violently. Long heavy rolls of thunder chased the wind across the night's sky. He wasn't ready for the next day and more time wouldn't help. He would never be prepared. Lionel just had to dig deep and get through it. Dercho and O'Reilly shared tremendous confidence in the inevitability of a guilty verdict. Maybe that would enable him to move on. There was nothing Lionel wanted more than closure. He wanted to feel normal again but more than anything, he just wanted Dylan back.

The rain outside was hypnotic. Its driving cadence entranced Lionel, causing him to drift off into memories of a happier era. He remembered bringing Dylan home for the first time, teaching Dylan how to play baseball and how to fish.

A bolt of lightning lit up the sky followed by an enormous crash of thunder. Lionel snapped out of his trance.

"That thunder sure is close," he said, gazing at the stars through the window.

To his right, he noticed the framed picture of Dylan and him at the Philipsville fishing derby when Dylan was only six years old. It was Lionel's favorite picture of the two of them. He picked it up and stared longingly at the old photo. The Wellington River flowed through the city and was stocked every year with trout for the annual angling extravaganza. Thousands of people lined the river banks for hours.

Lionel and Dylan went each year. When Dylan was six, he had caught the biggest fish. The five thousand dollar cash prize had gone into Dylan's college fund. Lionel treasured that memory. He had only started teaching his boy how to fish less than a year earlier. After Dylan had hooked the trout he had tried to hand off his fishing rod to his father but Lionel had refused; it was Dylan's fish to land. He remembered coaching his son through the forty-five minute battle with the twenty-pounder. At times, he had told Dylan to reel in the line. At other times, they had slacked off allowing the fish to wear itself down. Hundreds of contestants had watched the battle royal. Dylan had done it all on his own.

Finally, he had reeled the tired fish towards the edge of the river. Lionel had reached in with their net and landed the gigantic creature. A hearty applause had erupted all around them. Dylan's eyes had sparkled with pure joy as his Dad removed the fish hook then handed him the trout. It was almost as big as he was. He could barely hold it. Lionel had squatted next to him and given him a big hug. A photographer from the *Philipsville Herald* had snapped a picture of the father/son duo holding the fish. It appeared the next day in the newspaper with a caption praising the youngster for the win. From that point on Dylan had turned into an avid fisherman.

Lionel had walked into the newspaper office the Monday morning after the fishing derby. The photographer still had the original photo in his lab. He'd presented it to Lionel free of charge. Since then, the photo had rested in a frame above the Stockwell's television set.

"Oh Dylan, we need you here." Lionel said to the photo. "Please, come back to us,"

He ran his hand over Dylan's image. The fishing derby was one more sweet memory turned sour. Lionel loved telling the story to anyone who would listen. It was an example of the unique bond they shared. Now, it was nothing more than another painful reminder of what he had lost. He set the picture back on top of the TV set.

Outside, the rain fell from the heavens. It was the worst thunderstorm Lionel had seen in years. There would probably be damage around the city in the morning. As he gazed out at the weather, a figure appeared in the reflection on the window. Lionel turned around and saw his wife standing behind him in her bathrobe, her eyes filled with tears.

Dana looked at her husband — he was so tired and worn down by a broken heart. His hair had visibly greyed and thinned over the summer. He hadn't put on weight but his arms, chest and shoulders shrank considerably. It was as if Dylan was the source of Lionel's youth. When he died, Lionel became an old man,

"Are you okay?" she asked.

He shook his head. He knew that neither one of them looked forward to the trial. They would have to sit through a full account of everything Dylan had endured over the years. It would eat them alive.

"Are you ever going to come to bed again?" Dana asked.

The question hit him like a grenade. He meant to be there for her in the aftermath of the tragedy but he was consumed by his own emotions. Lionel had lost his bearings. He was drifting and his wife wanted him back.

"I know it's been hard Lionel but I need you. I'm sorry if I've made things harder for you at times but I need you to help me get through this."

Lionel acknowledged her words with a faint nod of his head. Everything she said was true. He hadn't been there for her. For twenty-five years, Lionel had been the bulwark and the shield of his home but this was one obstacle he had never anticipated. All of Lionel's energy now went into hating those who robbed him of his son. His desire for retribution burned incessantly.

"I'm so sorry, Dana," Lionel said, after a long pause. "I can't get those five boys out of my mind. I want them to pay for what they did. It was my job to protect Dylan and I failed."

"It's not your fault," she replied.

"But it's now my responsibility. I want them to suffer. I want them to fucking die."

Dana walked up to her husband. She put her arms around his neck and pulled his face gently towards her own. She focused in on his bloodshot eyes.

"Lionel, listen to me," she said softly. "I hate those boys as much as you do and I always will. Some things are unforgiveable. This is one of them." A tear rolled down her cheek. "You need to find a way to chase them from your mind. Every time they consume your thoughts, they win. Don't let them do that. Do whatever you have to do but don't let them take any more than they've already stolen."

She stared at his face but Lionel didn't react. He wanted freedom from the Vipers but he couldn't walk away until his sense of justice had been satisfied. He hoped the trial would provide that relief.

"They have to pay for what they've done," he replied. "I will have no peace until that's accomplished."

"The trial starts tomorrow," Dana said as she massaged her husband's neck. "We're going to sit through it together. After they're found guilty, I want you to promise me you'll move on."

Lionel pondered the request. He never made promises he couldn't keep.

"If justice is served, I'll move on." His reply left the door ajar.

"Just promise me, you'll find some way to make peace with the world when this trial is over."

"You have my word," Lionel said, without reticence. "I will make peace one way or the other."

Dana smiled and kissed him. It was the first time she had done so since Dylan's murder.

"Please, lie down with me tonight," she asked. "You need to rest before tomorrow." Lionel acquiesced. She led him into the bedroom. Just before they pulled the covers over themselves, every light and appliance in the house flicked off. The power died. Lionel set his cell phone alarm to go off at seven the next morning.

The rest of the night was hell for Lionel. Dana curled in beside him. She rested her head in the nook of his right arm and slept soundly next to the man she loved but he was restless. The Vipers haunted his thoughts. He needed them to suffer. He would never feel right again until it happened.

Like they had done to his son before him, Andrew Reed and his brood tormented Lionel's mind even when they weren't around. There was nothing he could do but wait. The night seemed to last forever. Lionel lay on his back with his wife at his side.

Outside, the rain pounded the roof. Lionel listened to its drumbeat. In the past, the drone of a storm acted as a lullaby. It was no longer enough. He just stared into the darkness.

# CHAPTER 50

**THE** next morning reporters hounded Lionel and Dana as they made their way through the crowd. Jonathan Pickett led the charge but he left his trademark sarcasm back at the office. The grieving parents answered no questions. Lionel wore a dark blue pinstripe suit with a striped shirt and grey tie. Dana wore a light purple summer dress. They had front row seats reserved for the entire trial.

Rex Hunter came over and shook their hands as they sat down. He had met with them a few times over the summer to get as much information about themselves and Dylan as possible. They liked him. Lionel had known Rex for years through his work as a police officer. The guy was aggressive and that's exactly what Lionel wanted. He watched Hunter stroll over to greet his main adversary.

"Good morning, Brenda. It's great to see you again." Hunter shook her hand and pulled her in for a kiss on her cheek.

"Thank you, Rex," she replied, as they exchanged charms. "It's great to see you too."

Lionel looked around the courtroom. It was jammed to the rafters. Reporters held impromptu interviews with anyone of importance. They scribbled feverishly on their notepads. A few of the reporters sent updates by the minute to Twitter through their Blackberries. The seemingly ridiculous social networking site enabled them to report in real time.

Chief O'Reilly arrived as well. He sat next to Lionel and Dana and told them he couldn't stay for more than an hour but he wanted to be there for his friends.

"Mindy wanted to come too but she knew the court would be a zoo," he said.

Lionel looked to his left. On the other side of the courtroom, sitting right behind the defense lawyers were the parents of Andrew Reed, Carl Hicks, Boomer Simons, Rocco Palermo and Bobby Johnson. Lionel glared at them all decked out in their gaudy jewellery and thousand dollar suits. None of them made eye contact with him. They didn't even have the courtesy to come over and offer their condolences. Lionel wasn't sure he wanted it from them anyway, but their inability to make eye contact convinced him they knew the truth.

Finally, the defendants were marched into the courtroom in handcuffs. All five appeared consumed with the "woe-is-me" mentality. They looked dejected and scared. Their mothers cried as their boys moved past them in shackles. Lionel was disgusted. If they wanted to know about true misery they should talk to him and Dana. He had to suppress his rage. Now wasn't the time.

As the Vipers walked down the aisle towards their seats, a young woman jumped out of her seat and attacked Reed.

"Andrew, you son of a bitch. I'm going to kill you!" she screamed, charging towards him.

The woman was able to get past the guards and slug him in the eye. The guards pounced on her and dragged her out of the courtroom. Lionel and Dana watched the whole thing unfold.

"Who the hell was that?" Lionel asked Dana.

"I don't know . . . but I like her."

Dana's comment made him chuckle. He didn't expect it.

"Yeah, me too." Lionel took a mental note of Reed's attacker. He hoped he could talk to her later. Lionel also wanted to pound the shit out of Reed. This young woman actually had the nerve to rattle his cage. Lionel was intrigued.

Reed was clearly hurt in the attack and had a black eye in the making. His mother tried to run over and help him but the guards repelled her.

"Get back Ma'am. I'm not warning anyone again," one of the guards commanded.

"I'm his mother. Let me see my boy!"

"Ma'am you have three seconds before I kick your ass out of this courtroom."

Walter Reed jumped up and pulled his wife back to her seat. Lionel was entertained by the spectacle.

Reed was still on the ground with his hand over his eye.

"All right, on your feet. Move it!" The guard appeared in no mood to mess around. Reed looked up at him but before he could say anything, the guard grabbed his arm and hoisted him up like a ragdoll. He then pushed Reed into his chair at the front of the room.

"You treat my client like that again and I'll ruin you," Brenda Munroe said to the security official.

"Sorry sweetheart," the muscular guard replied with a wink. "I'm already married but I appreciate the offer."

Munroe glared at him as he shared a laughed with the other guards. The other four defendants took their seats next to Reed. With everyone settled into their places, the Bailiff's voice filled the court.

"Order: all rise. The Honorable Judge Isaac Devereaux presiding. All those who have business before this court step forward and you shall be heard."

With those words, the trial opened.

"Good morning, Counsel," Judge Devereaux said to Hunter, while taking his seat on the bench.

"Good morning, sir," he replied.

"And how are you Ms. Munroe?"

# THE OFFICER

"I'm great, your honor. Thank you."

Pleasantries aside, the legal maneuvering began immediately. Rex Hunter moved for the defendants to be tried as adults. He served warning that he would also push for street gang charges. Munroe jumped up and declared their opposition to the motion. She was halfway through her objection when Justice Devereaux ordered them both to sit down.

"I anticipated you would do this, Mr. Hunter so I'll save the court a lot of time. The motion is denied."

The entire courtroom fell silent. In the front row Dana gasped. It was a major victory for the defence but both groups of lawyers appeared equally stunned. Around the room, eyes bulged and jaws dropped.

"Proceed counsel," Devereaux said to the prosecution.

"I'm sorry your honor, did you just deny this motion without any deliberation?" Hunter glowered.

"I did, Mr. Hunter. Now, do you have any other motions? If not, I'll hand it over to the defence then we can begin with opening statements."

Hunter, for the first time in his professional career, lost his composure. He launched a tirade against the ruling. He pounded his fist against the podium. It was central to their case that they be tried as adults. Devereaux hammered his gavel. Hunter ignored it at first until Devereaux shouted him down.

"Sit down, Mr. Hunter," Devereaux ordered, with his high nasal voice. "I will tolerate no showmanship or insolence in this trial. You pull a stunt like that again and the Bailiff will remove you. Am I clear?"

Hunter was fuming.

"Yes, sir," he said through his teeth. "It will give us something to appeal should your final verdict be as misguided as this ruling."

Devereaux's gavel crashed against his desk. He glared straight at the cocky prosecutor. The judge wasn't lacking an ego either.

"Mr. Hunter, I hold you in contempt of this court. Bailiff, take him away."

Hunter stood behind the podium, his fists clenched in rage. The Bailiff took Hunter's arm.

"Come on Rex, let's go."

The bailiff escorted the prosecutor out of the court. Cameras flashed in rapid fire as he was led away. Devereaux banged his gavel again.

"Order in the court. There will be no more pictures taken," he shouted at the reporters. "This case consists of five young offenders. Their identities are to remain confidential. If one more flash bulb goes off, I'll clear the courtroom." The journalists quickly put their cameras away. Devereaux turned to Hunter's deputy. "Do you have any other pre-trial motions, Counsel?

"No, your honor," replied George Schultz.

"Thank you; you may be seated. Does the defence have any business before this trial begins?"

Munroe rose to her feet and moved behind the podium.

"Yes, your honor," she said, flipping open her dossier. "The defence requests a change of venue."

A dozen conversations broke out in the courtroom. Devereaux slammed the gavel on the bench. The spectators quickly quieted down.

"I saw this one coming, too," Devereaux said as he set the gavel down. "The motion is denied."

Justice Isaac Devereaux had denied two huge motions within ten minutes. Combined, these motions were expected to tie up proceedings for weeks. Devereaux clearly wasn't worried about any appeals. He had just handed both sides grounds to appeal any verdict. Flabbergasted, Munroe tried politely to inform Devereaux of this fact.

"You obviously weren't paying attention to what I told the prosecution," he said to the lead defence attorney.

"No, your honor," she replied. "I heard everything you said but I feel we're at least entitled to an explanation. This case has been covered extensively in the media. There's no way my clients can have a fair trial in Philipsville."

"Ms. Munroe," Devereaux said, removing his glasses. "This case has been covered extensively all throughout North America and Europe. I've been told the media in Australia have even reported on it. Unless we move the trial to the Serengeti, which I'm not going to do, you're going to have a jury full of people who have read something about the case. Moving it would waste time and accomplish nothing."

Brenda Munroe nodded and moved on. Because her clients would be tried as young offenders, she requested bail. He immediately denied that as well. Even though they were youth, they were still on trial for murder, Judge Isaac Devereaux sped through all the pre-trial business in half an hour. He addressed the two thunderstruck legal teams.

"I suspect this morning didn't go the way either side expected. We'll break now until one o'clock this afternoon. At which time, I expect the Prosecution to begin opening statements."

"Understood, your honor," Schultz replied.

"This court is in recess until then."

He slammed his gavel down and rose from his chair. The courtroom stood with him. Devereaux retreated to his chambers.

Back in the courtroom, Lionel felt confused and Dana had a puzzled look on her face. Since they would be charged as youths, Dylan's killers would face severely reduced sentences. Although both sides lost that morning, the defence clearly came out ahead.

The Vipers were removed from the courtroom by the guards. The reporters emptied out to file their stories. Lionel looked at George Schultz, hoping the pudgy assistant prosecutor could provide some good news. Schultz kept his head down as he exited court. Lionel knew the prosecution was badly hobbled right out the gate. His gut told him this trial wasn't going to end well.

\* \* \*

# THE OFFICER

Back in his chambers, Isaac Devereaux poured vodka into a glass, mixed it with Pepto-Bismol and chugged it down. His nerves were shot. Devereaux had fought against a basic shyness his whole life. The high-powered lawyers intimidated him. He had needed to establish dominance early or they would eat him alive. He didn't like being a hard-ass but he had to knock the egos down early on. Devereaux wasn't mean by nature either. He hated throwing people out of court or yelling at anyone. It was only 10:15 a.m. and his stomach was already in knots.

As he mixed another drink, Devereaux flipped open his laptop. He sat down in his plush office behind a huge ornate oak desk. The desk was a family heirloom. The Devereaux family had a long history of working in the legal profession. Family legend held that the desk had been given to his great grandfather, also a judge, from Ulysses S. Grant himself. It was still in prime condition.

The laptop hummed to life. He scrolled to the homepage of one of the many banks he had accounts with. He clicked on the "Easy Banking" link, punched in his password, then waited for the account to load up. He loved online banking. Devereaux remembered the world before online banking was possible. He had been reticent to try it. Once he did, he never looked back. The speed and ease of it all made him wonder how they had ever lived without it.

Cringing, Devereaux took another sip of his drink. He hated it but it helped him relax.

At last, the web page with all his financial information came on screen. He clicked on the link to an account he had opened only two nights previous. It now indicated a cool balance of 1.5 million dollars. The judge heaved a sigh of relief.

"Good, it's in there. He had better deliver the rest as promised."

Devereaux logged out of his account, closed the window and shut down the laptop.

He looked down at the concoction in his glass. It was disgusting. He held his breath and swallowed the rest of it. Devereaux had to prepare for the afternoon. The trial had only just begun.

# CHAPTER 51

**OUT** in the courthouse lobby, Lionel and Dana grappled with the events of the morning. Their son's killers would, at best, receive meagre rehabilitative sentences. Dana knew that would never sate her husband's burgeoning blood lust. It didn't satisfy her either. She tried not to think about it.

Before they knew it, a dozen reporters surrounded them. There was no way in or out of the scrum. They launched question after question. Dana simply said "no comment" and pushed her way out. She grabbed her husband's arm to lead him out of the gaggle but he didn't move.

Jonathan Pickett was one of the journalists in the crowd.

"How do you feel about Justice Devereaux's decision to try the defendants as youth?" he asked.

"I think Isaac Devereaux is a two-bit liberal pussy, Jon," Lionel replied. The media had struck pay dirt. "It's yet another example of this goddamned criminal justice system respecting the rights of killers over the rights of victims and their families. It's infuriating but not really surprising."

Pickett suppressed a smile.

"What do you mean by that?" he asked.

Before Lionel could answer Dana placed herself in between her husband and the reporter's TV camera.

"Thank you everyone for coming," she said, smiling. "We'll talk again at the end of the day."

That was a lie but she hoped it would placate the scavengers for the time being. Dana grabbed Lionel's arm and dragged him out of there. She didn't disagree with him. She just didn't want him speaking to the media while angry, lest he say something he would regret later.

"What's wrong with you?" she asked Lionel after they had escaped the clutches of the media hounds. "Don't talk to them! You know what they're after."

"I'm sorry," he said, still visibly agitated. "I got carried away. I just can't believe what happened in there."

"I know," Dana said "I can't either, but angering the judge isn't going to help our cause."

Lionel cringed. "Like it really matters now."

# THE OFFICER

Dana stopped dead in her tracks. "What's that supposed to mean?"

"It means this trial is a joke. At best, those little brats are going to get a couple of years at some country club for boys where they'll be 'rehabilitated' and then sent back into society."

This truth hadn't fully dawned on Dana until then but it had obviously hit her husband the moment the motion was denied. She tried to look on the bright side as she had done all her life.

"The prosecution can always appeal the verdict, right?"

Lionel didn't respond. He continued walking down the long ornate corridor with his eyes focused on the room at the end. His pace quickened and Dana struggled to keep up.

"Come on," he said. "The cafeteria is right up here. I need a coffee."

Dana, practically running beside her husband, repeated the question. Lionel didn't break stride.

"There won't be any appeals, trust me," he said. "The courts have one shot to get this right before I do it for them."

Dana grabbed her husband's arm and forced him to a halt. She grabbed the lapels on his suit jacket and jerked him towards her.

"What the fuck do you mean by that, Lionel?" Dana said, using that expletive for the first time in front of her husband.

"Don't worry," he said in a reassuring voice. "I mean the prosecution probably wouldn't appeal a young offender's conviction. It's just not worth it."

Dana stared at him with suspicion. She didn't like the way her husband had been talking. This wasn't the first time he had dropped a vague hint about vigilante justice.

"Do you want a coffee?" he asked politely. "I'm buying."

She stared at her husband for a little longer then nodded her head.

"That would be nice. I'll meet you in there. I just have to use the restroom."

Dana disappeared into the ladies washroom.

\* \* \*

Lionel turned and walked into the cafeteria. There was a line-up at the cashier. He regretted shooting his mouth off. Dana couldn't know what he was thinking. She would never condone it. Lionel's meticulous brain was already plotting the unthinkable should it come to that. It was on his mind constantly.

While sitting in the courtroom, it was all he had thought about. He wanted to inflict pain on those who had brought pain to him. He wanted them to suffer for the suffering they had caused others. Part of him hoped the legal system would fail. Lionel's thirst for blood had grown steadily since Dylan's murder. The trial had only served to intensify his revenge fantasies to the point where they bordered on pornographic.

Lionel was lost in his own thoughts, standing alone in the middle of the criminal court's cafeteria. He didn't even notice the young bombshell approaching him. She was stunning and looked no more than eighteen years old. She walked gracefully up to Lionel and tapped him on the shoulder.

When he turned around, Lionel was blown away by the sight. He snapped out of his trance. She was gorgeous. Lionel's stoic demeanor cracked for a nanosecond. She stuck out her hand.

"Hi, I'm Sarah Jane Harnick," she said with a smile. "I'm guessing you're Lionel Stockwell."

Lionel extended his hand slowly. He wasn't sure what she wanted. He was also certain he had seen her some place before. He had the most unusual sense of déjà vu. He shook her hand but didn't say anything. Sarah Jane seemed to expect this reaction so she answered the question for him.

"I'm the girl from the courtroom." Lionel still couldn't place her. "I attacked Andrew Reed and got thrown out."

Lionel's original apprehension gave way to gratitude. He had hoped to meet her.

"Oh, well it's a pleasure to meet you young lady," Lionel said. "The world owes you a favor."

"Well, the trial's only just begun," she replied. "You'll have your chance."

Lionel rolled his eyes then changed the subject. "What can I do for you, Sarah?"

She was a taken aback by his bluntness. "My name's actually Sarah Jane," she replied. "I just wanted you to know how sorry I am for what happened to your son. I knew Dylan. We went to high school together."

Lionel raised an eyebrow. "He never mentioned you to me. How well did you know him exactly?"

"I, well, I . . . er . . . had a few classes with him," she said. Lionel's eyes focused right in on her. "Truthfully, we weren't that tight but he was a really nice guy."

"Let me guess," he said, moving closer to the young beauty. "You were part of the in-crowd at that school. One of the many spoiled rich kids who made my son's life miserable." Lionel took a step back and sized her up. "You seem like a nice person. I'm guessing you weren't one of the more active or aggressive bullies but you didn't have any time for a loser like Dylan. Now that he's dead, you're feeling a little guilty and want me to let you off the hook." Lionel moved even closer. They were toe to toe. "Sound about right?"

Sarah Jane's wide eyes said it all. She looked down at her feet.

"Something like that," she answered. "But there's another reason why . . ."

"It was nice meeting you, Sarah." Lionel went to get in line for coffee. He didn't know why he was being such an asshole to her. She was the only stranger that day to offer any condolence to him or Dana. She wasn't to blame for what happened to Dylan.

Sarah Jane ran in front of him to cut him off before he got into the line.

"I know what you're going through," she said.

Lionel looked at her with ridicule. "Listen, you seem like a sweet girl but you know nothing about what I'm going through."

"Oh, yes I do! I've been watching you today. I can see it all over you."

"Who the hell do you think you are?" he said in a hushed yell. "Just, go back to your Ferraris; go back to your cell phones and your castle on a hill. You have nothing in common with me; you know nothing about me and you clearly knew nothing about my son either." Lionel tried to get around her but the young woman was tenacious.

"You're right," Sarah Jane said. "I'm a spoiled rotten Jewish American Princess who knows nothing about the real world. I didn't do anything to help your son while he was alive and I can't relate to anyone who has lost a child but that's not what I'm talking about."

Lionel wanted to push her out of the way but he knew that wouldn't get rid of her. This one was a feisty and determined ball of energy. Something made him want to hear her out.

"Well, talk sweetheart, I'm listening," Lionel said. "What do you want with me?"

It was Sarah Jane's turn to get up in his face. Her voice turned icy.

"You want blood," she said to him. "You want to kill the Vipers. I can see it all over you. You hate them."

It was Lionel's turn to be surprised. Her assessment was accurate but he didn't want to give that away.

"So, what's your reason?" he asked.

"Excuse me?"

"Why do you want to kill them?"

Sarah Jane backed off a bit and appeared to collect her thoughts.

"I don't hate all of them," she said after a long pause. "I just want to kill Andrew Reed."

Part of Lionel wondered if this whole thing was a ploy by someone at the police department to see if he was planning to murder the Vipers. Or maybe Jonathan Pickett had her wired up. He decided to give nothing away.

"Okay, so why do you want to kill him and not the others?"

Another long pause followed.

"Because he date-raped my best friend. She now has herpes because of him."

Lionel processed the information critically. The whole thing sounded vaguely familiar but once again, he couldn't place it.

"What's your friend's name?"

"It doesn't matter . . ."

"Yes it does," Lionel snapped. "Give me her name and when the rape happened. Now!"

Sarah Jane looked away. "Ashley Hood. She was raped at a party I held at my place."

"On Rockliffe Street?"

Sarah Jane slowly looked up at the tall police officer.

"How did you know?" Her voice trembled.

"I'm a cop. I'm well aware of that party and that incident."

Lionel remembered referring the case to Dercho but didn't hear anything until a month later when Dercho called him out of the blue. Reed's DNA was found on Dylan and Ashley. It connected him to both crimes. Lionel pushed it all out of his mind.

"Why the hell was he at your party in the first place?"

"He was a friend." Sarah Jane answered honestly. "We knew his reputation but he and his buddies had always been nice to us."

"Yeah, I'm sure a bunch of young horny rapists were kind to a couple of attractive girls," Lionel said. "That's big of them."

"I want to kill him," she said. "I'm dead serious."

"Congratulations," replied Lionel. "Why are you telling me this?"

They stood there silently as the hurly-burly of the cafeteria moved all around them. Lionel had met many people in his line of work who said they wanted to kill someone. They were seldom serious. This fireball meant every word she said. Lionel needed to end the conversation.

"Listen, I need to find my wife," he said. "It was nice to meet you." Lionel extended his hand. Sarah Jane took the hint.

"Likewise," she replied.

They shook hands. Lionel felt her pass something into his palm. She then turned and walked away. It was a piece of paper. He opened it. She had scribbled her name and phone number on it along with a message.

*If you need help, call me.*

He tucked it in his pocket then looked at his watch. Dana had been gone for fifteen minutes. There was no longer a line-up at the cashier. He decided to buy the coffee and a couple of muffins then set out to find her. He ordered two larges. He liked his black but Dana enjoyed her java with lots of cream and sugar. He paid for the order and scouted the cafeteria. He couldn't see her anywhere.

\*\*\*

After the lunch break, Lionel returned to the court with Dana. He was worried about her. When she returned from the washroom it was clear she had been crying. Lionel asked, but she denied it. They drank their coffees in silence and made their way back to the courtroom.

The trial began. Rex Hunter started by withdrawing some of his remarks from the morning. He apologized to Devereaux. The judge forgave him and withdrew the contempt citation. They proceeded with opening statements. Hunter's three-hour opening statement was mesmerizing. He didn't slow down or back down despite the setbacks that morning. Lionel admired the prosecutor for his passion. It was something he sorely needed back in his life.

Hunter laid out the entire case. He vowed to expose the defendants as sadistic bullies. He outlined their alleged crimes and read from statements by the dozens of people who had suffered at the hands of the Vipers. He also described in excruciating detail the rape of Ashley Hood. The whole courtroom cringed. The Vipers sat woefully, looking down at the table in front of them. Rocco trembled with anger and glared at Reed. Reed glared right back at him.

Their hatred appeared mutual. The mothers of the accused wept openly. The fathers shook their heads, refusing to believe any of it.

Shortly after 4:30 p.m. Hunter finished his opening statement. The man was a magnificent litigator. Nobody could have made the case against the Vipers more eloquently, accurately or persuasively than he had. When it was over, Lionel allowed himself to feel optimistic about the trial. He didn't know why. No speech, however wonderful, could change the fact that even the harshest verdict would be a slap on the wrist. Regardless, it was nice to feel good again.

Isaac Devereaux adjourned for the day shortly after Hunter wrapped up. He instructed the defence to be ready for nine o'clock the next morning. Brenda Munroe acknowledged the judge's words. She looked more than ready to launch her counterattack.

As everyone filed out of the courtroom, Dana and Lionel smiled at each other. The prosecution team brimmed with optimism. The defendants and their families all had woeful expressions plastered on their rich faces. Lionel took pleasure in their misery. It was sweet revenge but fleeting. He knew he would have to endure Munroe's opening statement the next day and did his best to brace himself mentally for the torture. Still, he was pleased with Hunter's effort that day and he reveled in the positive emotion while it lasted.

# CHAPTER 52

**DEVEREAUX** drove his fist through the wall in the living room of his nine thousand square foot home later that night. The second payment hadn't arrived. He was supposed to get the full three million dollars that day plus an additional two million once an acceptable verdict was reached. He picked up his phone and called the source of the money.

"Hello," came the deep the voice on the other end of the phone.

"It's Devereaux. Where is it?"

"You didn't honor our agreement."

"What are you talking about!" Devereaux screamed. "They'll be tried as young offenders. That was the deal."

"You denied them bail. They should be home with their families," replied the voice, in a very even, emotionless tone.

"That was never part of what we had discussed," Devereaux shot back. "You wanted them charged as youths. I made it happen. Now, fork it over."

There was a long period of silence.

"Implicit in our agreement," the voice said "was an understanding that you would always rule in our favor."

Devereaux was furious. None of this was implicit, explicit or anything else. Devereaux was livid and sweating profusely. His white dress shirt was soaked and he trembled with indignation as he yelled at the phone.

"Listen you . . . you son of a bitch, that wasn't part of the deal. Also, nobody suspects anything now because I ruled against both sides but I gave you the big motion. You guys still came out on top."

There was another long pause. Devereaux could tell the man on the other end was considering what he just said.

"Very well," replied the voice. "I'll wire $750,000 into your account tonight."

"That's only half of what we had discussed."

"You only did half of what we had agreed on."

"I did not," he whined. "Give me all the money or I'll—"

"You'll what?" the voice interrupted. It was the first time any emotion or tone variation could be heard. "You'll go to the cops? You're not going to do that Isaac and you know it. You've already accepted a bribe. We'll both burn if this gets out." The voice paused for effect. "And you're the judge. Trust me, you'll burn more."

"Give me my money," Devereaux stammered. He had no leverage.

"You'll get half of it tonight like I said. The rest of it will come if the verdict is to my satisfaction. Do not attempt to go all righteous on me now or I will destroy you, Isaac. My boy serves no time. Is that clear?"

Devereaux's lungs expanded and contracted violently as he tried to keep his cool. He was genuinely afraid and at a loss for words.

"Just pay me my money. . ."

With a heavy click, the line went dead. Devereaux slammed the phone down into the cradle.

"Goddamn it!" he screamed.

The frazzled judge tore the phone cord out of the wall then pitched it at the window in his living room. The phone smashed the window and landed in his beloved garden in the front yard, surrounded by white orchids and shattered glass. His wife ran into the room. She wanted to call the police but he didn't let her. After reassuring her that everything was fine, she went back to bed.

Devereaux poured himself a triple of vodka and Pepto-Bismol. He drank it down in half a second. After cooling off, he flipped open the laptop on his desk. He logged into his bank account. The money was there—half of it, at least.

Devereaux leaned back in his chair. It was still a beautiful sum. The balance read $2,250,000. Not bad for a day's work. The aging judge was already feeling a little better.

\* \* \*

"Rewind. Back it up and make a copy of it on the computer."

Jack Dercho had heard everything. He had always possessed a sixth sense for anticipating criminal activity. He was guided by a very simple question: *If I was a criminal, what would I do?* Dercho knew he would never receive authorization to track a judge without probable cause so he did it under the table. He brought in a couple of loyal constables to help him out.

The phone tap was his idea. Dercho ordered it the moment Isaac Devereaux was announced as the judge in the Vipers trial. Dercho had told Constables Nicole Maloney and Eric Dejong there was a way they could help the legendary lawman and they had jumped at the chance. Dercho left them monitoring the phone line non-stop. Maloney called him back seven hours later. She had listened in on an explosive conversation and had recorded it.

Dercho raced over to the office and listened to the recording. It was indeed a bull's-eye.

"Once you copy the file," Dercho said to Maloney, "send a copy of it to our voice technicians so they can analyze it."

"Yes, sir," Maloney answered.

"Oh, and back trace the phone number. Find out who that was on the other end. Or, at least, where the call came from."

"Give me two minutes Sergeant and I'll have that information."

"Thank you, Constable." Maloney was about to leave Dercho's office when he spoke again. "Nicole . . ." She stopped and looked at him. There was an awkward pause. "Great job tonight."

She acknowledged his compliment then returned to work.

Dercho had a history with the young, ambitious constable. She was one of a number of affairs that had ended his third marriage. He felt worse than she did. Maloney had never been under any illusions about their "relationship." Dercho's reputation was well-known. After a few lackluster sexual episodes, she had broken things off. Dercho had been dumbfounded by her audacity. He was unaccustomed to women ending things with him and hadn't known how to handle it.

Although three years had passed since their affair, things still remained awkward between them and it was entirely his fault. She had moved on the day after it ended. Dercho was the one who didn't know how to act. He knew that nobody in the department had knowledge about their fling but had no idea that he was the brunt of many jokes in Nicole Maloney's circle of non-cop friends.

Just like she had promised, Maloney returned two minutes later. She dropped the name, address and contact information that corresponded with the phone number of the mysterious caller.

"You're not going to believe this, sir."

"Why? What do you have?"

She dropped the piece of paper on his desk. Dercho picked it up and studied the information. He felt a surge of nervous energy shoot up his spine. Goosebumps covered his arms. The hairs on his neck stood up. His instincts proved infallible once again. Even though he had predicted this would happen, he still couldn't believe it.

"Holy shit."

"Congratulations, sir," a beaming Constable Maloney said as she stood by his desk. "I see you haven't lost your knack for this game." Dercho looked up at the young female officer. He longed for another chance to redeem himself. He didn't have a prayer. She gave him no reason to think otherwise. "What's your next move?"

Dercho's eyes ran up Maloney's body then back down again. He was tempted to give a smooth, lewd answer but decided against it. "I'm going to have a friend of mine raid their financial files."

"How exactly do you plan to do that?" she asked.

Dercho's eyes lifted slowly from the phone number on the page in front of him to those of his old fling. He wasn't about to divulge his secrets. "That's for me to know and you to find out, Nicole."

Dercho stared at the address and phone number on the page in front of him. In his line of work, the initial jubilation of such a discovery was always tempered by the reminder of human nature's uglier attributes. Dercho shook his head in disgust, never once taking his eyes off the name. He wouldn't tell Lionel. He would sit on this piece of information until the time was right.

# THE OFFICER

"Do you still need me, sir?" Maloney asked.

Dercho didn't hear her. He was lost in thought. How should this information be handled? What was the best course forward? None of it could be used in court since it was obtained illegally.

"Sir?"

Dercho jumped, a little startled by Maloney's question. He'd forgotten she was there.

"No, you can go home, Nicole. Thank you for your help."

"Who's going to monitor the phone line?"

"Dejong will be here in less than an hour. I'll watch it until then."

Maloney shrugged her shoulders then turned to leave. "Okay, good night."

"Good night, Nicole and one other thing . . ." The words hung awkwardly in the air. After hesitating, Dercho finally spit it out. "Nicole, this goes without saying, but nobody can know about this. Not even Lionel. Especially Lionel."

Maloney exhaled a sigh of relief.

"Understood, sir," she replied to her former lover. "Not one word."

She left the building. It was 10:30 p.m. Dercho had been dozing off when Maloney called him with the discovery. He was now wide awake and jacked with adrenaline. He picked up the phone and punched in a number for Ottawa, Canada. He had a favor to call in.

# CHAPTER 53

**BRENDA** Munroe had no problem arriving on time at court the next morning. She knew Justice Devereaux ran a tight ship and would force any late-arriving lawyer to start unprepared. She shook Rex Hunter's hand before sitting down at the defence table.

Munroe couldn't wait for her turn. She had tossed and turned all night like a child before a trip to Disney World. This was going to be so much fun. When Devereaux sat down behind the bench and gavelled the start of the day, Munroe didn't wait to be called. She rose to her feet and moved to the podium.

"You seem eager this morning, counselor," the judge said.

"Sorry, your honor," she replied, smiling. "I'm ready whenever you are."

Devereaux nodded his head. With a gesture of his right hand, he motioned to her.

"You may proceed, counselor."

"Thank you, your honor." Brenda Munroe composed herself and then began. "Everybody wants to see every participant in this case in black-and-white terms." She looked around the courtroom. "They want the defendants to be demonized and the victim to be canonized. That's natural. We have a tendency as human beings to react like that to any tragedy but especially when a young person dies before their time.

"However, the world can seldom be seen in absolutes. Right and wrong, good and evil are never as clear-cut as I, or anyone else, would like. If it were so easy and obvious, our entire legal system would be redundant.

We already know this case is not as clear-cut as the Prosecution would have you believe. Proof of that is the fact that Justice Devereaux has wisely tossed out Mr. Hunter's dangerously absurd claim that my clients constitute a criminal street gang. The prosecutor's blind ambition and reckless zeal led him to throw everything plus the kitchen sink at my clients hoping something would stick. He wasted considerable time and tax dollars trying to illustrate a point that every citizen would immediately know is ludicrous.

"Look at my clients; listen to the story of their lives as recounted yesterday by Governor Hunter himself. Even if everything he said were true, does that fit your image of a criminal street gang? Of course not. You know it; I know it and, more importantly, Mr. Hunter knows it. The prosecution's case is an out-of-control freight train, fuelled by fanaticism, opportunism and half-truths.

"It's a runaway freight train that wants to pulverize the teenagers sitting in front of you because one day, they got a little too rough while they defended one of their friends and a terrible tragedy ensued.

"No law enforcement branch had ever even heard of the Philipsville Vipers before that fateful day in June. That's how menacing these boys were. No police reports had ever even been filed until after this case went public and a lynch mob mentality took hold. In fact, my clients don't even have criminal records. None of them! Now they're in front of you charged with murder and, had Mr. Hunter had his way, as a criminal street gang." Munroe did another gaze around the court, her eyes resting for a minute on Hunter.

"When this case went public, it transformed from a prosecution into a runaway train," she continued. "Those past incidents my clients are accused of are blown way out of proportion. They are minor misdeeds elevated by publicity and public anger, exploited by an overzealous prosecutor.

"And be forewarned; you may admire the prosecution's tenacity on this file just because you don't particularly care for my clients, but it's this same zealotry, exaggeration and bias that has led to countless examples of innocent people suffering guilty verdicts through the ages. It's the same perversion of our system that could be turned on any one of you should you ever find yourself in the wrong place at the wrong time.

"It is indisputable that what happened to Dylan Stockwell was horrible. It was unnecessary and it was senseless. But it was not murder. It was a case of self-defense. Had Mr. Stockwell not passed away there would be no question that the behavior of my clients was unintelligent but par-for-the-course in the hormone-filled lives of adolescents in the modern world.

"The evidence will show that Mr. Stockwell beat the living tar out of Lucius Simons earlier that day because he had accidentally ripped his backpack. When the boys confronted him about this in the school bathroom, he assaulted my client again yet much more violently.

"Due to the two assaults, Mr. Simons suffered a broken nose, shattered ear drums and a cracked rib cage. His friends affectionately refer to him as Boomer. When they saw this they intervened.

"Ladies and gentlemen of the jury, let me ask you this: what would you have done? Nothing? If you've ever had a friend, a sibling or a loved one whom you cared about deeply and assuming you possess even a shred of honor, you would have intervened. You would try to defend them when they're being hurt. You add in the rash decision-making and trumped-up machismo that is common to all young men, and you have the recipe for a really bad altercation.

"These types of mishaps happen all of the time in our taverns involving men far older than the accused. They usually don't merit a second thought because they are so silly and usually no real long term damage is done.

"The altercation in the boys' washroom at Wellington High on that tragic day in June is no different except a young peer of the accused was accidentally killed—a fact which will haunt my clients for the rest of their lives. They didn't mean to kill Mr. Stockwell and would have preferred there be no confrontation at all, but they felt the need to protect their friend Boomer. He has been their friend since they were kids playing in the sandbox in kindergarten.

"My clients are star athletes with dreams for the future. There are many well-respected pillars of this community who will vouch for these boys and who agree with me that, while they are guilty of being boys, none of their meager transgressions warrant the destruction of their lives as the prosecution would like to see.

"This case has become a battle between exaggeration and truth, reason and passion, but most importantly, it's a monumental struggle between Rex Hunter's ego and the futures of five decent young men who made a mistake." She gave Hunter another quick look.

"Please, don't do Mr. Hunter's job for him. If he wants to be elected to higher office then he should do it on his own dime and his own time but not at your expense like he's doing right now. Do not hop aboard his runaway train; a locomotive of ignorance and vanity paid for by the hardworking people of this region."

Munroe left the podium and walked towards Rex Hunter. She got right in his face.

"And I think when you consider the following fact you will know that this prosecution has been a runaway train." Munroe slowly raised her voice. "And that fact is that after Dylan Stockwell was supposedly kicked and stomped on mercilessly by my clients, which in itself happened after he brutally assaulted Boomer Simons twice, he then stood up, spit in Andrew Reed's face and said, 'Fuck you, I will get even, I promise you!'

"Choo, choo . . ."

# CHAPTER 54

**JENNIFER** Hickman was the closest Dercho ever came to having a sister. They grew up down the street from each other in Oregon when they were children. They had always been close, oblivious to the typical gulf which divides the sexes between the ages of four and twelve. Hickman and Dercho remained tight during elementary school and all through high school. They traveled in the same circles and their parents were friends. They hung out a lot.

After high school, the two had gone their separate ways. She went off to university while he pursued policing. She spent four years at the University of Virginia Tech studying engineering physics and computer programming. Hickman was one of the few women in her class. She excelled at academics and made it through entirely on scholarship money.

Despite never seeing each other, Dercho and Hickman had remained in close contact while she was away at university and he was at the Police Academy. She had spent many nights on the phone with him as he faced suspension, expulsion and other disciplinary measures for disobedience and poor behavior. Despite their closeness, the relationship was never more than platonic. Dercho truly saw her as a sister. Someone he could confide in and trust with anything.

After university, they had drifted. Dercho burned through marriages while Hickman focused on her career at Canadian Security Intelligence Service where her computer skills and mathematical mind had made her a rising star. They had reconnected ten years earlier when he was reassigned to Intel for the region encompassing Philipsville. Dercho had been reticent to call because so much time had gone by since they had last spoken. When he finally had the guts to call her, it was as if no time had passed. They spoke frequently from then on.

With their old friendship rekindled, she had become an integral part of his career. Despite Dercho's imperfections, he knew that Hickman loved him like a younger brother and wanted him to succeed. Dercho owed everything to two people: Lionel Stockwell; the man who saved his career, and Jennifer Hickman; the secret weapon that enabled his career to flourish.

Hickman had access to files and information Dercho could only dream of obtaining. When he hit a legal roadblock in an investigation he would call her.

She almost always found a way around it. It was Hickman who enabled Dercho to crack the biker gang years earlier. Lionel's assault on their leadership was based on the evidence she had compiled. Ironically, Lionel never knew about Hickman. Dercho told nobody about the ace in his hat. Like Jonathan Pickett, he protected his sources.

So, when Dercho asked her to hack into Isaac Devereaux's bank accounts, she agreed. He already knew who was pulling the judge's strings. Nicole Maloney's back trace on the wire tap provided him with that insight. He didn't pass this information on to Hickman. If her findings matched his, he would know beyond any shadow of a doubt that Walter Reed was guilty of bribery and a whole slew of other felonies.

# CHAPTER 55

**LIONEL** Stockwell limped out of court. He thought he was going to puke. Lionel absorbed every word. It penetrated him to the bone then into his soul. What he heard was vile, disingenuous and dishonest. White became black. Good made bad. Right transformed into wrong before his very eyes.

It was five minutes to noon. Devereaux recessed the court for lunch. Brenda Munroe's opening statement would resume at one o'clock. The morning had been punishing for the Stockwells. It was payback time for the defence and they maximized the opportunity. Dana ran out of the courtroom when Munroe told the courtroom her version of events in the bathroom at Wellington High. It was too much for her to bear.

The prosecution's chutzpah and bravado from Hunter's opening statement the day earlier had vanished. Hunter's confidence had already evaporated and Munroe wasn't even finished.

Lawyers and police officers tended to have uneasy relationships at best. Up until that day, Lionel believed defence lawyers served a valuable purpose in the process. By fulfilling the devil's advocate role in an adversarial legal system, they forced the truth forward. After Munroe's opening statement, his opinion changed. He loathed every one of them. He sat through three hours of listening to a smug, arrogant attorney blame the dead for the murder. In this case, the dead was his son. The victim was his own flesh and blood. He couldn't, no matter how hard he tried, observe the case with the same detached objectivity that he had viewed so many other cases in his long and decorated career.

When the trial recessed for lunch, the defendants were removed from the courtroom. It was clear one of them had regained his old swagger. Four of the Vipers remained pitiful while Andrew Reed reacquired his old cockiness. He sat behind the table in his suit and tie putting forth the best image possible for the judge and jury.

As he was led out of the court by the guards, he smirked at Lionel. Andrew Reed once again had the upper hand. During the lunch hour, John Paul O'Reilly joined Lionel in the courthouse cafeteria. He tried to talk with his broken officer but not a word was spoken. Lionel sat at a table and ignored everything around him. He was like a volcano waiting to erupt. Dana was gone. Lionel would face the rest of it on his own.

O'Reilly told Lionel he had cleared his schedule for the afternoon to spend it with him. They survived the rest of the day together. Munroe spoke for another two hours after lunch. The judge adjourned early. The prosecution would begin presenting its case the following day. Lionel knew in his gut it was a lost cause. There was no reason left to hope. He had slept reasonably well the night before thinking about Hunter's opening statement. That would be the last decent night's rest he would get for a long time.

Since Dana took the car, O'Reilly drove Lionel home at the end of the day. Again, they rode home in silence. O'Reilly hadn't seen it but Reed had winked at Lionel as he left the court that afternoon.

Lionel relived the moment in his head over and over again. He fantasized about retaliation; what it would be like to get his hands on that puny little shit. Lionel seethed all the way home. The Chief tried to start a conversation but it went nowhere. Lionel wasn't in the car. His mind was in a far off place.

When they finally reached his house, Lionel exited without saying thank you or good bye. O'Reilly stared at the once great deputy chief slouch and slink up the steps and across the lawn to his front door. The man had nothing left. Anger kept him going. Hatred gave him meaning. He had lost twenty five pounds since his son's murder. His shoulders slumped forward, replacing his trademark posture. Lionel Stockwell had grown old.

\* \* \*

Lionel opened his front door in a daze. Reed's wink tore him apart on the inside. He wished he had charged the little bastard then and there. The guards would have never allowed him to get close enough. It would have at least reassured him that he hadn't lost his nerve.

Lionel was immersed in thought as he entered the house. He walked upstairs towards his bedroom to change out of his suit. He had to pass Dylan's bedroom every morning and every evening before going to bed. He swore he wouldn't enter the room, which was kept as Dylan had left it. However, despite the pain, sitting on the bed for fifteen minutes every day brought him closer to his late son.

Today, when he walked past Dylan's bedroom, the door was ajar. Lionel pushed it open. He stared in shock at the room. The dresser that had held Dylan's clothes, his desk, the closet and the walls were all bare. Everything in the room had been packed up into boxes. The room had even been sprayed to eliminate the scent. Lionel stood there in disbelief. This had been his one sanctuary over the past two months and now it had disappeared.

"Dana!" he screamed from the bedroom. "Dana, where are you?"

There was no answer. She was also adrift in her own world. Lionel heard a noise coming from the basement. He ran downstairs and saw his wife moving boxes around. The room appeared emptier than he last remembered.

# THE OFFICER

"What are you doing, Dana?" he asked. She didn't respond. He walked up and grabbed her arm. "I said what are you doing!" Dana looked at her husband. Her eyes were vacant and distant. Lionel had seen this same look on the faces of the destitute while on patrol. He never dreamt he would ever look into his wife's eyes and see that same isolated expression. "Dana, what happened to Dylan's room? Why is everything packed into boxes?" She still didn't respond. "Dammit Dana, talk to me!" Lionel shouted.

"I refuse to live forever in the past Lionel," she said in a tone of voice he'd never heard before. Lionel shivered at the sound of her words.

"Don't do this Dana. We'll get through it, I promise." Lionel was desperate. He didn't recognize her. She didn't seem to recognize him either.

She shook her head. "No, it's over Lionel. I want to move on."

"So do I," Lionel replied. "But where is everything? Where are all the boxes that were down here?" Dana didn't move. Her demeanor never wavered. She shook her head again but said nothing. Lionel feared the worst. "What did you do Dana?"

"I won't stay in the past, I can't." There was a long pause. Dana was still shaking her head. "I'm removing anything that's a reminder of the past so we can start over."

Lionel pressed further until he discovered she had already taken a couple of loads to the city dump. She had been offloading anything that served as a reminder of Dylan. Lionel was furious. His face turned red with anger. He shouted at his wife, accusing her of betraying their son's memory. The stuff she had already removed was lost forever. Lionel vowed never to forgive her.

Dana remained stoic. She offered no reaction. Lionel circled the basement like a raging bull. He also wanted to move on but he refused to pretend his son had never existed. Confusion, anger and guilt conglomerated on Lionel Stockwell. Dana walked calmly up the stairs to Dylan's room. Her husband remained in the basement. He didn't know what to do.

The sound of Dana moving boxes upstairs spurred Lionel back into action. He burst through the basement door as his wife was carrying another box into the back of their car. Lionel ran towards her and pulled it from her arms.

"No, Dana," he yelled. "I won't let you do this."

Dana tried to retrieve the box.

"Give it back, Lionel," she screamed. "I need to do this."

"Not a chance. Now go back inside and cool off."

A fight ensued in their driveway over the box. It contained a bunch of Dylan's clothing he had long since outgrown. They held on to it for sentimental value. Things like the booties he had worn when they brought him home from the hospital and the white garment they had wrapped him in when he was baptized. They had planned to make them family heirlooms.

Dana struck Lionel twice in the face as she tried to pull the box from his arms. In a flight of rage, he pushed her. She flew back against the wall of the house then slid down to the ground. She sat on the driveway staring up at her husband. He stared right back at her not believing what he had just done. After a few stutters brought on by disbelief, Lionel finally mumbled his apology.

"Dana, I'm so sorry."

She began to weep. She stood up and walked back into the house. Lionel sat down on the steps leading to his front door with his head between his knees. He felt sick to his stomach. He couldn't blame her for how she felt. He also couldn't believe he had pushed her.

Lionel felt the surge begin in his gut. It ran up his esophagus and exploded out his throat. He vomited violently into his garden then spent the next half hour dry heaving. He sat back down on the front steps. He didn't know what to do about anything. He looked down at the paved driveway until darkness swallowed the sun.

He didn't even bother going up to his room. He could hear Dana up there sobbing into her pillow. Lionel removed his suit in the living room and stretched out on the couch. He had all night to reflect. It would be the longest night of Lionel Stockwell's life.

# CHAPTER 56

"**JACK** Dercho."

"Hey dipshit, it's me," came the voice on the other end of the phone line.

Dercho sat behind his office desk confused for only a fraction of a second. He quickly recognized the voice. Dercho smiled and shook his head.

"Oh, you're a bitch, Hickman," he said endearingly.

"I'll take that as a compliment, Jack," she replied.

"I'm sure you will. So, what do you have for me?"

Jennifer Hickman had taken longer to retrieve the information than Dercho anticipated. She told him she had hacked into Devereaux's accounts as soon as she got off the phone with him the night before last. The money wasn't well hidden. Professionals who are consistently on the take know how to spread large bribes around. They're masters of filtering, laundering and ultimately hiding the ill-gotten cash. It had taken her less than a minute to figure out they were dealing with an amateur.

The payment could not have been more obvious. Devereaux had several accounts. With the exception of the one holding the bribe, he hadn't opened a new account in seven years. A new account was suddenly activated and $2.25 million magically appeared within less than forty-eight hours. She had also traced the source of the money to an offshore account in the Caribbean. The mysterious account had over ten million dollars in it and was under the name "Black Betty." Dercho was blown away when Hickman told him about all the money. He then shared the rest of his information with her. After a little more digging, Dercho learned that Walter Reed's wife's name was Betty. He asked Hickman to raid the elder Reed's commercial and personal finances. Hickman did as requested. That took a little more time but it paid off. She came back with quite a scoop.

This Walter Reed character," Hickman stated with a pause, "he is one loaded motherfucker."

"Oh, I know," replied Dercho. "The man owns Country Clubs all over the free world."

"That's not all he owns," she said. "The bulk of his wealth comes from the stock market but his offshore account is very active. He seems to be sending piles of money to China and countries in the Middle East."

Dercho was intrigued. "Does that have anything to do with this case??"

"Not at all," Hickman replied. "I just thought it was interesting."

Dercho rolled his eyes. Hickman enjoyed her job way too much. "You're positive this offshore account belongs to Walter Reed?" Dercho asked.

"One hundred percent," she replied. "Much like the judge he bribed, this guy isn't that sharp either when it comes to covering his tracks. Usually, people will transfer money through multiple false fronts before it arrives at the intended recipient. This makes it harder to track. This guy transfers money directly from his business accounts into the offshore account."

"That sounds pretty loose, Jennifer."

"It's as good as we're going to get, Jack. It's really a no-brainer. This guy routinely wires huge wads of money from his legitimate business accounts into the Caribbean. The banks record the date and time of every transaction right to the second. The exact sum then appears instantaneously in this 'Black Betty' account. There isn't just one transaction that follows this pattern, Jack. I was able to compare every deposit made into 'Black Betty' with a corresponding withdrawal or transfer out of one of his commercial accounts for the past two years."

"When you say 'corresponding,' you mean the date, time and amount match perfectly?"

"Yes. Furthermore, the manner he used to pay off the judge followed the same pattern. In my opinion, he's in waters way over his head, as is this judge who took the bribe. They don't know how to operate under the table. This is a grease money account, Jack. That rich prick uses it to buy access to emerging markets. This time, he used it to save his bastardly son. Sadly, it's not unusual in many societies. We see it all the time."

That comment infuriated Dercho. He didn't care if it was common elsewhere. This didn't happen in the West. We were supposed to be better than that. Dercho's anger swelled when he thought about Walter Reed and Isaac Devereaux collaborating towards the miscarriage of justice. He thought about Lionel and Dana, two good people who had done nothing but serve their community. Every parent deserved closure but especially Lionel. The man devoted his entire life to the pursuit of justice. When other members of the force faltered or grew disillusioned, Lionel remained steadfast in his commitment to principles like due process and the presumption of innocence.

Dercho had gone silent. The phone was still to his ear but he had forgotten about the conversation with Hickman.

"Hey," she said sarcastically. "Does espionage bore you?"

Dercho chuckled quietly. His mind moved back to the present. He sighed and looked up towards the ceiling. He didn't know what to do next. He wanted so badly to expose this to the media but he couldn't. If his tactics were ever uncovered, he would lose his job and probably end up in jail. Hickman had helped him on many other cases but this was the first one involving bribery and offshore accounts. He didn't know how to proceed. From the other end of the phone, she seemed to sense his heaviness.

"So, what's your next move?" she asked.

"I don't have a goddamned clue." Dercho said. "I'll be honest Jen, I'm still not 100 percent convinced that you've adequately linked the bribe money to Walter Reed. I can't make any move unless I'm absolutely certain."

"What would you do if we could prove this connection beyond a shadow of a doubt?"

"I honestly don't know but I'll cross that bridge when I get there."

Dercho knew Walter Reed was bribing Devereaux. He had the phone conversation and now Hickman's discovery. He just didn't want to believe it.

"Jack, I have an idea. Are you listening?"

"Yeah, go ahead."

"There is a way we can prove this connection. First, you need to tap the millionaire's phone lines."

"Already done."

"Does that include his work numbers?"

"We're way ahead of you Jennifer." Dercho was curious. He had no idea where she was going with this.

"Okay, here's what I'm going to do and believe me, it will provoke a reaction."

Dercho listened to her plan. He couldn't believe what he was hearing. The woman had guts. Dercho had never once shied away from a good fight. Heavy-handed tactics were his stock-in-trade. What Hickman proposed took it to a new level

A knot formed in his stomach. In any other circumstance, he would never agree to it but this wasn't normal. If Devereaux and Reed were in cahoots, Dercho vowed to expose them somehow. He owed that to Lionel. With grim determination, he gave Hickman his seal of approval.

"Let's do it."

# CHAPTER 57

THE trial carried on for the rest of the week. Lionel went to court each day by himself. On Friday, the trial adjourned for the Labor Day weekend. A year earlier, Lionel had taken Dana and Dylan to a cottage in northern Maine for the long weekend. Lionel and Dylan had fished all day while Dana reclined in the boat with her Smirnoff Ice coolers and a stack of her favorite magazines. It hadn't been the most fruitful few days of fishing. They'd caught next to nothing but they'd had a blast doing it. That was only a year ago— a distant memory remnant from another life.

The day before the trial adjourned for the long weekend Dana packed a couple of bags and went to stay with her older sister. Lionel didn't say anything. They needed some space. She left without a word or a kiss goodbye.

He returned home from court Friday afternoon. The house was silent. Dana was gone. Lionel walked out to the garage and found a bottle of Johnny Walker Blue Label he hadn't ever opened. He enjoyed a glass of alcohol every once in a while but was never a hard drinker. The bottle was a gift from everyone at headquarters on his fortieth birthday. Lionel was saving it for a special occasion. He didn't know when exactly he would crack the seal but wanted it to be in celebration of something monumental. He always felt like he would know instinctively when it was time to open it. The right moment would be self-evident.

Instead, he opened it by himself on that cool early-September afternoon. He had nowhere to go, nothing else to do and no desire to do anything. He had waited ten years. It was as good a time as any. Lionel grabbed a snifter from the china cabinet. He poured himself a triple. He then filled another glass with ice water to clear his palette. He walked out on his front porch and sat down. The leaves on the trees were changing colors. There was a nip in the air and the days were growing shorter. Autumn was coming.

He took a big sip from the glass and swirled it around his mouth. The smooth smoky flavor was a heavenly mix of honey and rose petals. For the briefest of moments, Lionel felt good but the moment passed quickly. Lionel looked down at his snifter. He tossed back the remaining scotch. It burned as it went down his throat. The potent whisky hit his stomach and spread. It felt like fire shooting through his veins. Lionel poured himself another and quickly

# THE OFFICER

downed it again. This pattern continued for three hours until the entire twenty-six ounce bottle was obliterated.

By 8:30 that evening, Lionel was finished. He hadn't been drunk in years. He could barely stand up straight. With the help of railings, walls and sometimes the floor, Lionel made his way to his bedroom. As soon as he hit the mattress, he was out cold. Lionel didn't move for thirteen hours.

When he woke up the next day, his head felt like it was splitting in two. The foul stench of urine and phlegm filled the room. It took Lionel an hour to realize he had been lying in it all night. His stomach and bladder had failed him.

Lionel changed into new clothing. He stripped the old linen off the mattress and dumped it in the laundry. He opened a window to air out the room and went to the kitchen to brew a pot of coffee. The very fragrance made him queasy. He could still taste the bile in his mouth. He felt like he was going to vomit again but there was nothing in his stomach.

The officer ran back and forth from the washroom three times thinking he was going to pop. Nothing came. Out of desperation, trying to move beyond the terrible nausea, Lionel stuck two fingers down his throat. The attempt to purge made him gag. His eyes watered but nothing happened.

After several unsuccessful attempts, Lionel closed the toilet bowl lid. Kneeling at the toilet, he rested his head on the lid and closed his eyes. His body screamed at him. Everything ached. He rested there on his knees trying to catch his breath and muster the strength to move. Although he had a bad hangover, it was an improvement on sobriety. At least it distracted him. He had something other than Dylan or Dana to feel terrible about. A splitting headache was easier to handle than a murdered son and a broken marriage.

After thirty minutes in the bathroom, he made his way back to the bedroom. It still stank. Lionel lied back down on the bed. He couldn't open his eyes fully and the pain pulsating through every inch of his body provided him an escape from reality.

\* \* \*

Labor Day came and went. Life continued for Ashley and her tight circle of friends as they returned to school for their senior year. All the students were back after two delicious months of freedom. Wellington High tried to carry on. Mary Lou Baxter was the new principal. She had never worked or taught at the school and wasn't even from the area. The school board thought it wise to bring in someone with no prior history at the institution. It would be a fresh start. They wanted someone to clean house. Besides, nobody in the local system wanted the job.

The Wellington Warlocks sports teams cranked into high gear. They had lost a few star players to graduation and a handful to the legal system but the teams remained dominant. A new batch of athletes showed tremendous prestige. The coaches reassured everyone that Wellington High would remain the school to beat in sports.

Ashley had more to think about than Sarah Jane and the others. She knew she had made the right choice about her pregnancy. She also knew she might live to regret it later but at that point in her life, it was the best decision. At first only Sarah Jane knew about it but when she let the rest of the group in on the secret, they all rallied around her.

As she walked through the hallways of Wellington High, Ashley still could not shake the memory of that infamous day in June. Nobody could. Her locker that year was on the second floor. She walked by the boys washroom where it happened. She still couldn't believe Dylan was gone. She wished she had talked to him when they were in the stairwell. They had never been close but on that day, he was closer to her than anyone on earth.

Meanwhile, the Vipers' trial dragged on. Reed's betrayal haunted Ashley day and night. The prosecution assured Ashley she wasn't going to be called up to testify. She just wanted to move on. Her heart broke for Dylan's parents. They looked so distraught and forlorn in all the newspapers. She wanted to talk to them. She felt she owed them that. Their son noticed her when she needed it the most. She wanted to return the favor but couldn't muster the courage. What would she say anyway? What possible words of comfort could she provide them?

The bell rang out through the school. Students made their way to homeroom. With their eyes to the future, Ashley and her four friends started their senior year.

# CHAPTER 58

**BRENDA** Munroe glared at the blubbering, gibbering witness on the stand. She eyed him up like a hungry wolf closing in on the juiciest lamb in the flock.

Rex Hunter had just finished with one of his two key eye witnesses to the central crime. He had the fourteen-year-old boy in the Wellington High washroom testify about what he saw on the day of Dylan's murder. His sixteen-year-old friend, who was also in the washroom that fateful day, was scheduled to take the stand tomorrow.

The lad on the stand was Brent Dow. He walked the court through the events as he saw them and broke down repeatedly as he recounted the story. He told Hunter that images of Dylan's death give him nightmares every night.

Whether genuine or staged, the boy conveyed a deep sense of loss and trauma to the jury. He also shared a personal story of being verbally abused by Reed during his grade nine year at Wellington High and his full awareness of the Vipers' reputation around the school. Munroe knew he had had an impact on the court members. He had to be destroyed.

"Ms. Munroe," Judge Devereaux said as Hunter finished up. "It's your witness."

Munroe stood slowly, never once breaking eye contact with the boy on the witness stand. All that could be heard in the courtroom was the sound of Brent Dow whimpering.

"Are you finished?" Munroe said to the boy.

"I beg your pardon, Ma'am?"

"I asked if you were finished?"

"Finished with what, Ma'am?" Dow seemed bewildered.

"Are you finished feeling sorry for yourself? A boy is dead and my clients' futures are on the line because you did nothing. You stood there in that washroom and watched. You were a spectator."

"No," Brent Dow said quietly. "That's not true . . ."

"You told quite a brutal tale this afternoon about the actions of my clients on the day in question. I'm just curious as to why you, by your own admission, stood by and did nothing?"

"I was scared of them, Ma'am. There was five of them and . . ."

"And you left Mr. Stockwell out there all by himself? Cowardice is your excuse? Mr. Dow, are you a coward?"

"No, Ma'am."

"Oh really, so now you're courageous? A warrior! Since you consider yourself so brave Mr. Dow, why didn't you intervene if the whole thing was as bad as you say it was?"

"Ma'am . . . please, you don't understand . . ."

"Actually, I think I understand perfectly." Munroe approached the witness. She got right in Dow's face. "Either you're a wimp or a liar. You said yourself you hated Andrew Reed because he had once made fun of you and hurt your precious feelings so you saw your opportunity. You jumped on the prosecutor's runaway train to extract a pound of flesh from the alpha male of your school. This case is the great equalizer of Wellington High isn't it Mr. Dow! You and all the other whiners have piled on after-the-fact because you don't like my client. Truth be damned, you want him to fry because he was top dog, not you."

Hunter jumped out of his chair.

"Objection, your honor, this is nothing but irrelevant badgering of the witness."

Devereaux pounded his gavel.

"I'm going to sustain that, Ms. Munroe. Please, ratchet things down."

Munroe paused for a moment to gather her thoughts. She proceeded in a low, ominous tone. "You collaborated with that other so-called witness didn't you?"

"That is absolutely untrue."

"You both had petty grievances fuelled by jealousy against my clients, so you twisted the truth, distorted the facts and somehow, produced police reports that are absolutely identical."

"That should tell you something, Ma'am," Dow muttered. He was now completely trembling and his voice vibrated along with the gyrations of the rest of his tiny frame.

"I find it interesting that in both of your reports you neglect to mention the physical abuse Mr. Stockwell dished out to Lucius Simons. How exactly did you overlook that?"

"We must have just forgot. Everything happened so fast . . ."

"What else have you forgotten, Mr. Dow? If your memory is so bad, why should this jury take anything you say seriously?

"I'm telling the truth."

"You're a coward." Munroe spat right back right in his face.

"I am not . . ."

"Then you're a liar, Mr. Dow. It's one or the other."

"No, it's not. I'm telling the truth." Dow pointed at the Vipers. "They are bullies. All of them! They killed Dylan Stockwell . . ."

"Yet they never laid a finger on you that day or any other day?"

"I lived in fear of them. We all did."

"You hated Andrew Reed?" Munroe asked.

"Yes, I hate Andrew Reed!"

"Even before this incident?"

"I've hated him since the day I met him."

"You want him to suffer for what he's done to you."

"He deserves it, Ms. Munroe. Your client is evil."

"In short, Mr. Dow, you want revenge." Munroe let the statement hang in the silence of the courtroom.

Rex Hunter had steepled his hands and seemed to be praying the boy wouldn't answer the question but his prayers were futile.

"We all wanted to get even with Andrew Reed and the Vipers."

"Getting even, you say?" Munroe's tone turned sarcastic. "Revenge is the sweetest pleasure, isn't it, Mr. Dow?" He didn't respond. "And isn't that what this is all about?"

# CHAPTER 59

**LIONEL** sat in the courtroom every day as the trial progressed through the autumn days turning to weeks and then into months. The multicolored leaves fell from the trees and were carried away by the wind. By November, snow covered Philipsville. It had been a long, punishing summer for the Stockwells. Fall and winter weren't appearing any better.

Occasionally, a friend like O'Reilly or Dercho would drop in and sit through a few hours of the proceedings with him. Those were rare occurrences. He was alone the majority of the time. The prosecution laid out its case followed by the defence.

Lionel no longer spoke with Dana. She had stayed with her sister for a month after Labor Day. She came home in October and tried to go back to work at the hospital. It didn't go well but she refused to quit. Lionel watched her endure the same career setbacks he was suffering but did nothing. He was too preoccupied with his own issues and misery.

By early December when the prosecution and the defence made their closing statements, Lionel still allowed himself to believe in a noble outcome. He had to. It was all he had left. He hadn't been back at work since early September so he could focus on the trial. He turned to alcohol more and more to drown his sorrows. It numbed the pain, but it always left him sore and tired and drove him deeper into depression, causing him to drink even more. He hated what he had become. His hope for some form of justice was the only glimmer of light he had left.

Rex Hunter had put forth a gallant effort throughout the entire trial, but Brenda Munroe's dream team was too much. The prosecution's witnesses were torn apart systematically.

As the jury retired to consider the evidence, he waited at home with Dana in silence.

Six hours after leaving the courthouse, Lionel received a phone call informing him the jury had reached a verdict. This was a good sign. Quick decisions by juries are usually a good sign that the defendant will be found guilty. If deliberations drag on, the jury is divided. Lionel felt excitement for the first time in months and even a shred of optimism.

The next morning, Dana joined Lionel in the courtroom. Although they didn't speak, they both clung to the hope that justice would prevail. The

# THE OFFICER

defendants were marched in and put in their places. The jury entered and sat down. Finally, Judge Isaac Devereaux took the bench. Everyone rose to their feet. He pounded the gavel and everyone sat down.

The courtroom was packed. The media had lost some interest in the trial as it dragged on but this was exciting. Everyone wanted to know how it would end. Devereaux put on his reading glasses. They sat close to the tip of his nose. He turned to the jury.

"Madame Foreman, have you reached a verdict?"

The jury was comprised of eight men and four women. A middle aged woman rose.

"Yes, your Honor." She handed a piece of paper to the bailiff.

The large lawman carried it to the judge. Devereaux studied the verdict quietly then looked straight at the defendants with an unreadable poker face.

"Will the defendants please rise."

Andrew Reed, Boomer Simons, Carl Hicks, Rocco Palermo and Bobby Johnson rose in unison. It would be the last time they would stand together. Brenda Munroe and her team stood with them. The tension in the courtroom could have been cut with a butter knife. Lionel and Dana held their breath.

"On the charge of murder," the judge read slowly. "The jury finds the accused . . . not-guilty." Gasps could be heard in the courtroom. Rex Hunter's entire legal team sank in their chairs. The judge continued. "On the charge of manslaughter, the jury finds the accused guilty as charged."

Devereaux turned his attention squarely on Reed. "Andrew Walter Reed, the jury finds you guilty of rape and aggravated assault against Ashley Hood." He then turned to the jury. "Members of the jury is this your verdict?"

They rose one at a time and unanimously gave their ascent. Devereaux thanked them for their service and excused them.

He told the defendants to sit down. He would now pass their sentences. Devereaux removed his reading glasses and looked at the boys.

"It saddens me," Devereaux said, addressing the Vipers, "that five young men who have received every break in life would end up in front of me. I hope these proceedings have given each of you pause to reflect on your lives. I believe what we had here is a group consisting of one leader and four followers." Devereaux paused briefly. His eyes scanned the teenage boys for effect. "Robert Taylor Johnson, Lucius Willard Simons, Rocco Antonio Palermo and Carl Patrick Hicks, please rise."

The four stood back up. Bobby was in tears, Boomer and Rocco were shaking. Hicks appeared clueless.

"I believe you four need some lessons in self-esteem. You were blind followers of Mr. Reed. You need to start using your heads. I have no doubt you're all smart, capable young men and I'm not prepared to give up on you just yet but God help you, if you ever appear in my courtroom again. I sentence you to time already served, two hundred hours of community service each and three years probation."

By this point, the four of them were shaking violently. They openly wept as the judge dressed them down. Their mothers also cried but at least their sons were going home. It was now the leader's turn to face judgment.

"Andrew Walter Reed, please rise."

Reed stared defiantly at the judge. He rose to his feet and focused on Devereaux.

"Mr. Reed, you surround yourself with weak-minded friends. You're a bully and, in many ways, the most reprehensible of the five young men on trial. I also see in you more potential than any of the others. You have committed two terrible crimes. For that, you must pay a debt to society."

Devereaux broke eye contact with the defendant, looked down at his hands in front of him then exhaled. Nobody in the courtroom could breathe.

"I sentence you to two years at the Bearhawk Detention Center for boys. I strongly advise you to mend your ways."

Devereaux pounded his gavel and declared the proceedings closed. It was a pitiful conclusion to such an arduous trial.

Rex Hunter and George Schultz made a beeline for the exit. They were hounded by reporters every step of the way but said nothing. Far from being the case they had always wanted, the outcome was a disaster for the ambitious prosecutor.

Meanwhile, as Andrew Reed was led from the courtroom in shackles, Lionel glared at him. Reed blew a kiss in his direction. It was a parting slap to the face. One final poke. The families of the other four Vipers exchanged hugs and kisses. Lionel watched in disgust. His boy wasn't coming home. So consumed by the moment, Lionel didn't even notice Dana get up and leave.

Overwhelmed and angry, he charged at the four boys and their families.

"You bastards!" he shouted as he ran towards them. "Wait till I get my hands on you!"

The guards wrestled him to the ground before he could reach them. The families high-tailed it out of there. The celebration would continue elsewhere.

Lionel struggled against the four guards holding him down. He knew they weren't mad at him. The verdict infuriated them too. When Lionel finally cooled off, one of the guards agreed to drive him home. It was the least they could do for a father denied justice.

\* \* \*

Three hours later, Andrew Reed arrived at his new home. He stepped off the transport bus in chains and shackles. He looked up at Bearhawk. It was an intimidating structure. The original portion of the jail had been constructed in the 1850s. The huge spires and imposing gothic architecture were designed to humble felons as they entered its front gates for the first time. It worked. Andrew Reed finally realized there was nothing he could do.

Half a dozen prison guards lined the entrance on each side. The closest one to him was tall, young and not afraid to get physical. He grabbed Reed by the arm and pushed him towards the entrance.

"Come on tadpole, let's go," he said. "They ain't paying me by the hour here so get moving."

# CHAPTER 60

**AROUND** the same time as Andrew Reed was incarcerated at Bearhawk, Dercho moved in for the kill. He had postponed Hickman's idea until the trial was over. Constables Nicole Maloney and Eric Dejong were scheduled to work the Saturday morning shift the next day. Dercho pulled strings and got them relieved. He needed them that night to monitor the wire taps. Dejong covered Walter Reed's phone lines. Maloney kept an eye on Devereaux's.

At exactly 11a.m. on the Friday the trial ended, Dercho gave the go ahead for Jennifer Hickman to implement her plan. In less than five minutes, the CSIS employee seized close to thirteen million dollars from Isaac Devereaux and Walter Reed combined. She emptied Devereaux's recently opened account then froze 'Black Betty'. All the money was wired into a Swiss account under the name *Lynda*. The name was Dercho's choice. He wouldn't say why but he had his reasons. It would serve its purpose in time.

When all the money had disappeared, Hickman closed the accounts. Dercho, Maloney and Dejong then played the waiting game. If the account belonged to Walter Reed, they would hear about it. Nobody loses ten million dollars without reacting. Because it was Friday, the possibility existed that neither man would check his account over the weekend. They hoped it would be sooner; otherwise it was going to be a boring few days listening to nothing.

After nine long hours of waiting, the monitored lines were ablaze with desperate phone calls. Dercho listened in on the voices.

"Checkmate," he said.

The three officers sat in the hidden room over at Intel where wiretaps were carried out. It was a secret room beneath the basement of the building. It felt like a cold war bunker. They had got what they wanted but none of them wanted what they got.

\* \* \*

Isaac Devereaux had just poured himself a bourbon and now reclined on the couch in his spacious living room. He wore track pants and a warm, heavy sweater. He was looking forward to a relaxing weekend and had booked the following week off to unwind. He and his wife were going to take it easy. Maybe invite a few friends over for Sunday dinner. Devereaux was on cloud nine and a satisfied smile ran across his face. Christmas was coming and the family would be together. The community widely respected him. The trial had finished. He would retire in a few years and he had secured more than enough money for his wife and him to live comfortably. Additional money was on the way. The initial guilt from accepting the bribe had dissipated. Devereaux had been a good boy all his life. The feeling of being naughty gave him a thrill. Part of him wondered if he should have started doing this much earlier.

Devereaux's relationship with his bank account had turned pornographic. Several times a day he checked his account online to admire the balance. The cash excited him.

The aging judge took another sip from his glass. He had only checked his account an hour earlier but had an urge to do it again. It was addictive. He loved gazing at all those zeroes while thoughts of how great he was danced in his head.

"What the heck," he said to himself as he sat up. "Why not!"

Devereaux walked through the living room and into his office. There was a mirror on the office wall immediately to his right. He shut the door and admired his own reflection. He winked at himself.

"Damn, I'm good," he said.

He flipped open his laptop and logged in. He put his feet on his desk, waiting for it to load. He took another sip of bourbon. Finally, the bank's homepage was on screen. He punched in his username and password then pressed "enter." Instead of accessing his account, a message popped up.

*You have entered invalid login information. Please try again.*

"Oopsie daisy," he said. "I must have pressed the wrong key by accident."

Devereaux leaned forward and meticulously entered his username and password. He tapped "enter."

*You have entered invalid login information. Please try again.*

"What?" Devereaux typed in the information again very slowly. He even said every letter and number out loud so there was no chance for confusion. Absolutely confident he had entered everything perfectly, Devereaux used the mouse pad to click on "Login."

*You have entered invalid login information. Please try again.*

"Fuck." Devereaux said. He sat up straight, squared himself to the computer and entered the information again. Same response. "Maybe the whole system's down for maintenance."

Devereaux had other accounts with the bank. He entered his username and password for one of his many savings accounts. It opened instantly. He logged out and tried another account. He was immediately granted access. He went back to the new account—his pride and joy. The judge entered all the information again. He was starting to get nervous. Devereaux pounded the enter key.

*You have entered invalid login information. Please try again.*

"Fuck you, you stupid piece of shit computer!" He swore loud enough that anyone outside the office could hear him. He reminded himself to keep quiet, lest his wife become curious. Devereaux was confused and growing more terrified by the minute. Maybe it was just a technical problem but the account contained too much money to leave it to chance.

Devereaux scrolled through the bank's web site. There was a hotline people could call if they had any difficulties with online banking. He was reticent at first. Devereaux didn't want to draw any attention to the account. It was going to just sit there until he decided how best to spread the money around. He needed an answer. Devereaux picked up his phone and called the 1-800 number.

He was placed on hold. Elevator music hummed obnoxiously in his ear for ten minutes. The tension swelled. Finally, someone picked up.

"Good evening, my name is Jade. How may I be of assistance tonight?"

Devereaux hesitated at first then told the young woman he couldn't access one of his accounts. She told him there were no problems with the system that she was aware of. She asked if he had other accounts with the bank.

"Yes, I have many," he replied.

"And..."

Well, I can access those just fine."

The assistant told the judge he would have to go into his branch and access it from there. Devereaux cringed at the thought. No bank would be open until Monday. That was too long to wait. Also, he tried to picture walking into a bank and telling them he'd lost an account only for some seventeen-year-old teller to locate it and find over two million dollars sitting right there. That might seem a little erratic.

"All right, thank you."

Devereaux hung up the phone before Jade could say anything else. He was starting to panic. This hadn't happened before. He had never been denied access to any account online in his three years of internet banking. Every worst case scenario ran through his mind. He tried to push them aside. There had to be a rational explanation.

His phone rang. He wasn't in the mood to talk to anyone. He desperately wanted to find out what had happened. Devereaux went back to the bank's homepage. He entered his information again. The phone blared in the background. Devereaux ignored it. He pressed "enter."

*You have entered invalid login information. Please try again.*

"You goddamn motherfucking whore!"

Devereaux was about to throw his laptop across the room. The phone rang for the ninth time, then the tenth. Devereaux tried to block it out but it wouldn't stop. He tried to think of what he should do next. There had to be something he hadn't tried. The phone rang again. It grated on his last nerve. It rang again. Finally, Devereaux snapped. He yanked the phone off the receiver and prepared to verbally lash whoever was on the other end.

"What?" he said.

There was no response. Devereaux waited. He could hear someone breathing. It sounded familiar. The breaths weren't normal. They were deep and full.

"Helloooooo," Devereaux said again.

The breathing grew heavier. Finally, a familiar voice in an unfamiliar tone responded.

"You son of a bitch. What have you done to me?"

\* \* \*

None of the officers spoke. They had conned the con men. The two men had dialled dozens of numbers. Walter Reed had placed six calls down to the Cayman Islands where a clueless banker offered no answers.

The evening culminated in a screaming match between Devereaux and Reed. Both accused the other of stealing the money. The words were never uttered but one thing was clear; all deals were off. Reed's father vowed to take Devereaux down. The judge returned the threat but neither man could do anything. The conversation ended abruptly with nothing resolved. Dercho knew they would be in contact again.

The officers recorded everything. By three in the morning it was clear these white collar criminals were done for the night. Dercho and his team would continue monitoring the lines in the morning. It was always satisfying to nail a bandit to the wall, but there was nothing rewarding about this. For Dercho, it was a reminder. For the other two, it was a lesson in the darker aspects of human nature.

With his worst suspicions confirmed, Dercho had tough choices to make. He couldn't tell Lionel about it. Not yet, at least. Maybe in time he would share the knowledge but possibly never. He had to deal with these two cretins on his own.

# CHAPTER 61

THE universal reaction in the media and the blogosphere was that the Vipers' punishment was a joke. Widespread condemnation rained down on Philipsville. Several politicians expressed their outrage and vowed to get "tough on crime." Lionel and Dana received countless sympathy cards and letters of support. One stood out for Lionel. The handwriting was sloppy but familiar.

*If you ever need anything, and I mean anything, call me.*

*Jack Dercho.*

Lionel held onto it. The people meant well but there was nothing they could do. With the trial over, Dylan's memory would quickly fade. The public would have nothing to remind them about what happened. They would move on. The Stockwells were now truly on their own. They were without justice, without closure and without each other.

Lionel hadn't moved from his computer since the end of the trial. He gathered as much information as possible. He read every article about the verdict he could find. The four Vipers restarted their various social networking profiles on Facebook, Pinterest, Twitter and elsewhere. Lionel kept a close eye on all of them. To what end, he wasn't quite sure. He hated doing it; yet he couldn't stop. Every picture he saw, every word he read reminded him of their crime. They were free to roam around but his son wasn't as lucky.

Lionel spent anywhere from sixteen to twenty hours each day at the computer. He scrolled through web pages and chat rooms. He would Google his son's name then browse all the hits. He always had a glass of alcohol at his side. Johnny Walker Blue was too expensive so he turned to rye and ginger ale. It did the job and for a fraction of the cost.

Whenever he wasn't at the computer, Lionel pretended to sleep. Andrew Reed dominated those hours. The memories of Reed smirking and winking during the trial made sleep impossible. In two years, that little bastard would be free. Dylan would still be dead. Reed would most likely flaunt his new found "street cred" once out of jail.

One week after the verdict, Dana packed up all her clothing and a few other items. It took her two hours to load up everything. The whole time she packed, Lionel stayed at the computer. He was oblivious to her. He still loved his wife but he had nothing to say. Her plan was to stay with her sister while she searched for another place to live. In a year, she and Lionel could reassess the relationship and decide whether or not to get back together.

Her leaving pierced his heart but he ignored the sting. Over the past six months, he'd learned how to shut it down. That was how he coped with Dylan. The loss was too much to bear so he disconnected it from his mind. He hadn't been able to isolate his anger and hatred. Every day, those two emotions grew stronger and more potent. They were the only two feelings Lionel had left.

\*\*\*

Dana closed the trunk on her car. She stood in the driveway. She still loved the man in the house but they needed some distance. They both had to get to a point where they would be able to at least function again. Dana wanted to go back in to say goodbye but wasn't sure if it was the right thing to do. She sat down in the front seat of the car, placed the key in the ignition but couldn't turn it. She had to see him one more time before leaving.

Dana got out of the black, four-door Honda Civic. She re-entered the house and walked to the computer room. Her husband's concentration was completely centered on the online article in front of him.

"Lionel," she said softly. "I'm leaving now." Lionel's face didn't move. He nodded his head ever so slightly to acknowledge her words. After a long silence, Dana spoke again. "I'll come back later for the rest of my stuff. I'll be in touch, okay?" This time, there was no acknowledgement. Lionel's eyes remained focused on the computer monitor. He didn't say or do anything to indicate he had even heard her.

Dana fidgeted with the keys in her hands. She looked down at her feet then up towards the ceiling. She wanted to tell her husband she still loved him, but it was too big of a risk. If he didn't acknowledge that, it would leave her heartbroken again. She couldn't take another hit. Slowly, Dana turned around and walked out. Lionel didn't move.

She got back in the Honda and started the car. Dana sat there weeping for a few minutes, then quickly wiped away her tears. She put the car into gear and drove off. She had an hour long drive ahead of her.

\*\*\*

Lionel returned to the Google search engine. He typed in Dylan's name again. There were thousands of links. Lionel sat there clicking from Web page to Web page all night. He downed more and more rye hoping it would bring gentle rest. He went to bed at around 3 a.m. but sleep never came. After two restless hours, Lionel returned to the computer. He typed "Philipsville Vipers" into Google. Many hits came back.

The very first was from a discussion board. It was a comment made in response to an online article posted on the *Philipsville Herald's* web site. The article depicted the Vipers in a negative but accurate light. Hundreds of comments had been posted. This one was the most recent;

> *Whatever! Dylan Stockwell was a pussy. All you faggots can complain all you want. It doesn't change anything. I'm the man. That's all there is to it.*
>
> *Boomer S.*
>
> *Posted 38 minutes ago.*

"Boomer Simons . . ." Lionel gasped.

Unable to move, unable to breathe, unable to do anything, Lionel's whole body locked up. He slowly started to tremble. The shaking escalated into convulsions. He dropped the glass of rye and ginger. It smashed on the carpeted floor. Lionel's breathing became heavy. He rose from his chair and leaned forward on the desk for support.

He had snapped and there was no going back now. Memories of Dylan, the crime scene, the trial and Andrew Reed piled on him. The reality of his wife leaving suddenly set in. His shaking intensified. He looked up towards the sky. From the deepest reaches of his existence came forth a mighty war cry — six months of pain, agony, sorrow, hate, anger and disillusionment exploded all at once. Lionel's roar was long, deep and terrifying. It could be heard a block away.

With sweat dripping from his face, Lionel stumbled towards the picture of him and Dylan at the fishing derby. He gripped it with both hands.

"I'm not going to let them laugh at you," he said. "I promise you, they will pay for what they've done."

Lionel set the framed picture back on top of the TV. He had clarity of mind once again and a sense of purpose. He knew what he had to do and nothing would stop him. Justice was coming.

# CHAPTER 62

IT was a long week for Isaac Devereaux. The money had vanished without a trace. He had gone to the bank on Wednesday out of desperation. They had no record of the account ever being opened. Walter Reed refused to pay the remaining two million as they had agreed. He also accused Devereaux of stealing his money. Reed's week had been no better. His offshore account disappeared along with millions of dollars and his son was in jail. Things weren't going his way. This was not something Walter Reed was accustomed to.

On Friday, shortly before Dana arrived at her sister's house, Devereaux was sitting at the kitchen table going through the mail. The smell of cookies filled the house. His wife had shortbreads in the oven, his favorite. She baked up a storm every year around Christmas. Devereaux slit open one envelope addressed to him—only his name and a stamp that wasn't postmarked were on the cover. He looked at the card. He smiled at the Nativity image on the front and read the words *It Came upon the Midnight Clear* placed across the scene. Then he flipped the card open. The inside was blank except for some handwriting. The words were sloppy but the message was clear;

*I know what you did. I'm watching you now. You will suffer for the suffering you've caused others.*

Devereaux jumped to his feet. He frantically tore the card to pieces He was already paranoid but this pushed him over the edge.

\* \* \*

Across town at around the same time, Walter Reed ran an identical card through the shredder, then burned the remains. He was positive Devereaux had sent it and swore revenge.

# CHAPTER 63

**THE** lethargy and sluggishness brought on by the previous six months had disappeared. Lionel had his old fire back. His sense of duty resurrected. This time, his obligations were to his son, not the community. Lionel walked outside and smashed the bottle of rye against a tree on his front lawn. He vowed to never again touch alcohol until his boy could rest in peace.

Lionel ran upstairs to his bedroom. He opened his wardrobe and removed his police uniform. Before he could embark on his journey, he needed to protect the good name of the Philipsville Police Department. Lionel called John Paul O'Reilly first.

"Hey, J.P., it's Lionel."

"Oh my God," O'Reilly said. "It is bloody good to hear from you."

"Likewise, my friend." There was a long pause. "John Paul, there's something I need to tell you."

O'Reilly listened and pleaded with the top cop to reconsider but it was no use. As was the case his entire career, once Lionel made a decision he wouldn't turn. It was only fitting that it would end this way.

The conversation was brief. Lionel had other people he needed to speak to and there was no way he would reconsider.

Before hanging up the phone, Lionel told his Chief he would stop by the office on Monday to clean out his office and resign his commission. O'Reilly didn't argue.

Lionel called Dercho next. It was 10:47 on a Saturday morning. Dercho could be anywhere—at the office, at home, or at the house of a woman he'd picked up during a Friday night on the town. Even if Dercho was home, it didn't mean he'd be awake yet or that he'd answer the phone. Lionel punched in his best friend's home number. Low and behold, Dercho picked up.

"Hello," came Dercho's voice, sounding scratchy and tired

Lionel smiled. He could picture Dercho perfectly; dishevelled, standing in the middle of his apartment in only his boxers. He wiped the smile from his face and collected his thoughts.

"Jack," he said followed by a pause. "It's time to return the favor."

"Tell me what you need, Lionel. Anything."

Lionel closed his eyes and cherished the answer. Despite his shortcomings, Dercho was a loyal friend. Lionel could always count on him.

"I want all the information you can dig up between now and Monday morning on those five spoiled rich pricks. I want to know where they are now, if they have jobs, if they're in school, everything. I need locations."

"Consider it done," Dercho replied. "What else? Just name it. I'll take care of it."

"All in good time, Jack," Lionel replied. He would rely heavily on his friend over the next few months. "For now, you focus on getting me that information. We'll chat again on Monday."

"I'm with you, Lionel."

The comment made Lionel think. He knew Dercho was sincere but that commitment would be stretched to the limit in the near future. He needed Dercho to appreciate what he was getting himself into.

"To the bitter end, Jack?"

Silence followed.

"To the bitter end, Lionel and then some." Dercho sounded sincere.

*  *  *

Lionel went to bed that night feeling a sense of peace for the first time. The calmness came from his lack of options. There was no alternative. He couldn't carry on as he had for the past six months. Something had to be done or he would never find closure. He would honor his obligations as a father, then stand up and face any consequences that might flow from those actions. Lionel was done being a victim and done waiting for justice.

# CHAPTER 64

**LIONEL** woke up Monday morning, bright and early. He had time to kill before his meetings with Dercho and O'Reilly so he went to the gym. He hadn't been there since June. Lionel worked out his shoulders and ran on the treadmill. He was definitely out of shape but the exercise felt good. He had forgotten how much he loved going to the gym. After he had sufficiently blasted his muscles, he showered, dressed and hopped in the car.

Wanting to get the ugly stuff out of the way first, Lionel went to Intel. Dercho would have already been there for hours. O'Reilly, on the other hand, never showed up for work before 10 a.m. Lionel looked at his watch. It was five minutes past nine. He pulled out his cell phone and called Dercho's office. He just wanted to be sure he was there. His secretary answered instead.

"Good morning, Staff Sergeant Dercho's office."

"Hey Shirley, it's Lionel."

Shirley gasped. "It's so good to hear from you, sir."

"Thank you. Has your dough head of a boss arrived yet?"

Shirley laughed. "He's in a meeting right now. Do you want me to put you through?"

"No, no, no. This is nothing pressing. He knows I'm dropping by this morning. Can you just tell him I'm on my way. I'll be there in . . ." Lionel looked at his watch. "I'll be there in ten."

"I will deliver the message right now, sir."

"You're the best Shirley. See you soon."

Lionel flipped the phone shut. He was actually closer to twenty minutes away. Dercho had a tendency of chatting to people in meetings about subjects that had nothing to do with the the meeting's purpose. He could shoot the breeze about fishing, golf, baseball, politics. Damn near everything. As a result, his meetings never ended on time. This ten-minute cushion would ensure perfect timing.

\*\*\*

Lionel's grey Taurus pulled into the parking lot over at Intel fifteen minutes and thirty-seven seconds later. It took him three minutes and twenty-four seconds to get from his car to the elevator and up to the Dercho's office. As the elevator opened, Lionel could see Dercho standing right outside his office door. He was laughing with his deputy Carl Knox. He still hadn't noticed Lionel's arrival. As Lionel approached, he heard Dercho say,

"All right, so I'll call you later today and we'll set up a round of golf for Saturday."

Lionel laughed and shook his head. Some things never changed. He looked at his watch. Nineteen minutes and fourteen seconds. Not bad at all. Dercho turned around towards his old friend walking towards him grinning.

"I'm guessing that wasn't work related," Lionel said.

Dercho made a "meh, whatever" face.

"The first five minutes or so was. The rest was about what truly matters in life."

"Golf?" asked Lionel.

"You better believe it. Come on in to my office here. I've got lots to show you."

Dercho entered first. He cleared off the table so they could go over all the documents he'd found. Lionel said hi to Shirley. Her response was heartwarming. She threw her arms around him and squeezed him tight. It had been close to a year since he last stopped by Intel. Lionel then joined Dercho in his office. He shut the door behind him and locked it.

As Dercho pulled out a thick file folder and set it on the table, Lionel told him about his decision to retire.

"I'm not surprised," Dercho said. "You've gone through hell the past six months, Lionel. It makes sense to step out of the spotlight, but it still saddens me."

The two big men chatted about Lionel's resignation for close to fifteen minutes. They shared a few memories. Lionel explained his reasons. He would do nothing that violated his oath while he was a police officer. Dercho disagreed.

"There's no contradiction, Lionel," Dercho said. "You were denied justice. You have every right to go get it yourself."

"No, Jack," Lionel replied. "We are the guardians of civilization. Laws are the thin line between order and anarchy. I cannot, in good conscience, break the law and wear the uniform."

Dercho shrugged.

"We'll agree to disagree."

Despite the bad news, they got down to business. There would be time to reminisce later. For now, they had their work cut out for them.

"What do you have for me today?" asked Lionel.

Dercho flipped open the folder and removed the first stack of papers, held together by a clip.

"Here's all the information," he said, passing the papers across the round table. "It's pretty straight forward and detailed."

# THE OFFICER

Dercho gave him the rundown on the whereabouts of all five Vipers. Reed was at Bearhawk while the other four had been expelled from Wellington High. Hicks was moping around Philipsville trying to finish high school via correspondence while Boomer, Bobby and Rocco had been sent off to private schools far away from the city.

He also informed Lionel that, except for Andrew Reed, the other four were all doing community service as part of their sentences but they hadn't yet been assigned their tasks. Dercho's Intel contained meticulous details about the travel patterns, habits and schedules of all the boys, including Carl Hicks's monthly rendezvous with a local drug dealer.

"All right, is there anything else?" Lionel asked after nearly an hour of listening to his best friend run through all the information.

"Just this," replied Dercho, handing him a Glock. "You'll need this if you're turning in your badge and gun today. It's untraceable. As for the Vipers, like I said, they all have to do community service. We'll keep an eye on the databases. We'll know as soon as they've been registered somewhere to work off the punishment. It may present more opportunities. Otherwise, everything's in here," he pointed at the folder. "Contact me if you need something." Lionel stood up and extended his hand.

"Thank you, Jack. I'll be in touch." They shook hands and gathered up the papers. Lionel placed them neatly back in the folder. He wrapped the folder in a thick elastic band so it wouldn't fall apart, then made for the door.

"What's your plan going forward?" Dercho asked just as Lionel was about to walk out.

"I'll plan things out later but first, I have to head over to the police station now and disappoint an old friend.

\* \* \*

The stocky, former deputy arrived at the police station shortly after 10:30 a.m. Lionel walked into the main lobby. Six months earlier, it was packed as the community celebrated his appointment as deputy chief. Everything had seemed so perfect but Lionel squashed the memory. He was sick of self-pity. Lionel had longed nonstop for the past. But he couldn't have it back. All he could do was change the future.

Lionel started with his office. He packed up his belongings, placing everything in a cardboard box. He had never kept too many personal belongings at work. He was in and out in less than twenty minutes. Lionel had one more stop to make. He walked back across the front lobby towards Chief O'Reilly's office and knocked three times.

"Come in," boomed the voice from the other side.

Lionel opened the door and sat down.

"Hello friend," O'Reilly said as Lionel took a seat in the chair across from him. "I'm guessing there's nothing I can say to change your mind?"

Lionel smiled and shook his head. "No. I'm afraid not, J.P." Lionel reached into his jacket pocket and pulled out his badge and his police-issued sidearm. He leaned forward and set it on the desk. O'Reilly choked up. He moved both items into his drawer. The two men sat in the office not sure what to say.

"So, what's your next move?" asked O'Reilly.

Lionel couldn't divulge the truth. He needed to insulate his friend as much as possible should things end badly.

"I need to get away for a while," Lionel answered. "It sounds trite but I need to find myself. You know, make peace with the world." The answer wasn't completely dishonest. This was what he was going to do. He just didn't give O'Reilly the specifics on how he was going to do it.

"You know if you ever need anything, Mindy and I are here for you."

"I know, John Paul," Lionel said as he leaned forward. He placed his left hand on his friend's right forearm. "Words cannot express my gratitude for your patience over the past few months. Yours and Mindy's support during this ordeal made it possible for Dana and me to get through it."

"How's she doing?"

"Not great," Lionel said as he leaned back in the chair. "We're in the midst of a trial separation. She's with her sister right now. Dana's trying to find exactly what I'm looking for."

"Peace?" O'Reilly asked.

Lionel nodded.

"More than anything, we just need a little distance so we can get ourselves back on the mend."

With that, O'Reilly stood up and walked around his desk. Lionel also stood up. Their right hands grasped each other's in a firm handshake. Lionel placed his left hand on top, O'Reilly followed suit.

"It has been the honor of my life to serve with you, John Paul."

"The honor was mine, Lionel. Thank you for all you've done." Lionel smiled.

"Don't mention it."

The handshake continued for a good fifteen seconds. O'Reilly finally released his grip and put his arm around Lionel, then escorted him through the door and out the office. When they arrived at the main lobby, Lionel stopped cold. He couldn't believe his eyes. He looked over at O'Reilly. The Chief smiled and shrugged his shoulders.

One hundred police officers, all dressed in their finest uniforms, stood in the lobby. Three or four were on the second floor looking down over the railing. They removed a couple of straps and a large banner unfurled. In big, bold letters there was a simple yet poignant message for the retiree — Thank you, sir.

The banner was huge. It appeared to be about fifteen by twenty-five feet with orange letters on a yellow background. As soon as it completely unrolled, one young constable started to clap his hands. It was Eric Dejong. Standing next to him was Nicole Maloney. She joined in. The momentum grew until the whole room erupted in thunderous applause. It was a final farewell and thank you to the man who was the reason why most of them were officers. Lionel didn't know what to do. Dejong approached him and removed the cardboard box from his hands.

"Let me get that for you, sir."

Lionel thanked the young officer. Dejong had completely healed since one of Willie Hogan's bullets cracked his ribs during the raid. Lionel looked over at O'Reilly who was smiling ear-to-ear. He made the "after you" gesture towards the exit.

They walked out the front doors to a deafening ovation. As soon as they were outside, Lionel heard a Drill Sergeant's voice call out a command.

"Squad, general salute . . . present arms!"

Two platoons of officers, twenty-one in each division, faced each other. With bayonets fixed to the rifles, they held the weapons straight in front of their bodies with their right foot positioned slightly behind their left. It was a general salute. Between the two platoons was a pathway leading to Lionel's car. O'Reilly patted him on the back.

"Safe travels, my friend and good luck."

It was hard to overwhelm Lionel Stockwell but the outpouring of appreciation did the trick. He made his way between the platoons with Dejong by his side, trying to smother the wave of emotion washing over him. The young constable placed the cardboard box in the back of the car then brought himself to attention. He saluted the retiring deputy chief then shook his hand.

"Take care, sir."

"Same to you, young man."

Lionel looked back at the building. The officers in the lobby had all moved outside. The platoons maintained the general salute. The building had been his second home for nearly thirty years. He climbed into his car. Dejong shut the door behind him then stepped back. Lionel started the car and drove away. He could see the Philipsville police station in his rear view mirror. It grew smaller and smaller the further he drove. Before long, it disappeared over the horizon.

# CHAPTER 65

"THAT son of a bitch!"

Lionel pored over Dercho's files all night. He memorized every detail. Retribution would begin with Carl Hicks. The files confirmed Lionel's suspicion; Hicks was scheduled for another drug deal Tuesday night, the very next day. The area would be perfect. It was dark, secluded and Hicks wouldn't expect a thing.

Hicks's dealer, Jacob Brenner, was the source of Lionel's anger. Brenner was well-known in local police circles. He was a Rastafarian, born and raised in Jamaica. He seemed to have a monopoly on dealing pot in the region. Lionel had actually met the guy once before. Brenner was a remarkably gentle soul who preached the redeeming value of "the herb" as he called it. The police would lay off him due to his non-violent nature. Brenner never sold anything harder than weed. They caught him four years earlier making a deal in a local school yard with adolescents. Lionel read him the riot act. He had crossed the line. Brenner promised never to do that again and offered his assistance in tracking down the dealers pushing the more unholy narcotics.

Brenner was a man of his word, unusual in his line of work. The cops were able to make twenty-nine arrests based on Brenner's information and he never went near a school again. Lionel wasn't comfortable working with any dealer at first but he always felt the laws against marijuana were antiquated. The substance was widespread and victimless. Regardless, the success they had tracking down the pushers of heroin, crack-cocaine, crystal meth and other vicious street drugs had laid to rest any qualms Lionel might have had with Brenner.

However, things had changed over the last six months. According to Dercho's files, Brenner started dealing cocaine and heroine shortly after Dylan was killed and Lionel was out of the picture. The gentle Rastafarian turned out to be a shameless opportunist. Lionel's rage intensified as he read the details.

"That bastard lied to me," Lionel snarled. "I'll deal with him tomorrow as well."

Hicks normally only smoked pot but he had decided after the trial to sample cocaine. He liked it. And Brenner had plenty of it. Barring any last minute changes, the deal would go down at ten o'clock. Lionel drove past the site where it would happen countless times. He planned out everything in his head then went over it endlessly. Lionel's sharp eye for detail was back in full force. Convinced he had covered everything Lionel went home for food and a few hours of sleep.

The former proved easier than the latter. The adrenaline pumped feverishly all day. Despite fatigue from not sleeping the night before, Lionel couldn't rest. He couldn't even sit still. Questions had begun flooding his mind. Could he actually do it? Had he covered every possibility? Much to his surprise, Lionel grappled with self-doubt. Was this right? Was this moral? Any concerns were erased by memories of Dylan's bloody corpse on the floor of the school washroom. Hate silenced doubt but couldn't destroy it. The conflict proved resilient and tenacious. As the time drew closer, Lionel's second-guessing intensified.

With a picture of Dylan in hand, he drove over to the part of town where the deal would happen. He wore dark jeans, a dark heavy hooded sweater and a black leather jacket. He brought a black ski mask but wouldn't put it on until the last minute. He parked three blocks away from the alley.

As he walked towards the meeting place, the voices raged in his head. Lionel positioned himself in a dark corner of the alley behind a dumpster. It was warm for a mid-December night. The snow was falling calmly from the sky. His hands trembled but not because of the cold. He felt an icy chill run up his spine as his heart pounded against his ribs.

"Come on, Lionel," he told himself. "Don't chicken out now."

Lionel tried to think of something, anything, to distract himself. He had one hour to wait before either man would show up. Lionel swore earlier he would accept any consequences of his actions and these possible consequences now weighed him down. Was he prepared to go to prison for the rest of his life for revenge? Yet, if he didn't see this through he would be trapped in the prison of his own mind. Forever tortured by feelings of anger and guilt for not protecting Dylan.

Dusk came early this time of year. There was no moon in the winter's sky. The darkness of the night was made even darker by the secluded alley. He checked his watch. It was 9:27 p.m. He still had half an hour to wait. Lionel pulled out his Glock, screwed the silencer into the end of the barrel and clicked the safety off. He held it in his trembling hands. Lionel was a terrific marksman but he wouldn't be able to hit anything if he couldn't control his breathing.

He saw a crow perched on an eaves trough only twenty feet away. Lionel raised the .40 calibre pistol and took aim at the bird. He wasn't going to pull the trigger. He just wanted to practice aiming the gun. It had been a long time since he'd used one. Lionel adopted the kneeling position, raised the gun and stared down the barrel through the sights. He couldn't hold it still. Had he taken a shot, the officer would have missed completely and he knew it. Lionel sat down, with his back to the dumpster. Whether or not it was right didn't matter anymore. He didn't think he could physically pull it off.

"Pull yourself together man," he said, banging his head against the massive garbage can. "What the hell's wrong with you?"

Lionel gave himself a pep talk until he was interrupted by the sound of approaching footsteps and a muffled voice. He couldn't hear exactly what the man was saying but the accent was unmistakable. Despite living in America for over twenty years, Jacob Brenner still spoke with a thick Jamaican accent. Lionel scurried to make sure he was completely hidden. He crouched up against the dumpster on the balls of his feet with the Glock ready to go. Brenner was early. He wasn't scheduled to arrive for another twenty-five minutes.

"Dammit," Lionel cursed.

He peaked out around the dumpster down the dark, desolate alleyway. They were in the industrial area just outside of Philipsville. The alleyway separated two abandoned auto factories. He saw Brenner's tall, skinny frame standing about forty-five feet away. He was talking on his cell phone. He had many places to go that night and several people to visit

Lionel hadn't met Brenner face-to-face since the school incident four years earlier. It was surreal to see him there that night. Until he showed up, the whole scheme was still conceptual. Lionel now fully grasped that this was for real. There would be no going back after tonight. This was for keeps.

Lionel pulled his head back behind the dumpster. He set the Glock on the ground and pulled out the ski mask. Lionel pulled it over his head, doing his best to remain absolutely silent. He got back into position. He looked down at his watch for a time check at the very moment another figure appeared in the alley. Lionel's heart stopped. It was clearly a male physique with broad shoulders and narrow hips.

Brenner ended the conversation on the cell and greeted his client.

"Hey mon," he said with the hospitality typical of his culture. "Long time, no see."

The closer he got, the more clearly Lionel could see his face. There was no mistaking it. Lionel had looked at that face every day for four months. It was Carl Patrick Hicks. The hatred surged through Lionel's body. The mere sight of him made Lionel's blood boil. He was one of the three who had stomped and kicked Dylan on the floor of the high school washroom after ramming him into the counter and crushing his internal organs. The prosecution had outlined everything in painstaking detail during the trial. The image was seared into Lionel's mind.

A grim, icy focus consumed Lionel. His trembling steadied. With his right knee planted on the ground and his left foot forward, Lionel raised the handgun, closed his left eye and took aim. He slowed his breathing down then squeezed the trigger. They were trained at the police academy to pull the trigger so gently that the shot would surprise the marksman. If you pulled it any harder, the gun would jerk upwards and miss the target.

The sequence unfolded in slow motion. Lionel saw the first bullet sail from the end of his barrel. It hit the Rastafarian in his left leg. This was intentional. Lionel couldn't have the guy following him. Brenner collapsed. His body thumped the pavement hard. The gun didn't make a sound. Hicks remained utterly clueless to the third man in the alley. Before he could react, six rounds

# THE OFFICER

riddled the sixteen year old in rapid succession. Seven shots fired. Seven entry wounds.

Hicks was dead before his body hit the cement. Lionel ran towards the wounded dealer and kicked him in the face. He grabbed Brenner's cell phone so he couldn't call anyone and ran out of the alleyway. Less than fifteen seconds separated the first shot from his exit. It was over before it had started. Lionel tore off his mask and tossed it in the dumpster.

He had planned to stroll inconspicuously back to his car but that wasn't going to happen. Even if he had had his wits under control, his body wouldn't have allowed it. Lionel ran as fast as his legs could carry him back to the parked Taurus. He slipped twice on icy patches along the way. Undeterred, he made it back. His lungs burned from breathing in the winter air. He jumped in, rammed the key in the ignition and floored the gas pedal. The car tires squealed until they gained traction. He was off like a shot.

As he drove away, Lionel remembered that he hadn't checked Hicks's body for a phone. That was only the first of many mistakes piling up in his mind. He drove 120 miles per hour for fifteen minutes until he was a safe distance from the alley. He drove in a different direction than he came, away from Philipsville.

Delirious, he pulled off the main road and drove down a back country road until he couldn't be seen from the main line. Lionel had brought a change of clothes. He was in the middle of nowhere and his nerves were completely shot.

Lionel stood outside to get some fresh air and cool off. He pulled off his sweater. The t-shirt underneath was drenched with sweat. He wrung it out like a soaked beach towel. He hadn't thought to bring deodorant either. It took nearly an hour for some sense of calm to return. Lionel got back in the car and drove towards the main road. A motel was only four miles away. He would park in the back and spend the night there.

The Rosewood Inn was a cheap, dingy hole-in-the wall. A seedy-looking man took his money and showed him to his room. All things considered, it wasn't bad. Lionel had on his game face the entire time as he tried to look relaxed and at ease. As soon as the man was gone, Lionel crashed on the bed. Every noise made him jump. Every sound made him nervous. He would leave in the morning.

After a hot shower which did nothing to relax his muscles, Lionel sat in a chair and stared out the motel room window. Every time car headlights lit up the road, he would panic. He stayed their all night making sure nobody had followed him. It was another long night.

\* \* \*

Lionel showered again in the morning. He did his best not to look stressed out and tired. Those are the signs he would look for if he was a cop on a manhunt. Lionel left the motel at 6:00 a.m. He walked over to the gas station next door, filled up his tank of gas and went into the convenience store attached. He purchased what appeared to be a two-day-old cinnamon bun and a newspaper. To his relief, there was nothing in it about Hicks or Brenner. He paid for everything, then began the drive home. The physical exhaustion started taking its toll. When he turned onto his street, he half expected to see police cruisers in his driveway. There was nothing. People were either asleep or just beginning their day.

As he entered his house, he immediately began to relax. Home was still comforting. After the motel room he stayed in, the modest house felt like a castle. Lionel wanted to call Dercho but it was too early so he decided to wait.

The events from the previous night still seemed surreal. Lionel removed his shoes as a hundred conflicting thoughts and emotions flooded his mind. Of all the sentiments, remorse was the last one he expected. It was only one of many sensations but it was there. Lionel was still an officer at heart. He had preached against vigilante tactics his whole life. Too many innocent people had died over the centuries from lynch mobs and witch hunts for him to condone such violence.

Something else gnawed on his mind; Hicks would never know who killed him. He died instantly and without any clue it was coming. When Lionel sat in the courtroom fantasizing about what he would do to the Vipers if given the chance, it always seemed so sweet and satisfying. For some reason, the previous night was anything but. Hicks died thinking he had bucked the system. To the very end, he believed he'd won. That grated on Lionel. The kid never experienced the fear of impending doom or the knowledge that he'd lost. This wasn't right. He'd let him off easy. This wouldn't happen again.

The next time would be perfect.

Lionel went up to his room and changed clothes. The conflicting sentiments pounded mercilessly on his psyche. He sat down on the bed to remove his socks. As soon as his ass hit the mattress, Lionel felt himself slowly fall backwards until his head reached the pillow. He swung his legs up on the bed just before everything went black. Fatigue had finally caught up with him. Lionel was asleep.

# CHAPTER 66

**IT** turned out Lionel's fears were baseless. Dercho monitored the situation from his vantage point at Intel and kept Lionel informed. Jacob Brenner didn't call the police, or anyone else, obviously because he was in the middle of a deal. In the weeks between Hicks's death and the discovery of his bullet-strewn body, snow blanketed the entire region. Carl Hicks' parents filed a missing person's report two days after he was killed. By the time police found Hicks's corpse, it was buried under nearly a foot of snow.

Christmas came and went. Dana had invited Lionel to join her at her family's place for the festivities but he declined respectfully. Mindy and John Paul O'Reilly extended a similar invitation. Lionel also turned it down. It was the first time in Lionel's life he spent Christmas day alone. The memories of past Christmases haunted him the entire day.

He remembered vividly Dylan's first Christmas. Relatives all had wanted to spoil the newest addition to the family. His presents had been stacked a mile-high, yet he'd been too young to understand what was happening. Dylan received countless toys, books and clothing; however, it was the wrapping paper that had most fascinated him. When it was time for the Christmas feast, Dylan had tried everything. He was such a chubby baby but he grew up to be such a string bean. Lionel and Dana had snapped hundreds of pictures from that day. It had been such a pleasant memory. Not anymore. Just another reminder . . .

Lionel spent Christmas planning his next hit. The loneliness of the day supercharged his animosity towards the Vipers. Bobby Johnson would die next. The initial traces of guilt from killing Hicks had vanished. When it became clear he'd pulled off the perfect murder, Lionel experienced the thrill of beating the system. He had tried to suppress the satisfaction but it was too strong. Murderers often suffered from inferiority complexes. Committing a crime and getting away with it made them feel invincible. Lionel had never felt inferior to anyone but the thrill of the kill was undeniable.

The newspapers, radio stations and TV stations covered the search for Carl Hicks daily. When the body was finally discovered three weeks later, the local television station interviewed the devastated parents in their posh, spacious mansion. Lionel watched the interview with a smug grin on his face.

*Now we're even.*

He waited until the school year resumed in January for the next hit. Bobby's parents had shipped him off to Upper Canada College in Toronto, Canada. It was an elite private school and one of the oldest in the country. Lionel wouldn't need his Glock this time. There would be no quick death from a distance. This would be face-to-face, up close and personal.

# CHAPTER 67

**LIONEL** made the trek up to Toronto in his Ford. Dercho had called him up one week earlier with new information—Bobby was permitted to work off his community service hours at the private school's massive swimming pool. He would do general maintenance after hours.

Upper Canada College is a stunning campus. Its old buildings give it a well-earned aristocratic feel. The campus spans seventeen hectares in Toronto's affluent Forrest Hill community. Lionel parked his car a few blocks away from the intersection of Avenue Road and St. Clair Avenue West in Canada's biggest city. He made the fifteen-minute walk to 200 Lonsdale Road. The pictures online hadn't done the campus justice. Lionel stood in awe of the school's architecture and size. From the moment he set foot on the campus, Lionel was in observation mode. The place would be too easy for a determined individual to penetrate. He was also on the lookout for Bobby Johnson. Thankfully, their paths didn't cross. Lionel feared he would kill him on the spot.

He walked to the school office and spoke to the lady at the front desk. She was an attractive woman in her mid-thirties with a big toothy smile.

"How may I help you, sir?"

Lionel, wearing a suit and tie along with fake eyeglasses for additional affect smiled at her.

"Good afternoon Ma'am," he said. "I'm considering enrolling my son here in the fall. Is there any chance I could get a tour of the facilities?"

The woman smiled and flipped open her calendar. She scanned the different days. "We have a tour coming up on Friday this week. Would you like to take part?"

Lionel pretended to consider the option. "I'm afraid I'll be out of the country on a business trip that day." He paused again for dramatic purposes. "Listen, my boy is a big swimmer. Is there any chance I could sneak a peak of those facilities today? I'll bring him back later for a full tour."

"I don't see why not. Do you want me to take you over there?"

"I would like that a lot."

She escorted him across campus. He asked questions about the school's storied history and recent accomplishments. She informed him that there were only four Olympic-size hockey rinks in the province of Ontario. One of them was at the college. Lionel feigned amazement. He had extensively researched everything he could find about the school before making the journey.

They arrived at the building. It contained that Olympic-size swimming pool and three gymnasiums. The place was mammoth. He thought Wellington High was good but it had nothing on this place. She walked him around the building and explained every little detail.

The woman was more than generous with her time. Lionel thanked her. Before leaving, she slipped him her business card. Her home phone number was written on the back. Lionel gave her a slight nod to acknowledge the information and slid it into his suit jacket pocket.

He then left the campus and went back to his hotel room. He was registered under the name of Gabriel St. Pierre, the fake identity Dercho had cooked up with the assistance of Jennifer Hickman before Lionel left for Canada. Lionel made some minor adjustments to his plan but nothing drastic. He would return that evening around eight o'clock.

\*\*\*

"Hey Bill, I'm going to start in here first then I'll clean the change rooms."

"Sounds good to me, brother," said the chief custodian of Upper Canada College. He grunted at his young temporary assistant.

Bobby Johnson walked into the main pool area. It was empty. The water was calm. It was shortly after nine in the evening. The pool was closed for the night. The students had either gone home or back to the dorms to finish homework and other assignments. The community service was a huge inconvenience for Bobby. It cut into his study time but he had little choice in the matter and the work could have been a lot worse.

He started by reeling in the lines that divided the pool into different sections. This enabled the pool to be used by different groups simultaneously. One side could be used for laps while the other hosted a game of water polo. It took Bobby about two hours every night to complete all his tasks. He hated cleaning the change rooms. He saved that for last.

Bobby worked quickly but meticulously. If he did a bad job he would be reassigned. God only knew where he would end up. After an hour, the pool area was spic and span. He shut it down for the night.

"Well," he said to himself, "I guess there's no putting this off any longer."

The sixteen year old opened the janitor's closet. He picked out the cleaning supplies he would need. The floors had to be mopped, lockers emptied out, toilets and sinks scrubbed. Bobby placed all the cleansers, sponges and scrubbers he would need into a mop bucket and pushed it towards the first change room. He stopped at the door, pulled out a pair of rubber gloves and slid them on his hands. He heaved a heavy sigh then pushed open the door.

\*\*\*

# THE OFFICER

As soon as the door opened, a pair of powerful hands reached out and grabbed Bobby by the shirt. They dragged him into the change room and pushed him across the floor. Bobby rolled along the cement floor and slammed into lockers on the other side. The attacker, wearing a black ski mask, locked the door.

"Bobby Johnson?"

"Who . . . who are you?" Bobby asked.

"Lionel Stockwell . . . Dylan Stockwell's father." Lionel paused to allow the revelation to sink in. Bobby's eyes instantly filled with horror. "I would stay quiet if I were you," he said to the boy.

Lionel reached into his pocket and pulled out a metallic object. It was eight inches long. With a quick flick of the wrist, a metal rod shot out two feet. It was an ASP baton, straight from the lockup of the Philipsville Police department, courtesy of Jack Dercho. The ASP had replaced nightsticks because of its collapsibility. When not in use it compacted down but with one movement, it extended into a lethal weapon.

Bobby cowered in the corner. Lionel could hear him whimper. He was a quivering mess. The boy was so weak and helpless. Lionel looked down at him. He felt a brief but intense wave of pity flow through his mind. With one violent choke, Lionel replaced it with the image of Andrew Reed winking at him. That was more than enough.

Lionel walked up to Bobby and pounded him with the ASP. The kid tried to resist but his efforts were futile and his cries for help went unheard.

"I said shut the fuck up," Lionel shouted at the pleading, sobbing teenager. After four fierce blows to the skull, Bobby was knocked out. Lionel stuffed a rag in his mouth and rapped duct tape over it. He used plenty of it to make sure it didn't come off. He bound Bobby's hands behind his back and his feet together.

"Let's go," Lionel said to the battered and bloodied kid. "We're going for a swim."

Lionel took him out to the pool and dunked his head under water. Bobby woke up. Lionel looked into his eyes. They were wrapped in tears, begging for mercy.

"This is for Dylan, you son of a bitch."

He turned the kid around so he faced the pool. Bobby began flailing and screaming as best he could but he wasn't going anywhere. Lionel delivered a knee to Bobby's spine. It sent him sailing into the pool. Lionel stood on the side. He watched the kid struggle underwater as he sank like a rock. Within a minute, Bobby Johnson was dead. His lungs flooded with chlorinated water, removing all buoyancy from his body.

Lionel watched Bobby's body sink to the bottom of the pool, then gathered up everything he had used in the crime's commission and made his way for the exit. His adrenaline was pumping but he controlled it. He walked casually out of the building and off the campus. It was a beautiful tranquil winter night in Toronto, clear as a bell. He took the scenic route back to the hotel so he could admire the beautiful houses in the upper-class neighborhood around the school.

# CHAPTER 68

**A WEEK** later marked the beginning of February. Ashley Hood was tired but excited—it was almost time. She had gained forty pounds over the past nine months. The last month in particular was excruciating. Her friends and family doted on her. Three days after she was due, her water broke.

Ashley's parents rushed her to the Philipsville General Hospital. She spent twenty-eight hours in labor. Her mother had warned her about what to expect but words could never convey the enormity of the pain. Finally, only minutes after midnight on February 4th, Ashley Hood brought a beautiful, healthy baby boy into the world. The baby screamed upon arrival. The cries filled the delivery room with joy. The baby was breathing on his own.

The nurses cleaned him off, cut the umbilical cord and wrapped him in a blanket. Ashley was exhausted and wanted to sleep but she had the strength for one more miracle. The nurses handed her the baby. Cradled in her arms, with the cadence of a familiar heartbeat next to his ear, the infant rested. He bore an uncanny resemblance to his maternal grandfather. Although asleep, mother and son bonded for fifteen minutes. He was then wheeled away by the nurses. Both he and Ashley slept all night under the watchful eyes of her parents and four closest friends who would become like Aunts to him in the years to come.

# CHAPTER 69

**LIONEL** woke up the next day to a media frenzy throughout Canada. Bobby Johnson's water-logged corpse had been found a few hours after his death. It was a murder at one of the finest boys' schools in the country. The police were investigating. Nobody had a clue how it happened. None of the janitors saw anyone enter or leave.

The following day Lionel checked out of his hotel and drove to Pearson International Airport. He left his Taurus in the parking lot and boarded a plane for Boston. He drove around using a pseudonym for everything including booking reservations, cars and flights. He had given his credit card to Dercho so Dercho could make small, silly purchases around Philipsville. If an alibi was ever required, the receipts would help out.

Boston was a beautiful city. Lionel had never visited it before. He planned to stay for a while until the media coverage of Bobby's death had settled down. Boston, called the "Athens of America," contained over a quarter-of-a-million students living there at any given time. Lionel went on student housing Web sites. Many students in university would study abroad on exchange for a semester. Unable to get out of their leases, they would sublet to offset the cost of renting. There were so many units to choose from. Lionel found a perfect spot and negotiated rent for a month with a sophomore at Harvard.

It was a stone's throw away from Boomer Simons.

\*\*\*

Jonathan Pickett rubbed his eyes in disbelief. It was too much of a coincidence. He scrolled from one Web site to another of the various media outlets in Toronto. The *Toronto Sun* and the *National Post* featured huge write-ups on the murder at one of the country's most elite private schools. The news dominated the airwaves at CFRB 1010 and CTV News made it their lead story on the evening news three nights in a row.

Pickett sought and received confirmation that Bobby Johnson was the second of Dylan Stockwell's killers to be found murdered. The two murders were so vastly different and so geographically disparate that nobody made the link. Pickett started making a few unofficial inquiries.

He called Lionel Stockwell's home. His cover reason was to get a quote from Lionel about the news that two of his son's tormentors were killed. The phone rang and rang but no one answered. He tried repeatedly throughout the day but still no answer. He even drove over to Lionel's house and knocked on the door. Nothing.

Not easily deterred, Pickett spoke to neighbors. He told them about the news that two of the Vipers had been killed. He just wanted to get a reaction from Dylan's family. Did they know where he was?

One of Lionel's neighbors barked at him and told Pickett to leave the family alone. They had been through enough. Another was polite and said she didn't know and couldn't help him out. He went door to door until someone finally spoke to him. It wasn't much but it was a lead. The neighbor four doors up from Dana and Lionel saw the former cop pack his car and leave a few days earlier. The neighbour hadn't seen him since. He had no idea where he was going or what he was doing.

Pickett thanked the man for the information. He hopped in his car and drove back to the newsroom. He placed a call to the Chief of Police. He knew John Paul O'Reilly was close to Lionel. Maybe he knew something.

He went back to his cubicle and picked up the phone. Pickett was excited. He pulled a cigarette from the pack in his pocket, put it between his lips and fired it up. He took a long pull and exhaled slowly. The phone, pinned between his head and his shoulder, rang over and over in his ear. Finally, someone picked up the phone.

"Oh, hello, this is Jonathan Pickett of the *Philipsville Herald*. May I speak to Chief O'Reilly please."

The feminine voice on the other end told him she would redirect his call. She placed him on hold. Without warning, the Chief's booming voice came on the other end.

"Chief O'Reilly."

"Good afternoon, Chief. This is Jonathan Pickett of the *Philipsville Herald*. How are you today?"

"I'm busy, Jonathan," the Chief grunted. "Make it quick."

"No problem. I'm trying to reach Lionel Stockwell. Do you know where he is?" O'Reilly rolled his eyes.

"As far as I know Jon, his number is still listed in the phone book."

That wasn't the reaction Pickett had hoped for. It wasn't defensive or combative. If something was going on, O'Reilly was probably not involved in it.

"I've tried to reach him at home but there's no answer. His neighbors say he's been gone for a few days." Pickett let the words hang there. It was an old trick in journalism. Allow a statement to linger until someone filled the void. Most people would do anything to avoid awkward silence. Usually, what they said proved useful and often for unintended reasons.

However, O'Reilly didn't take the bait. Pickett could hear the Chief's breathing through the phone line. Finally, the Chief broke the silence.

"Well, it's been great chatting with you, Jonathan. I need to get back to work. Take care."

"No, wait," Pickett blurted out. He didn't want the call to end. "Do you have any comment on the deaths of Carl Hicks and Bobby Johnson?"

"Who?"

Pickett was stunned. O'Reilly didn't even know what he was talking about.

"Carl Hicks and Bobby Johnson. They were two of the five boys who killed Lionel Stockwell's son. They've been murdered."

O'Reilly sounded incredulous. "Is that what this is about?" This time, the Chief allowed for a silent pause. "No, Jonathan, I have no comment on that."

"How about the whereabouts of Lionel Stockwell?"

"I have no idea. Have a great day, Jon."

Click.

The phone line died before Pickett could ask another question. Pickett slammed the phone down and finished off his cigarette. He crushed it out in the ashtray on his desk. He got nothing out of the Chief. Pickett knew from the conversation that O'Reilly was clean and would be of no assistance to his little crusade.

"I'll have to take care of this myself."

With that, Jonathan Pickett booked off the next three days from work and ordered a plane ticket to Toronto. He had a few questions he wanted answered.

# CHAPTER 70

**LIONEL** had all the information about Boomer Simons. His father Abner Simons was able to enrol his son at the Commonwealth School in Boston. A small private school, it accommodated a student body of around 150 children that spanned all grades from kindergarten to grade twelve and a tiny student-to-teacher ratio. Boomer had only needed one more semester and the school had an opening. Abner, after pulling a few strings, got him in there.

Boomer lived a twenty-minute drive from the school. He'd brought his truck that had carted the Vipers around Philipsville; otherwise he couldn't have commuted to and from the school. His father put him in an apartment in West Somerville to isolate Boomer from the other students and keep him out of trouble. It seemed that he just wanted his son to get through high school then to on to university

Lionel also had a detailed description of the truck. Dercho's agent had tracked it while they were following Reed. For two weeks, Lionel trailed Boomer and watched his every move. Lionel waited for him at the private school the first day. His car showed up just as scheduled. He spent the rest of the day waiting, then followed Boomer on his drive home. Boomer's life ran like clockwork. He didn't mix things up. His routine was set and he drove the same way to and from school daily.

Lionel was looking forward to this one. It was Boomer's boasting on a discussion board that awoke the sleeping giant. Dylan had twice kicked Boomer's ass, a fact his lawyers made central to their defence. Brenda Munroe argued it had been self-defence. His son taught this little shit a lesson twice. It was clear from his online chest thumping that he hadn't learned. Lionel was going to finish what Dylan had started.

Boomer's predictability made it much easier to plan out an attack. Lionel wanted to vary things. If all the murders were the same, it would be too easy to draw a connection. This one had to be different. He knew exactly what he would do. After two weeks of planning and another week getting together everything he needed, Lionel was ready. The trepidation he had experienced before the Carl Hicks and Bobby Johnson murders no longer existed. He now had no doubts or second thoughts.

# THE OFFICER

Lionel rented a car for his time in Boston. It was expensive. He had already burnt through a lot of money since Hicks. However, there was no going halfway. He would see this through or die trying.

\*\*\*

Pickett's three days in Toronto proved fruitful. He flew in on a Tuesday and made his way directly to Upper Canada College. The Toronto Police Service had already faxed him a copy of the police report. Nobody saw anything. There were no witnesses. Everyone was baffled. Pickett refused to believe it. There was either bribery going on or the killer planned things out in advance. If that was the case, the culprit had probably been on the property before the actual murder to scout out his possibilities. Somebody must have seen something.

Pickett went straight for the UCC front office and introduced himself. An older woman with silver hair was behind the desk.

"Good day, Ma'am," Pickett said, removing his hat. "My name is Jonathan Pickett. I'm with the *Philipsville Herald* . . ."

Before he could finish, the secretary cut him off. "If you're here about the murder, we're under strict orders not to speak to the press. You need to go through our Public Relations department."

Pickett nodded his head. He wasn't about to do that. The woman seemed like the inflexible type so he told an outright lie.

"No Ma'am, that's not why I'm here," he said.

The secretary crossed her arms. She appeared more than a little skeptical. Pickett opened his briefcase and pulled out a picture of a police officer. It was a clear, professional 5x7 of the man in his uniform. He set it on the counter in front of the woman.

"Have you or any member of the staff here seen this man on your campus in the past two weeks?"

The secretary took a long look at the picture. She shook her head. "He doesn't look familiar. May I ask what this is about?"

"We have reason to believe he was here. I wish I could give you more information Ma'am. All I can tell you is that it is very important that I find him."

She took another look at the picture.

"I'm sorry, young man. This picture's not ringing any bells," she said. "I can't circulate it to our staff unless you give me a reason. For all I know, you could be a stalker."

The old lady had him there. Pickett was out of options.

"Okay, let me ask you this; are people allowed to look around this campus unescorted?"

"Absolutely not," she replied.

"They would have to come here first?"

"Yes."

"Are you the only secretary who would handle such visitors?"

"Actually, I don't handle them at all. There's another receptionist who provides impromptu tours but she's on lunch break right now. She would be the one to handle that."

Pickett felt a surge of excitement. This was the connection he had been waiting for. He decided he had pushed the matter long enough. He would leave it in their hands.

"Well, may I leave this picture with you? Whenever she gets in have her take a look at it. If she recognizes this man, have her give me a call." Pickett pulled a business card out of his pocket and passed it to the woman. "Like I said, feel free to circulate this to anyone who may have seen him."

The woman reluctantly took the card. She was still suspicious. Pickett smiled at her. He tried to exude trustworthiness and confidence. Finally, she broke the tension.

"I'll see what I can do."

Pickett heaved a sigh of relief.

"Thank you, Ma'am."

Pickett put his hat back on and left the office. He then went for a walk through the fancy surrounding neighborhood to relax. He wanted to be close by if his cell phone rang. If anyone recognized Lionel's picture, Pickett wanted to speak to him or her personally.

# CHAPTER 71

**LIONEL** set up his rental car at the corner of Conwell and Curtis. Boomer lived on Conwell Avenue only a few blocks away from Tufts University. He would always drive up Curtis Street, then turn on to Powder House Boulevard and follow it until it turned into Broadway street right after Nathan Tufts Park. This comprised the bulk of his journey each way.

Lionel waited until 5:10 p.m. to pop the hood. He had timed it meticulously. Boomer always drove around that corner at about the same time each day; give or take a couple of minutes. It was close to his house. He rented the apartment in the basement from the owner. Lionel currently rented in a house a block away on Stirling Street. The girl he was subletting from had gone on a student exchange over in India for the semester.

Boomer had developed quite an interest in car engines after his dad bought him his own truck. Dercho somehow had found this out. The files back at Lionel's apartment said the kid could be seen daily working on his truck in his father's garage. Lionel noticed the same thing during the three weeks he was in Boston. It gave him an idea. It was a long shot but he thought it might work.

Lionel saw the truck approaching as it turned on to Curtis from Powder House Boulevard. It was unmistakable. Lionel quickly raised the hood and stood by his car looking all depressed. Boomer's truck slowed down as it approached Lionel's position, then pulled in behind him. He jumped out of his truck and approached the man he had seen each day during the trial for murdering his boy. Lionel had anticipated this problem so he had grown a beard and wore dark sunglasses.

"Car problems?" Boomer asked, walking up alongside Lionel.

"Yeah, this damn engine keeps conking out."

"Oh, do you mind if I take a look?"

Lionel looked at the seventeen year old. He gave him a "what can you possibly know about this?" look and shrugged. "Be my guest."

Boomer walked to the front and peered under the hood. Lionel moved into position.

"You know," Boomer said, "it may just be your car battery. I have booster cables in my truck. It's worth a shot."

The bearded man nodded as if considering everything Boomer had to say. "Indeed."

At that moment, Lionel pulled a Taser out of his back pocket. He put it to Boomer's neck and sent fifty thousand volts through his body. Every single muscle in Boomer's body, including his rectum, clenched then released when Lionel removed the charge. He fell like a wet noodle to the ground while soiling himself simultaneously. It happened so unobtrusively that nobody in the neighborhood noticed. Lionel shut his hood. He moved the kid into his backseat where he slapped handcuffs on him and placed a towel over his head.

Lionel jumped into Boomer's truck and drove it the rest of the way to Boomer's apartment. The owner wasn't home. He parked it there then walked back to the rental car. Dilboy Field was only five minutes away. They drove there for cover. Once there, Lionel properly bound and gagged Boomer so he couldn't move. He even Tasered him one more time for the hell of it. He stuffed him in the trunk and made his way to Logan International Airport. Gabriel St. Pierre was booked on the 7.30 p.m. flight out of Boston.

Lionel scouted out a secluded area that was a thirty-minute walk from the airport. It was cutting it close but he had a first class ticket. The flight wasn't leaving without him. After filling his tank at a nearby gas station, Lionel drove to the place and parked the car. The area was closed in by trees. It wouldn't take long for someone to find the car but it would give him enough time to get away.

He stepped out of the rented Hyundai Elantra. He removed his two suitcases from the backseat. He knew he wouldn't be heading back to his house after this so Lionel was already packed. He opened the trunk. Boomer was a mess. The foul odour from Boomer's unplanned defecation hit Lionel like a freight train. The stench made him gag. He had stuffed a hand cloth in to Boomer's mouth and wrapped it with plenty of duct tape to hold it in place.

"Lucius Simons," Lionel said, introducing himself for the first time. "Or, should I call you Boomer?"

The kid blinked his eyes. He was barely cognizant from being Tasered twice.

"I'm Lionel Stockwell, Dylan's father. You do remember Dylan, don't you?"

Boomer didn't react or respond. He was bound and gagged in the back of the trunk and completely disoriented.

"Yeah, you remember him, I knew you would." Lionel grabbed his Taser and shocked the boy again. "How does that feel, motherfucker!" Lionel shouted as Boomer convulsed in the confined space. "Let's see you call my son a pussy now."

The officer continued the electric torture for another five minutes. Lionel zapped Boomer's legs, arms and testicles with multiple bursts. He would have done it for longer but he was on a tight schedule. He also wanted Boomer alive for what would happen next so he said good bye.

"Burn in hell, you rat bastard."

Lionel slammed the trunk shut and locked it. The faint sound of Boomer's weak struggle to escape could be heard for a moment before he gave up. Lionel walked back to the driver's seat. Beneath it, slightly to the left was the lever to unlock a small hatch on the left side of the car. Lionel walked around, opened it all the way and unscrewed the cap sealing off the car's gas tank. He pulled a pack of matches out of his pocket, lit one and dropped it down the hole.

As soon as he released the match, he ran as fast as he could. The gasoline caught fire and the tank exploded. The blast pushed Lionel fifteen feet through the air. The car was a smoldering wreck. The explosion was far bigger than Lionel had anticipated. He looked back and marvelled at the carnage but not for too long. He had to get moving.

It was approaching six o'clock. He had a plane to catch and more importantly, an explosion that big tends to attract attention. He ran out to the road, out of sight from the smoldering Hyundai and then began to walk. As luck would have it, a taxi cab was idling outside a nearby store. Lionel figured it was worth a shot.

"Hey bud, anybody got you booked?" he asked the cab driver.

The man had his MP3 player blaring in his ears while reading *Sports Illustrated*. Lionel tapped him on the shoulder. The cabbie, off in his own little world, didn't see or hear the man standing in the passenger window. He jumped out of his skin.

"Holy shit, buddy," he said, laughing. "You scared the hell out of me."

"Sorry, I didn't mean to."

"It's all right. Do you need a ride somewhere?

"Yeah, I need to get to Logan International Airport. Can you get me there in ten minutes?"

The cab driver nodded confidently. "Saddle up partner."

# CHAPTER 72

**LESS** than a week later, John Paul O'Reilly sat in his office working away on a stack of paperwork. The police station still felt empty without Lionel. He hadn't heard from the guy since Christmas. He hoped he was all right.

O'Reilly's thoughts were disrupted by his phone. He had a lot of work to do and was tempted to let it go to voice mail. He decided against it. He signed his name to a report then answered the phone.

"Chief O'Reilly."

"Hi John Paul, it's Bonnie." Bonnie Smith operated the switchboard at the station. She directed all incoming calls.

"What can I do for you Bonnie?" he answered as he opened another report to read through.

"Umm, I have a man on the other line who wants to speak with you . . ." She paused not sure how to continue. "I know you told me to hold your calls because you're busy today but I think you may want to take this one."

O'Reilly didn't like the sound of this. "Who is it?"

"He says his name is Agent Jeff Black. He says he's with the FBI."

"The FBI?" O'Reilly said confused. These guys were never pleasant to deal with. "Put him through."

"Yes, sir." Bonnie put the Chief on hold then connected the call. O'Reilly girded himself for battle. The FBI could get pushy and arrogant when it wanted to.

"Chief John Paul O'Reilly here."

"Chief O'Reilly, it's a pleasure to speak to you," came the boisterous voice on the other end. So far, so good. The man seemed nice enough. "My name's Jeff Black. I'm with the Federal Bureau of Investigation."

"So I've been told," O'Reilly replied with a hint of suspicion in his voice. "What can I do for you Agent Black?" O'Reilly held his breath. Jurisdictional disputes between law and order branches could make boundary disputes on the West Bank seem mild. Everything had been going smoothly around Philipsville. The FBI was the last group he expected to hear from.

"Oh not much, sir," replied Agent Black. "In fact, I only need one thing from you but maybe you don't know the answer." There was a moment of silence as papers ruffled in the background. It sounded like Black was looking for something. "Ah, here it is. "Sorry about that. I needed to find my notepad." This was followed by another pause.

"I don't mean to be rude Mr. Black but I have a pile of work I need to get done. If we can move this along, I'd really appreciate it."

"Fair enough," the agent replied undeterred. "I'll make this quick. Do you know the current whereabouts of Lionel Stockwell?"

O'Reilly froze. He set his pen down, sat up straight in his chair and composed himself. The young man on the other end now had his undivided attention.

"Not at the moment," he replied honestly. "Lionel Stockwell retired from the force a few months ago. Would you mind telling me what this is about?"

"Oh, probably nothing," he replied, brushing off the question. "I just need to speak to him."

"About what?"

"I'm afraid I can't go into that right now. You're sure you don't know where or how we could reach him?"

O'Reilly wanted to tear the young man in half but thought twice. They always invoked confidentiality to keep everyone else in the dark. However, yelling and screaming would accomplish little. He tried a different approach.

"I'm afraid not Mr. Black," he said. "But the more information you give me the more I can help you out."

"Rest assured Chief O'Reilly," he said. "We'll be in contact with you again should the need arise."

"Very well," O'Reilly replied, doing everything he could to maintain a steady demeanor. "You have a great day."

"You too, sir."

The line went dead. O'Reilly set the phone down. The conversation didn't make sense. Why did the FBI want to speak to Lionel? O'Reilly thought about it. There was no scenario in his mind that ended well. He knew Lionel was closer to Jack Dercho than anyone else on the force. O'Reilly didn't care much for the brash, cocky officer. He had wanted to fire Dercho ten years earlier but Lionel had pleaded with him to spare the man's career.

O'Reilly conceded that Dercho was one of the finest Intel officers in the country. He had developed a begrudging professional respect for the man over the following decade. That's as far as his praise went. He didn't relish the thought of calling him, but he knew it was his best chance of uncovering something. O'Reilly picked the phone up and pressed zero.

"Hi Bonnie, get me Jack Dercho on the line right away. Thank you."

*　*　*

Pickett's trek to Toronto one month earlier paid off huge. His cell phone rang less than half an hour after his visit to the front offices of Upper Canada College. The other receptionist did recognize the handsome face. She had given that man her business card, hoping he would call her later that evening but the call never came.

She couldn't remember the man's name but she remembered thinking it sounded French. If that was true, Pickett knew Lionel was using an alias. She could also have been mistaken so he didn't waste too much time on that theory. However, he got what he had wanted—an eye witness who could vouch to seeing Lionel there.

Pickett took the woman out for coffee after she was finished work. She told him everything about her meeting with the mystery man. She took him for an impromptu tour of campus but all he really cared about was the aquatics area. Pickett scribbled everything she told him down and read it back to her to make sure it was accurate. He also recorded the whole session.

The reporter then told her not to go to police with any of her information. He claimed they wouldn't be interested. His real reason was that he wanted to break the story first. He still didn't have a lot to go on but he knew he was on the right track. He would continue building his case until he could smash Lionel Stockwell in the media. His gut told him the guy was being helped by people at the Philipsville Police department. If that was true, he could bring down the whole police force.

Pickett spent the next three weeks trying to find Lionel but to no avail. However, he had finally acquired an inside source at Lionel's old place of employment and the informant was starting to pay off. The source didn't have access to much information but informed Pickett that Lionel was closest to Jack Dercho on the police force. That was a name Pickett hadn't heard in a long time.

Jonathan Pickett had cut his teeth on the local scene during the fiasco ten years earlier when Dercho nearly lost his job for assaulting a suspect. Pickett shredded him in the media. After that, Dercho fell out of sight. Pickett never realized he had been reassigned to Intel. He couldn't believe he'd missed it. He thought Dercho was long gone. If his source was right that Lionel was close with Dercho, Dercho would be in a position to supply his friend with oodles of information on the Vipers.

For the time being, Pickett focused on finding Lionel. He needed to speak to him before he charged ahead with a conspiracy theory this big.

When Lucius Simons was found burned to death in a car in Boston, the journalist figured out the pattern.

Pickett jumped on a plane. This time, he flew to New York. His instinct told him that's where Lionel would go next.

* * *

Lionel flew from Boston all the way to California. He needed to lay low for a few weeks following the explosion. He realized his mistake in setting the rental car ablaze. It could be traced back to Gabriel St. Pierre. Lucky for him, he never actually met the student whose place he had rented for the month. Everything had been over the phone and the Internet. Regardless, he needed to take cover to let everything blow over.

Reporters from all over the New England area were at the flaming Hyundai within an hour. They almost beat the cops there. Lionel had considered cutting the break lining on Boomer's truck. It would have been easier and ensured anonymity. After Carl Hicks, Lionel vowed to do the job face to face. Boomer was also the one who had the gall to boast about the murder online. He needed Boomer to know it was Dylan's father who killed him or it would have been meaningless.

It was a long tense flight from one end of the USA to the other.

Despite extensive coverage, nothing was reported in the media that connected the deaths of the three Vipers. Trying them as young offenders turned out to be a perverse blessing in disguise. Had all five of them been exposed to daily media coverage during the trial, someone in the general public might have already made the link. Lionel had friends in San Francisco. He called them while he was in the air. They were delighted to have him. He stayed with them for the next two weeks.

Lionel spent those two weeks quietly planning his next move. Rocco Palermo was next on the list. Dercho's Intel indicated he was now somewhere in New York City. He was staying with relatives there while attending the St. Agnes Boys High School. Lionel knew he would have to keep this one simple. His last plan was too elaborate. Rocco would be taken out with a gun at close range in a hidden area. It wasn't original. It wasn't creative but he no longer had the luxury of time.

His last conversation with Dercho confirmed the worst: the hunter had become the hunted.

# CHAPTER 73

**JACK** Dercho's ability to network made him a legend over at Intel. He was never able to crack the CIA but he had Jennifer Hickman in the Canadian counterpart. He also had an old friend from the Philipsville Police department who went on to work for the FBI. They often helped each other out. More than anything, they were drinking buddies. Dercho asked him to keep an eye on the investigation into Lionel Stockwell. It turned out the FBI had picked up on the connection between the Vipers but had little else go on. They were working hard to develop more evidence.

Meanwhile, Dercho decided it was time to get his hands dirty. There wasn't a chance in hell he was going to allow his best friend to serve jail time. He simply wouldn't allow it. Lionel Stockwell had done too much for society during his lifetime. Dercho would not stand by while an ungrateful community placed a hero behind bars. He had a plan. Isaac Devereaux still had no clue where his money had gone. The time had come to educate the man.

Dercho waited outside the judge's office. It was now the first week of March. The days were getting a little longer and the snow was starting to melt. Spring was still a ways off but the early signs of it approaching were faint and subtle. Dercho sat in the police cruiser for two hours waiting for Devereaux. As soon as the man walked out the front door, Dercho drove away.

He sped across town with sirens blaring. Cars moved out of his way as he ran red lights and weaved in and out of traffic. The twenty minute drive from Devereaux's office at the courthouse to the judge's palatial home took the speeding cop only seven minutes. As he approached, Dercho slowed down and killed the siren. It was 7.30 in the evening. The sun had already set and Dercho had the cover of darkness to his advantage.

He parked the police cruiser a block away from the judge's mansion and donned a ski mask. He was wearing a full SWAT suit minus the seventy-five pounds of body armor. He wouldn't need it for this target. He just needed the black outfit to blend into the night.

Dercho sneaked around Devereaux's home. He positioned himself in a nook just off the walkway between the house and the shed. He could hear people inside. He knew this had to go down quickly and quietly or the whole world would hear it. As he positioned himself in the shadows, he heard an SUV engine purr down the road. It grew louder and louder until it pulled into the drive way. Devereaux was home.

The judge took his sweet time getting out of the car. At sixty years of age, he was no spring chicken anymore. Devereaux carried his briefcase in his left hand. With his right hand he fished his keys out of his pocket. For whatever reason, he seemed to prefer entering through the side door rather than the front. A crouching tiger waited to pounce.

Dercho remained absolutely silent even as the scrawny judge walked right past him. He controlled his excitement, stepped out of the hiding place and followed him. Devereaux didn't appear to notice. In one powerful motion, Dercho slapped his left hand over the prey's mouth and tackled him into the bushes. Devereaux's briefcase flew in one direction, his keys in the other.

Even without the element of surprise, the fight wasn't fair. It was a tiger versus a tabby. Dercho had a twelve-year age advantage over the judge and easily one hundred pounds of muscle. He pulled a dumbfounded Devereaux to the ground, then delivered three crashing blows with his right fist to the man's chest and stomach. He rammed a gag into the guy's mouth and covered it with a gloved hand.

"Shut the fuck up and listen good," Dercho said ominously with his deep, commanding baritone. Devereaux had already pissed himself. The look in his eyes told the cop he was so scared there was no way he'd hear what he had to say. "Shut the fuck up," Dercho repeated as the man whimpered and struggled in vain to break free. "I'm not warning you again."

Devereaux's whimpering continued. This was taking too long. Dercho had to get it over with quickly. He drove his knee into the judge's groin and pulled out his gun. He pointed it at Devereaux's head. Devereaux froze.

"Isaac, if I kill you tonight, it will be entirely your own fault," Dercho said trying to get the guy to listen. "Chill out and you'll live to see tomorrow." Dercho was on top of Devereaux, hand on mouth, eyeball to eyeball. "I know about the bribe Isaac. I know you took money from Walter Reed to rig the trial."

The words had a sobering effect on Devereaux. The look in his eyes went from terror to comprehension. He stopped shaking and took note.

"I'm also the reason the money's all gone. If you do as I say, your secret will remain safe with me." Dercho paused to ensure he had his full attention. It was an absolutely silent evening. They had been on the ground for close to a minute. Devereaux's family had to have heard the car pull in the driveway. They would soon come looking to see where he got to. Dercho clicked the safety on his pistol. It rendered the gun incapable of firing a shot but Devereaux didn't know that. He thought the opposite which was the intended effect. The clicking noise made him tremble. Dercho delivered the ultimatum;

"If Lionel Stockwell ever comes before you, you will immediately throw out the charges. That man doesn't spend a single day in prison. Do I make myself clear?" Devereaux nodded his head feverishly. "If you don't do as I say Isaac, first I'm going to shame you publicly. Everyone will know you're a slime bag." He allowed his threat to sink in. "Then I'm going to kill you. Any questions?" Devereaux shook his head, indicating that no more clarification was required.

"You sicken me, you greedy fuck," Dercho said. "How can you look at yourself in the mirror?" The judge didn't respond. He looked like he was about to cry. Dercho flipped him over and pushed his face down into the snow. "You stay like that and count to a thousand," Dercho ordered. "You so much as sneak a peek and you will die tonight, you piece of shit."

Dercho stood up and backed away. His gun pointed at Devereaux. He then holstered it and sprinted back to the car. He jumped in, removed the ski mask and drove back to the station. He wasn't going to visit Walter Reed that night. Devereaux still served a useful purpose. He could keep him on a short leash forever. Reed was useless. Dercho had racked his brains trying to conceive of an adequate punishment. Then he remembered that the man was about to lose his son. Lionel was preparing to dish out a punishment far worse than death for any parent. Had Walter Reed not bribed the judge, Andrew would have faced more prison time but he would at least have lived to see adulthood. The fact that Walter played a role in writing his own son's death warrant was deliciously ironic to Jack Dercho. Both of them would soon get their just desserts.

Dercho went home that night satisfied that Devereaux had understood his message. As for Reed, both father and son, their day of reckoning was fast approaching.

* * *

As the FBI investigated Lionel Stockwell, Jonathan Pickett took his investigation to the next level. He knew he was on the verge of completing the story of a lifetime. This was going to be huge. Every major magazine and newspaper in the free world would want it. He could probably even turn it into a book. Then maybe Hollywood would come knocking. He would be the next Woodward and Bernstein. Anything was possible.

It took Pickett two phone calls to get one step closer to catching Lionel. He called the Boston Police. They faxed over the report of the murder. The rental car was the compelling factor. It had to have been rented under someone's name. Pickett tracked down the company that owned the car and got what he was looking for . . . Gabriel St. Pierre.

Pickett called his contact back in Toronto. He said the name to her. She confirmed that was the same name he had used while meeting with her. Pickett now knew what to look for. He told his contact back in the Philipsville Police to keep an ear out for that name. It might be how people referred to Lionel when talking about these murders.

In the meantime, Pickett had set up shop in a New York apartment across the street from Rocco Palermo. Pickett had home field advantage. New York City was his old stomping ground. He knew it too well.

Pickett had a fifty-fifty chance that this would be Lionel's next target. The other target was in jail and harder to kill. Pickett kept an eye on the teen from a distance. If Lionel were to appear, he would be waiting.

# CHAPTER 74

**LIONEL** had to move quickly. He purchased a fifteen-year-old Pontiac from a used-car dealership just outside of Sacramento. The place was a little sketchy. They were prepared to accept cash for the old piece of junk. It didn't have much life left in it but it would enable him to finish his journey and get home.

Lionel had everything worked out for New York. He would make the 3,000-mile trek across the country. That would give him time to organize the two final acts of vengeance. He would arrive in New York City two days later, finish off Rocco Palermo, then immediately make his way to the Bearhawk Detention Center. He would spend no more than twenty-four hours in New York. If the Feds were on his case, he wouldn't be able to wait three or four weeks between hits this time. It was time to end it.

Lionel said good bye to his friends in San Francisco. It would be a long time before he would ever see them again. For obvious reasons, Lionel never told them what he was up to. He did his best not to be emotional. His friends made him promise to visit again before too long. Not wanting to offend, Lionel agreed. It was the first time in his life, Lionel Stockwell made a promise he knew he couldn't keep.

With all that behind him, the officer began the final leg of his journey. He hadn't been home since early January. He pined for his wife. Lionel had thought of nothing but murder since December. With the end in sight, his vision was shifting to life after the Vipers. He longed for Dana. At night, Lionel would dream about returning to their house in Philipsville after the Vipers were eliminated and find his wife, the love of his life, waiting for him.

It was a long, tedious drive across the USA. As Lionel prepared his final two hits, he also suffered from flashbacks. Anxiety gripped him at every turn. Every time he saw a police cruiser, fear gripped his mind. Were they looking for him? He never imagined that one day he would ever have reason to fear the police uniform. It was a complete perversion of how he'd lived his life.

Lionel was also plagued by Boomer's death. He had tortured and tormented the seventeen-year-old before burning him alive in the trunk of a car. What had he become? Lionel had trained an entire generation of officers to use a Taser only in defence and as a last resort. He used it twice on a kid he could have taken down a hundred different ways.

The fact that Boomer stopped to help him with his engine added another layer of guilt. Lionel had convinced himself that the Vipers were demons. Every day in the courtroom, he loathed their weak, pitiful, meaningless existences. In his mind, they were worthless scum capable of nothing but evil. Lionel tried to suppress a scary notion but it refused to yield;

Was there good in him after all?

This nagging question kept haunting him.

Lionel stopped in Lincoln, Nebraska to rest. He pulled over and tried to fall asleep in his car. Lionel didn't rent a hotel room. He didn't want to leave a trail. Unable to sleep, he found a local tavern. He broke another promise he'd made to himself. Lionel hoisted four pints of Budweiser and downed several shots of hard liquor. He had hoped the alcohol would dull his conscience and help him sleep. It definitely accomplished the latter. Lionel passed out in his rusty old car at around midnight. He was halfway to New York City.

His cell phone woke him up the next morning. His head throbbed from the booze and his back ached from the awkward position he'd slept in all night. Groggy, he answered the phone.

"Hello," he said, barely awake.

"Lionel, is that you?" Dercho asked. "Is everything fine? You sound like shit. Where the hell are you?"

Lionel had slept in the driver's seat. He had reclined it all the way back for the night. He pulled the lever by the floor and returned the seat to its upright position.

"I'm in Nebraska right now," he answered. Lionel's head pounded and his stomach boiled. It took him a moment to remember exactly where he was. Dercho was concerned for his friend. Their sporadic conversations were always brief. Lionel finally composed himself enough to formulate a question. "What's going on?"

"It's about Bearhawk," he said hesitantly. "I made a few discreet phone calls like what we had discussed. If you still want to do this," Dercho paused. "It's going to cost you five hundred thousand dollars."

It was a staggering amount. Far more than either man had anticipated. Lionel sobered up.

"Five hundred thou—" he said aghast. "They can't be serious!"

"I know it's steep Lionel, but they do have a point," Dercho said. "You're not just asking them to turn a blind eye. You want them to help cover it up. They said that would cost extra." Lionel had already burned through his money over the past two months. This would throw off everything.

"Do you think I could maybe talk them down a bit?" he asked.

"Not a chance. They said that's their only offer. Take it or leave it." The pause suggested he had something else to say. "And they want every penny of it in advance."

# THE OFFICER

Lionel felt the world spin. The mere thought of parting with that amount of cash made him queasy.

"They want an answer by tonight at the absolute latest," Dercho continued. "Do you want me to tell them to forget it?"

That wasn't an option. The financial sacrifice would be painful but Lionel had no choice. He had not come this far to leave the job unfinished. He sucked it up and spit out his answer.

"No, tell them I'll get it to them. Every dollar." He stopped and looked at the date on his watch. It was Tuesday morning. "Tell them to be ready to go Friday night. I'll have the money for them forty-eight hours from now."

"Okay, I'll give them the message."

"Thanks." Lionel ended the call.

The amount of money had knocked the wind out of him. He got out of the car and went for a walk. He needed some air. With his stomach rumbling, he found a little diner less than a block away from where he'd parked for the night. He devoured two orders of pancakes and four cups of coffee. The food hit the spot. His energy levels returned and he had to keep going. The timeline was tight. He was going to need more than luck to keep to it.

Lionel climbed back into the car and turned it on. He flicked the radio on to a local morning show and began the final half of his cross-country trek. Lionel reached into the pocket of his leather jacket and pulled out a piece of paper. There was a phone number and a brief message written on it;

*"If you need help, call me.*

*Sarah Jane"*

He needed her now. Lionel flipped open his cell phone. He had one last call to make.

# CHAPTER 75

**ROCCO** never got home before nine o'clock Wednesday nights. His mother and father had enrolled him at the Saint Agnes Boys School on West End Avenue in New York City. That was Adriana's choice. She thought it would do her son some good to finish high school in the warm cradle of Catholicism. The all boys private school in the big city was an adjustment for Rocco but he enjoyed it.

The semester was half over. Rocco joined the Varsity Cross Country Track team to make new friends. Between school, practices and community service, Rocco was busy. He preferred it that way. It helped pass the time. The packed schedule also provided him with a much needed distraction. The kid wanted to forget about the past and move on. There wasn't a day where he didn't feel remorse for Dylan. He was ashamed for ever getting mixed up with Andrew Reed. He had nothing but hatred for Reed and wanted to kill him for what he did to Ashley.

The track team practices were on Monday, Wednesday, Friday and Saturday. If there was a competition, they wouldn't practice Saturdays. On this particular Wednesday in mid-March, Rocco went to practice, then hit the gym with two of his new buddies. He lived in an apartment on 83rd Street with his older cousin Tony who oversaw all the restaurants in the city owned by Rocco's father.

It couldn't have been a more convenient location. It took Rocco less than ten minutes to walk to school each morning at a leisurely pace. He enjoyed taking the scenic root home at the end of the day. He lived close to Broadway. It was a slight detour but a pleasant one. Despite fatigue from a long day, he decided to walk along the famous thoroughfare that night.

It was a beautiful evening in the city that never sleeps. Rocco left his school on West End Avenue and began his short but sweet saunter home seemingly oblivious to the predator lurking behind him.

\* \* \*

Lionel's approach was remarkably basic. He had parked the car across the street from Saint Agnes and waited. As soon as Rocco emerged, Lionel got out and followed on foot. As expected, he strolled down Broadway. This provided more time and more ambush opportunities.

# THE OFFICER

Lionel maintained a healthy distance. He had shaved his beard and cut his hair since leaving Boston. He looked exactly the way he did at the trial. Rocco would know who he was if he saw him. Lionel walked casually behind the young lad for five minutes. He slowly and steadily closed the distance between them. Rocco didn't appear to have the foggiest notion there was any threat.

They turned off Broadway and on to 83rd Street. So far, everything was as expected. Lionel planned to ambush Rocco in a secluded area between two buildings. The area of 83rd Street between Broadway and West End was closed in and quiet. At this hour, it would be perfect.

\* \* \*

Jonathan Pickett hovered around Rocco's front school entrance. This was his daily routine. It was starting to wear him down. He knew Lionel would strike. He had to be ready and he had to remain inconspicuous.

As Rocco left school, Pickett hopped in his car and headed back to his apartment. The journalist had followed the student home the previous week but had grown concerned with the tactic. It was too risky. The last thing he needed was Rocco accusing him of stalking.

He would wait back at the apartment to make sure Rocco arrived home instead. If he did, he knew Lionel had waited for another night. If he didn't . . .

\* \* \*

Lionel made his move. He pulled out his beloved Glock, screwed in the silencer and moved up to Rocco Palermo. He placed his left hand on the kid's shoulder and poked the barrel into his hip. Rocco didn't stop. Instead, he looked straight ahead, slowed down and raised his hands.

"Lionel Stockwell," he said with no concern in his voice. "I've been expecting you."

This was the first unexpected twist all day. The reaction so surprised the seasoned policeman, it threw him off for a brief moment. Had Rocco wanted to fight back that would have been his opening. Lionel was flabbergasted.

"Is that a fact?" he replied, trying to conceal his astonishment. "Don't make a sound. Go, over there." Lionel led his compliant target into a secluded area between two big establishments. When he was satisfied they were alone, he pushed Rocco down to his knees in traditional execution pose. Lionel took position behind him and raised the handgun and pointed it at the back of Rocco's head.

"Your son died courageously," Rocco said. The comment sent rage through Lionel. He flipped the Glock and pistol-whipped the boy's skull. Rocco keeled over on the cold cement holding his head. The pain was sharp. The blow to his head appeared to make him weak and he couldn't regain balance. Lionel pointed the gun in his face.

"You ever mention my son again you little prick and you'll be begging me for death before I'm through with you." Rocco calmly acknowledged the man's instruction. His demeanor confused Lionel. The boy either had no fear of death or a whole lot of arrogance. Maybe both.

"I know you killed the other three," Rocco said, massaging his throbbing head with his hand. "I don't blame you. I would have done the same thing. I'm a dead man. I knew it was only a matter of time before you came for me. May I say something before you pull that trigger?"

Lionel stared at Rocco. Bobby and Boomer whined, sobbed and pleaded in the face of death. This one had his wits about himself. Against his better judgment, Lionel granted him his request.

"You've got thirty seconds. Talk!"

Rocco informed Lionel of the details he had never known about the day Dylan was murdered. He told him about Dylan standing up to Boomer in the morning because of the ripped backpack. His son became a hero around Wellington High. So many students were amazed anyone would have the balls to do that. In the bathroom at lunch hour, he mocked the Vipers and manhandled Boomer before they all jumped him.

The story got to Lionel. He still had the gun pointed at Rocco's face but his mind wasn't there. He could picture the confrontation. Rocco wasn't finished. He told the retired officer about Dylan rising to his feet then spitting in Andrew Reed's face right before taking a pair of brass knuckles to the temple of his head.

Lionel slowly lowered the gun. Rocco got back on his knees. He apologized for being too weak to stop it from happening. The apology was given in a steady, matter-of-fact manner. It wasn't delivered by a coward looking to save his ass. It was genuine contrition. Rocco had one last thing to say.

"I know you're angry, sir," he said. "I also want to kill Andrew Reed."

Lionel shot him a weird look. "Why is that exactly?"

"I'm assuming you know about Ashley Hood." Lionel remembered her all too well. He would be meeting her best friend in forty-eight hours.

"What about her?"

Rocco paused then became very animated. "I loved her. I wanted to be with her but Reed would never allow it. He wanted her too. When she refused to have sex with him he raped her." Rocco stopped. As Rocco knelt down on the ground in front of Lionel, he tried to hide his face. He seemed able to hold it in but Lionel knew he was pained. "I want him dead. If you give me the chance, I'll take care of it for you. I'll suffer all the consequences alone."

The Glock was now down at the officer's side. Rocco, like Boomer, was a follower. He was desperate for acceptance and approval but he also appeared repentant. Lionel studied him with his eyes. The kid had played a big role in Dylan's death and had spent years bullying him. However, he gave him the truth about Dylan. He died on his feet defending himself. He died a man. A long, sad look crossed Lionel's face. He missed his son. He was always proud of him but never more so than at that moment.

# THE OFFICER

"All right, let's go." Lionel said to Rocco. He motioned with his head towards the exit. Rocco heaved a sigh of relief. He stood up and walked in front with Lionel keeping an eye on him. Rocco shared his ideas for killing Reed. Lionel stopped, raised the Glock towards the back of Rocco's head and pulled the trigger. Rocco's face flew off his skull. His dead body hit the cement. It shook and trembled on the ground. Lionel pumped two more bullets into the kid's back. It was probably unnecessary but he had to be sure.

Lionel stood over Rocco Palermo's dead body. His mind was blank. This murder would haunt Lionel longer than the others, but at the moment he was frozen. He felt nothing. Lionel looked around. The place was desolate. Lionel made a discreet exit.

Four down. One to go.

* * *

It was taking Rocco way too long to get home. After waiting for twenty-five minutes, Pickett went out to see what the hell was going on. He knew Rocco's route. He retraced it on foot. Sure enough, he found Rocco's body riddled with fresh bullet wounds lying on the ground less than a block away from the apartment. He knew Lionel was close by.

Pickett stood slack-jawed at the sight of the boy. He felt a wave of emotion roll over him. Maybe he should have alerted authorities before the kid was killed. He had had the power to stop it from happening but his precious feature article mattered more.

Pickett looked around to see if anyone was with him in the alley. The slightest movement or sound made the already uptight reporter jump. He had to get out of there before someone noticed him standing by the corpse. His alibi would not sound too convincing to any judge.

He was about to leave when he decided he needed to do something. He couldn't just leave the teen on the cement for the rats and the vultures to munch on. Pickett pulled out his cell phone then quickly put it back in his pocket. He couldn't risk having the call traced back to him. He had an idea.

Pickett walked up to Rocco's dead body. He patted the kid's jean pockets and felt a cell phone bulging out. He removed it and dialled 911. The phone rang once then a woman's voice answered. Pickett cut her off before she could complete the standard greeting.

"Hello. Get down here immediately someone's been murdered." The operator asked for his location. He supplied it then added; "Send this out to every police officer in the city; the man they're looking for is Lionel Stockwell. He's probably already on his way out of the city. I repeat, Lionel Stockwell."

The operator asked for his name. Pickett quickly closed the phone and ran back to his apartment. Along the way, he tossed the phone down a sewer. He packed up his stuff and drove out of New York City as fast as he could. He knew where Lionel was going next but he had to get back to Philipsville. If he didn't leave immediately, he feared he would become a suspect in the murder of Rocco Palermo.

# CHAPTER 76

**GIUSEPPE** and Adrianna were notified the next morning. Rocco's mother was devastated. Her husband, although reeling on the inside, remained stoic. Their son was murdered and nobody saw anything.

Lionel drove through the night. He had made it out of the city, unobserved. He was oblivious to the fact that every police officer in the city was out to get him. As a result, he drove casually out of New York City. Any police cruisers that passed by barely took notice. He seemed like an ordinary commuter who was just passing through.

Lionel found a cafe with Internet access about one hundred miles away from New York City. He needed to transfer money. He was able to pull together the requisite funds. The bulk of it came out of his savings. Lionel also drained Dylan's college fund. There was fifty thousand in that account. It had been meant for the future. Instead, it would be used to avenge the past.

His concentration was interrupted by the ringing of his cell phone at around 3.30 a.m. Only one person knew the number.

"Jack, what's up?" Lionel asked quietly.

Dercho heaved a sigh of relief. "Oh, thank God you're all right," he said. "When I heard the news I thought you may have been arrested already."

Lionel was confused. "What are you talking about?"

"You mean you don't know?"

Lionel shook his head and shrugged. "No, what happened."

"The New York City police did a massive search for you last night. The call went out around 9:20 in the evening. What the hell happened?"

Lionel knew what he had done. What didn't make sense to him was how they could have possibly known so definitively it was him. There were no witnesses. This unknown element terrified Lionel. Was someone on to him? Dercho chimed in.

"By the way, Jonathan Pickett has been calling every officer in any position of authority here in Philipsville. Apparently the editors stopped the presses just for him. He's already working on an article about the NYPD search for you."

"So, what does he want to talk to you guys about?" Lionel asked.

# THE OFFICER

"I don't know," Dercho said, "but I strongly recommend you do whatever you got to do and fast. Your cover has been blown and we're out of time."

Lionel acknowledged the instruction. He thanked Dercho and hung up. He needed to keep moving.

# CHAPTER 77

**WITH** the funds wired and the plan in place, Lionel drove to Bennettburgh. It was a town of eight thousand people and the closest town to the Bearhawk Detention facility. There was nothing but farmland between the town and his final destination. Lionel spent the night at a motel in town. He double checked and triple checked the arrangements. Nothing could be left to chance. This was the big one. Of the five, Lionel believed this one would be the sweetest.

Lionel's accomplice met him outside the Bennettburgh Motel the following afternoon. Sarah Jane Harnick did as she was told. She dressed in the sexiest outfit she owned. The red dress fit snug along her body. Her makeup and long dark hair were done to perfection. She brought along a secret weapon in her purse. She was the bait. Lionel needed her to draw the beast out into the open and distract him. She was more than happy to play the part.

They drove through the countryside. It was a forty-five–minute ride through the wide-open spaces of rural life. The smell of cow manure occasionally wafted through the car windows. It was a beautiful sunny day. Most of the snow had melted, although it would probably return before the permanent arrival of spring.

Sarah Jane tried to make small talk. Lionel wanted none of it. They had already gone over the plan when he had called her from Nebraska. They sat in silence the rest of the way. Sarah Jane hadn't seen him since she introduced herself in the cafeteria at the courthouse. Lionel's steely-eyed focus was both reassuring and disconcerting.

When they arrived at the prison, the Captain of the guards greeted Lionel enthusiastically. He and two of his close friends had made a lot of money for very little work. The Captain tried not to overtly ogle the bombshell next to the renowned police officer. As they walked into the building, Sarah Jane turned heads everywhere but she pretended not to notice. Lionel actually didn't notice. He was scope-locked on the task at hand.

There was no one Lionel Stockwell hated more than Andrew Reed. In a matter of minutes, they would be together again.

\*\*\*

# THE OFFICER

Around this time, the *Philipsville Herald* hit the news stand. Pickett's article was front page and dominated much of the third page as well. Dercho read it with a heavy heart. The information in Pickett's article confirmed things were worse than he expected. The journalist had a source in the department somewhere. Pickett's article also insinuated that Intel may have aided and abetted Lionel in his efforts.

Dercho was stunned. Nobody knew about his involvement. He was determined to plug the leak but he had bigger fish to fry. The press was already on the war path, O'Reilly was seething and the FBI was on its way.

\* \* \*

Inside Bearhawk, the young prisoners were in school. Two guards approached what was the equivalent of a grade twelve English class. Inmates were not obligated to see visitors. If they weren't interested, the guards would make the visitors leave the premise. They walked into the class and apologized for the interruption.

"Reed," the smaller of the two guards said loudly. "You've got a visitor." Reed wasn't expecting anyone. His parents only visited on weekends.

"Who is it?"

The other guard looked down at the clipboard. "Her name's Sarah Jane Harnick. She wants to see you."

Reed's eyes lit up. They had been friends back in Wellington High but he knew she hated him for Ashley. "What does she want?" Reed asked as they exited the classroom.

"I don't know," said the smaller guard as he patted Reed on the back. "But, there are times when I wish I was a young badass in prison. This is one of them."

He gave the two guards a confused look. They were smiling ear to ear. The bigger of the two looked back at the clipboard.

"She's waiting for you in Room 101," he said with a wink. "Knock yourself out."

\* \* \*

Sarah Jane sat in one of the many visiting rooms in the prison. She touched up her makeup and made sure she was showing maximum cleavage. The room consisted of a rectangular table, two chairs and a large one-way mirror for observation. There was also a security camera in the corner of the room above the entrance. This one happened to be unplugged.

When Reed entered the room, blood immediately rushed to his groin. He took one look at the vixen sitting on the table with her legs crossed and couldn't mask his lust.

"Hello, Andrew," she said; sultry and seductive. "I have something to tell you. Sit down please."

The chairs were positioned at opposite sides of the table. Reed sat in the one closest to the entrance. With his back to the door, he gazed towards Sarah Jane. His eyes were enormous as he took in the scenery. Sarah Jane relished the moment. He wanted her but she wasn't going to give it to him. She never knew revenge could be this much fun.

\* \* \*

The shorter of the two guards shut the door behind Reed as the young inmate entered the room. The guard walked around the corner. Lionel Stockwell was leaning up against the wall. He nodded at him.

"Come get us when you're done."

Lionel stood silently in the corridor alone. He slowly walked around and looked through the mirrored window. There he was—the ghost that haunted two generations of Stockwells. Lionel glared at him. Every ounce of anger, hate and loathing swelled inside of him.

The officer readied the electrical cord and waited for the sign. He admired Sarah Jane. She played Reed like a violin. The filthy mutt was salivating at the piece of meat in front of him. Lionel couldn't wait to kill him.

\* \* \*

"I missed you, Andrew," Sarah Jane said as she walked around the table. "I'm sorry about that day in court. You can forgive me, right?" He nodded his head enthusiastically. "Aw, you're so sweet. Thank you."

She walked behind him and ran her index finger across his neck. The physical contact sent electrodes through Reed's body. Her fragrance was intoxicating. She walked around the table and back to her chair. Reed got a good look at her backside. He reached out to grab her when Sarah Jane slapped his hand away.

"Not yet, Andrew," she chided, playfully. "Soon, but not quite yet."

Sarah Jane opened her purse and pulled out an envelope. She slid it down the table until it stopped in front of Reed.

"Take a look," she said as she winked at him. "I think you'll like what you see."

Reed tore open the envelope. He looked at the first one . . . but was confused.

It was a picture of a baby. He flipped slowly through the dozen or so pictures. They were all of the same infant. The child looked to be no more than two or three months old.

This was the sign. Sarah Jane saw the doorknob turn. Reed looked up at Sarah Jane with a perplexed look on his face. He appeared to be trying to form a question. She cut him off with the answer.

"That's your son, Andrew," she said. "He was born a month ago. Take a good look. It's amazing something so beautiful could come out of something so hideous."

Lionel entered the room. He shut the door without making a sound. Reed was locked on the pictures.

"Ashley named him Dylan," Sarah Jane continued, now ignoring Lionel like he had instructed her. "He's an absolute sweetheart. It sucks you'll never get to meet him."

Reed's eyes narrowed with confusion. He looked up from the pictures. Sarah Jane blew him a kiss.

Lionel pounced. He wrapped the electrical cord around the prisoner's neck twice then pulled both ends with every ounce of strength he could muster. Lionel was a strong man but his hatred for Andrew Reed made him ten times more powerful.

Reed jumped up and struggled against Lionel. He was surprisingly strong. Sarah Jane stood and moved into a corner to get out of the way. Reed clawed at the cord that was choking the life out of him. He began flailing away at Lionel. He reached back for Lionel's eyes trying to gouge them out. Lionel readjusted. Reed pulled forward as far as he could then jerked his head back. He connected with Lionel's nose, breaking it.

The wounded father let out a roar. He lifted Reed off his feet by the cord around his neck, swung him to his right then reversed direction and drove Reed's head through the table. He pulled him back up and rammed him into the wall. Reed's face changed color. His energy faded. Like a bull terrier, Lionel pulled tighter and tighter until Reed fell to his knees. The room was turning black. Before he exhaled his last gasp, Lionel leaned forward and whispered in his ear;

"This is for both of our sons."

With a powerful jerk, Lionel choked the last breath out of Andrew Reed. The kid was dead. Lionel maintained the choke hold for another five minutes. He just couldn't ease off. Finally, Sarah Jane walked over and placed her hand on his shoulder.

"It's over, Lionel," she said softly. "It's time to go."

\*\*\*

Lionel was possessed by unbridled hate. Sarah Jane served as a reminder of civilization. For the time it took to murder Andrew Reed, Lionel's entire universe became his son's killer. He temporarily forgot everything around him. He released Reed and pushed his lifeless head to the ground. He hovered over the seventeen-year-old's body. He took in the image. Before him was the source of all the misery and loneliness Lionel had endured over the past year. Lying on the ground was the guy who had murdered his son, then antagonized Lionel for months in court.

Lionel kicked Reed's head and spit on his dead body.

"Let's see you wink now, you little prick."

Sarah Jane wrapped her arms around the officer.

"Lionel, can we please go now?" she pleaded.

Lionel, staring at the body, nodded faintly.

The two left the room. They found the Captain and his two prison guard friends. They took Reed's body back to his cell where an improvised noose made from various items around the prison was tied up. It was hanging from the bars covering the only window in the enclosed space. They placed Reed in the noose and planted a note on his bed. The three of them left and waited for another guard to come across it honestly.

Reed hung by his neck for two hours. An investigation into the incident concluded it was an obvious suicide. The Philipsville Vipers were finished.

# CHAPTER 78

**LIONEL** drove Sarah Jane back to Bennettburgh. Her car was waiting back at the motel. Lionel never spoke but that didn't stop the girl. She told Lionel about Ashley's baby and how she named him after his son. Ashley had finally told Sarah Jane the full story about Dylan. She was confused by Ashley's extreme sorrow the day he was killed. It was like she had lost a brother. Now she understood. When she told Lionel, he didn't react or respond. His eyes remained focused on the road ahead.

Lionel said nothing to the girl until they got back to her car. He thanked her for her help. Sarah Jane gave the burly cop a big hug then kissed him on the cheek. She jumped into her car and drove off. Lionel sat alone in his car. He had a lot to digest.

He began the three hour drive back to Philipsville. A million thoughts raced through his mind. The Vipers had been his distraction since the tragic day back in June. With them gone, he had nothing left to distract himself from his loss.

He refused to break down. Lionel hadn't cried in years. Not even when he held Dylan's dead body in the Wellington High bathroom. He was determined to keep it together. There was work to be done. Dylan wasn't ever coming home but his wife needed him. He needed her. He hoped she'd be there at home waiting when he returned. It was that one happy thought that held the tears at bay.

Lionel drove through the evening without stopping. He arrived back in Philipsville at 9:37 p.m. It was a clear but cool night. He drove through the town he'd called home since shortly after Dylan was born. He didn't know what to do next. His career was over; the Vipers were dead, and his finances severely depleted. None of that mattered so long as he still had Dana. His house was only five minutes away. If she was there they would work through the problems together.

As he pulled into his driveway, he saw that the house was completely dark. The outdoor lights were off. It wasn't a promising sign but he thought maybe she was inside sleeping. Lionel hadn't been home since January. The newspapers and mail had piled up on his doorstep. The newspaper from that day was on the top. An article by Jonathan Pickett dominated the front page. The headline screamed:

*Former Deputy Chief Hunted by NYPD.*

Lionel approached the door with trepidation. He noticed Pickett's headline at the top of the bundle. He picked it up then kicked the rest of the newspapers out of his way. He prayed Dana was in there willing to start over. It was the last hope for his continued sanity.

As Lionel unlocked the deadbolt on his door, he heard footsteps in the bushes. Lionel stopped and pulled out his Glock. A familiar figure emerged from behind the shrubs.

"Hello, old friend," said the deep voice through the darkness.

"Jack?" Lionel asked. "Is that you?"

Dercho moved closer. Lionel heaved a sigh of relief. He placed the handgun back in his underarm holster. They exchanged a firm handshake.

"Did you hear about Reed?"

Dercho nodded. He had a pained expression on his face. Lionel knew he had some bad news. After working with the man for thirty years, he could anticipate him.

"Lionel, you need to go," Dercho said with his trademark bluntness. "Get out of here; lay low for a while, but you can't stay here."

Lionel was taken aback. "Why, what's wrong?"

"The FBI is sending agents to town tomorrow. They're going to question people about you and they'll definitely come here. This place will be under surveillance. John Paul has been able to keep them out of our jurisdiction so far but that won't last any longer."

Lionel felt sick. He was tired, lonely and just wanted to sleep in his own bed. "What am I supposed to do Jack? Where should I go?"

Dercho could barely look at his friend. The man had gone through hell and back. The year had not been kind.

"Lionel, you need to lay low. This will blow over. The FBI has bigger problems to deal with. If they can't solve the case quickly they'll reallocate their resources. The media probably won't be as kind but we'll endure. You just need to stay off the radar."

Dercho pulled a piece of paper from his pocket. He handed it to Lionel. "This information will provide you with access to a Swiss account I've set up for you." Lionel was suspicious but Dercho cut him off. "Don't ask."

Lionel looked at the information. He had no idea there was close to thirteen million dollars sitting in the account.

"Whatever you do, don't forget the password," Dercho continued. "It's *Lynda* spelled with a 'y'. If you ever get confused, just remember it contains all the same letters as Dylan." Lionel did a double take. Sure enough, Dercho was right. Before he could thank him, Dercho looked at his watch. "I have to go, Lionel. I beg you; please don't be here in the morning."

"I'll be gone," Lionel replied vacantly. "Don't worry."

Dercho quickly turned around and started walking away. Right before he totally faded back into the night Dercho turned around and faced his old friend.

# THE OFFICER

"Lionel . . . I really am sorry about everything." He searched for the right words but found nothing. "You didn't deserve any of this."

"It's okay, Jack," he replied. "Get out of here. I'll be all right."

Lionel folded the paper Dercho had given to him and placed it in his jacket pocket. He then turned the key and entered his home.

\* \* \*

Across the street, camouflaged by thick bushes, the digital camera with a massive telephoto lens clicked non-stop. The man behind the camera struggled to contain his glee. His source told him Jack Dercho was planning to meet Lionel Stockwell that night at his home. The fact the meeting took place outside was manna from heaven. The camera snapped hundreds of pictures. It also recorded the date and time each picture was taken.

When Dercho retreated and Lionel slipped into the home, Jonathan Pickett sat down on the wet ground and looked through his pictures. They were clear, focused and unmistakable. A shit-eating grin covered his entire face. This piece of information cost him a lot of money but it would make him far more in the future.

Once certain the coast was clear, the reporter snuck away. He finally had what he wanted.

# CHAPTER 79

**THE** house was pitch-black. Lionel flipped on the living room light. His heart sank—the place was empty. All the furniture was gone and the walls were bare. Dana had come back like she said she would to remove the rest of her stuff. Lionel felt his chest grow heavy. There was only one comfortable chair left in the living room. She had taken everything else.

Lionel looked briefly at Pickett's article in the *Philipsville Herald*. He rolled the paper up, put the elastic on it and tossed it into the corner of his empty living room. Lionel walked around his home. There wasn't much to see. He now truly had nothing left to distract or comfort him. They were either dead or he had driven them away. In a sense, Dana was the last thing Andrew Reed had stolen from him.

One thing caught his eye. There was an envelope on the counter. It said *Lionel* on the front in pencil. It was Dana's handwriting. Lionel wasn't sure he wanted to open it. He held it up to his nose. He could still smell her perfume. That alone brought back a thousand splendid memories. He walked back into the living room and ripped open the envelope.

Before opening the note, Lionel noticed something small lying on the floor where the TV once stood. He walked over and picked it up. It was the framed picture he loved so much; the photo of him and Dylan at the fishing derby. Lionel wiped it off on his shirt then sat down.

He opened the letter. Dana's handwriting was unmistakable;

*Dearest Lionel,*

*If you're reading this letter, I'm guessing your journey is now complete. I know what you've been doing. I'm not mad at you. I share your hatred for those boys and still do but I fear they've driven a permanent wedge between us.*

*I know you miss Dylan. I know you're angry at the people who took him away from us. You're angrier at the people who denied us justice for our murdered son. I used to think love could conquer everything. I'm not so sure anymore.*

*I refuse to live in the past Lionel. I still love you. I will always love you but we cannot be together until you've found some way to move forward in life. I'm not suggesting we forget Dylan. I'm his mother. I'll never forget him nor will I allow anyone to forget him. I am saying we need to move on. Every day you spend wallowing in anger, hatred and bitterness is one more day wasted. Every time that happens, the Vipers win. If their deaths can provide you with closure, maybe some good will have come from your actions over the past few months.*

*I won't ever forgive them. I don't expect you to either. But we must move on. If you can find some way to do that, I'll be waiting for you. Until that day comes, please don't try to contact me. If you ever truly returned my love, you will honor this request.*

*Take care of yourself. May our paths cross again before too long.*

*Forever yours,*

*Dana*

The letter left him paralyzed. Lionel sat crippled in the chair. He wanted to crumple it up and throw it away. He was angry that she wasn't here with him. He needed her but he also knew she was right. The poor woman had gone through everything with him. She was dealing with the same pain. He would be nothing but an additional burden.

Lionel sniffed the note again. Dana's heavenly fragrance transported him to better days when the house was as full as the life they once shared. The officer looked down at the framed picture in his other hand. He could see his reflection in the glass. Out of nowhere, a tear drop landed on it. Then another. It took him a minute to realize they were his own. Lionel wiped them away with his shirtsleeve.

Hunched over in the darkness of his living room, Lionel Stockwell clutched his wife's letter in one hand and his son's picture in the other. He wept.

## THE END

# ACKNOWLEDGEMENTS

I AM indebted to so many people who assisted me over the last four years. Their commitment to this project helped make my dream come true.

First off, I must thank my biggest supporter; my mother, Debbie. Her enthusiasm and advice proved invaluable. She was instrumental in helping me push through the monotony of rewrite after rewrite. She taught me from an early age to finish what I start. That lesson was sorely tested with this novel. I can't thank her enough for her love and support through the years.

My two editors Kat Exner and Sharon Crawford did Yeoman's work bringing my manuscript up to par. Their tenacity, patience and wisdom were seemingly endless. Thank you for your professionalism and dedication.

To Craig Riehl for designing the original cover to the novel; it helped out enormously for our promotional material and it motivated me to see this project through to completion. Your assistance and friendship mean the world to me.

Steve Rae is not only the man who gave me my start in radio he was also one of the earliest supporters of this novel. Steve's advice on the manuscript was critical. For many reasons, I owe him a debt gratitude that I will never be able to repay.

My old friend Al Walsh has always been there for me and this time was no different. Her advice for my novel was very specific and very important. I can't thank her enough for her assistance.

I must also thank Friesen Press for bringing this novel to the public. I couldn't have done it with their expertise.

I wish to thank the wildly talented Jake Nothdurft and Rian Schaefer for their work on my online promotional material. Both guys can work wonders with a camera and a laptop.

Finally, to the reader; I hope you enjoyed *The Officer* as much as I enjoyed writing it and thank you for your interest in my work.

I beg the deepest forgiveness from anyone I may have omitted. It wasn't deliberate. Literally, dozens of people contributed in small ways to this book and I'm grateful to all of them.

Ethan Rabidoux
Stratford, ON, 2013